Voices of the Nomadic Genes:

An Enigmatic Journey

Book 1
A Narrative Memoir

STEPHEN WOLFE

Copyright

eBook ISBN: 978-1-965431-87-0
Paperback ISBN: 978-1-965431-88-7
Hardback ISBN: 978-1-965431-89-4

Table of Contents

Dedication

After spending several days with the verbal functions of her brain shut down, within two hours of her death, my incredible wife Patricia turned to me as I held her hand and said, "I love you, Stephen." No words can express the intensity of my feelings for the love and respect for this woman with whom I collaborated, hugged, worked, and traveled together over the decades. Like two pieces of a jigsaw puzzle, we were partners in mind and flesh. Her encouragement and tolerance made this deep dive into writing possible. Thank you, honey. The world is a better place because of your gifted accomplishments and ability to help all of us feel better about life.

Foreword

A Cossack brutally rapes a young woman in a Russian shtetl. What repercussions does this one event have? It unleashes a two-hundred-year history of excitement, mystery, creativity, trauma, pain, and survival for four generations of a family. The family members and their stories, as told by Elijah to the Sonoran Desert Storytelling Group, are discussed by the reading group members:

Larry: "I'm a financial advisor and always deal with risks. I've never seen such risky people in my life!"

Mary Ann: "It is a wonderful love story that struggles to succeed. Sometimes I felt like a voyeur. But it was fun to talk with others about it."

Charlie: "All these other people kept trying to figure it out. Why bother? Enjoy the mystery. It was like a mountain road with cliffs on one side and steep canyons on the other, winding up and down. I just went with the flow and let them entertain me."

Harry: "It was like living in the historical times. I'd studied the events in school. Yet, experiencing the impact of the events through the eyes of the people involved made those events more incredible than what I read in the history books."

Tim: "Quirky people with guts and creativity."

Nancy: "I'd feel angry, sad, and adoring all on the same page!"

Author's note: Yep, those are my people. As a physician specializing in psychiatry, individuals, families, and organizations have routinely requested my help to solve problems. We'd look at the events, facts, decision-making challenges, and emotions together. Pursuing solutions, we'd asked:

How do you feel?

What can we do?

Why do it?

What are the upsides? Downsides?

Should we do it?

Did we do it right?

How did we get in our own way?

And maybe most importantly, after deciding, we'd ask, "Do you still like the person who stares back at you each morning when you look in the mirror?"

All these questions have been discussed for generations, whether rolling cigars in early New York, quilting in Vermont, sitting on a beach in California with a friend, or chatting in reading groups in your own hometown.

Now retired, I decided to investigate how my family had answered these questions. What have they bequeathed me? I hope their journey entertains you and provokes your self-reflections or discussions, as it did for the group.

Thanks,
Stephen Wolfe

Prologue

On New Year's Eve Day, the weather was surprisingly warm. Dressed only in a light sweatshirt, Lucas walked through the deep wash. The desert floor, recently abused by an early monsoon, was rearranged into the landscape du jour. The rocks had been newly located and tumbled to different locations as torrents of water rushed through the wash, moving everything in its way. The night before, the skies above the Arizona Sonoran Desert spewed lightning, and the wind played soccer with the loose elements on the land below. Lucas loved these changes. They made everything seem fresh and new. They also created opportunities for finding gold. He stooped to pick up a small piece of quartz and turned it over and over in his weathered hands. Nope, there was not even a hint of color. No gold. Speaking of gold, it wasn't his lucky day.

Today, Lucas kept striding carefully and slowly with his eyes glued to the path before him. If asked, Lucas would laugh, explaining that his pace was a wise older man's way of prospecting for gold. That answer was more romantic than true: he didn't want to trip and fall at his age. Even avoiding a twisted ankle was foremost on Lucas's mind.

He looked forward to this day. His tale was to be told. The Desert Storytelling Group met throughout the winter months. This was to be their first meeting of the snowbird season. The visitors came from far and wide along the Western United States and Canada to rough it in Quartzsite,

Arizona. This tiny town of two thousand people, lacking even the simple conveniences of their abodes back home, expanded to become a winter home for nearly two hundred and fifty thousand campers and snowbirds in the winter.

How and why did Lucas and many other people seeking warmer winter weather show up to "rough it" at this crossroads in the desert? Why not go to the posher winter locations away from home, in Florida or Palm Springs? For five years, Lucas had come and been perplexed by the force that drew him to Quartzsite. Just as Issac Newton wondered why the apple fell straight down, Lucas had been entranced by the stories people told about the magnetism of Quartzsite. Over the months, he finally understood his decision to be there. It was a fascinating and life-saving story. Today, it was going to be told.

Dragging his camping chair behind him, Lucas bent forward to get a handhold on a deeply embedded rock to help him climb the steep side of the newly reshaped wash. He walked towards a group of big and small RVs, circled like wagons of the old West, but just with 1990s amenities. Stopping a fair distance back, He unfolded his camping chair and talked to no one but sat to the side like a ghost waiting to observe those he'd left behind.

Assorted campers soon arrived. They sat and enjoyed talking and joking with each other. Their stomachs were full, except for the room left for the sweet desserts that always came before any campfire event in Quartzsite. Some were locals who routinely enjoyed the regular storytelling group sessions. However, most were winter residents, meeting with this group for the first time. They had all gathered to attend the New Year's Eve inaugural meeting that had become a tradition. For this group, the pleasure would be to hear and share a good story while leaving the drunken debauchery behind. Those years of youthful frivolity were long gone.

A tall, thin man sat across from Lucas behind the group of strangers. His name? Elijah. Nothing distinguished him from the rest of the residents dressed in old jeans and a long-sleeved shirt, the kind that was worn daily to offer protection from the sun. From beneath his low-slung cowboy hat, he just stared at the back of the heads of the group. When he saw Lucas across the way, he merely nodded. Elijah and Lucas observed the group for over an hour. People mingled, laughed, and enjoyed being together to celebrate the holiday. They also speculated about the story they would hear over the next few weeks.

After a time, the straight-backed, weathered man loudly cleared his throat and began to walk to the front of the group. He remained silent as he moved through the crowd with a slight smirk and a penetrating gaze in his eyes that may make some turn away. After all, they were there for fun. Elijah appeared more somber than fun. Finally, he moved closer and spoke with a raspy voice that was barely above a whisper, as if Sam Elliot had suddenly appeared from nowhere. Elijah said, "Let me tell you a story from long ago. Soon, you will hear of a painful tragedy. It is the beginning of my friend's story. My friend is a descendant of Sophia, whose experiences we'll listen to first.

Her story takes us back over 150 years, where we will find the origin of four generations of her family. As we talk about all these people, feel free to jump in with any thoughts that tickle your fancy. As you hear their stories, you may want to think about your own. Discuss it among yourselves and share your thoughts and feelings if you'd like. The characters will entertain and fascinate you. You'll wind up hating some, loving some, and seeing bits of history differently.

One of Sophia's descendants and my friend is someone named Lucas. He lives here in Quartzsite. I've come to know Lucas well. In some ways, he is like all of you. By telling you his story, you may hear some of your own stories. Lucas calls Quartzsite the adult playground, an Exploratorium for grownups. Our spot of land in the desert is barren of condos, golf courses, water fountains, swimming pools, and fancy restaurants or art galleries."

Raising his voice in emphasis and widening his smile in appreciation of his surroundings, Elijah continued: "Just as the proverbial rising of the mythical phoenix from ashes that occurs every five hundred years was interpreted by older cultures in different ways, so too, our city at the crossroads that arises from the sand each year excites visitors new and old, giving different meaning and opportunities to their lives. To Lucas, Quartzsite meant salvation. Whereas the more profound reasons for Lucas's salvation may remain hidden, we know they are adorned by a sky like an art gallery of changing colors. Orange, red, and purple colors flow across the canvas above us. Performance art, some would call it. But, whatever the label, it is a never-ending work in the sky of an artistic master called nature.

We share a consistent camaraderie among the snowbirds on the ground in Quartzsite. The activities range from risky four-wheel driving and listening to bluegrass music to immersing oneself in craft land heaven. There exists a shared experience of exploration and discovery each day.

Each season here, campers have their own stories to tell that are full of excitement, pleasure, sadness, and mystery. I got to know Lucas better when sitting with a group like today. He was talking about his great-grandmother from Russia. Many reacted in horror and commented on her story. They kept asking for more and more. Finally, someone suggested he tell his entire story to The Desert Storytelling Group.

Lucas and I began sharing coffee as we met in the morning at sunrise or for a beer while enjoying the sunset. One day, we were high-centered on some rocks on a jeep ride in the desert. I didn't have much experience with that, but I observed Lucas examine the situation and devise a plan to get us moving again.

Later that evening, we slowly progressed back toward town, and I commented on how organized he seemed in that crisis. There we were, alone and miles from town. I was worried, but Lucas didn't seem to share that discomfort. Instead, he laughed when I called it a crisis. So then, Lucas just began to spin another yarn about how problem-solving seemed to define most of his and his family's blessings and curses. He then continued with stories about his own experiences and those of his family until we finished our ride. It was then that I, too, urged him to share the story at the storytelling group the following season.

At first, Lucas was not so keen on telling his story. I'm unsure of whether he was shy, embarrassed, or reluctant to be that open about his life. However, when we met again this

October, he said he'd finally decided it would be OK for the story to be told. I asked him what had changed his mind."

LucusLucas explained, "I wasn't sure what the family story was about. Then, one day, my wife Emily was listening to the DVD of Mama Mia. It opens with an old ABBA song. I was struggling to find the simple truths of my life, but my story was right there in that song."

At last, he said, that if he were struggling to find the simple truths of his life, his story was right there in that song. He asked Emily to listen to it with him again and told her that would be the message of his story. He then shared those impactful words with me.

I Have a Dream, a song to sing

To help me cope, with anything

If you see the wonder of a fairy tale

You can take the future, even if you fail

I believe in angels

Something good in everything I see

I believe in angels

When I know the time is right for me

I'll cross the stream. I Have a Dream

I Have a Dream, a fantasy

To help me through reality

And my destination makes it worth the while

Pushin' through the darkness, still another mile

I believe in angels

Something good in everything I see

I believe in angels

When I know the time is right for me

I'll cross the stream. I Have a Dream

I'll cross the stream. I Have a Dream.'

"Emily knew of your suggestion to tell my story. She knew it would become her story, too. Feeling reluctant to have our issues, our dirty laundry washed in the desert. She indicated that hanging it out to dry in the hot sun won't make it cleaner or smell better! She asked, 'Why that song anyway?' I told her that it reminded me of a fairy tale. And I felt that my life was like a fairy tale. Why not?"

He told Emily that his family history is a series of dreams. Part of these dreams was the countless angels met along the way. Angels, who Lucas believed deserved recognition. Lucas questioned her about why he shouldn't share his fairy tale. Her response was intense and challenging. She was exasperated. Her antagonism showed no bounds. Emily persisted, 'I'll tell you, why not? Because fairy tales are for children. Not for adults."

Lucas countered. The ones with witches and wizards might be. But stop and think of a fairy tale's purpose. It's not only to entertain but also to teach lessons. He reminded her of the day they found petroglyphs on some canyon walls. Together, they wondered about what they were communicating. They were probably sharing warnings or stories passed down from the elders, in other words, fairy tales. The Greek and Roman myths they studied in school seemed sophisticated, but they, too, were just stories, fairy tales. Today, we look back at those myths as fabricated, creative, magical explanations. But there were lessons in all of them.

I don't think Emily was ever totally on board with Lucas telling this tale, but Lucas told me the story could be told as long as it was not by him. It would lead to too many personal questions and tangents. So, instead, he asked me to tell his fairy tale as I had come to know it. So now, I'll say a formal good evening to you all and wish you a happy new year. My name is Elijah Rosenovitch, and I'll be Lucas's storyteller."

Lucas was as yet unidentified and sitting way behind the group. Next to him sat a young Navajo/Dine descendant, Kristina. A junior in college, she was fresh and youthful and felt that music could express the essence of any event. Her long hair tied in a formal French braid matched the classic elegance of her attire in a loose black top with matching wide-legged pants. She was dressed more formally than the group before her, but it reflected her deep feelings about the importance of New Year's Eve. She was on Christmas break, visiting her parents, who were wintering in Quartzsite. This evening, she gladly accompanied Lucas to the gathering.

Elijah said, "Before we break for this evening, let us hear from Kristina, who has deep feelings that New Year's Eve is a time for remembrance of those who've gone before us as well as hopeful expectations of what is to come."

The girl in black rose and carefully walked around the edge of the sitting campers. Short in stature, she stood tall and moved with grace. Her presence was immediately felt. The hush was quick and total. As she walked toward the front of the group, two coyotes had a brief conversation- meaningful, no doubt. Then, as if sensing the human feelings around them, the coyotes paused, allowing the girl in black her turn. Elijah held Kristina's hand so that she could keep her balance. Then, with boots clicking on the makeshift wooden platform, echoing in the otherwise silent desert, she lifted her legs one at a time to climb the stairs to the platform above the group.

Elijah let go of her arm and stood straight, a statue in black. The flickering flames of the campfire added occasional crackles and pops as if they were a rhythm section for the girl. Kristina stared ahead into the darkness high above the heads of the sitting campers. Her ancestors created smoke signals to rise above the desert floor, serving as a beacon to those far away. This beautiful apparition was to send deep, resonant tones that musically remastered the nostalgic memories of Lucas's heart. She nodded once, then brought a black clarinet to her pursed lips. The campers listened as Kristina played solo, with no sounds in the desert other than Auld Lang Syne's clear, haunting, penetrating tones.

The notes also passed through the campers' hearts and into the desert sky. Nearly all present silently heard the song's words and the tribute it offered. Then, finally, the girl in black concluded her song. She was carefully helped down, taken behind the nearest RV, and then, she disappeared. There was nothing but silence for two or three minutes before anyone moved.

Elijah stood and turned to thank Kristina, who had vanished into the darkness. There was no applause or shouts of a happy new year. Instead, Elijah quietly said, "The words to that song and the melody will likely bounce around in your heads tonight. But let's not forget the middle verses and the theme of our story; the ones about meaningful memories and gratitude.

We two have run about the hills,

And picked the daisies fine;

But we've wandered many a weary foot

Since auld lang syne.

We two have paddled in the stream

From morning sun till dine;

But seas between us broad have roared

Since auld lang syne."

The group's nostalgia level was high. So was their curiosity. There was more than a tear or two as people were bombarded with memories of times gone by. Soon, they returned to their homes on wheels, perhaps some to think of their own stories.

Chapter One

The group gathered after lunch the next day. Elijah, standing with a big grin on his face, offered his observations. "Well, I see that all of you tempered your festivities and are alert and awake, seemingly not hung over. Walking over here, I hear snoring still pouring from more than one rig. I'm glad to see so many of you free from being hungover. Welcome to this year's first storytelling session."

Elijah paced up and down twice in front of the seated campers. Then, in anticipation, everyone just stared and waited.

"Let me tell you a story from long ago."

He began, "Sophia screamed, but nothing could come out. Frightened, fearful for her life, and in pain, Sophia shut down. She could only wonder. *'Yesterday was nice. Why couldn't today be nice?'* She screamed, but it was not heard. The scream was in her head but could not be heard by any observer. She shook as if in ice-cold water, but her body, nude from her dress being torn away, stayed stiff to the eye of any observer. She stared up into the eyes of the man on top of her. The man with a knife to her throat demanded, "Look at me. Look at me, you Jewish whore." He shouted this repeatedly as he invaded her body. But suddenly, it stopped. His yelling stopped as red appeared on his throat. In a state of shock, Sofia was removed from reality. She thought, *oh, he must be choking on something,* as his shouting metamorphosed into a gagging gurgle. Then, just as quickly, he fell back as a passing teenage boy who had slit the Russian's throat pulled him off Sofia. Sofia lay bewildered, bloodied, shaking visibly, and impregnated as shock set in.

Hours after being attacked, a fellow villager found Sophia exposed, lying on her back on the dry, dusty street. She was motionless, staring at a cloudy sky. Patchwork splotches of dirt stuck to the Cossack's dried blood on her body. She was helped up and accompanied home. As she was being carried through the streets, some people glanced at her state. But Sophia was not unique. Others were suffering the same mayhem. The villager laid her gently on a bed as they reached home and quickly left.

The rest of her family slowly safely came home. There needed to be more help from her five children. But none was forthcoming. Their father, Efraim, as an afterthought, casually suggested they may want to take care of their mother. But Efraim himself barely bothered to look at her. Such was their relationship. She was mainly left to clean herself up and was soon expected to make dinner. Efraim went off to attend to his friend and business associate whose son had been killed. Sophia looked at her family, who were walking around her. *I must cover myself up,* she thought. Someone handed her another smock.

The Russian translation for pogrom is "To wreak havoc, to demolish violently." That is precisely what Sophia experienced. Still dazed and in shock, Sophia pulled herself up and wandered outside. The attack had not yet fully ended. Straggling Cossacks, feeling safe from interference, were pillaging and plundering at will. The shouts and the screams enveloped her. She dragged herself with a weakened, painful leg up and down the streets, looking everywhere as if she were in another world, a play being performed all around her but not involving her. She felt nothing. She had no purpose. The was no fear or even anger. She wasn't a part of this play. Bodies were everywhere. Some people were dead; some people needed help. She kept walking. She wasn't part of this play. She was an observer, a member of the audience.

She recognized a dead Cossack on his back, knife still lying in his hand. Someone had cut his throat. She stared at him, bent down, and slowly removed the knife from his grasp. Calmly, staring into his eyes that were gazing at the sky, Sophia sank to her knees and then stabbed him in the chest, the belly, and the groin over and over, and yet once again. She did all this slowly, methodically, feeling nothing, as if she were butchering meat. She stopped. Then she dropped the knife on his chest and walked home. Only now did she notice her limp from the sharp pain in her leg. A leg that had been bruised, lacerated, and stretched unreasonably in an unseemly manner in her own attack.

As she entered the door, only a few of the gathered household members bothered to look up. The Russian soldiers had begun to leave as she walked home. This had occurred before. It would happen again. Those surviving wanted normalcy. Her family expected Sophia to provide that. They had no feelings towards her other than irritation that she was late. Everybody wanted to return to the household's routine of yesterday. As they watched her dragging her leg across the floor, there was little concern for what she had just experienced. Like a robot, Sophia started to make the soup.

But what was "the nice yesterday" like for Sophia and her fellow villagers? Over the past few decades, the Russians had taken control of more and more land from the Poles. The Jews, who often experienced relative quiet under Polish rule, were now settled into shtetls, the Russian word for 'small towns.' They were not allowed to travel outside of the territory set aside for them. Fearing business competition from the Jewish population in the 1790s, Catherine the Great ordered Jews to live in these dilapidated, impoverished areas.

The Jews, a minority group, had known persecution since biblical times. In the years surrounding Sophia's rape, the attack on the shtetl was not unique. Anti-Jewish attacks were frequent during the 1800s in the Russian Empire. Thousands of Jewish homes were destroyed, many families were reduced to poverty, and numerous people were injured, killed, and raped. Tragically, Sophia's experience was typical.

The Jews were not allowed to own land that would enable them to compete with the nobility. Instead, their financial and organizational acumen benefitted their nobleman employers. Further, their contacts within the extensive network of farmers and other Jewish shtetls throughout the countryside proved valuable in helping their employers with the marketing of products and all matters of commerce and finance. This was the source of Sophia's husband Efraim's financial independence.

Sophia's life before the rape benefitted neither from her husband's position nor financial stability. Not even the positive aspects of the Jewish culture in the shtetl could create any comfort for her. Sophia's mother had died while delivering Sophia, her only child. Sophia's father, Abe, was always resentful of Sophia for killing his beloved wife, Sarah. He raised Sophia with some help from his sister, Eva. Aunt Eva occasionally provided guidance and brief encouragement to the young girl, who needed it while growing up.

However, much of the physical responsibility for Sophia's rearing was left to her dad. Although he was never physically abusive, frequently, when upset or drinking, he would tell Sophia clearly that she "owed him" for creating his loneliness and taking Sarah from him. Her Aunt Eva attempted to counteract her brother's emotional abuse and reassure Sophia that she had done nothing wrong.

Abe, considered an eligible bachelor in the eyes of the matchmakers, would never recommit to another woman. He never healed from his loss and avoided facing any other loss. This, likely, also kept him emotionally distant from Sophia. He knew that he would someday lose her, too. As a young girl growing up, she received occasional attention, but the only love she witnessed was when listening to her father talk about her dead mother.

Despite often feeling like an orphan, Sophia was lucky in ways she might not have realized at the time. Abe often talked of his wife, Sarah, in favorable terms. Sarah was bright and strong. Abe saw Sophia's mother as capable, depended on her advice, and especially loved her sensitivities. He could have seen these traits in his daughter if he had looked. Sophia inherited good genes from her mother. Sophia sought and had many close friends. She was warm and kind.

As she entered adolescence, her father became more restrictive in what he allowed her to do. Of course, he felt he was protecting his daughter. But when other kids would get together, even for religious holiday experiences, he would keep Sophia home as a companion for himself. Sophia became more resentful of her dad's control. On the one hand, she felt sorry for him and cared for him. Even wanted to take care of him. But, on the other hand, she did everything to create distance between him and herself.

When she was fourteen, she started liking a boy her age, Seymour. As the months went by, they became inseparable. Aunt Eva warned Sophia about certain boundaries that she must maintain, and Sophia did that. But Seymour was her go-to person. He was that person in life she could trust, talk openly with, and rely on. In many ways, he was the mirror image of herself. Their mutual respect grew into love.

When Sophia turned sixteen, Abe suddenly died, likely from a heart attack. Although Sophia had grown even further apart from her father as she fell in love with Seymour, this loss was still an unexpected tragedy. More so than she realized at the time. Some say that placing flowers on a coffin gives a sense of release that one cannot express verbally. As Sophia walked forward and bent to put one flower on her dad's wooden box casket, she felt no such release. She was torn between love and hate. Only a week before his death, Abe had told Sophia that he had arranged a marriage for her to a man she had never met, Efraim. She would have to immediately sever her ties with Seymour, who had an uncertain future. The man she would be betrothed to, Efraim, could provide stability and a lovely family for her.

The Torah explains the common practice of a man paying the father of an unmarried virgin a price, a dowry, to sleep with her and make her his wife. Did Efraim have a subconscious awareness of his heart condition, therefore trying to protect Sophia by providing for her? Or, knowing that he was losing her to Seymour, maybe Abe decided to follow a common custom and line his own pockets? We'll never know. But the dowry was paid, meaning the contract was signed. The community would see it that way. Sophia had no wiggle room in this situation. Running away was not an option.

At the graveside service, Sophia asked her aunt if she could spend some time alone at her home. She needed some time alone. In the comfort of her tiny house, Sophia screamed, cried, threw things, and tried to empty her emotional basket of all the feelings she'd never be able to release in public. They may have to stay bottled up forever, given the future Sophia saw ahead.

She hoped to see and speak with Seymour, hold and hug him. Unfortunately, Seymour was young and not ready for marriage. His father wisely chose to have Seymour accompany him on his monthly trip, where he would peddle goods and arrange agreements. They would be gone for about two weeks, long enough for Sophia to have been moved to Efraim's shtetl. After that, Sophia never saw or heard from or about Seymour again. She was about to enter her new marriage, angry and despondent at the loss of her lover.

In Jewish tradition, it is common for the family to have seven days of formalized mourning, which is called sitting Shiva. This is expected behavior, especially for children. Although this was to be held at Aunt Eva's home, Sophia would be the center of attention for those shtetl members coming by to express condolences. Many people are steeped in this overwhelming commitment to religious piety. But not so a bereft, traumatized sixteen-year-old girl, looking at the task of lying with an older, grotesque husband and then raising his spoiled four-year-old boy.

Efraim, a widower, was well thought of by his community. He had married late so that he could save money made from his many brokerage-like contacts. His first wife died right after childbirth, and he quickly rose to near the top of the list of available males on the marriage broker's inventory. His residence was populated by over a thousand people. Sophia's father chose Efraim for the marriage transaction.

By the time Sophia had bred her first child with Efraim, growing up and living in a shtetl in the old country was challenging and frightening for everyone. It was even more problematic when your role was one of near servitude and a breeding machine. Sophia was also expected to care for Efraim's oldest son full-time, who had already been schooled in entitlement. In his obnoxious, child-like manner, he quickly let Sophia know who the boss was. He forever maintained the perch at the top of the pecking order. Efraim did not discourage this behavior. He promoted it."

The group, in rapt attention, waited as Elijah paused. He then stood up and suggested that it was time for supper. The evening before, the group had voted to share a desert stew on New Year's Day. A large black kettle was placed on the stand over a prepared structure of wood, designed to burn just high enough to heat the heavy cauldron. One by one, the campers opened their can of veggies, meat, or sauces and emptied them into the pot that was soon labeled a stew. Desert stews became a metaphor for the blending together of any diverse group in the desert. One of the newbies was doubtful, questioning whether there might not be too much of one ingredient or not enough of another. Charlie, a seasoned expert, told her not to worry. "There is enough salt in that boiling pot that even the biggest hater of Brussels sprouts won't taste them. Instead, you'll have a mixture of goodies bathed in a sauce designed to preserve our meal throughout the digestive process!"

Sitting around satiated and sipping coffee, many campers felt incomplete. They wanted more. They were angry at Efraim, even at Abe.

The campers all settled in that evening. The fire to heat the stew had been fed more logs to serve double duty, becoming the evening campfire. There were many conversations among the group members as they shared curiosities, assumptions, and confusion. They wanted more. Any superficial gaiety merely covered feelings of agitation. Sophia's story couldn't help but create discomfort. Many campers would be further burdened that night once they heard the rest of the story. There would be more than a few who wouldn't sleep well. But for now, the campfire was stoked. People moved their chairs so that most sat with the prevailing wind at their backs. But it was a calm night. The wind was less of a bother than the story they'd heard. Elijah came out of his rig, knowing he could provoke them even more.

"Nine months after the rape, Morris was born. The pregnancy was terribly difficult for Sophia. She had horrible morning sickness and was operating in a weakened state throughout. Yet, Efraim demanded that she continue to function as a housekeeper, cook, and lover. She would be roused to make a meal for one of their older children if she were found asleep in the kitchen, overcome by exhaustion. They were not sympathetic to their mother because their father would not allow it. Any goodness shown towards her, or any help given, was done in secret. Efraim's oldest son wondered if the "bastard baby" couldn't be put up for adoption. The culture in the house was not one of a home consistent with Jewish tradition or belief. It was a culture designed for Efraim's comfort and his son's ego.

When Morris was only two months old and crying from hunger in the next room, Sophia stopped cleaning the kitchen to take him to her breast. Morris's oldest brother told her that Morris could starve for all he cared. He took Morris from Sophia and told her to return to her chores. Morris's one sister had been aloof to her own mother's struggles. She, too, seemed bitter of Morris's existence and preferred to ally herself with her full-blooded brothers and father. Morris remained the youngest son and child of his family. No children were born after the rape. Sophia appeared infertile.

Not being Efraim's biological son, Morris was forever called the bastard child. None of his brothers considered him a genuine part of the family. Morris grew up resented by his older brothers, sister, and father. The trauma Morris faced was painful and significant in that he was frequently reminded he was inadequate and unworthy. His response was not anger or revenge but a herculean effort to gain approval by doing what others would value and consider good, loving deeds. It rarely worked to benefit him. He grew up feeling like an underdog and was forever unsuccessful in striving to achieve acceptance.

Sophia understood well what was going on in the family and its impact on Morris. She did her best to reassure him of his worth. As he got older, his mother explained why others disliked him. She was a loving mother who taught Morris well and saw in him her own ability to assess a situation and calculate a response. Morris loved and respected his mother. He was caring towards his friends. He showed creative skill in working with his hands. Sophia did everything she could to counter the negative impact Morris's siblings and stepfather had on him. She told Morris that someday he would have better circumstances and enjoy success. But Sophia died relatively young. Morris was then left to raise himself. Sophia's tragic demise was likely from a broken heart, a body wrecked with exhaustion, and a will strangled by sexual and emotional abuse.

Chapter Two

The tall, weathered man became silent as he hung his head in thought. He just stared at the group, processing the tragedy of Sophia's life of abuse and degradation. Then, quietly pacing in front of the group and staring down, he muttered, barely above a whisper, "Let's jump forward a generation to events in the United States. I want to tell you about Rachel. The year is 1928. In the late afternoons and evenings, Rachel usually flirted with men standing in the hotel lobby where she worked. Her job? Encourage them to put money on the counter as she turns the cage holding the dice. It was fun and safe, and she made great tips."

Then, Elijah turned his back to the group as if he were contemplating. Suddenly, he whirled back and shouted animatedly,

"A cracking gunshot reverberated in the large hotel lobby! Rachel recoiled at the unexpected noise. Stunned, she saw blood pooling by her feet. She stared. Was it hers? Horrified but not wounded, she tried to run but slipped, falling on top of an outstretched arm. She felt angry that the arm was there. *Nobody should have left it there on the floor,* she thought. Suddenly, nothing made sense in her world. All Rachel knew was that she wanted a different world, not here, not now, not covered in blood...

SHIT! I'VE GOT TO HIDE. WHERE CAN I HIDE? Maybe run? The mind is not rational at this time, just paralyzed or impulsive. She had no plan but knew that she had to be somewhere else. She got up, screaming and weeping, and ran, trying to fight through the panicking crowd. Her thoughts and legs were swimming in all directions as she slipped and fell into the blood again.

She struggled to get up and then ran towards the door of the hotel. It felt like she was moving in molasses. Others blocked her way, pushing and shoving her. *Why are they so inconsiderate? Why won't they let me through? Why are they trapping me?* Fighting for safety, she couldn't find the strength to open the door. Finally, being tiny and bashed by guests trying to escape from the danger, she was almost flung onto the sidewalk. The cold cement was a momentary reprieve, almost a comfortable feeling. Rachel's only thought was to escape. She got up and bolted from the hotel.

Gasping, short of breath, she could run no more. She walked quicky, first in one direction and then in another. She had no plan. Suddenly, Rachel saw a bus approaching. She got on without a thought about where it might take her. She was desperate for immediate relief by fleeing the scene.

Immediately, bus riders began to stare at her. She shivered and wondered why. The bus went for blocks, stopping and starting every few minutes, with people getting on and off as they walked in front of her. No one chose to sit next to her. She wondered why. She was as yet unaware of her torn, bloody clothes. The stares scared her even more. Looking away to avoid their glances, she sat huddled up, her eyes only focused on the floor. The disgusted stares made her shiver. Serendipitously, Rachel looked up and recognized a neighborhood grocery store as it went by the bus. This gave her a welcomed but brief relief because it meant home was nearby.

Suddenly, she looked down at her torn blouse covered with tear stains and splashes of blood. This was not the outfit she wore when kissing her mother goodbye that morning as she supposedly left for her clerking job at the hotel. No, a dress short enough for a ballerina or a cigarette girl would only infuriate her mom. Once again, panic set in and quickly turned to fear, confusion, and, for the first time, doubt. She wondered what she was doing in a job that could be this dangerous. Her life seemed to change in an instant. Rachel lost all semblance of stability and security. She tightened her arms around her body to try to control her shivering as she realized why everyone had been staring at her.

Rachel had begun the job nearly a year before she was only seventeen. She was dating Saul, and an opportunity arose right after graduating high school. The woman previously running the dice game in the lobby of the Book Cadillac, the largest hotel in Detroit, was leaving to get married. Saul knew the hotel manager and suggested his girlfriend, Rachel, for the job. Saul alleged that she was eighteen and an Honors high school graduate who was well-suited for such work. The manager was dubious about anyone so young handling the job, but Saul called in a chip and asked that Rachel be given a chance. The manager suggested that Rachel come for an interview with Darlene, who was departing and knew the job well. If Darlene felt that Rachel could handle the job, the manager would give her a try."

Elijah continued, "some of you may find it strange that a seventeen-year-old girl was mixed up with a debonair twenty-five-year-old man. How did these two become a pair? Let's look at their lives.

Rachel and Saul came from a bustling city that was being industrialized quickly by first-generation immigrants and their descendants. While the city offered a wonderful future to many, for others, it was full of barriers and hurdles. Prohibition also led to troubled waters because of the organized mobs that were engaged in illegal trades in alcohol and sex. There were also endless conflicts between labor and management. There were wars within families at the dinner table and between families on the streets.

So, where do Rachel and Saul fit in? Saul was an immigrant who arrived on these shores as a young child. He witnessed his parents start as peddlers and work hard to become self-sufficient and raise five children. Saul, being the oldest, witnessed each bump and hurdle his parents encountered. Because he knew immigrants had to work twice as hard to survive, he spent his life trying to fit in and make money.

Contrary to Saul's experience of witnessing and often participating in the immigrants' struggle, Rachel grew up with parents who established a successful electrical business. Her older brother adored her, and she had an older sister who acted like a second mother. Rachel knew no real struggle. She was bright in school, even starting half a year ahead of most kids and skipping a grade. She had no dreams other than being the perfect homemaker, mother, and wife.

Although Saul was eight years older than Rachel, they grew up in the same neighborhood, only a few doors from each other. Saul considered her a cute girl, and Rachel drooled over this older guy, more suitable for her older sister.

Because Rachel often tagged along with her sister, she was in crowds of older kids accompanied by her sister and brother. Even though she was young, the older kids tolerated her presence. They actually liked her and didn't consider her a nuisance. As she matured through adolescence, the boys took notice of her. She became a full-fledged member of the group. As the jokes between her and Saul progressed, they started flirting, and a relationship of mutual respect and caring began. Soon, they were officially dating, and the future relationship was cast.

Rachel's parents initially objected fiercely to her dating Saul. However, he was charming and had managed to make Rachel's mom fall for his charm. He had complimented her cooking by repeatedly pleading with her to invite him for dinner- an approach that would seem forward to some won her mother over. Saul was also very respectful of Rachel's father, not just to his face but behind his back to Rachel, too. Saul definitely respected her father's success in building a business that employed others. He respected that kind of success.

Rachel never imagined herself doing much beyond secretarial work. She was a very fast typist. But the interview prospect at the hotel Saul had arranged excited her. Yet, she was apprehensive. The routine of taking the bets and handling the money would be easy. But she needed to get more information from Marlene. This departing employee was happy to be open and frank with Rachel.

Darlene explained that the job involved two main things. The first was encouraging the betting, the play. "Honestly, dear, that job is all about being enticing, using a low level of flirting, more teasing than seductive. Charm them so they show off their gambling prowess and challenge them to win. Suggest that you might even bring them good luck- that is an open-ended promise that can stimulate all types of vague fantasies.

The second thing you will need to do is diplomatically handle any overreaction to the flirting, especially if the man involved happens to be drinking too much." Darlene said, "The job is really easy and fun unless some guy pushes too hard. But the tips are well worth the occasional aggravation. Hey girl! Nothing ventured, nothing gained. You are tiny and young. Some guys may try to try to take advantage of you, but the boss doesn't want any trouble. There are security guards roaming to protect you. After all, dice in a hotel lobby is just a game, not big-time gambling. So, emotions don't run too high. Do you think you would be up to this kind of challenge?" Rachel could see no reason not to jump at this opportunity except one, her parents.

Rationalization is a wonderful tool for moving forward when we like. It works because it minimizes the negatives and accentuates the positives. Rachel had grown up hearing the need for occasional "little white lies." At this moment, she kicked down the guilt of lying to her parents by convincing herself that a clerk taking money from someone checking into a hotel was not significantly different from a clerk taking money selling cigarettes or playing a game.

Yet, truth be known, Rachel's life had more than just a few white lies to smooth the way to do what she wanted to do. She was not always forthright with her parents when it came to her relationship with Saul. Many of the "movies" they went to see were, in fact, parties of Saul's older acquaintances. There, she learned how to handle the advances from older men and enjoy a bit of scotch. Also, many alleged "meals out" were eaten at clubs with dancing, booze, and mostly adults, who were much older than her. But Rachel had never caused her parents a moment of worry or trouble. Besides, her older sister and brother liked Saul, were close to his age, and could and did vouch for him. They also watched over their younger sib at some of the super clubs.

Rachel, now only eighteen, enjoyed the good times of the roaring 20s in Detroit. She enjoyed the social life she had with Saul, who cared for her and respected her. She valued her job. Many friends were jealous of her unique opportunity. She secretly enjoyed their envy but never stopped to consider the risks and benefits of being part of a bigger, more complex organization and social environment. She never considered what the downside could be.

In the spring of 1928, Rachel and Saul got married. Initially, she thought of quitting this job to start a household of their own. But most of the houses she wanted in her parent's neighborhood were too expensive. Moreover, the young couple was not yet ready for children. So, they planned on finding an apartment nearby and saving some money until they had the right place. Till then, they stayed with their parents. There was plenty of room in the house, and their company was appreciated. Rachel kept the job. Her long-term goal was to be a good mother and wife and run a household that would make her husband proud. This was typical of the time.

So Rachel took the job at the hotel and thoroughly enjoyed it until today. Suddenly, her fairytale life with Saul and keeping the job did not seem so wise. Rachel had never realized what that meant: Saul could get her a job at seventeen running a lobby dice game in a big hotel! Her parents knew nothing of the activity or the fancy dresses she wore. She could not go home in that dress, bloody at that!

Rachel thought, *"I can't let my parents see me like this, see my deception. They will be so hurt and disappointed in me. They'll never trust me again. I hate the thought of treating them so poorly."* Her parents knew nothing of the activity or the fancy dress she wore. There was no way she could go home dressed like that.

She got off the bus and ran to her friend's house. Likely, Sally's parents wouldn't be home YET. Neither would Sally, but Rachel knew where the house key was hidden. She could sneak in, ditch the bloody dress, wash up, and borrow some of Sally's clothes. Luckily, Rachel and Sally wore nearly the same size. When she got there, her shaking fingers couldn't find the key. *It has to be here. It has to be here.* Fruitlessly, she reached all around, groping at the dirt and searching under the rocks. Finally, she fell to the ground, feeling hopeless and in despair. She was sobbing at the thought of what had happened and in fear of her parents' response when, luckily, Sally got home. Rachel cried, and Sally helped her clean up and change clothes. Eventually, Rachel calmed. She knew that her parents would question any unusual emotion.

She took a quick shower and let Sally help her rub the blood from her arms and legs. She stood frozen in front of the mirror as Sally asked her what had happened. Numb and frightened, she recounted the whole story in monotone. Sally, understanding that Rachel was in her own head, gave her a pair of clean jeans and a button-down shirt to put on. She sat her down on her bed and said, "I'm going to give you 5 minutes. Quickly wear these clothes and listen to me. Hey, look at me. You're okay. I'm here. You need to get home before my parents see you like this and get suspicious. Remember, everything is alright. Perk up before they notice something is wrong."

With that, Sally left the room. Rachel forced herself to snap out of the trance she was in so that she could put on the clothes set out on the bed and leave. Sally was right. Even though she still had a few hours left before her official pack-up time, she needed to get out of there before Sally's parents got home.

As Rachel bid Sally goodbye, she quickly made her way back home. Once inside, her parents questioned why she was home early from her job as a clerk.

Taking a deep breath and plastering a fake smile on her face, she said, 'Oh, things were relatively slow at work. I was having some stomach issues. Just not feeling up to par. So, the boss suggested that I go home and rest. He's so thoughtful, you know.'

Once safely upstairs in her room, Rachel sat at the edge of her bed, fearful of what would come next. She was too anxious to think straight. She put her face in her hands and sobbed. For weeks, Saul had been dragging his feet about looking for another house to rent or buy. Failing, he'd been saying that it was time they left Detroit. But leaving was never a part of the plan Rachel had in mind for the future. She wanted to live close to her family. She and Saul lived in their house, and she wanted to look for a place in the same neighborhood. She had always imagined life in Detroit. Her long-held vision of the future was to marry, have children, and live close to her family, enjoying the support she'd always known. Saul's desire to leave DETROIT threatened her vision and dream. She wondered, *For what? A life so separate from those I love, a life of uncertainty? Why should we do that?*

Saul had begun going on and on about how the economic conditions in Detroit were changing. He said the struggles with the unions and mobs made everything seem uncertain, even potentially dangerous. Economically, too, things were getting more challenging. Rachel knew little of this. She had always lived in the sheltered existence of her parents' world. Her father had a good business and seemed stable. Saul's family also seemed so adoring and stable. They, too, had a good income. Neither her parents nor her in-laws expressed the same concerns as Saul did. Usually, sitting around the dinner table, there was non-stop information, gossip, arguing, and discussion of current events. *Was Saul uniquely informed, or was he the one out of touch? Or maybe he was exaggerating?* Rachel wondered. She was beginning to feel that she was the knot in a heavy rope being pulled in a tug of war.

Rarely was Rachel privy to the specific details behind Saul's reasoning and concerns. He was eight years older and seemed so sure of himself, so successful. But now, she wondered, *successful by what means? And how could he have such a different view of her hometown from her parents?* She tried to ask him, but he offered generalities in discussions, not giving enough details to make a convincing or coherent story. Rachel wondered if she was too naive or stupid to understand the complicated intricacies of the business world. With dice, you win or lose. That was a simple and profitable business for the hotel. Life was more complex. Life with Saul would really be more complicated. Rachel understood that. Scared as she was, she would often laugh, imagining living out a destiny she couldn't even fathom. Saul had never described his long-term goals. His lack of direction stirred up her anxiety.

In truth, what did Saul even do? He had told her of his numerous activities with newspapers and various businesses, but no names of employers or descriptions of daily jobs were given. When others asked him what he did, he replied that he was a consultant. Her dad was nice to Saul and liked him. But Dad acted differently when discussing Saul than he did when talking about other businessmen he knew. Her father seemed suspicious of Saul. Dad was always bothered that Saul was always vague about his employment. Her father acknowledged that Saul was very bright but didn't like how he was also so elusive. But she thought Dad was so old-fashioned, from the old country. Saul was an immigrant who grew up in America at a young age. He was sweet, fun-loving, and well-dressed. He always seemed to have money and was so adoring of her. Dad needed to understand that Saul was part of an economic scene, more complicated and sophisticated than Dad knew.

Rachel was bright, beautiful, caring, and in love. Also, she was naive and yet unaware of the dangers of Saul's itinerant employment. She talked to her girlfriends about the gangs, impressing them with Saul's money, savoir-faire, and power. They said the gangs, such as the Jewish mafia and the Purple Gang, were connected to Capone. In quiet times, the possible danger seemed more exciting than threatening.

Rachel had often taken some of her friends to parties at the hotel. Dancing, beautiful women with extravagant gowns, laughter, and booze. It was all there. All her parents knew was that the hotel put on parties for their registered guests. To Rachel, life in Detroit in 1927 seemed like playtime. She and her fellow first-generation immigrants knew better than their parents. These new ways of doing things were part of the culture of a blossoming America. They must leave the old behind. People were going to drink, regardless of prohibition. Someone had to provide the booze. The temperance movement couldn't stop progress.

Rachel and her peers knew about the reality of the liquor trade and the gangs. They could hardly avoid this common street knowledge. What Rachel didn't fully know or understand was what SHE experienced as playtime, good light-hearted fun, was becoming ragged and dangerous around the edges. Her current impressions had once been correct. For a while, there had been significant stability. The gangs divided up territory. But the more recent Chicago influence from Capone stirred things up. The Purple Gang controlled much of the whiskey flow across the border from Canada. Capone found the gang to be a convenient ally. But there were always some young rebels who wanted more influence. Organized ethnic crews fought with each other and among themselves. Men postured. People died. Unknown at the time was that the chaos and the gang killings were sure to get worse, as was the economy. But neither Rachel's parents nor Saul fully anticipated what was to come.

The Valentine's Day Massacre occurred shortly later, as did Black Tuesday, marking the beginning of the Wall Street Crash. Saul hadn't expected the latter but had long feared some form of the mob massacre.

But so much of the danger that Rachel sometimes heard about was outside the reality of her day-to-day fun, easy existence. The gangs were not in her part of town. The problems were still across the river in Windsor, Canada, separated by a river without a bridge. Truth be known, all of Rachel's friends' parents and Rachel's parents were worried. The Jews have a Yiddish word, nudnick, that refers to ne'er do wells, who were seen as harassing or troublesome. Rachel's parents' generation had seen plenty of mayhem spewed from these people. They could be dangerous as they sought and gained more money and power. Her parents were not as naive as Rachel in many ways. They knew of the dangers but rarely talked about it in front of the kids, who were all, by then, adults. Yet, her parents knew little of Rachel's exposure to these gangs. Indeed, no one knew the extent, if any, of Saul's involvement. But her father, Joseph, often worried that Saul was a nudnick.

Now, an unknown shooter frighteningly brought Rachel into the world of her parents and Saul's awareness. The sudden lack of stability made playtime at the hotel seem uninviting, scary, and bloody. The noise in the lobby at the Book Cadillac Hotel was no longer joyous but now seemed chaotic and threatening. Rachel was beginning to think that maybe Saul was right. They'd better make themselves scarce. Her mind was like a whirling dervish dealing with all these racing thoughts and observations.

When Saul rushed in after arriving home, he was relieved that Rachel was physically okay. But, tremulous, tearful, and confused, she nearly fell into Saul's arms sobbing. Why? Why?

'Honey, this is what I've been worried about all along. Detroit is a growing economic powerhouse. There is tremendous opportunity here. But the struggle between unions and management, the lure for territorial rights to alcohol sales, the gambling, the numbers game, and prostitution make the landscape fraught with danger. The status quo out there is pretty unstable and unpredictable.

We need to be better situated with an established business to jump in and compete in that melee. But we have no such business. So we have to leave, and the sooner, the better.' Saul became insistent that they had to leave. Likely, he personally had to go, and that would include her. 'Let's find a quieter place, a safer place. Let me take care of you.'

Saul had been saying similar things for weeks, but Rachel paid little attention to him. Now, her experience made his words feel more urgent and vital. It wasn't Saul's reasoning that persuaded her to leave. It was her own newly found fear, pure and simple.

Rachel now accepted that Saul was right. She would deeply miss her friends and all the lovely girls who were by her side at her wedding. Rachel's history was simple. She had done well in school. She was a fast typist and determined to get an excellent job to help her family. However, the lobby hostess job Saul got her was better, not just because of the salary but because of the tips. But she never thought of the job as dangerous or permanent. Sure, there were the constant approaches from the many men who passed through, but she was intelligent and clever in knowing how to deal with all the advances. It had become a game of its own that she thoroughly enjoyed.

Her older brother and sister were as dear to her as she was to them. Her parents, aunts, uncles, and cousins were all a tight-knit family from whom she'd never been away. So, leaving would be more than problematic. It was something she never expected to happen. Her siblings married and stayed in Detroit, living a few doors from the family home. Rachel had hoped to do the same.

Saul had been trying to soften the idea of leaving in the last few weeks by suggesting they take a trip. He called it "sort of a honeymoon.". Now, she was ready to do as he suggested. But she was worried about leaving her parents. True to form, they were in tears when she told them she was going, even for a brief trip, a delayed honeymoon. Her father did not believe that they would come back and settle down in Detroit. He never really trusted Saul, a man he continued to see as very bright but perhaps shady and unreliable.

'But, Dad, it is like a honeymoon for a little while.'

All of Saul's younger brothers lived in Detroit and attended the wedding. Rachel told her mom and dad that the first trip to Chicago was to visit Saul's sister, whom she had yet to meet. Even though the shooting was a major news item on the radio and newspaper, Rachel had told them nothing about being at the shooting. Rachel and Saul packed and left.

Rachel acted bravely. She trusted Saul because now, she was scared and didn't have much of a choice. No longer could she keep her present job. Saul had no benefits or responsibilities of permanent employment. Rachel chose to leave her home town with Saul by her side and doubt in her mind. Many family stories detail what happened in Detroit that motivated Saul's going. You'd have to dig hard to find the truth about why the couple, especially Saul, seemingly enmeshed in Detroit, had to leave while others stayed. Many Detroit citizens, potentially exposed to the same chaos as Saul and Rachel, remained in Detroit. Why didn't Saul and Rachel stay?"

With this, Elijah stopped his story. In a voice less intense, more friendly, as if becoming a large cuddly grandpa teddy bear, he said,

"So begins our story of Rachel, someone I knew pretty well. But that is probably enough of our story for tonight. I'm sure all of you will have some thoughts to share tomorrow."

Chapter Three

Sitting on the edge of their seats, wanting to know what would happen next with this unusual couple, the campers moved their chairs closer to Elijah. Some wondered if he was toying with them, teasing. True, his tale had created tension, but that was his intention. The winter events in the desert created camaraderie. For many, the real gold in the desert was not something bright and shiny but rather the opportunities to share, learn, and explore with others. Elijah sensed the tension in the air and began to reveal more.

"If you are confused by Saul, welcome to the club. Here was a good-looking, well-spoken, bright, successful, charming, and helpful beyond belief young man who nobody really knew. If you asked, "What does Saul do?" no one could tell you. "What does Saul think or feel?" Same answer. Some person could reveal a thing or two he'd done with them, usually successfully, but that is hardly a full picture of a man. Similarly, each person in Saul's life had his or her version of why Saul was so intent on leaving Detroit. Of course, the real historical incidents of Saul's past were lost, but rumor, rumors and secrets were plentiful among friends and family. He was especially a source of gossip for his many cousins. Some speculated that he probably owed money to some bad people and needed to skip town. Others said that he was in trouble with the law, or no, he pissed off some gang hotshot. And on and on it went. Seemingly, Saul had no close friends. No one knew him well, knew what he felt or what motivated him. He was truly a mystery to those around him.

Once Saul arrived home on the day of the shooting, Rachel began to calm down. They needed to talk in private. Rachel told her mom they were going out and hoped to see "The Singing Fool," a new Warner Brothers production with some talkie features and a post-production accompanying musical score.

"But isn't your tummy hurting, dear? Don't you want to rest a while?"

"Oh, I'm feeling much better now. It will be fine," Rachel tried to sound convincing. She stretched and smiled at her mother, trying to portray how well she was feeling. As soon as her mother looked a little convinced, she left with Saul and went for a long, long walk.

"Well, I'm certainly not singing, but I feel like a fool for working in that damn place," she said as soon as she was away from the concerned stare of her parents.

"Honey, I'm so relieved that you weren't hurt. It must have been a terribly frightening experience for you. I can't even begin to imagine. It's over now, so don't worry; you absolutely don't have to go back to work there. I will speak to whoever necessary to ensure that they don't force you to come back."

"Well, I'm certainly not going back tomorrow. I'm still shaking."

"I'll let Horace, the manager, know. He'll understand. What matters is that you're okay. Can you tell me what happened?"

Rachel was mostly silent but kept debriefing Saul about what had happened as if somehow she could make it pass into oblivion. After listening to Rachel attentively and offering support where needed, they stopped for a coke, and Saul felt it safe to voice his thoughts.

"Honey, you know I'd never encourage you to go back to work again at that place. You'd always be looking over your shoulder. Even as you are walking with me this evening, you keep looking back to see what is behind you."

"Yeah...you're right. I hadn't noticed, but I'm still pretty shook up. It was all so quick. It seemed like the worst part wasn't the pain of falling or being mangled by the crowd but the utter feeling of having no control. For a minute, I didn't think I'd make it out alive. That damn place, I hate it."

"I hate to tell you, honey, but that's the city we live in right now. It wasn't a product of the hotel. It's a fine hotel with very high-class guests who are known to be polite and pleasant people. We live in a city of conflict with big money at stake. I think it would do us both some good if we took a little vacation, get your mind off what happened, and go have some fun somewhere else for a couple of weeks. We've never really had a honeymoon. And you haven't even met my sister, Rebecca, who lives in Chicago. We could go there. It's a great city, lots to do and see. Then, we could hop on a train and head West. Maybe even go to sunny California and swim in the Pacific. Our whole lives here are focused on work and living in small places. We deserve a vacation. What do you think, honey?"

The conversation was left in the air. After the shooting, Rachel didn't return to work and spent a lot of time at home. It was not long before, day after day, she began to feel like the walls were closing in. Saul would occasionally have something to say about some fun or interesting events happening in cities far away, like in Dallas, Boston, Kansas City, and even New York. Rachel began to look at these places as opportunities.

Rachel started helping her mother cook and clean and visiting older women in her mother's group to keep herself occupied. However, it wasn't long before all this began to take a toll on her marriage. In many ways, she and Saul were opposites. Saul's life was defined by his ongoing personal challenges. On the other hand, Rachel's life, which was usually calm and smooth, was now challenged by feeling displaced. She didn't have a home of her own, a family to attend to, or even a purpose away from her family home. Her marriage could only be defined by her looking forward to Saul's return at the end of the day and hearing superficial reports of his experiences. They shared little else.

Friends and relatives could understand why she dated "Dapper Dan" but not why she chose to marry him. They ruled out pregnancy about four or five months later but had no real idea what had pushed her "go" button. Maybe it was lust or puppy love at her young age, perhaps. Just old-fashioned lust, they speculated.

Rachel was the one who now brought up the idea of a vacation. Saul offered muted enthusiasm for the idea, trying not to look so obvious. But he was not without a plan. He suggested only a weeklong trip to visit his sister, Rebecca, and explore Chicago. Rachel, afraid of being confined to the limits of Rebecca's day-to-day activities, suggested that maybe three days in Chicago would do the trick.

Saul replied, "That doesn't seem much like a vacation. It seems like a long weekend getaway. Chicago is a good jumping-off point, but I'd like to have more fun exploring new places. It may be years before we have the time and freedom to do this again. Once we are both working and have kids, it may be decades before we see beyond the city limits of Detroit!"

Rachel began to smile at Saul's enthusiasm as if he were a kid pleading for another chance on the merry-go-round before leaving the park. Saul thought he also saw some enthusiasm in her smile. He gilded the lily. He reminded Rachel of his family's history.

"Think about it, dear. My grandmother went through a pogrom, rape, abuse, and lived most of her life in a few square blocks. She brought up my dad in a way so that he could be successful in life, and he is. She had little to live for but more abuse. Her only loving relationship was with her one son, Morris. All her other children mistreated or ignored her. Efraim's oldest son sounds like he was a tyrant toward her. I suspect that she might not have expected to live very long. She certainly experienced man's inhumanity toward man in the worst possible ways. What I found most impressive about her was that she didn't teach Morris negativity, to constantly be careful and look over his shoulder, to hunker down and hide. Instead, she encouraged him to envision a better, freer future for himself. His excursions were at great risk and effort. Now, our parents have helped us arrive at a position of what would have seemed like unlimited possibilities to my grandmother and likely your grandparents too, and you're afraid of going beyond the city limits for more than a long weekend? Is that what they struggled for? Now is our chance for something new, different. But of course, I won't force you. The decision lies in your hands."

When he saw that Rachel was quiet, Saul sighed, hunched his shoulders, expressing defeat, and went to the bathroom to pee.

After weeks of discussion, but little actual planning, Saul and Rachel did get on a train to Chicago. Well-dressed and groomed, they looked like the successful couple they had hoped to become. Saul was in a gray suit with white pinstripes. Intended to lengthen his short stature, he eschewed the bow tie, preferring the more recent silk long neck ties tucked neatly behind his vest.

Rachel wore her best suit, a classic cut showing off her silhouette. She decided to forgo wearing a hat. Her long blond hair, beautifully coiffed, spoke of someone of high class. Her cosmetic carry-on contained lunches packed by Celia, Rachel's mom. The two sat side by side as the train quickly left behind the only sense of home Rachel had ever known.

Rachel leaned her head against the window, not to rest but for support. The countryside whizzing by was not perceived as beautiful new scenery, only miles measuring the distance between her and her once secure life., Rachel still thought of herself as a teenager living at home, even if she were married. Her train seatmate was her life partner, but she wondered what kind of life they were set out to have. They needed to create a home, look for jobs, and talk about specific plans to re-establish the peace and comfort Rachel had known. Sometimes, Rachel would feel they were an organized partnership. Today, she felt hopeless and exhausted. Saul was similarly exhausted. He had walked a tightrope of fending off the competing recommendations, explanations, warnings, and pleadings that bombarded them as their families made their feelings known. Saul wanted to help Rachel feel safe in what they were about to do. He was wise enough not to deny the realities of what others were saying but had to put them in a different context for Rachel. To create a different paradigm, he emphasized the idea of a delayed honeymoon, likely a round trip. Yet, he bought only one-way tickets. That was a product of optimism that kept his anxiety level in check, at least to a tolerable level. There was no denying the possibility that this could be a fool's errand. Both parties were excited but looked better than they really felt on the inside.

We know two things for sure: having survived the family onslaught, Saul and Rachel did leave. Second, perhaps more importantly, Saul needed to be farther away from Detroit than Chicago for him to feel comfortable or safe. They stayed over a day and a half in Chicago, not to look around but to introduce Rachel to Rebecca, Saul's sister. The visit was short. Rebecca was often suspicious of her own brother's motives and intentions. But she cared dearly for him and wanted the best for him. Their bond went back to early childhood when Rebecca mothered and cared for him, especially when they had emigrated from Russia years ago. Having already left the family behind as she moved with her husband to Chicago, Rebecca was less critical of Saul's leaving Detroit. She also saw his creative side but warned him against rushing into anything based only on his unyielding optimism.

Rachel and Saul then got on an early night Rock Island train from Chicago and headed southwest. Unlike their first train trip, this time, they were both exhausted and fell asleep quickly. Saul's head lay against the window while Rachel's head lay comfortably on his shoulder. They arrived very early in the morning. The couple had a full day's layover in Des Moines before they could choose to hop on a connecting train to Kansas City or Omaha. They had yet to decide which. Rachel and Saul, but both expected to depart Des Moines that evening. Rachel was no longer looking over her shoulder for the first sign of trouble. Their long walks and excursions in Chicago erased the fear she'd briefly carried from the Detroit hotel fiasco. Her confident side that handled daily confrontations in the lobby was now suitably back in place. Yet, experiences in a new place were making her both excited and apprehensive.

After several hours of sleep on the train, Saul was antsy. He couldn't imagine sitting around the train station all day. He thought that it might be fun to explore Des Moines. Saul began to wonder if Des Moines was outside of the influence of the power brokers of crime in Chicago. Illegal booze was still a sought-after and consumed product in Des Moines, but local easy agricultural access to alcohol-corn in the surrounding farmland supplied plentiful raw materials for the illegal booze trade. Also, rural and away from the big city action, the local bootleggers could center their businesses in the state's more rural areas, miles away from the law or the influence of the mobs in Chicago or Detroit.

In Rachel's mind, they were ostensibly waiting for a connecting train going West. However, Saul was curious. He didn't want to pass up what might be a good opportunity.

Since they were in no rush, he suggested to Rachel that they take a cab to the city central and explore a bit of Des Moines. Not wanting to just sit in the train station for hours, Rachel quickly agreed. They checked their bags at the station so they could look around town. They sat for eggs and coffee at the station lunch counter as soon as it opened for early morning service.

When finished, they hailed a cab so that they could look around downtown. Many shops had not yet opened. They wandered for what seemed like hours to Rachel, who was burdened with traveling in high heels. She suggested that she take a cab back to the station, rest, and meet Saul for lunch later while he continued his exploration of the city.

Saul agreed and helped Rachel find a cab, then they both headed off in different directions.

Rachel returned to the busy station. She was like a petite, pretty China doll who sat quietly in the corner. People would expect little of her, she'd hoped. Indeed, she was out of her element but was not worried. Since she did not want to walk around with Saul, her only alternative was to be patient and wait for him as she rested.

She was an avid reader and had her book, but she after a while, found it hard to

concentrate and still looked up periodically to see if Saul was walking across the lobby.

Saul kept walking the streets.

He wandered up one street and down the next. He was still determining what he was searching for, perhaps something that spoke to him. Only his father, Morris, really understood how complex Saul was. The many threads of Saul's personality often yanked him in different directions. Having been down a similar road, his father knew that tug of war quite well. Both men, having the same struggle, were forever optimistic. Many experiences magnified Saul's optimism. Mostly, he was successful in his endeavors because of his curiosity and sense of an entrepreneurial and fun-loving spirit. The fact that he was a bit manipulative also helped. But Saul lived with the competing forces only his father knew and saw. Saul was very socially minded. In seeking to satisfy his own wants, he strongly believed and was committed to making things work out well for everyone. He cared for the welfare of others. That concern motivated him, but his inbred cynicism and skepticism made him wary of which path to choose. Though his optimism often overpowered his cautious worries, he frequently found himself at odds with himself.

There was one final ingredient to the son Morris saw. Saul had no sense of ultimate purpose or goal in life. Yes, he was successful in managing brief opportunities here and there. He was self-sufficient. Before Saul left, Morris advised him, "You are going on an odyssey, son. Will you return quickly? I know that you say the trip will be short. I believe that you believe that. But a man on a journey seeking a long-term future does not always find an answer quickly. You need to find a way to start a family to have stability. But keep going until you find what you want, or at least figure out what you want."

Walking, Saul remembered his father's words. His anonymity while exploring and wandering was a relief. Other than Rachel, he would have no one to report back to during the next evening meal discussion. The feeling of freedom and safety he experienced on the streets of Des Moines were a pleasant gift.

He found a city of 100,000 without all the decay of some of the larger cities. New buildings were going up. He stopped and chatted with locals living in the area. Folks were friendly, unexpectedly so. More than that, they seemed happy and proud of their city. He learned that Des Moines was Iowa's cultural, governmental, and business center.

Before starting the trip, he had no preconceived notions about or any expectations for Iowa. For people living in Detroit, the country's agricultural center housed just two cities, Chicago and Kansas City. Saul was pleased to find another alternative that felt decent and dynamic. Such a place could accommodate an opportunity worthy enough for them to move here.

Glancing far ahead as he walked down a main street, he saw a sign hanging perpendicular to a large building that read "Newsroom."

Saul was intrigued. In the middle of the next block, the shop had "Hyman's Book Store and Magic Shop" written on a large plate glass window. "Hyman's Book Store and Magic Shop," Saul thought, *how ironic but clever and appropriate to wed those two things.* The optimist saw opportunity everywhere. The cynic? Well, he was just off the streets of Detroit, figuring that there were many paths out of any deep, dark forest. Saul chose to walk in. But he stopped a few shops away and lit a cigarette first. Favoring cigars, Saul only smoked cigarettes infrequently. Right now, he needed to pause and think. This might be his first foray into a significant person-to-person dialogue on this expeditionary trip. It was easy to gather the basic facts of city life from the casual people he had encountered. But Saul and Rachel would not be entering just the community of Des Moines or any city they chose but also the Jewish community that functioned there. How the Jews were treated and accepted in Des Moines would be an important issue. You could walk into a store or office and enquire about local employment opportunities or the winters. It was not easy to ask, "How much anti-Semitism do you have here?" That would be a key concern, no matter where they decided to settle, especially if it were a smaller city that had not been a recipient of the Jewish immigrants coming out of Western Europe or Russia.

Saul gave himself a pep talk. *Each day in my adult life, I get up, Wash, and put on my suit and tie. I've always been well-dressed and groomed, ready to do business. I'm similarly groomed today. I should be alright.* He knew that he was outgoing, exceptionally personable, and presented well. He had become a keen observer of people, events, and conditions around him. Saul was not tall, but he was good-looking, with wavy hair, a winning smile, and a good sense of humor. When he smiled, he beamed. Saul was good at schmoozing. He knew that he had demonstrated all the qualities needed to make an excellent first impression and prosper but still needed to steer clear of the worst chaos in Detroit. *I am ready*, he said to himself as he flicked the cigarette and walked towards the shop.

Stepping inside, Saul needed to figure out which way to look. Hyman's was crowded with newspapers and books. There were chairs and tables in all corners. A large glass display case full of tricks and gadgets stood at the back. Somehow, the arrangement felt welcoming and homey, less like a store and more like a gathering place. Saul was given a friendly greeting. Not busy with other customers, the owner, Pinky, came over to see if he could help this new customer. Pinky, like Saul, was an engaging person. That was the lifeblood of running such a shop. Soon, he and Saul were joyfully sharing stories.

Of course, coming from Detroit, Saul appeared to Pinky to be a reliable purveyor of exciting insider news, some expert in the know. What could be more attractive to a newsstand proprietor than a private news source from the big city? And Saul? Well, he wanted to learn more about the ins and outs of Des Moines. Notably, both men quickly established their Jewish connection and bonded despite their differing agendas. For this, Saul experienced a big sigh of relief. A good omen? Perhaps. The dance for information began. Their relationship was sometimes to be like a samba and at other times like a waltz, but they were consistently successful in the short conversations that they had.

In a light-hearted way, they began talking about the news business. After all, Pinky was a newsman, and they were standing in his news shop. The commonality of bullshit is often the mortar of friendship. However, the conversation was superficial, more about the recent news than the news business. Pinky was interested in the news but knew little more than what he read in the more widely circulated national papers. That was enough to have brief conversations with many folks in and out of his shop for whom the news seemed secondary to the local gossip.

"I guess, all-in-all, Saul, I'm more of a conduit than a newsman. Irun a news shop version of a beauty salon or barber shop. Enough about me. Tell me about yourself. What is living in Detroit like?"

"Well, you know there is much to enjoy in Detroit. There is a lot of growth going on there, especially in manufacturing. Socially, there is endless fun to be had with key clubs, music and dancing, and, of course, good whiskey. And we enjoy our family life. We have six brothers and sisters. Until we got married, Rachel was still living at home. She has a good job in a hotel. I work with the newspaper, learning the printing side as well as the reporting side. We're doing fine, but Jews have been moving west, looking for something more for decades. Rachel and I have felt that same yearning. So here we are, West of Detroit. We never took a honeymoon. So, this is it. A trip to explore if there may be a place more comfortable for us to settle down."

The pause was profound.

"Is Rachel as yearning as you are?"

"Good question. Likely not. But until recently, she has been more sheltered from the chaos and dangers. Gangs, unions forming, strikes, and wars with management, all along with the antisemitism, were creating conflicts everywhere. Operating in the business world, I found things pretty nasty. But Rachel had a simpler existence with home, work, and friends. Our families' loud cross-talking and arguing dinner conversations were familiar from childhood. They seemed like normal daily events. She's very bright but probably saw most dinner arguing or expounding as superficial chit-chat, revealing little that concerned her. The discussions were about the lifeblood of what I was involved with every day. I hoped that we could set out on our own and get away not just from the family squabbles but from the chaos of the city, too. You know, look for something new, someplace with less turmoil where we don't have to fight so hard for acceptance. We both yearn to establish something better and new, just like our parents did. I'm proud of what they did. In some ways, I measure myself against my dad's accomplishments and guts."

It was nearly noon. Customers began flooding into the shop, and Pinky got busy.

"Well, Saul, I can see that we have much to talk about. If you want to talk more, why don't you return to the station and get back to Rachel now? The two of you should look around town, maybe get a cup of coffee or a bite for lunch, and then come back. We can continue this conversation in a few hours. How does that sound? I really would like to hear more about your story. Things will get quieter later. My helper, Lenny, can handle most of the afternoon traffic. Let's meet at, say, 7 pm?"

"Sounds good. I'm excited for you to meet Rachel. We'll see you in a few hours," said Saul as he shook hands with Pinky and made his way back to the station."

Chapter Four

The campers wandered back to their seats, beginning to enjoy the camaraderie. Elijah was pleased to see their interaction. He loved to tell stories and get different views, but people needed comfort to open up. Informal compatibility was like a built-in support system allowing for disagreement. He didn't fully understand it, but he knew sharing gossip and chocolate chip cookies helped facilitate a more interesting discussion. He continued with the story as the last few women rushed to sit down.

"Pleased to have an opportunity to talk further with Pinky, Saul was grateful for the break and briskly walked back to the station to join Rachel for coffee and give her some rest from the monotony of the train station. They found a coffee shop nearby and shared a piece of pie with their coffee.

"So, tell me what you saw and found there. Anything exciting?"

Saul shared his general positive thoughts of what he'd seen. He also told Rachel about Pinky and his shop. He proudly informed her that he was already steps ahead in his exploration because his concerns about the nature of the local Jewish community had been answered.

"Are you going back there after we eat?"

"Sure, there is a lot to learn there."

"I can't see what is so exciting about a place where they sell fake poop to fool people."

"Point well taken. But I'm shopping for local community information, not tricks. It is more than a magic trick, gimmick, or newspaper shop. Such a bookshop is a hub of activity and information transfer. Being Jewish and seemingly open and forthright, Pinky could be a great source of information. I can get the two of us to talk about things beyond the fake poop."

"Well, I'd love to meet him with you."

"I'm glad you would. I'd like that too, but not on this visit. This must be man-to-man. But, believe me, your lovely, engaging presence would change the dynamic."

"Well, am I just supposed to just sit in that train station like a piece of luggage? And do what? Just fiddle my thumbs while you socialize?"

"Sit, yes. Fiddle your thumbs, no. A train station is a hub, too. You learned quite well how to schmooze with people in the hotel. There, you talked them into gambling, for goodness' sake! Stations have lots of people milling around, waiting to leave. Many are from Des Moines, and others are mid-transit. Trains are so frequently late. We're looking for information about Des Moines or any city in the Midwest. People love to talk, to tell you their stories if you ask. Become a one-person, forward scouting party out for information. Just stay safe doing it. Come on, I'll walk you back."

Rachel hesitated. "Go ahead. I'll return to the station once I have another cup of coffee and maybe even a piece of the pie. Then I'll meet you there, say by 4:30 or 5:00?"

"Don't you want me to walk you back?"

"I navigated the streets of Detroit by myself. I think I can handle Des Moines. So go ahead, go...go. I'll be fine. Just come back as an encyclopedia full of Des Moines knowledge. Be productive. There's a reason why I brought you along on this trip, my good man. Prove your worth. Go forth, discover."

They kissed goodbye, and Saul left, shaking his head. He was always slightly taken aback when Rachel seemed so self-assured and forward. In awe, he smiled, glad that there was someone to have his back.

So, each member of this expeditionary force set out to survey the territory in their own way, follow their own path, and come back to report to the other. Would their findings be confirmative or contradictory? Would some minor excursions lead to potential information? Or would each draw a blank and head back to the train station to check on the next train going West? Let's look at Rachel's path first.

For Rachel, their lunch had been productive. The food satisfied her hunger, but an awareness of Saul's investigative work showed her how beneficial casual conversation could be. Rachel was petite, pretty, quiet, supportive, and even compliant. But she was also bright and painfully a worrier. She realized she acted like a passenger on this trip rather than a participant. Yes, Saul was wise, sometimes incredibly so. He was intelligent and well-informed. But he was also creative and enthusiastic. That is where the potential rub came in. Rachel recognized that she could see pitfalls that Saul would excuse. She must be on her toes to keep informed and be strong enough to demur when necessary. Frequently, in her relationship with Saul, Rachel had been passive. She didn't want to nag, nor did she want to go along to get along. That would eventually sabotage their relationship. However, now, she had to step into a new role. Being assertive was nice to think about but more challenging to implement. She had to be on her toes and be more assertive with Saul.

Rachel had been a shopper in Detroit. Why not in Des Moines? She used her walk back to watch people and enter a few stores. Unfamiliar places made her anxious, but she decided to watch people shopping and talking rather than engaging herself. Pretty soon, she couldn't resist. She checked out a scarf or two but was mainly interested in seeing the response of the saleslady. Everyone seemed pleasant. She felt comfortable. She tried several stores along Grand Avenue. Each created the same feeling inside of her. At last, with her feet hurting, she took a cab back to the station. She wasn't about to do a widespread reconnaissance at this point. *Maybe that can come later*, she thought. Besides, there were many people she could talk to right there at the train station.

An elderly woman sitting a few chairs away had smiled at her earlier before quickly turning away. She was still sitting in the same place when Rachel returned. She watched the woman as her hands fidgeted with her bags, purse, and hair.

Sensitive to others' feelings, observant, caring, and helpful are all words one could use to describe Rachel. Being an individual who was always anxious about what could go wrong made her acutely aware of when things were going wrong for others. As she sat back on their shared bench, Rachel turned to the woman and gently asked,

"I'm sorry to intrude, but are you alright?"

The woman started to tear up but looked straight ahead as her hanky was moved to her eyes. Rachel moved over to their shared bench to try to comfort her. Eventually, the story came out. Her name was Charlotte. Her husband William had died a few months before. That was horrible to deal with, being alone after being married for nearly forty years. But now her son insisted that she move to Kansas City, where he lived, so that she could be closer and he could help take care of her.

"Oh, how I appreciate Samuel's concern, but I've lost my husband, and now I'm losing all my friends with this move. I'll know no one in Kansas City but my son. I don't want to hurt his feelings by telling him no."

"I can see that you're really in a bind. Let's go over to the lunch counter. I'll get us a couple cups of coffee, and you can tell me more about your son." The change in physical location broke the downward spell the woman was experiencing.

And so, it happened. Soon, the woman laughed as she told Rachel about her husband and son. She had had a great marriage and was proud of her son, Samuel.

"I am at one of the crossroads in life that we all face sometimes. I don't know what to do."

"Well, I can't answer that for you, but I can give you some advice if you'd like."

"Sure, tell me."

"Well, you have a lot of respect for your son, and you want to please him. But, Charlotte, let's assume for a moment that he wants the best for you. Maybe he doesn't know what that is, either. Be honest with him. Tell him about your dilemma. Make him a part of your team solving the problem, not the source of the problem. Have you told him everything you've told me?"

"No, I haven't talked to him about this yet. I agreed to come without raising any concerns."

"Well, I sincerely believe that you and your son will feel better about everything if you talk with each other."

The woman smiled, nodded, and reached out to hug Rachel. Soon, they were talking about many things, including Rachel's rather unique lifestyle at the hotel in Detroit. Ida, the woman serving behind the counter, overheard all of this. Pretty soon, she chimed in.

"I don't mean to interfere or insult you, but where did a woman like you, looking like someone just out of junior high school, get so smart and have the experiences you're describing in Detroit? Do all the young kids in that city run amok?"

"Well, I'm not a young kid, and I never thought of myself as running amok, but I can see how you'd get that impression. I married quite young, but my parents knew nothing about the true happenings at the hotel. The hotel had been a safe, protected spot until the shooting. And I'm not all that smart, just a practiced chameleon. And please, tell me I look older than a junior high girl. I'm a married woman off to explore and conquer the world!"

"Chameleon? How so?"

"Well, to my parents, I seemed like the perfect young Jewish princess waiting for Prince Charming to come along but destined to be a proper housewife. So then, in the late mornings, I'd leave home, prim and proper, to supposedly cover my clerk shift at a large downtown hotel. But once I got there, I would change into another outfit, not scanty, yet provocative, to run a dice game in the lobby. Naturally, my young looks make many men want to parent, watch out for me, and care for me. But, of course, I don't wear my wedding ring at work. That led to some pretty good tips. An occasional guy seemed to want to be an incestuous parent!"

"Goodness gracious," said Charlotte. Ida laughed and asked, "How did little missy handle that?"

"Well, I changed my stripes once again. First, I tried just kidding with them, laughing it off. If that didn't work and they kept pushing, I'd put on my jaguar stripes, using stronger language to tell them they had no idea who they were dealing with and who my friends were. That threat did the trick."

"But what about your friends and that husband of yours I saw walk out before?"

"Out pops another persona. Most of my friends didn't know what I did at the hotel. They thought I just had special privileges there to attend parties and dances. My immigrant parents didn't know how much fun the parties were. But I did have to keep a necessary change of clothes or two at a friend's house. There are always costume changes when living in a live drama and a stage presentation."

"Are you really old enough to drink?"

"Well, legality is an issue for everyone now. But I am absolutely legal except anywhere my parents might be!"

"What about your husband? What stripes do you wear for him?"

"My true love stripes. He is bright, kind, and thoughtful. He is very creative and has a wonderful sense of humor. He is also very good-looking, if I may say so myself."

"So, he sees the real you? Whatever that is?"

"My real me is what my parents want me to be, raised me to be. But I'm more youthful than they are and enjoy having fun. I am a good actress, too. But Saul has seen all sides of me. So, when we're together, we feel mutual love and respect. We share risk mutually."

"How so?"

"I was 17 years old and started running a dice game in the lobby of one the most prominent hotels in the city. Stop and think. You don't just waltz in and apply for that kind of position at my age or any age. So how do you get it?

"So, how did you get it?"

"Saul got it for me."

"Oh, well, that's good, I guess," said Charlotte.

"It was good because I had great fun and a lucrative job. But those gambling jobs were controlled by the mob. So how did he get it for me? I worry. Is he connected? Or was this just someone returning a small favor, as he claimed? I need to find out the extent of his involvement."

There was a long pause, both women reflecting. Then, finally, Rachel spoke up. "Part of me has been hoping that Saul and I could have a fun trip. That we wouldn't find any place better than Detroit. Then, we'd return to our families and their way of life. But Saul is more motivated to leave and look for someplace new and different. His older sister did. Maybe he sees her as paving the way."

As time went by, the train station became more congested. Finally, an announcement was made that the train connections heading west to Omaha and Kansas City would be delayed even more by a few hours. Many travelers, soon arriving or already present for departure, were left to wait. The waiting room got considerably more crowded.

The lunch counter became unusually busy. Rachel saw that the waitress, Ida, and the young man helping to prepare food needed to catch up. Feeling like she was now part of the train station family, Rachel said,

"Hey, do you guys need any help behind the counter there? It looks like you're getting swamped."

Ida exclaimed, "Well, I'll be. I've never had anyone offer anything like that before. But does a well-dressed lady like you know how to cook?"

"Well, I'm an expert on strudel, liver and onions, and pot roast. But I doubt that any of that would be helpful here. How about I get behind the counter, take a few orders for you, and serve some people who look famished and irritated by all the waiting? I also make a mean pot of coffee," she winked and jumped briskly behind the counter to help Ida.

Chapter Five

As Saul walked the streets, writing his own story of why he left Detroit, he struggled with how to approach Pinky. His background might sound frivolous and without gravitas. Some would consider him a fixer. He was, but not in an illegal sense. He helped disputing parties negotiate conflicts or fulfill needs that would be less complicated than needing an attorney.

On the other hand, he was an opportunist, using his best asset, understanding and evaluating issues and conflicts in situations, and then formulating and executing a plan.

Most of the issues presented to him were minor, annoying, or even confounding for others. Yet, people were happy to have someone else deal with the aggravation. He met lots of people and seemed to have many connections. But none were permanent. It was inevitable that Pinky would raise the question of who he was. What did he want? And, most importantly, why did he want to leave Detroit and move to Des Moines now?

All good questions, thought Saul. He stopped and got a coke. As he sat at the counter, he looked at himself in the mirror and stared at his image as if he were having a conversation with that person. He thought, *who are you, mister, and how did you get that way?*

He started to talk to himself. *The only consistent business connection I had was with the newspaper. But even there, I had no regular employment. I hung around and did favors and small tasks for which I got paid. But that's where I was the happiest. I'd love to be an investigative reporter, but I don't have the background or education to qualify for that in a big-city environment. But hanging around, I loved asking everyone questions about how you do this or that, covering everything, from writing to copy and content editing to buying the newsprint and setting the type. I learned and loved it.*

Somehow, after my bar mitzvah, I felt freer. It was as if there was truth in the belief that I was seen as a man, a full-fledged member of the Jewish clan. Everywhere I turned, I grabbed that freedom that truth had given me and ran with it. I worked odd jobs; some were known to my parents, and others were not. When I did manage to get to school, I frequently asked questions. My curiosity and interest appealed to teachers, who subsequently tolerated my frequent absences.

But whatever I got out of classes, there was more to be learned outside of school. All that pontificating, gesticulating, criticizing, and philosophical arguing at the Jewish dinner table was just a way of life. Even there, much could be learned by simply listening. I was a patient listener. I gleaned elements of wisdom that proved to be graduate school education. On those evenings when there was little to be learned, I was at least entertained by what appeared to be these old men talking over one another and hearing nothing.

As many kids did, I became streetwise. I began to run errands for questionable people and hear their conversations. I came to understand the many economic schemes, from running numbers and dice games to pyramid schemes. I saw bullying and brutality at its worst. But, most importantly, I learned to avoid getting involved in situations where I might later have to say no, quit, or depend on my meek physicality to be safe. Maybe being smaller actually protected me...Yes, I had many contacts, some with people of questionable character but no alliances. I never became ingratiated with anyone on the street.

Every one of these experiences tells a story. I witnessed the building blocks of Detroit's culture. They are, at times, just as warm and admirable as they are despicable and frustrating. But each experience and event, good or bad, is a story, and I want to dig deeper into more humane stories, not just about corruption but the plight of workers or bigotry that was so prominent in America.

The problem is that I am impatient, but I don't want to wait 20 years to get a chance to write those stories. There are too many well-trained people in front of me in Detroit. I need a new, smaller, less sophisticated place to make my mark. The paper here is pretty well established. But it couldn't hurt to inquire there also. I'd be willing to work my way up. We have quite a bit saved, but that won't last. He looked straight in the mirror and said aloud, "If I see a real opportunity, I will go for it." The self-induced pep talk was motivating, missing only one part: an opportunity.

The reality was that Saul's newspaper experience was chaotic but not to be diminished in importance. Saul worked in the press room, saw editors at work, and read their revisions. He talked to the drivers about distribution. He learned the business. Most importantly, he had a mentor, not a formal one, but a formative one, "Old Harry."

Saul found Harry easy to befriend when hanging around the Detroit Free Press. Harry had had his day in the sun, but his day had long past dusk. By Saul's time there, Harry had started drinking in the early afternoon and was pretty much useless by dinner. However, his history and successes made him a staple in the newsroom. All tolerated him. He was harmless, but he did take up a desk. As a young kid, Saul ran errands for Old Harry, who in turn befriended Saul, regaling him with story after story. Saul knew embellishment was at play, but the other reporters said there was much truth in the stories. Old Harry had been quite the reporter in his day. But now, he was pretty useless. He probably hadn't lost his talent, but he was unmotivated, and booze often muddled his thoughts.

After Saul's graduation, he and Harry would hang out more, sometimes even at Harry's apartment. He felt sorry for Harry. He continued to help him, buying groceries, booze, cigarettes, and ensuring he was okay every week. Harry still worked on the paper but did little there. He covered occasional social events or accident scenes. Nothing special, just straightforward who, what, why, when, and where type reporting that they were taught in journalism school. It was simple enough for Harry, even when he was drunk. Saul smiled, remembering his special relationship with Harry.

Saul remembered an afternoon not long ago when he brought some groceries to Harry, who hadn't felt up to going out that day. When Saul entered Harry's apartment, the phone rang. Saul picked it up. The editor was on the line. He wanted to talk with Harry.

"He's not here. He had to go to the store. He should be right back, though."

"Well, we need him to cover something. Nothing special. But we need it before the deadline. So, when he gets in, have him call me right away."

"Okay, can I tell him what this is regarding?"

And so, the editor told Saul all the details. It was a big industrial accident. People had been injured, likely killed. The editor knew there would be much to follow up on in this story, maybe even fraud or corruption, but Harry could get the initial facts. That could precede the many following investigative reports that need to be done. They wanted the first story by press time. Other reporters would then follow up.

"Okay, I'll tell him as soon as he gets back. Does he need to call you?"

"No, give him the facts as I told you. He'll know what to do. Just get me the story."

Harry was passed out on the sofa, and despite rigorous attempts to shake and wake him, he refused to wake up. Saul decided to go get the story himself. He felt terrible about deceiving Harry, but he was in no condition to walk, much less go and interview people. Plus, it wasn't Saul's fault that Harry refused to get up. Saul grabbed Harry's credentials, hung them on his neck, and turned them backwards. He justified his efforts as trying to save Harry's job. That was likely true. This could have been the last straw that necessitated Harry's retirement, so really, he was just doing Harry a favor.

Saul typed the story on Harry's old Remington, which he'd used since journalism school. It was excellent, brief, and just what the editor wanted. There, Saul opened the door to ask why the accident had occurred. He speculated about unfulfilled safety regulations and the company's financial problems. He had no facts to back any of this up, but by interviewing employees standing around, he got the main gossip and decided that it would make great news.

Saul rushed the story over to the paper and delivered it personally to the editor. He told him that Harry was exhausted from running and being on his feet for so long at the scene, so he sent him to deliver the story personally. The editor read the story and laughed.

"What's so funny?" Saul asked, trying to mask his worry.

"Well, I'll be damned. This is Old Harry reborn. He was always doing this stuff early on, the factual reporting and all, and then he couldn't help but show he wanted to be an investigated reporter by throwing in all this speculative stuff. His last editor told him he couldn't do that without getting more facts. Those stories would be for follow-up, not for the original piece. But Harry, being Harry, kept at it. He was eventually rewarded by getting the follow-up stories when his last newspaper's investigative reporter retired. I guess Harry had to try it one last time. Yes sir, vintage Harry at his best!" the editor chuckled.

He drew two red lines through the last two paragraphs, signifying "delete." He then handed the story to the runner to take it to be set to print.

"Harry and I will laugh about this tomorrow when he gets in. Thanks for bringing this over. I imagine it was pretty tiring for Harry to cover this last minute."

Saul smiled at the editor, "Yeah, he was flat out in exhaustion."

Saul, done reminiscing, looked at himself straight in the soda fountain mirror, smiled, and said to himself, "Well, now it is time for you to go." Saul left the counter and started walking toward Pinky's news shop.

Walking down the street, he thought to himself, *so what? What does all this mean? The truth is that I am not running away, as much as it might seem to others. I think I am running towards something that I haven't been able to find in Detroit. Maybe connection, a sense of belonging, and my work... I want to be a real newsman. I have carefully watched reporters work. I have gone with them when they covered stories. I should be able to make a good newsman myself.*

As he stood in front of the news store, Saul thought, *so that's it, in a nutshell. I'm leaving at a great time. Maybe I'm rushing a little bit, but it's only so that I don't have to wait 20 years to write about the many stories I see around me. I have my story to tell about why I'm leaving and what I want, whether that something is here or, more likely, in Kansas City or Omaha,* he thought as he walked towards Pinky.

He was ready. He had written his story.

Chapter Six

Saul walked back into a now nearly empty store. Pinky, free from his customers, was glad to see Saul. He motioned for him to join him at a nearby table where customers often perused magazines or books.

"Sorry if I was impolite when I kicked you out before. It was going to get busy, and I wanted to be able to pursue what we were talking about in a more meaningful way. I hope it worked out okay for you. Rachel probably needed some Saul time, stuck in that station. I'm sure she was pretty interested in what you were discovering about our city in the hicks, am I right?"

"Well, I've discovered that it is no hick city. Rachel and I had a nice lunch, and she fully understood why I wanted to come back and talk with you some more. She wanted a woman's opinion of the city and decided to walk back to the station while I meandered back this way. Growing up in Detroit, she's pretty used to downtowns and discovering new places, although I'm not sure how long her feet will last, walking around in those high heels."

Saul briefly looked around the shop. He saw a few customers. "Is now a good time for us to chat some? I don't want to become a nuisance for you and interfere in your work."

"Now is a perfect time. I'm glad Rachel will have a chance to look around by herself. In fact, it's good she is exploring as she will soon learn how safe it feels here. Occasionally, you may have to excuse me for a few moments when duty calls.

But my customers are used to always seeing me chatting with someone. Besides, I'm always interested in hearing new stories," Pinky winked.

 Saul may have appeared casual and relaxed, but at that moment, he sensed this was a pivotal opportunity. It was no longer merely simple chit-chat for him. In strategic cases, Saul always had a plan. Whether or not he could implement it was another story. But, he pondered, *was sitting down with Pinky going to be like a job interview? Or more like getting a friend's help to search for a job? Perhaps both?*

Saul had his way of sizing up people in work situations or groups. There were leaders, facilitators, worker bees, and followers. He saw Pinky as an excellent facilitator and a very empathetic man. Saul, sweating emotionally, if not physically, knew he needed help and support to make the inroads he desired in Des Moines. Finding Pinky as a facilitator could help smooth that pathway.

"Tell me, Saul, how does Des Moines strike you as you walk around? I imagine it is so much smaller than Detroit," Pinky interrupted Saul's thoughts, stopping him from spiraling.

"I'm sure it is, but I'm not quick to judge, and honestly, I have seen so little of it so far. I'm looking for more information from you, a good sales pitch worthy of a member of the Chamber of Commerce. How did this place come to be what it is?"

"Well, Des Moines started off as a Fort established in 1843. It was made at the confluence of the two rivers to protect the rights of the Sauk and Fox peoples, who then lived in the area. I think it was in the 1850s when the 'Fort' appellation was dropped, and a city was founded.. Over the years, Des Moines has grown organically, probably because of the location. Then size begets size. Now, enough about Des Moines, tell me about you! I'm more interested in hearing how someone starts in Detroit and finds himself wandering the streets of our fair city."

"Well, Pinky, my story has a zillion twists and turns. It's probably longer than you want to hear, but it begins not in Detroit rather in Russia."

"So, you are a Russian immigrant?" Pinky asked with his eyebrows raised.

"Yep, I am."

"When did you come over to America?"

"Well, I was born in a shtetl like many in Eastern Europe. I've been told that years before I was born, the pogroms from the Poles who ruled the land were not so severe. But when the Russians took over the land, the pogroms were so severe that no one apparently felt safe. I was too young to remember it, though."

"But I bet you know enough about it to entertain me. I love hearing immigrant stories. In many ways, they are all so similar, but they each have their unique quirks. So, don't hold back!" Pinky, looking like an overexcited child, nudged Saul.

Smiling, Saul continued, "my father, Morris, was an ironworker. He was one of the lucky ones as he was an especially skilled ironworker and an excellent designer. That led to him having a special privileged pass to go outside the shtetl gates to do wrought iron gates work for wealthy locals' estates. That was lucrative, given the time and the place. He saved enough money and turned some into diamonds and gemstones. Even though it was a good job, it did not improve the day-to-day life of our family within the shtetl. , Instead, the outside work allowed him to accumulate more diamonds and gemstones. Eventually, his savings were enough to help his large family escape and emigrate to America.

"So, you all just left and came over together?"

"No, it wasn't all that simple. You had to escape the shtetl and find a way over. My father made the journey alone, leaving the rest of us behind. It was all so strange. I never even understood the full story. You know the tradition. You ask your parents what happened then, and the answer is, 'Better you shouldn't know.' They always wanted us children to look forward in life, not dwell on the past."

"So, you know nothing about how you got here? It seems like such a shame to let a story like that die."

"Well, Mom, my sister and I came later. Dad didn't come home for long periods. His work outside the shtetl often kept him away for several weeks as he designed and built these huge gates for the estates. So, Dad didn't tell my Mom that he was leaving. He was fearful that telling her would lead to an argument. Mom would become upset and confide her concerns to a good friend, who would likely then leak the "secret" to another friend. Once that happened, it would have been difficult to keep his plan a secret. Even your neighbors would rat on you if that gained them benefit from the guards. However, his prolonged absence, at first, didn't faze Mom. She was used to his absences.

The rest of the family did not like my Dad. His brother-in-law, Ben, was his employer. They worked closely together, were best friends, and trusted each other. Dad only told Ben of his plan to escape. He gave Ben the gemstones, along with instructions to wait weeks before telling my mother about her husband's attempt to flee the country. The gemstones were left behind to help Mom bring me and my sister to America once I got old enough. So, I was two when I made the trip with my Mom and sister," Saul said, lost in thought.

"Why did he leave in that manner? Did he want to get established in America first? Your Mom must have been really pissed!"

"She was angry and felt that she was given no good reason for why Dad would leave without us.

During the entire time he was gone, Mom had never heard from him or anything about him. Then, out of the blue, once he arrived in America, he arranged for one brother and a nephew to come over even before my Mom, sister, and me. That was as much as my mother would stomach. She told Ben that she was going to take us kids and go to America and look for her husband, who abandoned her. It was only then that Ben told her about Dad's plan. Then, apparently, she didn't explode but instead became dead set on fulfilling a plan of her own, to find him no matter where he was hiding. No discussion from Ben could change her mind. It was nearing winter, and Ben wanted Mom to wait so that he could at least help her arrange a safer, even more organized trip, but no, she was leaving, and she was leaving now."

"That sounds horrible. Why would your Dad do that to her?"

"I don't know for sure. My grandmother, Sophia, became pregnant when a Cossack raped her and nearly killed her during one of the pogroms. Unfortunately, that was all too frequent then. Life in the shtetl was scary and unpredictable. That much I know. My Dad came from that pregnancy but was raised as the bastard son by my non-biological grandfather. Sophia's husband oversaw some wealthy man's estate or farm, where my grandmother worked in the kitchen. Growing up, his brothers resented my Dad. He was always referred to as the family bastard. Dad had reddish hair and looked nothing like his four brothers, who belittled him constantly.

"How sad, such pain caused by so much abuse over the centuries. And in many ways, it continues," Pinky offered some sympathy to Saul.

"The abuse of the pogroms was bad enough. In our case, the pain festered way into the aftermath of the event. Apparently, Dad always had to prove himself to his brothers. They always called him "the little bastard." He was the youngest. That's why he brought one of his brothers over first. He wanted to prove to them his worth and be accepted. Choosing siblings first was a sign of his allegiance to his birth family. Dad is the most religious of the family, too, not in a practicing orthodox way, but in consistently acting on his beliefs in faith, hope, and charity. He smuggled three Torahs out of the country and brought them here. He's promised to give me one of them."

"So, your father's need for acceptance was the driving force in his life? Even to the point of abandoning his wife and kids?" Pinky seemed to be in shock.

"On the surface, it would seem so. But in his mind, his plan was solid. If he made it to America, everyone else would then be brought over. If he died on his trip, it is likely that his wife and kids would have died, too, especially if they were with him. He figured if he made it once, he could go back for Mom and us kids, as well as his brothers. But we would be alive back in the shtetl if he had died alone. Ben would have watched out for us. For him, satisfaction didn't come from his brothers' acceptance. It was all about proving to himself and to them that he was as good as they are, maybe even better. They depended on him to create safety and freedom, not vice versa. Once they were brought to America, they never again called him. 'The Bastard.'"

"Where in all this excitement were you, your sister, and your mother?"

"Well, that's another story. My father had left the gems with Ben to finance passage for Mom, me, and my sister. The other brothers and their wives soon found that he was gone, but it was a while before Mom knew. When she insisted on coming to America, they gave her the gems. My mother had sewn the jewels into the hem of her smock. She refused to let her brother-in-law accompany us. She didn't want to put him in danger. When we escaped, I was two, and my sister was five or six years old. We all walked nearly a thousand miles in the winter to get to a port where we could afford steerage."

"How in the hell did she manage that?!" Pinky asked, looking like he was going to drop off the chair.

"I don't really know. I don't remember much of it, really. The story, as best I know it, was like a horror story. But immigrants forever have had their own horror stories. Living comfortably as we do, it is hard to imagine the bad being so bad and the appeal of the promised good to be found elsewhere so good that one would set out on such a journey.

Mainly, our trek was just acknowledged by my parents but never discussed in detail. Mom knew the ports where we might get steerage and set out in that direction. But there were no maps, escorts, or horses to ride. She walked. My sister and I walked hundreds of miles. Sometimes, mom had to carry me. I was small, tired, and often grumpy, according to the notes in Dad's diary. He wrote the story as Mom told it to him. But it was clear that I didn't make it easier for her. Sleep was often in fields or barns. Food was where she could find it or sometimes beg for it. People were generous. I do have some images of being cold and huddling in the hay. All these are occasional flashes of memory. The trip was never talked about while I was growing up. We just proceeded to be here and do what we did. If I pushed and asked too many questions, Mom said we must look to the future, not the past. Without Dad's diary, I'd know next to nothing. But I'm sneaky and not done pushing quite yet!" Both men smiled.

"Occasionally, we got a ride in a wagon. Some people were undoubtedly kind when they found out about our journey. Others ignored us or glared as they were all competing for available food. Mom was not the only woman on the road alone or with children. Unlike living with Dad's family, she didn't feel like an outcast or excess baggage out on the road. She felt free, and now part of a large family of unnamed people mortared together by mutual fear, hope, and caring. Sometimes, she provided food for others even when she, although not the children, would remain hungry. Others did the same for her. 'That's just how they are,' people would say.

There were problems of violence and abuse. The story is vague about the details of the abuse en-route. People didn't talk about that kind of thing readily. But, no matter what happened, there was no turning back. Dad wrote that she never wanted to stop going forward.

"She tried to make a game of it for us kids, but we soon tired of the game. Yet, each day, we would begin the game again. Sometimes, she tried to break the game up into small parts. She'd say, 'If you win by helping get us to that town, your prize will be a big piece of bread!'

The story of this fantastic journey, with harsh weather, freezing nights, rugged terrain, and competing companions, will forever remain vague for me. At a young age, we children were poor historians of the trip's events. I have just slivers of memories, like riding in a man's cart, getting wet wading across a stream, or sleeping in a shed with animals. I've talked with my older sister about it. She remembers crying when we left. We had to be so secretive about it that she thought we were doing a bad thing. She was scared she'd be punished. She also remembers the boat voyage. She was sick the whole way, and I was too. But she'd laugh and say that my crying all the time was more annoying than her own nausea.

Eventually, after months, we arrived at Bratislava, where Mom could arrange waterway transportation to America. Our experience in steerage was just smelly, crowded, hunger-provoking, and dangerous from rats and disease. I do vaguely remember feeling nauseous and that everyone around me was vomiting, too. Mom told dad that we cried more in the boat than when walking. While walking, there was also an opportunity for respite. The situation could be changed just by sitting on a rock. But not on the boat. He wrote that some kids cried the whole trip. That included my sister and me, but according to my sister, it was mostly me. Mom and many adults wept, too, packed into the cramped, dark quarters with the sea around, threatening in so many ways.”

“What did your dad do when he got here?”

“He was a very skilled iron worker. When he landed, he quickly got a job in New York, but then, he had an accident that caused significant problems in one eye. His depth perception suffered. That interfered with his industrial construction work. Of course, it wasn’t long before he lost his job. That's when he decided to look for greener pastures in Detroit. He heard that the battle for unskilled employment was easier there.”

“So, how did this extraordinary trip effect you? What was it like for you?” Pinky’s curiosity seemed unmatched.

“To tell you the truth, I don’t know if it was like hearing about someone else’s vacation trip that you’re sorry or glad that you missed. I know that it took up a good part of the second and third years of life, but I couldn’t begin to even guess how much impact it had. It got me to America. I know that I am thankful for that.”

“So, what are your earliest memories of being here?”

“Playing with two older kids and hearing words like neighborhood and boundaries, I think these kids, whom I remember as being kind and looking after me and my sister, were older cousins. But that was when we were in New York.

Mom knew about the family connection in New York, and they had already gotten a letter from Ben that we were en-route and received us warmly. Once Mom got used to the hustle and bustle of bigger cities and gained some grasp of the language, she was hell-bent on going to Detroit to be with Dad. And we did."

"Was that like a big fight or a big reunion?"

"I just remember it as being casual, almost like when we arrived at our relative's house in New York. Then, it was pretty much a matter of Mom and Dad working as a team to survive and raise us kids and the others that came along."

Since your dad lost his eyesight, what did they do to survive?"

"In Detroit, his only option was to work as a peddler."

"I can't even begin to imagine...Tell me, what was that like?"

"Well, he never talked much about it. But my mother told me that I reminded her in some ways of what he must have gone through."

"You, really? How come?"

"Well, peddling was the springboard for many migrants out of Europe. It was really the first ladder of the American dream."

"What did they do? Was it like the panhandlers we see on the streets today?"

"Not really. These were not people who were down on their luck but working and organizing to build a clientele, hoping to make enough money to open a small shop or business.

Mom said that when he arrived in Detroit, a few Jewish families gave him some goods to sell, and then he had to develop a territory, usually out of town. So, he became a traveling salesman, left town on Sunday, went to his domain, spent the week there, and then returned to restock. He both bought and sold during his trips."

"So, are you telling me that is what you did, too? That was how you were like your dad?"

Saul laughed, "Hardly! No, I didn't have it that rough. But peddlers then had to learn to talk their way into peoples' homes and often communicate in different languages with other immigrants from all over Europe. By then, these immigrants had established homes and spoke different languages, depending on where they came from. My Dad was not fluent in the same languages as my Mother, but he was skilled in selling and communicating with a few words from each language. But he wasn't operating out of one store as you do today. Instead, he moved throughout his territory, making new contacts and renewing old ones.

My territory was much smaller than my dad's, just the boundaries of greater Detroit. But my peripatetic existence growing up was similar. I wasn't selling goods, but my services to varied folks in Detroit. I had to learn their cultures, values, and sometimes the words of their languages. This reminded her of what Dad did when he arrived. She nostalgically describes this. I'm not sure he saw it as positively as she did. For him, it was just hard work. But my mother appreciated his efforts. That is why she tolerated what I was doing when I didn't have a specific job. Other people saw me as lazy. I had the peddler blood in me."

"And he made enough money to raise a family doing this?" Pinky raised his eyebrows.

"No way," Saul chuckled. "He was a typical peddler for a while. But eventually bought a cow and kept it way out of town. He would walk out there to care for it and begin making cheese to sell in town. Eventually, he had a dairy."

"Rags to riches story."

"They were not quickly or exactly rich, but both my parents were industrious. Once my mom adapted to the hustle and bustle of a big city and learnt a new language, she overcame her original immigrant fear. She was thankful that our older cousin watched out for us in the neighborhood and was soon comfortable with my sister and me playing in our own yard. She paid close attention to how business things worked. I guess she had an intuitive understanding of what we call networking. This fits right into her tendency to support and help others. Graciously, she accepted the help others gave her, especially at the beginning. However, helping other immigrants, regardless of religion, was always foremost on her mind.

I'd have to say my mother and father were true partners. They might not have appeared to be the most romantic couple, but they consulted one another on most issues. So yes, they went from peddlers to dairy farmers. The cheese they made was unique. They developed a good clientele and used the money saved from the dairy to buy property and enjoy a comfortable life. As Dad became prosperous, both parents pushed for a good education, especially for the boys. I have one brother who is in osteopathic college and another who is studying law. He offered to do the same for me but not for our sister, who badly wanted to attend college."

"What about you? The professions didn't interest you?"

"Not really. I am the oldest boy and had to help my dad with the dairy. When I started school, I, being the oldest, still had responsibilities for chores. The schoolwork was easy, but I had little time for play. Serendipity took over. Spending so much time around my dad, I heard him and others when business transactions were being made. At first, they were small, like any peddler. But then, things progressed. I liked listening to the wheeling and dealing.

When nighttime came, I'd be exhausted. I was too tired to study, and I didn't need to. So, I began to pick up books and magazines Mom and Dad had around the house. There weren't any radio broadcasts then. The silent movies were in their prime when I got to my teens, but no talkies yet. My parents, exhausted as they could be, were avid readers before bed. Dad seemed to be into the deeper stuff... philosophy. Mom liked magazine short stories. Imagine at 13 or 14 picking up Kafka's Metamorphosis and digging in. I searched and dug and needed help understanding. But I was enthralled by someone doing something that seemed so deep and thoughtful. Mom had been reading "The Rainbow" by D.H. Lawrence. That was a story about a struggle growing up. It was different from my effort, yet similar.

That was it. I was going to be a novelist, too. Pretty soon, I'm lying in bed and making up my own stories. When other kids were thinking of being a doctor or fireman, I thought it would be wonderful to be an author, a novelist."

"It seems you didn't exactly stay on that path. Forgive me for being so frank."

"Well, that's where serendipity became advantageous. Being around my dad, once I got into 10th grade, I saw business deals all around me. Not just my Dad's, but other stuff. Mostly, at that age, it was neighborhood bartering. But then, things got more involved, especially with the onset of prohibition in the 20s. By then, I'd sold papers, gotten to know the delivery men, and begun hanging around news desks so that I could do errands for people.

I didn't have personal knowledge of what life was like in the old country, but spending long hours with Dad at the dairy, I heard many "old country stories." He is quite a man with significant accomplishments and an excellent storyteller. Recounting the reality of his past, I saw why he was the way he was. Success for him was critical. He was proud of his capabilities but also looked for respect from his family. He hated authoritarian abuse. He is a devout humanist, and I think that rubbed off on me. Investigative news reporting seemed like being a first cousin to being a novelist. I fantasized about discovering the abusers. Besides, there were jobs in newspapers. There are no jobs for novelists in waiting."

"Wow. What a story you have, Saul. So, tell me…How does this intriguing tale lead you and Rachel to Des Moines, Iowa?"

"What's the long and the short of it? This is a combination of delayed honeymoon and exploration trip."

"What exactly are you exploring?"

Chapter Seven

"To be honest, Pinky, I was more certain of what I didn't want than passionate about what I did want. I knew something was burning within me but wasn't sure what that was or is, even today.

After graduation, my parents knew little of my work activities. I'm sure Dad has had some idea. He knew I hung around the papers a lot. But by the time I decided to be a journalist, I'd also become impatient. I wanted to avoid returning to school or college to get a degree. I thought my time had passed. It was now my brother's turn at the expensive education my dad offered.

I'd learned a lot from my father. After high school, I had been doing small business deals of my own. Small and likely unsustainable. It was not a career, but I lived well and enjoyed life. I made good contacts. I was not one of the go-to guys or a big shot.

With all the competing forces of men with extensive experience or degrees competing at most city newspapers, working your way up to be a lead or investigative reporter seems like quite a climb, especially in a large city with many people chasing the same golden nugget.

Once Rachel and I got married and knew that a family would soon be underway, I wanted more stability. So, I decided to climb the mountain, leave everything behind, and see what was on the other side of the hill. Dad thought it was silly. You know, the grass is always greener and stuff. He offered to bring me into some of his dealings but was focused on real estate then. But that wasn't journalism. I wanted what I wanted. After a while, my dad laughed at me when he heard me obsessing about what I wanted to do. He said, 'You spend more time trashing every other profession. Let's face it: you have a passion. Wake up and follow it! Be a writer, or at least try it. If you don't, you'll always regret it.'

Rachel and I talked a lot about this. Her feelings about the problems had been far different from mine. She saw an easy path to stability as living a comfortable life in Detroit under the umbrella of her parents. She optimistically, somewhat naively perceived that we could easily recreate that. She enjoyed her family and good friends and envisioned a future as a homemaker just like her mother. The only change she aspired to was getting a house down the block from where we were raised and our families still lived. But she didn't see or know what I saw. In a city where she saw an easy path. I saw the local battles and economy as fraught with obstacles and potentially even dangerous. Also, it was a city where I could no longer easily do consulting as I had in the past. Further, it offered no possibility for me to pursue my journalistic passion. A passion. By-the-way that she saw as frivolous" Saul broke eye contact with Pinky, looking around the shop, almost as if he was embarrassed.

Pinky, trying to get him to focus on the conversation again, said, "I get it. Did she know how badly you wanted to be a reporter?"

"Not really…That was such a long shot that I didn't want to confuse our conversation about leaving by limiting our opportunities so narrowly. I'd given up hope for a good newspaper future in Detroit. Doing all the other business I did, one is bound to burn a bridge or two. It was time to leave.

The only thing that helped to move the needle on her comfort scale was there was a shooting in the hotel lobby right next to where Rachel was standing. Up to that point, she thought that job could supplant being a homemaker until we were better established. She wasn't wounded or hurt badly, but certainly bruised and shaken up. There was pandemonium. She slipped and fell into a pool of blood and finally ran out. But in those few minutes, she went from unaware to being somewhat aware. At least, she became a willing traveling partner. Her fear created strength. She stood up to her parents and insisted that leaving was best for her. They didn't agree, of course, but Rachel and I were adamant. We are willing to struggle and pay our dues, but not in the middle of gang wars.

So, we are looking for a suitable place to settle down and raise a family. We want to join an accepting community, both Gentile and Jewish, free from gangs, shootings, and daily conflict. We want a comfortable place to raise a family where we don't look over our shoulders daily and are scared to go out.”

“You're not talking about a desire to find a place to be a reporter. So, I’m assuming that isn't an issue in your eyes?”

“Not at this point, no. That would prematurely eliminate too many other opportunities. Being a reporter or writer may be my dream, but it’s not my immediate goal.

Rachel and I started just heading West. We have no plans or commitments anywhere. We wanted to look around. Kansas City and Omaha were high on our list. But we never thought about Des Moines. Finding this wonderful community was serendipity. We had a long layover here, so I began walking around. It seems like a nice town, prosperous but not frantic. Everyone has been congenial. So, tell me about this town of yours, Pinky. It's your turn now," Saul took a deep breath, smiling up at Pinky, waiting for an answer.

Pinky tried to reassure Saul that the intra-religious skirmishes were minimal. There were three synagogues to which people self-selected, avoiding many head-on clashes over religious differences. Instead, there was respect and cooperation between the groups. However, each congregation could choose its own level of traditional worship. He told him about the many social support groups. There was a Jewish social service group, women's groups, and a religious school. Similar resources had developed in other surrounding cities. Cooperation among the cities was good. In Des Moines, Jews were accepted and involved in the business community, even if excluded from many parts of the Gentile community's social life.

"You know, Saul, your dad, and others like him benefitted from their arrival in America from a start they got from other immigrants before them. Even as a peddler, he had to get his first merchandise from others, a product of their goodwill to a fellow Jew, Irishman, or whatever. The same goodwill still exists in smaller places like Des Moines. I have yet to learn about Detroit. I'm sure that they are very welcoming too. But you will find that the Jewish community here will welcome you with open hearts and hands. There is plenty of room and opportunity here."

Saul was impressed. But he was used to hearing good sales pitches. He nodded his head as if in agreement but said nothing. He didn't know what factors would make him say, "Here. This is the place. Let's plant our future here." His dream, as distant as it seemed, would make it difficult to commit to fulfilling his goal. At times, mixed feelings and ambivalence can be rough waters to navigate. This may be one of those times.

Saul's novel plots still needed to see a word put to paper by a writer. But ideas arose spontaneously, seeming to have an impulsive driving force. He could quickly develop two or three pictures on a short bus ride. Unfortunately, Saul was more creative as a writer than a productive one. That was the way his mind worked. He'd be off to the following plot before he'd set pen to paper on the first one. He often blurts out these ideas while reading a newspaper article in the evening. Overwhelmed with the voluminous compendium of ideas, Rachel often acknowledged his newest excitement with a brief "uh huh" as she read her magazine.

As Rachel knew, if anyone were within hearing distance of his newest brainstorm, Saul would likely blurt it out. And it happened that warm spring day in Des Moines. Impulsively, he had one of his not infrequent inspirations.

"Pinky, I have an idea. Is there support in town for a Jewish newspaper published in English? Maybe even a state-wide paper for the Jews of Iowa?"

Pinky, gazing over to ensure that a customer was being cared for, responded with little thought or enthusiasm. It was as if Saul had asked whether he thought it might rain tomorrow. The question had little impact on Pinky. For Saul, each inspiration was the golden path to a bright future.

"I don't know, Saul. I've never thought about it. This is the first time anyone has brought it up. It could be a nice thing. That would be much work and require the support of many people."

"Work aside, Pinky, would such a paper be appreciated, wanted?"

"I don't know about what people want. I've never heard anyone even bring up the idea. I'm unfamiliar with that type of rag, so I'd like to know whether it would be appreciated. But, on the other hand, no one is knocking down the doors to set up another newspaper. We already have a strong paper here in Des Moines."

"I'm not talking about competing with the Des Moines Register, but a paper for the Jewish community about issues relevant to that community. But more than a newsletter, a paper with more depth and editorial content. What do you think?"

Pinky seemed to be deep in thought before he said, "the Jewish Community is not all that large. You'd have to sell many papers to be financially successful. And if you suggest something with editorial content advocating political positions or community activism, that might open a can of worms. Newspapers often have a strong political bent. Something like that here would have to be generic from a religious point of view. You know, avoid pushing the orthodox or reform agenda. Also, best to stay out of political differences unless it was generic, such as helping the Jews still abroad. We don't need a bunch of Jews arguing with each other in letters to the editor. We can get that at family gatherings!" Pinky chuckled at his own joke before continuing, "It would have to be something newsy- what's been going on with the clubs, civic groups, and women's groups. For solvency, you could also reach out to other cities, Rock Island, Davenport, Sioux City, and places like that."

"Sounds interesting, Pinky. We could stay here a few days and look around. If I were interested in doing something like that, who are some of the folks you think I should talk to?"

"Saul, this would be a huge undertaking. Starting such a thing from scratch. Wow? Let's get you and Rachel acquainted with Des Moines first. See if you like it and what other opportunities might be here before you go off half-cocked on such a huge undertaking when you're still living out of a suitcase?"

"Haha, Pinky, it's 1929. We're only 150 years or so from the founding of this country. Everything around us started from scratch. The peddlers often carried only a small satchel of personal belongings in their wagons. I'm not talking about the New York Times here. You already have a city paper. I'm talking about a small but informative, pertinent rag that would be one more element in the mortar binding the Jewish community together. And it would also say to the larger community, hey, we are here and to be reckoned with."

"How would it do that?"

"By being a new avenue for advertising for the non-Jewish businesses."

"Saul, it sounds intriguing. How would you go about it? I sell books, papers, magazines, and tricks. I've not been involved in anything like what you are talking about. So where would you even start to work on something like that?"

"Well, Pinky, from my experience, the first step is to get community interest and support. See, you're already interested."

"Hey, don't get me involved in this cockamamie idea. I'm small fry around here."

"I'm sorry. I'm not trying to burden you. But you underplay your importance to this community. You and your store are a hub in this community. You have the pulse, a sense of the feelings, attitudes, likes, and dislikes of the community you serve. You're like the blood pressure cuff for a doctor or the retail version of a barbershop. So, I want your reading. If I were to ask three people in town about this idea, whom would they be?"

"Hey, come on, Saul. I'm nothing but a shopkeeper. I'm no big wheel around here. I'm not even that well connected," even though he was embarrassed, Pinky seemed to enjoy the importance Saul was giving him.

"Pinky, every town, community, and group has power brokers. Who are the power brokers in the Jewish community here?

"Brokers?"

"The wheelers and dealers. Who seems to have the most influence?"

"When you put it that way, you need to talk to the top dog. The prominent power broker."

"Okay, Pinky. Who is that?"

"Hold on a second. Let me take care of Mrs. Perkins here."

Pinky, relieved, rushed off, allowing Saul to catch his breath. The excitement of being onto an idea felt like a rush. A rush that he'd frequently experienced. When it came to his literary career, the satisfaction of completing the idea had yet to occur. He scratched his head and wondered. "This time? Maybe?"

Pinky returned, looking flushed from dealing with his customer.

"The first person to meet is Rabbi Mannheimer."

"Tell me about him."

"He is a kingpin, maybe right now the kingpin in Jewish society in Des Moines."

"Kingpin? Coming from Detroit, that appellation causes my stomach to cramp up. That sounds a little nasty for a Rabbi."

"No, no, you're wrong. Your Detroit experience is coloring your feelings. He's a kingpin, not a king or kingmaker. He is the top-notch facilitator in our community. Do I have my pulse on things? He's the doctor-in-chief. He looks after the welfare of this community like no other. Imagine a wise, loving father who is stern but gentle and doesn't try to boss you around or tell you what to do. He's in the central position to know if this is a good idea, how to go about it, and how to help it happen. He will help you, never boss you or try to control things. He will tell you if he thinks something is a bad idea or the wrong time. Unless he sees it as destructive, he won't fight you. He might even still help you.

The Rabbi has a way of allowing things to happen by encouraging compromise and cooperation among competing groups, even groups that drastically disagree. And goodness knows we have a long tradition of disagreements among Jews! People trust him to analyze and assess. He is amazingly thoughtful and fair and understands the politics of compromise and pacing. Once the talking is done, he is good at promoting action groups. He's helped bring about the Jewish Federation, charities, and the community center. As you put it, lots of the mortar that holds the communities' bricks together came about because of his efforts. If interested, he could be accommodating in bringing your paper to fruition."

"What does he do?" Saul asked, intrigued.

"He's a rabbi!"

"I know, I know. But how does the rabbi function? Does he have any positions in town, on any boards?"

"He is the rabbi at the most reformed shul but started a Hebrew school for orthodox kids who didn't know how to read the English language. He is also very active with the Christian Community and Des Moines' welfare projects. He is involved with the school board but has yet to become a member. I gotta say, he's a loved and respected man. This rabbi is a gentle, loving soul. He'll know what our community needs and is ready for. If you get his blessing, you'll get his support even though you might not always see that it is there."

Saul said little but just nodded his head, thinking. After a while, he said, "So, you'll introduce me?"

"Hey, it's not like I can just call him and tell him I just met this guy he ought to talk to. I don't have any clout with him. But, of course, we know each other. I'll call him, ask him about meeting you, and see if he would want to meet with you. Of course, I can't guarantee what he'll say."

"Of course. Thank you. I'm very interested, excited even, and appreciate your help," Saul said excitedly, genuinely feeling respect for Pinky in his heart.

"Consider it done. But there is a second issue. Raising money. I suspect you didn't come to town with pockets overflowing with money for such an endeavor. If I am right, you'll need funds. A state-wide paper would need support. But, if it is going to succeed, it should have community involvement too."

"We live just fine, Pinky. But a big project like this is largely beyond our means. So yes, I'd love additional help and would certainly need it. What is the pathway there?"

"Well, let's not get too far ahead of ourselves. I'll see if you can talk with Rabbi Mannheimer first. Let's see what he says and ask what he thinks is the best way to make all this happen. He is very straightforward and savvy.

It's up to you. If you're serious, stick around and explore Des Moines. I'll be glad to help. If you decide to stay, I'll investigate things with Mannheimer. Meanwhile, you and Rachel have a good time. Look around. You'll find a fine town, an excellent place to live. And if it's okay with you, I'll be back in touch at the hotel, or you can stop by here."

"Sounds great, Pinky." Both the men shook hands, saying their farewells for the time being.

As Saul left Pinky's store, he wondered if he would spend more time looking around or over his shoulder. Hurrying back to the train station, he realized he was already a half hour late. But Saul knew the wife he adored. He knew Rachel likely expected him to be late but would still scold him. He also knew she was finding ways to entertain herself and those around her. That was who he had married.

Chapter Eight

Elijah came out of his ring. The group had gathered! Were they so interested in the story that they were early? Probably not, he mused and smiled. Older folks in the desert were always early to every event. Potlucks and music events were the most overrun with enthusiasm. He hoped his story might compete. Elijah continued:

"Any thoughts about where we've left off, folks?" Everyone chatted. Thoughts were plentiful. It was more like a free-for-all, with concerns, recommendations, and enthusiasm from all directions.

"All I know is that if I were gone that long just looking around without her, Fran would be pretty pissed by the time I got home," Al offered.

"No, probably relieved that you were out of my hair," Fran retorted.

"Well, that's true, but your basic starting point each day is wanting me out of your hair. Poor Rachel was abandoned. They had set a time limit for Saul to get back. Not only wasn't he back, but when he did come back, he had a shit load of stuff to dump on her. Lots have happened. Married, Rachel is now an unknowing silent partner in Saul's wheeling and dealing lifestyle, with daily changing plans. How is she going to handle those potatoes?

Fran got more serious. "Al's right. I'd be pissed off. So many changes in such a short time. They never even discussed Des

Moines as an option, much less starting a statewide newspaper. When he enthusiastically dumps all these notions in her lap, he might see her packing her bag and heading back East. Saul's intentions already seem way out in front of her. It seems like he is aching to stay in Des Moines. He seems like someone who likes challenges and truly likes the community atmosphere. But he's left his wife behind. Where is she in all this?"

Nancy wondered. "In addition to the paper idea, she doesn't know anything about Des Moines. I don't see how she'll be able to enjoy his enthusiasm. Her view of Des Moines has been minimal. And we really don't know how committed she is to leave Detroit. Does she think this is a vacation, a temporary reprieve from the problems back home? Or a true departure or escape? The newspaper idea would seem risky for someone barely old enough to leave home."

She continued, "It'll be fun to see how this is resolved. We're getting mixed messages about how assertive Rachel is. If she doesn't bring up how she is feeling, Saul better hear it in her voice or see it in her actions. He needs to include her in all this, not exclude her. If he sees his wife as a drag in his negotiations, he'll be barking up the wrong tree."

David, quiet up to now, was more forthright. "I think the whole thing is a big gamble any way you look at it. OK, I guess anything is possible. But to me, Saul seems to be an interesting guy with interesting ideas. But he is also a guy who doesn't act without data. Saul is good about observing people, figuring 'em out, and maybe even bringing 'em together to help fulfill his dream. After all, that's why Saul and his folks had emigrated here, even though he remembered little of his own trip. Saul seems to share his father's ideas for doing things in new ways for himself.

Amused, Elijah decided to pick up where he left off before the group started to come up with their own narrative of Rachel and Saul. Hushing them, he said, "Okay, everyone, let's find out what really happened.

After Saul left Pinky's store, he slowly walked back to the station, going up and down the streets. He saw large theaters, department stores, restaurants, office buildings, and a big building housing the local newspaper. The Des Moines Register was known beyond the borders of the state. They even had an evening paper, as well as a morning one. Des Moines was the commercial and political center of the state. In comparison, Detroit was huge, with about one million people, and it was dynamic and unmanageable in many ways. It was in a messy stage of new industries creating conflict for power and control by different parties. On the other hand, Des Moines was smaller at about a hundred thousand people and was the state capitol. To Saul's eyes, that seemed 'full service' but manageable and ideal for a new person starting out.

Saul and Rachel had set off with an unspoken understanding that they'd probably not return to Detroit to live, but the group was right. They hadn't clarified that. They were mutually mollified just to be getting out of town. They left their permanent intentions purposely vague. No actual words to describe the "adventure" were consistently used. Sometimes it was a "vacation," and sometimes an "exploration" or even a "delayed honeymoon." They never said to each other, "Let's look for a new place to live. A city where we want to set up shop." Saul knew, though, that he had to give the trip structure so that he talked about going west to see more of the country, maybe as far as Kansas City.

His friends at the paper in Detroit had some experiences in the Midwest. Of the three major cities of Kansas City, Omaha, and Des Moines, KC seemed, to many, the most problematic.

It had an established political machine, the Prendergast machine. Going there, you had to take sides. It was a Detroit-style conflict all over again, maybe more sophisticated and even less violent, but still conflict. Omaha was the furthest from Detroit or home but less dynamic than Des Moines, which had the state capital. But beyond that, Saul knew little.

As he entered the train station lobby, Rachel saw him coming and smiled in relief. She stood up and took off her apron when she saw Saul enter the station. Serving others distracted her from the intense anxiety that she had been feeling. Now Rachel had at least some relief, even encouragement, because of the smile on Saul's face. She had such respect for Saul but still felt dependent on him. His energy coming across the room excited her. Indeed, she had a smorgasbord of emotions. They hugged without saying a word. The inspirational words would come later. Now, Rachel's curiosity had just about outlived her patience and dampened her anxiety.

"Did you have a nice walk and meeting? You were gone a lot longer than I expected. I was really beginning to get worried."

"Yeah, I'm sorry about that. Look, there is so much to tell. We'll stay over for a day or two, maybe a few days. I met some people. They suggested a hotel, The Brown. Let's get a cab and go over there, sit down, have a drink and some dinner, and I'll tell you all about it."

"But the train leaves for Kansas City soon. We'll miss that. I thought we were going to Kansas City," she said, sounding panicked.

"We will, maybe, we can if we want, but not tonight. Tomorrow if we wish to. But now, let's catch our breath. Let me tell you about this place and the people I met. It has been a long day."

"Okay...if that's what you want, but I'm worried about changing the plans....."

"We didn't have specific plans, so we haven't changed anything. Remember, we're exploring, just like shopping for clothes. You may wander around a department store, just looking. Then something grabs your attention, and you begin to move to a different department, maybe even try on some other things. All those things can delay you. You can leave if you don't find anything you like. Same process here. But we need to take time out to talk and figure things out. Let's discuss what we see on the rack and consider what it might feel like on your body."

"Well...okay. Dinner sounds good, but I'm unsure how we get that drink. This isn't Detroit, you know."

"Rachel, prohibition is almost a dead issue. Finding a drink is the least we need to worry about."

They got in a cab and headed toward The Brown Hotel. Walking into the lobby, Rachel exclaimed, "My goodness, I didn't know they have huge fish like this in Iowa!" The walls were covered with deep-sea trophies.

"The place is probably owned by a wealthy guy who loves deep-sea fishing. Doubt these came from a couple of rivers here or rivers anywhere." They settled in their room and made dinner reservations. Saul said, "I'll be back soon. I'm just going down to the lobby to deal with something."

"Today or tomorrow?" Rachel said sarcastically, the unpredictability of the situation finally getting to her.

"What?"

"Today or tomorrow?" she said, only louder this time.

"Today or tomorrow, what?"

"Will you be back today or tomorrow?"

Saul looked at her pleadingly, saying, "Honey…"

"Just go, just go. Why start explaining now? Do what you want!" Rachel retorted, feeling more annoyed by the second about the change in plans.

I guess she's more pissed than I thought, muttered Saul to no one in particular. *She'll get over it. She always does,* he thought. Finding the head bellhop, Saul slipped forward a bill and inquired, "My wife and I are thirsty. Are there any reasonable solutions for two parched wayward travelers around here?"

"If you don't already know, sir, Iowa is a dry state. We can't sell you anything. Nobody can. We can only accept tips, the usual bags, making reservations, helping you with directions, things to do, places to go, etc. No, sir, we don't do anything unusual here at The Brown."

Saul knew the game. If you were in a city where the cops were paid off, as part of the "Untaxed prohibition commerce," you could deal for illegal booze quite openly. In other parts of the country, it had to be more indirect. If you were an unknown customer, a bit more caution was taken.

"First time in Des Moines?"

"Oh yes, our first time."

"Liking it?"

"Just beginning to explore."

"What sort of things are you interested in?"

"Well, obviously business opportunities, but first, maybe even a job."

"What sort of job?"

"I like charitable work, social service organizations, helping with settlement houses, helping people out who are in need, that sort of thing."

"You know, I know a guy you ought to chat with. He does a lot of charitable work, providing people with what they need."

"Is he around here?"

"Yes, sir, right down the street. His name is Tony, and he works at the cleaners around the corner."

"Great, I'll drop by and see if he's there."

"I'm sure that he can help you out. He's very nice to many people I send down there. You know people for whom I make reservations. I get a lot of guys who stay in the hotel who are very charitable, just like you. Give me big tips too. I send a lot of these guys to Tony. He's so charitable himself. He gives lots of things away."

Bullshit, without self-incrimination, was the national language from the Atlantic to the Pacific, well especially prominent in the Atlantic if you considered D.C. in the equation. After having upped the bellhop's tip, Saul sauntered toward the cleaners. The bellhop pocketed his second, larger tip, and Tony received a quick phone call, a heads up that a new philanthropist was coming his way.

After his excursion to find some drinks to calm their nerves, Saul returned with a brown paper bag. He and Rachel walked toward the dining room. "Oh, I see you went shopping for brown bags. How pretty." Calmer, friendlier, and indeed hungry, Rachel sat down as Saul pulled out the chair for her.

"Nice place, linen, stemware, the works."

"Nothing but the best for my wife."

The busboy filled the water glasses. The waiter approached. "Welcome, Madame, Sir. I'm looking forward to helping you tonight. In addition to your water, would you like any other beverages? I, of course, cannot serve you liquor, but if you'd care for an extra smaller glass, perhaps with some ice and a bit of water or sparkling water, I can help. Then we can consider hors d'oeuvres if you'd like."

"Thank you. Ice and sparkling water will be fine. Small glasses, please."

When the drink glasses arrived. Saul added the scotch, acquired via a very mild form of the underground railroad. "L'chaim," they uttered and clinked glasses. The hors d'oeuvres arrived. Rachel sipped her drink and said, "Okay, Saul, talk, all of it. The whole thing. Don't leave out an 'if' or 'but' out. I know you're up to something. Talk now!"

Saul did, bringing her up to date. He told her all that he had learned about Des Moines, Pinky, the lack of a Jewish newspaper...everything that crossed his mind at that minute.

Rachel sat listening silently to all that Saul had to say. She felt overwhelmed, as if being overtaken by an avalanche. They sat staring at one another; Saul, overwhelmed with excitement, Rachel with fear. Saul finally broke the silence, hoping to find Rachel as enthused about his ideas as he was.

"Honey, you look like you've seen a ghost. What's the matter? Don't you like the idea?"

"I don't know what to say."

"You must have some thoughts and questions. How do you feel about what I've found out?"

"I'm not exactly sure what you've found out. But how do I feel? I feel confused, overwhelmed, scared, and deceived. I was on a trip to look around a few hours ago. Just a short cab ride ago, I thought I'd soon board a train to Kansas City. Now I'm told I'm staying in Des Moines, perhaps to live permanently, and I will help start a statewide newspaper. This is also a riskier plan than our current situation in

Detroit. A plan that almost certainly takes me away from my family.

"Before the cab ride, I felt curious and sad simultaneously. But it was okay. Do you know why it was okay, Saul? It was okay because it was just a new experience, a trip, an excursion, a substitute honeymoon, a trial balloon. Now I feel like I've been hit by a truck, and I'm lying on the ground bleeding, and my husband walks right on without noticing me."

In his excitement, Saul didn't wait for any further explanation, "No, we're not staying here permanently. Extending our stay is just part of the exploration. And we're finding some interesting things. Come on, don't overreact. Look at the bigger picture."

Regaining some semblance of composure, Rachel added, "No, Saul, you're finding some exciting things. So far, I've just found a nice department store that doesn't begin to rival Hudson's back home, and there are some friendly people in the train station where you dumped me off. How do I feel? I feel like I started a nice leisurely walk through the meadow, and then suddenly, I was faced with a mountainous volcano and told to climb it and peek over the edge. That's how I feel!"

"But don't you think the idea of a statewide Jewish newspaper published in English is good?"

"It could be. It is an interesting idea, but is it good? I'm in no position to evaluate that. But it isn't the idea that concerns me."

"Okay... if not the idea, then what?" Saul sat quietly. He felt as if he'd been slapped aside his face. In some ways, he had been. But his mind immediately went into calculating mode. He knew the next thing out of his mouth was important.

He continued, "Darling, I'm sorry. You are one hundred percent correct. I was like a diesel train running on the track out of control." He figured an apology would be best for sheltering him from the raging storm. It may have been the best he could have offered, but it was a horrible metaphor.

"You know Saul, I don't know much about Diesel engines. They're still new and, in some ways, untried. But I'm also beginning to see you in a new light. You go off half-cocked with this grandiose idea of you creating a statewide paper. I thought you might want to get a job. You know, one of those activities that ordinary people go to daily. And you know what? They get a paycheck for doing that job at the end of the week."

"But this would be a job!"

"No, it would be a creation. You're building a huge stone sculpture and have never even picked up a chisel. You have no experience as a reporter, much less as an editor and publisher. And we certainly don't have the money to do something like that. So, it all sounds like a pipe dream. This is your fanciful idea, and you know what bothers me the most?"

"I thought I'd heard most of it?"

"Don't be sarcastic with me. You are forty miles down the road in discussing this, planning it in your head, already arranging to talk to important people about it, and I am just finding out about it."

"When did I have time to talk to you about it?"

"The moment it came into your head! If you were acting like a teammate, you'd have considered bringing the idea to me first, not going off and getting knee-deep into the planning process. Rather than impulsively telling Pinky first, you could have discussed it with me. What was the rush? I bet you've spent a good deal of time in your own head figuring out how to sell this to Pinky or whoever, but did you once think that this may be a horribly wrong idea for us? I'm not worried about the people in Des Moines. They'll take care of themselves. Who will care for us if you're not careful in considering the risks?"

Saul stared at Rachel in disbelief. Deep inside him, an unreliable force suggested that a puppy-dog stare would change her mind. It didn't. Finally, he said.

"Okay, maybe I deserved that. I'm sorry. I should have discussed all this with you first. That being said, we have lots to talk about. Help me think. Let's finish eating and head back to the hotel. We can brainstorm there."

Even though Saul apologized, Rachel felt no sense of victory. She never felt marriage would be this hard and complicated.

Chapter Nine

Fresh, after-dinner treats were abundant. The group gathered, more silently than usual, and reseated themselves around the campfire. Elijah questioned whether they ate so much that they felt too satiated to talk.

Fran said, "No. I think many of us were revisiting our early years of marriage. Our two newlyweds sure have a lot to work out. I'm beginning to think they didn't know each other all that well when they got hitched."

Elijah responded, "Well, some friends and family wondered what the rush into matrimony was all about. But, no, there was no pregnancy or other urgency beyond their passion, if that's what you're wondering."

Nancy added, "I'm not sure either of them knew themselves very well."

Fran replied, "Who of us does at that age?"

Elijah began, "Well, to be sure, there are many issues on the table. Is Saul sure he can handle the project he is suggesting? Does he know the newspaper business well enough to pull this off? If he does, can he convince the Rabbi of his character? After all, as an editor, Saul will be catapulted into a position of authority in the Jewish Community. If you were Saul, with his background, would you be prepared for a one-on-one with your clergyman when you knew he was not there to console or help you seek forgiveness but instead, to evaluate you? What should his strategy be? Should he approach this meeting as a casual one, an opportunity to get to know one another? Bide his time, get established, make other contacts, then broach the subject of an Iowa Jewish News?

Nancy enquired, "What do you mean by 'his background'?"

Elijah continued, "Good question, Nancy. He's used to dealing with people regarding specific tasks or transactions. Either someone thought he was trustworthy and capable, or they thought he wasn't. The job, editing, and publishing responsibilities are far out of his wheelhouse. A Rabbi would be concerned not as much about the task, but in that position, you are an influencer. Any clergyman will look deeper at character issues before backing him or turning the reins over to him on some massive project. Creating, publishing, and editing a religious-oriented newspaper that will have sway over the clergyman's minions is far different from running numbers or any errands in Detroit.

Or should Saul risk getting off on the wrong foot with a community leader by pushing the matter of an Iowa Jewish News? What do you guys think? Left fork or the right fork in the road?"

Harry remained doubtful. "I wonder if he is gutsy enough to go head-to-head with the Rabbi. That's a lot of moxie in my book. I'd expect to see that much confidence in a fraud, a con man. If he isn't a fraud, maybe his sense of self-esteem, or whatever you want to call it, is blown out of proportion. I agree with you, Elijah. There is a choice Saul must make. He has to be sure of what he has to offer and not take a long shot. If he overshoots and doesn't deliver, that will bite him in the future."

Nancy, feeling uncomfortable, stood up to put another small log on the fire. The flames were doing fine, but she wasn't. Facing such a multitude of ifs and buts seemed overwhelming. That was something she could identify with. She added, "Even with what Harry says, we still have the cart before the horse. There are so many other balls in the air. Is this a good place for the couple? Is he willing to explore that openly with Rachel? How will Rachel respond? It seems to me this meeting with the Rabbi is premature."

Larry added, "It seems to me that Saul is taking a risk before he needs to do it. Almost like setting the newspaper idea solidifies a decision to stay in Des Moines. It would be more appropriate to decide on Des Moines first and, subsequently, to pursue the possibility of starting a newspaper. It's like Saul sat down at a poker table and is going 'all in' on the third hand with little knowledge of the other players. I'd be scared shitless doing what he's doing. But I wonder, is he fearful, confident, or excited?"

Cindy added, "Well, if his story isn't all true, he better be cautious about how much he makes up! He could get his man parts subsequently caught in a ringer. I guess lying, overreaching, or being truthful all have risks in this situation."

Everyone laughed. Cindy was the only one of the group who lived full-time on a ranch and was used to impulsively speaking her mind.

Elijah knew that the speculation could be endless. But it was time to see what happened when Rachel and Saul were awake and rested. He cleared his throat and continued.

"The following day, Saul awoke, anticipating that the tension from the night before would still occupy the hotel room space. He was surprised and, in some ways, outfoxed. Rachel was also a good strategist. When Saul was ready to sleep, she told him, "You go on to the bedroom, honey. I'll be there in a bit. I'm not all that tired right now. I'll sit in this easy chair and enjoy my book until I feel sleepy." She pondered, strategized, and decided there were ways to take control without winning an argument with Saul.

When Saul was up, Rachel ordered room service coffee and breakfast. She was dressed and met Saul in a happy, content mood. If she'd learned anything hosting a gambling game in a hotel at seventeen, it was how to manipulate the ambient temperature in a hot situation. She sat down to eat, poured a cup of coffee for Saul, and spoke, "Well, aren't you going to join me? The eggs will go cold."

Saul, now in his robe, sat down. "Oh, you got a newspaper too."

"Yes, I made sure they'd bring up a couple of copies so we could read more about Des Moines. We know so little. Considering your shopping analogy, I don't always buy the first dress I try on, even if it looks pretty good. I'm wary if the saleslady is pushing especially hard for that choice when there are others to consider."

They both read in silence. Saul was warned by the message he was receiving.

Chit-chat followed by a good breakfast and a second cup of coffee. Then, Rachel got up and said, "While you shower and get dressed, I'm going for a little walk. Be back soon if that's okay." She left without waiting for an answer.

Saul had been shaken by Rachel's confrontation the night before. Her saleslady innuendo was less than subtle this morning. But she was right. He had operated as an independent operator and salesman since high school. He made decisions and dealt with the consequences when things went south. But mostly, his efforts, plans, and deals worked reasonably well. Now, he was married. He had to act as a partner. The benefits and discomforts of that were new to him.

The night before, he had his first real taste of those discomforts, but he wondered if the benefits were not so hidden in Rachel's words, too. Was he sledding downhill too fast with his idea of the newspaper? Was that way beyond his skill level? Was he biting off more than he could handle? On the other hand, maybe Rachel was doing him a favor by slowing him down, perhaps even stopping the runaway train. He needed perspective but felt like he had no one to talk with besides Rachel. He already knew her feelings about the matter.

Saul had only one current confidant in his life. He'd kept the details of his life to himself and never shared much with his brothers and very little with his parents. But one person who knew him well was "Old Harry," his true mentor and friend at the Detroit Free Press. But Harry was in Detroit, and Saul was in Des Moines. Saul rarely felt desperate, but this was one of those few times his feelings overtook him. He decided to try to call Harry for advice. This was a significant decision. A long-distance call would cost over four dollars for just three minutes. The average hourly wage in those years was in the ninety-cent range. But he needed help. Had he overestimated his abilities?

He glanced across the room at the phone, staring at it as if it were Pandora's box and about to open. Rarely did Saul feel that scared. But he had no other options. Saul was looking for a way to comfort Rachel. It had nothing to do with wanting to win. It had more to do with crossing the stream to fulfill his dream. Rachel would fear they'd drown. He was looking for a life raft or two to carry them both. Saul needed an objective opinion from someone who knew him better than his wife. He picked up the phone and was slow to respond to the operator on the other end. Finally, he placed the call.

Harry was an unusual drunk. He rarely had a hangover. Mornings were his best time. Describing him as energetic in the mornings would be an overstatement, but he was at least coherent and clear-headed. He, too, enjoyed his morning coffee while reading the paper. He was not all that interested in the day's news but more in critiquing how "those young fellers" were doing the reporting. Harry was disappointed when he heard Saul had suddenly left town without even saying goodbye. But now he was glad and relieved to hear from Saul.

Saul gave Harry a speedy summary of the trip to date. He then explained what had happened with Pinky, the idea of the Iowa Jewish News, and Rachel's reaction. He said to Harry, "Look, you know how much I value your advice. But unfortunately, I don't have much time. Rachel will be back any moment, and I don't have much money to spend on long-distance phone calls. You know me. Do you think I'm getting in over my head?"

"Okay, Saul, brief it will be. First, you're on your own with Rachel. Second, I'm no expert on love and marriage. My two ex-wives will verify that if you need my bona fides. That being said, you don't have to worry about your head, but your heart."

"Harry! Don't be cryptic. What do you mean?"

"Look. You've seen enough of the workings of a large paper to know what you need to start a small weekly rag, no matter how wide the distribution. You've been in every part of the Free Press. You know how to typeset and how the presses operate. Granted, what you'll have to get will be much smaller, but type setting is type setting. You've learned the skill. If you're going statewide, you'll need reporters, but you know nothing if not the ability to schmooze and encourage interest in people from other cities. No, you have the head and the know-how of how to organize this thing. However, you need your head pointed in the right direction and your heart to be your editorial assistant."

"Cryptic Harry, you're being cryptic."

"Okay, okay. It's all about your mission. You are not doing investigative reporting or presenting the news of the day. Base level, what are you all about? What is your purpose? You would be doing community organizing. That is the mission. It can't be done just with facts; the heart will ultimately be the motivating power. Your work must be focused on creating a strong emotional connection within the community. Imagine the drawstring on a bag. A lot in the bag can fall everywhere if the top is left open. But nothing will fall out if you, as the editor, can pull the drawstring together. That is what that type of newspaper should do."

"Harry, you are a gem. What would I do without you?"

"Frankly, my boy, I don't want to know about everything you've done without me. And by the way, thanks for covering that story for me when I was asleep."

"You mean passed out?"

"Yeah, yeah, whatever.

"Oh, you found out about that?"

"Yeah, when the editor thanked me for covering the story, I didn't remember that I had. Then, when he kidded me about not being able to resist sticking my nose in the investigative part, I realized that wasn't something I was likely to forget. I told him that it was most likely you were using my little nap to your advantage. Since you'd left town, I felt it would be okay to fess up. Also, I told him that he should have been smart enough to recognize a diamond in the rough and keep you aboard. Anyway, good luck, kid. Have a nice trip. Keep in touch now and then."

Saul was pleased and reassured by talking with Harry. But he couldn't ignore the possibility of failure. Harry was honest and experienced, but could his loyalty make him a biased observer? He knew the newspaper business and appreciated what Saul had done for him in recent years. Harry put the issue in finer perspective for Saul. Of course, Harry could not know whether Saul had the editorial heart from which the Des Moines Community could benefit. But that was the primary issue for Saul to consider. He was sure he had the strength to face the adversity likely to come with bumps in the road. But could he rise to the level of a savvy and responsible community organizer?

He knew Rachel would be back soon, but he had to make one more phone call. He rarely, if ever, asked his father for advice. Nor did Dad offer unsolicited opinions. Now Saul felt that he needed an opinion from someone who knew what it was like to reach and get that extra horsepower to climb to the next level. If that someone also knew him well, all the better. That was his father.

He called Morris and brought him up to date on what had happened on the trip thus far.

"I'm not sure what to do, Dad. I passionately want to push ahead with this, but the idea seemed to come out of nowhere, and I wonder if I'm trying to go too far too fast. The risk of letting down Rachel and the people in Des Moines is scary."

Morris responded, "First, is Rachel onboard with this?"

"Not yet. But I think she will be."

"It would be a mistake to threaten your marriage in addition to the other risks and downsides you can see. That would not be very smart. If you like Des Moines and that suits you, you can find some honest work there. So, stay and enjoy starting a family. You don't need to start such a big experiment out of desperation because you are not desperate. Don't act as if you are."

"But what if Rachel is on board?"

"That's a different story. Then, you are stepping way outside your comfort zone to rise to a new creative type of life for yourself and your family. You know at least some of your grandmother, Sophia's, pain and suffering. She was desperate but could do little, nothing really, to improve her own plight. But from birth until she died, she encouraged me to groom myself for something different and better. She never told me what that would be, but she urged me to do something different than living with daily abuse and subjugation. She told me that someday I would have freedom. I was still young when she died, but I continued to groom myself mentally for something better than the life she had.

Your Uncle Ben and I argued intensely about my escaping the shtetl and immigrating to America, especially without your mother, you, and your sister. I couldn't rationally make sense of it to him or myself. I was making a good living as a skilled artisan. We weren't being abused daily. But we weren't free. Despite my success and skill, I was demeaned by almost all in the family. I was the insignificant bastard, not recognized as a legitimate family member.

I felt that your grandmother had forced herself to stay alive, to feed me when others didn't care if I was dead or alive. She intended that someday I could have the freedom and respect that she never had. She told me that if I could have independence, my story would be different from hers, and my children's stories would likely be other than mine. My passion was to have that freedom, even if it meant risking death to try. But I owed it to my mother to try. How can you owe a dead person anything? That doesn't sound very smart, even to me. But that is how I felt. Your mother and sister would be looked after by Ben. You all would be okay. I saw an opening and had to take it.

My mother made her children her project, especially me, because I was a boy. But your sister, Rebecca, lived in that same environment and has exceeded what many women her age have accomplished. Rebecca does not live in daily fear of rape. She and I can live openly as Jews in bigger cities with many opportunities.

So, all I can say to you, Saul, is that I've watched you flit here and there over the years. Each time, you believed your new idea would benefit others even more than yourself. That benefit motivated you to pursue what you imagined. It's like when your mother and I decided we could make cheese that other people would like better than what they had. We would benefit only if we pleased them and helped them to have something better. It worked.

Many have seen that a mysterious helter-skelter employment activity has been successful most of the time. Consider all your activities to be your practice runs. Have they prepared you well? I don't know for sure. But what seems to run deep in the heart of your grandmother, me, and now you, is that our passion drives us, maybe more than our talent or wisdom. Your grandmother lived long enough, over incredible odds, to pass the message and the mantel to me. I am happy with what I've done. I have delivered freedom to you and your sister and brothers born here. But, aside from some unique cheese years ago, I've created nothing new. Not even a wrought iron gate. So now, maybe, it is your turn to respond to your passion and create something new. No one will shoot you if you fail."

Saul teared up hearing his father pass on his life story to him. Even though he knew most of it, he deeply appreciated his father's words of wisdom. Thanking him and bidding goodbye, Saul took a deep breath, preparing himself for Rachel's arrival.

When Rachel got back, Saul was prepared. She was in a good mood, shared a story about the exciting department stores in Des Moines, and then made some tea for Saul and herself. Saul wondered if this were a peace offering but quickly dismissed the idea. The peace offering was his to give, not hers. A good opening, he thought.

"Okay, honey, I have a peace offering."

"I'm listening."

"As I said before, all your concerns and fears are valid. So are my dreams. The fact of the matter is that, as you've pointed out, I've already started the ball rolling downhill. But if we keep ourselves focused on our process and progress step by step and not always debate the endpoint, we'll work together and not invite tragedy."

"That sounds good, but I have no idea what you are talking about!"

"For example, today, the issue for us is to refrain from debating the risk versus rewards of a dream, a passion. Instead, we need to step back and define the goals of what we both want. Once we have defined our needs, we can make our plan."

"Be more specific, please."

"Okay. Let's investigate the issues on the table one by one. First, does Des Moines seem like a welcoming city where we could enjoy living and raising a family? If it is, we will continue to explore Des Moines. The newspaper idea is a secondary issue. It is relevant only if we feel very positive about Des Moines as an option. If we see Des Moines as mediocre, no worries. We leave the newspaper situation on the table and do not commit to it. Then, we will head west and explore some other cities."

Maybe we will return to Des Moines, and maybe not. If Des Moines seems out of the question for you, we don't consider pursuing the newspaper, even if I fall in love with the idea. That approach pretty much puts the brakes on my overly enthusiastic ball rolling downhill."

"What do you mean by 'pretty much'?" asked Rachel.

"I was honestly shaken by your lack of confidence in me. I never had to face that before. I've operated as a loner. Even though your concerns were genuine and worthwhile, they shook me. Was I barking up the wrong tree, or did I have a shot at pulling off this newspaper idea? Des Moines was not the first concern on my mind. It should have been. We'll either both like it here, or we'll move on to a better option. The big issue is Des Moines. We could even stay in Des Moines with a different job in mind."

"Hmm, go on."

"Well...I called Harry."

"Who the hell is Harry?"

"That's the old guy at the paper that I sometimes talk about."

"The old drunk who is too soused to work anymore? Did you ask him for advice? God help us."

"No, really, he's been a great mentor to me at the paper. He is an alcoholic, but he's not stupid or demented. He's old and wise, well, except about alcohol and women. But anyway, he gave me some great advice. He put things in perspective."

"Tell me what he said."

Saul repeated the details of the brief phone call as best he could. Rachel was still dubious but glad to hear Harry's confidence in Saul to deal with the details of physical planning and execution. She had no idea what capabilities he had. But if an old newsman said Saul could do it, he probably could. Somebody who was that old, unreliable, and alcoholic yet still had a desk at the newspaper must have some credibility. The issue of the paper being a community organizer appealed to Rachel.

Rachel rose to a new leadership position in the partnership. She said, "Okay, we can chew gum and walk simultaneously."

"Now you've got me confused."

"I've been reframing things in my mind. Rather than seeing everything as a threat to our magical and rapidly deteriorating plan, I'm going to be open but skeptical about seeing new events as opportunities. So potentially investigating the paper, meeting the Rabbi, and maybe even some successful, well-connected people in the Jewish community is a way to learn more about the community here. You may see them as investors. I see them as investigative sources. It beats just walking the streets, going into the shops, and even schmoozing with people in the train station.

The way I see it, the critical question of staying in Des Moines is why? If the why is first and foremost to fulfill your dream, no dice. I'm aboard if the why is because we've fallen into a pit full of potential gold information about a place we might like to settle down. But you better be sincere about that. And you know that all these months working a dice game has created a great sense of smelling a skunk if one is lurking. Don't become a skunk, Saul."

Ultimately, Rachel agreed to let the process continue if her full participation was included.

Laura exclaimed, "Is that it? Is that all? Didn't Saul tell her about the conversation with his father?"

Elijah looked at Laura. He was thoughtful before answering, "It appears that he didn't. That is a good question. Reviewing the story, I wondered why he didn't tell Rachel about that call. Lucas said to me that Saul was strategic. He needed the reassurance that his passion was a legitimate motivator. He trusted that he and his father were on the same wavelength about the advantages and disadvantages of imagination, creativity, and passion. None of these qualities could be evaluated rationally or necessarily understood by someone who hadn't been torn, pushed, or shoved by passion. Saul loved Rachel and her father. He was such a gentleman, tolerant and understanding. But he had his limits defined by his own experiences. Anything beyond those boundaries was likely considered foolish. So, Saul figured that neither Rachel nor her father, whom she would call with the advice Saul garnered from his father, would be on board with decisions based primarily on imagination, creativity, and based on one's passion.

Okay, let's leave it there for now, folks."

Chapter Ten

The campers gathered after dinner. No one said a word. Instead, all looked at Elijah expectedly.

Elijah continued, "What? No questions, comments?"

Kathy calmly said, "Get on with it, Elijah. What happened?"

"Okay, okay, I'll tell you how the morning went.

Pinky was able to successfully set up a meeting between Saul and the Rabbi. The shrill ringing of the phone set off different feelings in Saul and Rachel. For Saul, it was as if the bell had rung in a boxing match, a message that he must emerge from his corner and walk into battle. For Rachel, it was far different.

Rachel experienced the noise as if a curtain was to go up on a Greek tragedy where she had a leading role. Her loving parents both assumed that their daughter's trip was folly. For them, she was a child and belonged at home where they could look after her. She may be married, yes, but she was still their little girl. Her older sister already had children of her own. She was a grown-up mother. Petite, innocent Rachel was not ready for adulthood yet. Before she and Saul left, her father had told her that the life they had created for her was good enough. They felt shame that she was off seeking something better.

As the curtain rose for the first act of the imagined play rushing through Rachel's mind, Rachel started with a monologue to reassure her parents of their wonderful care, love, and parenting. Just like a Greek chorus, she danced around the truth and expounded about how her parents should not see her honeymoon as her being ungrateful for the life they had worked so hard to create for her in Detroit. No, they should be happy for her. She had always dreamed of a wonderful honeymoon that she would soon have.

Act two: point, counterpoint. Enter stage left another section of the chorus, her parent's rebuttal. They did not see Kansas City or Omaha as resort destinations. Why couldn't she and Saul go to the wonderful resort of Charlevoix up on the Great Lake just as her brother and sister-in-law did for their honeymoon? Rachel's mother and father were equally glib at extolling the virtues of a real honeymoon. The more they talked, the more excited they got about the change in plans they were mentally arranging for their youngest child. Most of this conversation took place in Yiddish. There were definitely a few words about Saul from her father, who rarely cussed, so we won't bother to translate any of it into English.

But alas, the phone did ring. The protagonist, Rachel, had incredible qualities and experiences that her parents hadn't seen. However, if things went well for Saul with the Rabbi, she sensed that a tragedy was about to befall her. She would have to make the phone call to her parents that would wound them forever. That imagined play would open in Detroit and likely never reach Broadway.

Saul would respond to the bell by meeting with the Rabbi. Rachel was shaken by the thought of the phone call she might have to make to her parents.

Let's look at how it went for Saul.

So, there they sat. Two short-statured men. One older, seemingly wiser, with a tiny mustache and penetrating beady eyes. The other dressed nicely but obviously travel-worn and apprehensive.

"Thank you, Rabbi. I appreciate you taking the time to meet me."

"Uh-huh."

Silence.

Saul cleared his throat. Looked down. "Rabbi, you like cigars?"

Silence.

"If you don't mind, sir, I like cigars and would like to offer you one."

Saul took two cigars from a case and handed one to the Rabbi. Mannheimer hesitated but accepted it. Saul rolled and moistened his, then lit it.

"Rabbi, with all due respect, Pinky got me up to date with the structural aspects of the Jewish community in Des Moines. He was also sufficiently intrigued when I suggested that you and I meet. I look forward to being here with you. You must have many questions for me. What would you like to know?"

Rabbi put the cigar in his breast pocket. "Why?"

"Why what?"

"I was told that you were wandering around town without your wife, asking questions. Why?"

"Because I was curious and wanted answers."

"Obviously, but why?"

"We, like many others, are traveling and looking for a new place to settle down. The train had a long layover here. Rachel stayed at the train station while I took the opportunity to explore a bit."

"Where are you traveling to?"

"Kansas City."

"What are you going to do there?"

"I'm not sure. Look around, maybe get a job."

"What kind? What do you do?"

"I've done lots of things. Worked everything from dairy and cheese making to assisting in hotels and newspaper offices and helping my father manage some apartments. What Pinky told me about Des Moines and the Jewish community seemed appealing. I want to lay over, spend a few more days here, and speak with more people. We've lived in Detroit most of our lives. Rachel moved there from Cincinnati when she was quite young. I immigrated as a toddler.

Our families are still in Detroit, well-established, comfortable, and happy. Unfortunately, things are more chaotic for someone like me looking for a career. The battles between union members, management, and the gang can occur at the same dinner table! Rachel worked at a large hotel, and there was a shooting right where she stood. She, too, no longer found Detroit comfortable. We both want someplace smaller and dynamic like Des Moines but without the chaos and hectic pace. In Detroit, there is confrontation and competition even within the Jewish community. We hoped to find something different. Hence, our trip west."

There was silence. Saul squirmed, but very little. He'd sat with Rabbis before! He knew the silence could be a challenging technique as well as an opportunity to redirect the conversation.

"You know, Rabbi, I've been asking why Pinky suggested that I meet with this one Rabbi in a reasonably large city. I'm not asking to join a congregation. I'm not trying to enroll a child into a school, and I need the acceptance of the headmaster. So, what's this all about?"

Silence again. Saul waited calmly. He knew that this was a pivotal point and that he must wait.

More silence. Saul re-lit his cigar and reached for the ashtray but glanced at the Rabbi for acceptance. The Rabbi nodded. Saul took the ashtray.

"So, how have you answered that question, Saul?"

"Well, Rabbi, may I be frank?"

A nod.

"It's not about me. It is about you and the newspaper."

"How's that?"

"You are a powerbroker, a prime mover in this community. The newspaper is a big idea. It isn't likely to go forward and succeed without your blessing. The meeting isn't about Rachel and me joining the Jewish community in Des Moines. It's about the idea, the paper."

"Wow, you come into town, young man, and right off the bat, give me a promotion, powerbroker, prime mover! How gracious of you. But from where do you get such power?" The Rabbi's voice was slightly more intense than before, maybe even harsh and scolding.

"You know, Rabbi. I really felt lucky to have met Pinky. I found someone friendly, gracious, welcoming, helpful, and seemingly honest. Newsstands, barbershops, salons, and deli proprietors significantly represent communities. People gather there. They are like a Catholic priest without the power of forgiveness. But they hear everything. They know how the community thinks. "

"And so?"

"And so, I'm not being arrogant or giving you a promotion. I'm just respecting and reflecting on the esteem and thoughts that others in Des Moines have about you. This is not an effort on my part to falsely suck up to you. Whether or not Pinky is a pretty good judge of character, you know better than I do. Wear his compliment with pride. You've earned it. If not, you can deliver the message that he overestimates and glamorizes you. Tell him to knock it off if you must. But for my purposes, I choose to believe him. I believe in your wisdom and experience and would value your opinion. I'd gladly listen, even if you thought the idea was horrible. Whatever you say, good or bad, should prove instructive."

Saul knew that this was a break-or-make moment with the Rabbi. He wanted to get him to soften up towards him and accept that he did not mean any harm. He wanted to show that he wasn't a threat to the community, and so, he chose his next words wisely.

"Rachel and I can be like any other couple moving into a town. We can look around and investigate the way anyone else would. In doing so, we may have had a reason or opportunity to meet you on some occasion, social or religious. I'm delighted to be meeting you now, but under ordinary circumstances, that would not be a vital part of our moving to Des Moines. This meeting is primarily about my idea for a Statewide English Jewish Newspaper."

"So, I am to decide if this new idea of a newspaper is to be?"

"I hope not."

"You hope not! Then what?"

"I want you to be an essential part of the discussion. Not to make the decision."

"Fair enough, Saul. I'll think about that. But Pinky could have brought the newspaper idea to me alone. So why are you, pardon the reference, the delivery boy?"

Saul recognized that Rabbi was letting him know the hierarchy here with the "delivery boy" reference. *But why did he need to do that,* Saul wondered. *Have I ruffled his feathers by being frank rather than just sitting and trying to impress him? Did he really need that fawning admiration from me? I'll file this one away but tread lightly.* Saul gently moved forward.

"Delivery boy... It's been a long time since I wore that hat. But it brings back feelings of pride. The direct answer to your question of why use me as a "delivery boy," as you put it, is because Pinky is a smart man. He wants to kill three birds with one stone..."

"And what might those birdies be?"

"Well, as I've mentioned, the paper is the first. The second is your assessment of whether I was a good fit to be involved with the newspaper if it were to be pursued. Lastly, Pinky wanted to use the best salesman he knew to convince me about the values and benefits of living in this community."

"Big agenda, I must say."

"True, Rabbi, only if we can manage it," Saul smiled. "You know, Rabbi, since I'm somehow part of all three birdies, there is an important question you'll want to know the answer to. So, you might want to just go ahead and start there."

"Now, I'm not sure who is running this interview," laughed the Rabbi. "Okay. We'll get to the paper later. What should I know? What should I ask you first?"

"Rabbi, we're talking, getting to know each other, exchanging information. We're not running a high holiday or even maariv service here. No one has to be in charge. The question is, why did we leave Detroit?" Long silence. Saul played with the cigar.

"Rabbi, I respect what and who you are. After talking with Pinky, I know the incredible things you and others have done here. But I'm not looking for a power struggle with you or anyone else."

"Well, what are you looking for?"

"We left Detroit to find a better place to settle, where I can feel we belong and can contribute. And for my own ego to create something that doesn't already exist."

"How will you know when you find it?"

"Good question. I ask myself the same thing. My decisions have always involved observation, fact-gathering, and analyzing the pros and cons, excellent decision-making steps. Honestly, my desire to build something creative is a passion. Those imagined 'somethings' create unknowns that circle around my current decision-making. So somehow, this time, my decision seems different."

"Different, how?"

"Look, if you are crossing a stream, hoping not to fall in and get wet, you carefully look for a rock to step to and step, then stop, look for the next rock, and so on until you get to the other side. That's the way to do it. But somehow, that analogy feels empty in this situation-"

"In what way, Saul?"

"Well, I'm twenty-seven and have already gone across many streams. The other side has usually been okay. My crossings were a success but could have been more satisfying. So, this time, as I walk my path, I'm looking for a more opportunistic stream or a more exciting bank."

"What would that stream or bank look like?"

"It is not what it would look like, but more what it would feel like."

"Go on."

"I want something bigger than me. Something that feels important and challenging. That is what defines a career for me."

"Well, with all the union stuff and political conflicts in Detroit, you could find fertile ground there."

"True. But in Detroit, well, it just feels too dirty. If it were just unions and management, that would be one thing, but it's messy with organized gangs and crime syndicates getting into the auctions. That will soon invade politics if it hasn't already. Plus, more power brokers protect turf than you can shake a stick at."

"So, you're looking to become a power broker?"

"No, that isn't a responsibility I'd want to shoulder. But people make decisions. Communities make decisions. They should have good information to help them to do that. Power brokers, like in Detroit, don't always want outside good news or facts influencing the people who live in their voting districts. Power brokers just as often benefit from the chaos of misinformation."

"Well, Saul, maybe sometimes that's what progress looks like."

"True. But I'm in favor of the free flow of factual information. To mix opinion and fact is tricky and often messy and distorts the truth."

The Rabbi stared at Saul, not understanding where he was going with this information.

"So, when push comes to shove, I'll know when it is right when it feels right. I can't describe it. But I want something that challenges me but gives me opportunities. An opportunity to expand who and what I am and a chance to contribute and help make something better than already exists."

"Saul, it sounds like you might not be looking for a more appealing bank to cross to but a much larger rock, a boulder in the middle of the stream, where you can stand comfortably and safely, look around, and enjoy the scenery around you for a long time."

"I like that imagery, Rabbi, as long as I don't feel stranded on that rock."

"There will always be other smaller rocks to get off on and cross to the other side."

"I'd add a caveat, Rabbi. If I left the rock, it was of my own volition and not being pushed off."

"That's always the risk. There are no guarantees."

"None expected."

"Saul, Saul, I'll tell you what. You have already decided to stay a day or two, which seems wise. Why don't you go and get your wife? I'm sure that she must be worried. I'll go home and enjoy this cigar, maybe with a bit of after-dinner wine, and we'll meet again in a day or two if you'd like and talk more about the paper idea. I know we've left that untouched, but we can discuss it later."

"Sounds like a good idea, Rabbi. Thank you for your courtesy. I'll look forward to both of us learning more soon."

Saul waited for the Rabbi to stand, then followed him out. Watching as the Rabbi went North, Saul decided to go South.

He was in a hurry to get back to Rachel. Yet, he chose to walk more slowly and observe. Saul felt different than in the city center of Detroit. He liked the difference but couldn't quite name it. "Dynamic!" *Yes, it is not as busy,* he thought. Yes, people moved more slowly, but there didn't seem to be any pushy conflict that made him feel everything was moving in several directions simultaneously in Detroit. Here, people noticed him and said hello as he passed. Then, they stood, taking the time to look into shop windows.

From talking with Pinky and the Rabbi, Saul felt that within the Jewish community, there was less of a feeling of "taking sides" that always seemed pressured, even around the dinner table back home. Living in Detroit, there was always some pressure to take sides. Management vs. labor, Jews vs. Gentiles, each nationality with its' own fiefdom and often enforcement group. It took a lot of energy to exist in Detroit. This place seemed like it could be better. Starting over was always hard, but that decision had really been made when they got on the train leaving Detroit, their home. Leaving was always hard, but staying would have been hard, too.

Unbeknownst to Saul then, the forthcoming depression would lead to hordes of folks to start over by having to go and look for work or stand in line just for bread. This should never be seen as just another event in history. It was a human tragedy marked by human pain, suffering, and feelings of helplessness and desperation.

Saul quickened his pace. Rachel was waiting.

Saul and Rachel had known each other for quite a while, but their marriage was still relatively young. It was a beautiful formal wedding and a lovely party. But their life together made them feel like allies fighting against being anchored by family demands. For Saul, there was pressure from many conflicts in Detroit, including being too close to power brokers who could do you as much harm as good.

Anyway, he and Rachel could be allies in building something new. Time would tell. But now, he had to discuss it with Rachel."

Elijah stopped his tale, stood, and stretched. He'd thrown the last log on the fire for the night. Now everything was embers. Even the coyotes seemingly had settled in.

"That's all for tonight. We can pick up this story around tomorrow's fire. But think about what you've heard. We can talk about it if you'd like."

The fire was adequately cared for. The campers quickly found their way to their own RVs, and all was quiet. Elijah loved this time of night. He took his chair and walked to the edge of the camp. Sitting in darkness punctuated only by the moon and the stars. He loved staring and wondering. So many things out there, both in the desert and the sky. It seemed never-ending.

Chapter Eleven

The group gathered. Elijah continued, "Well, where do we go from here? Do you think Rachel will feel Saul stayed within their guidelines? Or did he begin coloring outside the lines in how he talked with the Rabbi?"

"In their shoes, I'd have been up all night worrying about everything that could go wrong, especially if the Rabbi jumps on the idea of the paper." Maxine seemed overwhelmed, fearing that Saul might over-commit without discussing events with Rachel.

"Yes, you would have kept me up all night, too!" her husband responded.

"Okay, let's take a look," said Elijah, clearing his throat as he continued.

Well, worry, Rachel did too. She peppered Saul with endless questions after he returned. For many issues, Saul only had a few answers. Rachel could see that Saul seemed devoted to the process of understanding the culture in the city. Although his ideas may come quickly and impulsively, his decisions were usually carefully thought out. He believed suitable methods would bring about the best results, in the end, usually anyway. He also believed in being prepared to cover your rear end if things didn't work out as planned.

Saul was nothing if not optimistic. He also knew his role was to reassure Rachel, and he did his best. Saul didn't argue about her concerns and gave them credence. Rachel was comforted that Saul was going back to further clarify things and talk with Pinky and the Rabbi. She knew that Saul would get no help from Pinky and his other contacts without the go-ahead from the Rabbi; for Rachel, that might be a relief. Nevertheless, Saul felt a door had opened. Successfully walking through it might be more challenging than negotiating with the Purple Gang back home, but failure would not be as permanent.

Let's hear how Saul did.

Looking dapper as usual, he arrived at the newspaper shop. Pinky had become excited at the prospect of getting to know this possible new family addition to the Jewish community. He was equally enthusiastic about the possibility of Jewish News. Being in on the original discussions gave Pinky an elevated sense of importance. The reality was that the wider community already loved Pinky, who was more than generous with his time, showing kids tricks and patiently answering any of their questions about the gimmicks and gadgets he sold. The fact that the kids rarely had the money to buy anything was of no concern to Pinky. He just loved to entertain them and see them giggle.

"Ah, welcome back, Saul. I hope that your meeting with the Rabbi was fruitful. He is very kind, but he carefully assesses what he hears."

"Yes, he was pleasant and encouraging, but we must talk more." Saul picked up a copy of the Des Moines Register and Detroit Free Press and put the money on the counter. Pinky let it rest there.

"But is there anyone else I can talk with before I meet with the Rabbi again? I'd like to get as many views of Des Moines as possible. I know he will want some idea of a plan from me. But it is best to understand the body size you're trying to fit when picking out clothes. The same is true of any chore. Plans need to meet the need. You and the Rabbi have told me so much about the city. Enough to generate great hope and enthusiasm but not enough to create a plan."

"Well, whom would you like to speak with?"

"People who know what the community is hungry for. What more would they like than what they have? At least a couple of Jewish community leaders. Then some regular members of different congregations."

"Anyone else?"

"Actually...yes, a couple of the leaders of the gentile community, including some clergy and the chairmen of the republican and democratic committees here and, if possible, the editor of the Register."

"Wow, not the Governor?" Pinky said sarcastically.

"I know, I know. I'm sorry the request is so huge, but anyone planning a project like this should do homework. If I were already established here, I'd take my time and do this over weeks or months. I'd have my own contacts. But frankly, I don't have the time to start and scratch my way up. So, I hope you and the Rabbi might be able to help or at least give me some leads and contacts. I don't expect that I'll be able to talk with all these people right away. But that is my laundry list. Even getting to talk with a few would help."

"Well, I understand your interest. Obviously, the entirety of that list is a little much for me. But let me chat with the Rabbi and see what he thinks, and we'll get back to you. What room number are you in at the hotel? One of us can give you a call later."

"Well, I'd rather not sit around waiting. I think I'll return and get Rachel, and we can walk around today. How about a call around 7 or 8 tonight when we return to the room?"

"Sounds good. In the meantime, why don't you drop by with Rachel? I'd love to meet her."

Saul agreed and waved goodbye. The money for the papers remained on the counter.

Walk around, the couple did as they enjoyed all the storefronts up Walnut St. and down Grand Ave. Saul suggested that Rachel would enjoy exploring all six floors of the Younkers Department store. They'd meet after he had tried to meet with some bankers. Rachel readily agreed and enjoyed each floor as the elevator operator, in white gloves, stopped each time "Mezzanine books and periodicals, second-floor children's wear" was heard across all six floors. It was not quite as large as Hudson's in Detroit, but it was still very nice. Later, she took Saul back to the Younkers Tea Room for lunch and briefly explored Wolf's Department store across the street while Saul went to another appointment.

As they continued walking to Pinky's store, Saul asked, "So? What is your first impression of the town?"

"Well, this is far from the hick town I mistakenly expected. I haven't seen a live cow or cornstalk anywhere, but the people seem nice, friendly, and not pushy, actually sort of slow."

"Slow? What do you mean by that?"

"Not mentally, dummy! I mean that they stroll. I'm short and take small steps and have to try really hard to keep up with the people on the street. However, I felt like no one was rushing by me here, and after a day on my feet in high heels, my toes are not crying for escape."

"You did have those shoes off under the table at lunch."

"Well, every part of the body should relax and rest at lunch. What did you learn from meeting bankers or other people and sticking your head into various businesses?"

"Nothing."

"Nothing?"

"No, I didn't mean that negatively. Everything seemed relatively standard. Folks were open and liked the idea of new people coming to town. Business practices seemed routine. All that is good. I didn't see anyone reacting negatively when I mentioned the Jewish newspaper at the bank or insurance company. There was no negativity in their voices, much less their words."

Rachel, with fingers crossed, asked, "Did they react positively?"

"No, one guy was curious at best. But I didn't go into detail and didn't expect any encouraging reactions.

As they walked through the front door of Hyman's News shop, one customer was talking with Pinky. He excused himself from his customer, Celia, and quickly ran over to meet Rachel. "Rachel, how wonderful to meet you," he said enthusiastically as he gave a bear hug to this petite woman.

"My goodness, this is a friendly city," exclaimed Rachel.

"I'll be right with you guys. Just let me finish finding out what Celia needs."

Rachel gave Saul a strange glance, but Saul shrugged his shoulders and smiled.

Pinky returned. "I know you want to hear about my talk with the Rabbi. But first thing first. My wife and I want you to join us for dinner tonight. So, before you say anything, we won't take no for an answer."

"Oh, we don't want to impose and put you out!"

"Rachel, since when is enjoying a nice dinner with new friends an inconvenience? Besides, you want to know more about Des Moines, and we would like to learn more about you, Detroit, and your current plans."

Saul knew that this was a heartfelt invitation and a valuable source of information for the Rabbi's evaluation of the couple. He quickly accepted the invitation, saying that they would find it an absolute pleasure to get to know Pinky and his wife better.

"Lois and I will pick you guys up at the hotel at 6:30 pm, and then maybe we can drive around for a while, show you the town, and eat around 7:30 if that isn't too late?"

"Thank you, thank you," said Saul. "We'd love to meet Lois, and a tour would be great. We look forward to it. But Pinky, please don't make me wait until then to hear how it went with the Rabbi!"

"Of course not. Lenny, who works here part-time, covered for me so I could lunch with the Rabbi. He was glad that the two of you were looking around by yourselves and thought your plan of meeting people was excellent. He didn't rule out his role in arranging that. But he wanted to meet with you first and talk more about things. If he feels that he is interested in participating, he'll pull in a favor from others and request that they meet with you."

"No problem, Pinky. I feel the same as the Rabbi. It's sort of like a job interview. He certainly needs to dig into who I am, and I need to dig into what Des Moines is. I wouldn't dare want to meet a list of folks without knowing anything about them. So, yeah, the Rabbi and I have lots to talk about. Did he give any indication of when we could meet again?"

"He respects that you two are traveling and doesn't want to ask you to drag this out. I suggest you just go about your own exploration. Likely, you'll hear from him, one way or another. He is not the type to just neglect you."

"I'll do that, thanks."

With that, Saul and Rachel bid Pinky a hearty goodbye. They hugged and decided to meet later that night.

The couple took a cab for the short ride back to the hotel. Despite her earlier enthusiasm, Rachel's feet were now crying for relief. Before heading to the room to prepare for dinner, they sat in the lounge, sipping their stash of Canadian manufactured scotch and talking.

"I don't know, Saul, this is all going so fast. So many uncertainties. How are we going to make a living? We have money put away, but I don't want to burn through that. Where will we live? What will my dad say? He'll think we are crazy! Des Moines? Who would ever consider living in Des Moines, Iowa, when you have family and opportunities in Detroit? Detroit has been good enough for them and good to them. Why not us?"

"Okay, you've got quite a list there. The way I see it, there are three things we need to figure out. First, do we want to find a place other than Detroit to start our family and life together? Sure, I have opportunities in Detroit, but not the kind I like. And don't forget we left problems behind too! And those problems are not insignificant. Also, if we stay in Detroit, all the family help and support come with a cost. They'll always be the judges of everything we do and decide. I've already felt that, fought against it, and I don't want it hanging over my head all the time.

Second, if we want a new place, the question is, can Des Moines be that place? We're in the process of finding that out right now. To choose Des Moines, we must want Des Moines, not the newspaper opportunity. That's like frosting on the cake. But frankly, from what I'm seeing so far here, I can't imagine that Omaha or Kansas City would be much different or better. I'll find a job anywhere. But I would prefer a job that excites me.

The third is the whole issue of the newspaper. Again, that's a vast unknown. It's going to take a lot of energy to figure it out. But I don't want to waste our time and energy if we aren't interested in staying in Des Moines."

Rachel was silent; she absorbed what Saul was saying and tried to present a cooperative stance. "You're right. In Detroit, I just kept things simple. Work in the hotel, go out with friends, have a good time, live with my folks, and keep blinders on about problems and arguments. I guess I just thought that's what life was to be. But if we are starting over, I ought to at least be more open to exploring. Hopefully, I may even get excited by doing something different on my own. I mean with you, of course, but without my parents trying to direct every decision."

"I know it's hard, but..."

"You know, even waiting in the train station, someone would ask me where I was going or what we were doing, and I would describe it as a vacation, trip, or a delayed honeymoon. I guess that's how I thought about it deep down, not as an exploration or as 'starting over.'"

"I know it feels risky. I completely feel your anxiety."

Rachel laughed. "Sort of pitiful, isn't it? Our folks took the horrible risk to escape a miserable, dangerous situation in Russia. And here I am, being a crybaby, thinking of moving just a few hundred miles away from Detroit. How did they know how to start over in a foreign place, across an ocean, not speaking the language, and I'm whining about this? Pitiful."

Later, at dinner, Rachel felt comfortable as they were welcomed into Lois and Pinky's world. Their host couple wasn't patronizing but, to the contrary, comforting. They treated Saul and Rachel truly as equal adults. Especially more adult than Rachel felt, especially when she was back home. It was indeed a step in growing up. The conversations led far and wide. Ultimately, each couple grew to find the comfort they'd hoped for. The food was great, and the talk was informal and gossipy, with lots of laughter.

Once settled back at the hotel. Rachel asked, "When do you meet again with the Rabbi?"

"I'm not sure. We didn't set any definite time. The Rabbi wants time to talk about the paper idea with other folks. Check up on me. For him, it is not about us coming into the community- that is solely up to us. It is about the newspaper idea and whether to include me. But Pinky told me at dinner that I'll be meeting him again tomorrow morning."

"So, what do we do in the meanwhile?" Rachel asked, sounding tense.

"We wait and continue to do our own investigating. In our conversation with Pinky and Lois, they mentioned several businesses run by Jewish families. So, I'll drop by a few and see what I can learn about the community. Also, I'll call some guys I know at the Free Press in Detroit and see if they have any contacts at the Des Moines Register. There is also that guy I met at a union meeting, Jacob Norwak. I think that was his name...he reports for the Detroit American. He talked about having worked in Des Moines a few years ago. Maybe he knows someone here for me to contact."

"So, you want me to sit in the hotel room all day waiting?"

"No! Having you sit in the hotel room would leave my greatest asset unused. I think getting audiences with some businessmen will be easier if they see that we are a family who are interested in settling here. They need to know that we are not random people or bachelors who want to find a house here. Instead, we are looking to be part of the community, and it's important for them to know that".

With that, the couple proceeded with their exploration. It was more enjoyable than they originally anticipated. Luckily, getting a couple of good contacts at the local paper and foraging the town for information, Saul and Rachel spent some exhausting but exciting three fruitful days as investigative reporters.

On one of those days, they had a good lunch with Pinky, a good chance to thank him for the dinner and all the help he'd given. Pinky readily accepted the couple's invitation and emphasized that they needed to be patient. Eventually, just before going out for dinner, the long-awaited call from the Rabbi came. Saul had long thought about how he would react if and when the call came. For Saul, this call was not just to be informative but strategic. And come, it did.

"Yes, Rabbi, it's good to talk with you again. Thank you, of course. I'd like to meet again."

Chapter Twelve

Elijah continued. Saul's pause was part tactical, for effect. A longer extended hesitancy resulted from his anxiety about what he would do next. He had played out the upcoming conversation with the Rabbi in his mind repeatedly. But his life was changing. No longer could the next meeting be only a two-way conversation. To exclude Rachel from the critical interactions with the Rabbi would be inappropriate. To act as if this were just "business talk" between two businessmen would be misleading. Yet, having a three-way conversation would significantly alter the dynamics of the discussion. Furthermore, it would change the tactical approach he had rehearsed.

Think about the conditions at the time this phone call occurred. America was a male-dominated society. Men made the decisions, and women lived with them. The 19th Amendment, giving women the vote, had only recently been ratified. It had been a messy fight, hard-won. Jewish families were still male-dominated, and at least for the orthodox Jews, women were kept separate, even in devotion. However, Saul and Rachel were not orthodox or traditional.

For Saul, this was a touchy moment. To exclude Rachel would be an affront to her. Yet, assuming she should be welcomed could create animosity with the Rabbi. Saul took a deep breath and continued.

"That time is excellent, but Rabbi, my wife, Rachel, would also like to meet you. By now, she has heard so much about you. She would like to come with me. I would like that too, if it is alright with you."

The Rabbi had many dealings with women in the Jewish community. These were women who had been instrumental in creating the very community organizations they were now running. He was comfortable with that. Encouraged it. But there still seemed to be a line, usually not crossed. Saul couldn't be sure of where the line was in this situation. The Rabbi appeared to stumble in answering. Was that from surprise, hesitancy, or irritation? Regardless, the Rabbi was somewhat boxed in. But to demur would be impolite. Finally, after clearing his throat, he responded.

"Of course, Saul. How delightful! I would love to meet Rachel. Yes. I'll tell you what, let me call you back in a few minutes so I can make all the arrangements. Would that be satisfactory?"

"Yes, Rabbi, of course, but I don't want you to go into any trouble."

"No trouble, Saul. Please give me a minute. I'll call you back," with that, the Rabbi hung up.

Eavesdropping on her husband's side of the call, Rachel was concerned. She felt that he had significantly broken protocol. "Saul, what did you just do?"

"Rachel, up till now in life, when you met our Rabbi, you were Phillip and Hannah's daughter, a child, no matter your age. Now, we are adults, and the Rabbi will see us as adults. You have experiences in many ways beyond your years. You've seen political wars, union battles, government corruption, and family shouting matches. Your parents tried to hide much from you, but you were out in the community and saw much more than they knew and did much more than they knew about you. I overheard many of the conversations you and your girlfriends had. They were not just about tea parties and dollies. You'll be just fine. Just don't be timid."

They had little time to wait. The call from the Rabbi came shortly.

"Marian and I would love to have you over for dinner tomorrow. Shall we say six o'clock? We can pick you up at the hotel?"

"We'd be honored, Rabbi, but we don't want to put you and Marian, especially Marian, out. I say that by being presumptuous in suggesting you're not the chef."

"Actually, my matzo brei is to hold your breath for. I have many culinary talents you don't know about. First and foremost, I pour a delicate glass of after-dinner schnapps. 6 pm, okay?"

"Six it is. We'll be out in front. Thank you."

Each day, Saul had gone to Pinky's bookstore for his daily papers. The day of the meeting was no different. He talked with Pinky and others, learning more about Rabbi. Rachel, worn out being an investigative reporter, worried about what to wear. Pinky's advice was simple.

"Just be yourself, warts and all. Let the Rabbi see you. There have been enough conversations, not about you, but about the idea of the newspaper. There seems to be a reasonable breadth of community interest and support for the idea. I think it is going to happen. So it appears that the agenda for you and Rachel to decide is whether Des Moines is for you and if you can successfully politic to get the newspaper gig. But remember, the Rabbi doesn't make the final decision. If you get his approval, you'll be passed over to the people who can make it happen. That will then be round two of the job interview.

But the next meeting with the Rabbi, I agree, could be a make-it-or-break-it moment, but not necessarily the most difficult one. In the long run, he'll look at it from the point of view of the attitude and philosophy you'd have for the paper in this community and likely even for the state. The backers will be more focused on whether you can do the job. At all levels, trust will be the issue.

But don't be naive. The business leaders in this town are no second-string players. On the contrary, they're bright and not likely to go along with anything they see as counterproductive for the community or a barrier to their well-being. They know that starting such a paper demands skills. They'll want to be assured that you have what it takes."

The dinner and overall meeting went very well. There was much camaraderie and laughter. The Rabbi was not stuffy or formal. Marian was warm and encouraging. Saul and Rachel felt very comfortable and welcomed. But the conversation had followed a wide berth around the specifics of a deeper dive into who Saul and Rachel were. As the dessert plates were removed, Saul noticed that the Rabbi did not attempt to move only the men and their talk into the den to be enjoyed with cigars and brandy. Instead, Marian suggested that they all move into the den to enjoy the coffee she brought out. Agenda items were hanging loose in the air, like so many piñatas waiting for an attack. Yet, so far, no one seemed to want to swing. There was silence. Saul and Rachel took small sips of the newly brewed hot coffee. Marian glanced at the Rabbi with a knowing smile. He eventually broke the silence.

"We've been unkind, even selfish in some ways. We've asked you many questions about yourselves and life in Detroit. But we may not have given you two enough chances to ask us things you may want to know."

Saul paused a bit too long as he searched for the correct question to ask. Rachel's mind, randomly skimming over seemingly unrelated options, strangely saw an image of the low-stakes poker game her father and his friends sometimes played. She remembered the phrase 'going all in.' She remembered that as a grand gesture. She decided that if she were to annoy the Rabbi a little bit, she would do little additional harm by annoying him a lot. To everyone's surprise, even hers, Rachel made a grand gesture. She stole the floor from her husband and spoke first.

"Well, you know, Rabbi, I only heard his side of the conversation when Saul received your call. But there seemed to be a longer pause than expected when he asked if I might join you. Were you uncomfortable with that?"

Saul, surprised, swallowed noticeably hard. The Rabbi smiled and nodded his head. "Very perceptive, Rachel. I'd like to say no, of course not. But in reality, the discomfort came from a feeling of surprise, not dislike of the idea. I just never expected to hear that you might want to come, to what I perceived, a business meeting. I guess that is pretty insensitive. I apologize. I did not intend to insult you."

"No insult perceived, Rabbi. After receiving such an incredible meal and conversation, I feel honored. Marian, you've got to give me the recipe for that casserole. It was scrumptious. But I'm going to ask you to pardon my frankness. I think you've made an understandable mistake, Rabbi."

"Mistake? How do you mean, Rachel?"

"First, I may have had more experience with business than you know. But more to the point is what was to occur between you and Saul was for us, not a business meeting. It was a life decision-making meeting. I think where we as a couple go from here is making a life commitment. Not necessarily permanent, but undoubtedly very significant. The 19th Amendment and all, I do get the vote, Rabbi. Saul and I have to make this commitment together. We need it to be that way, and you, pardon me for saying, should want it that way."

Marian choked as she laughed while trying to swallow some coffee. Then, finally, she actually had to get up and leave the table. In 15 years of marriage, she had heard only a few men speak to her husband, so frankly, indeed, never a woman.

The flabbergasted but not annoyed Rabbi, only pleasantly surprised, responded, "Saul, how disappointing and deceptive of you. You made yourself the chief applicant for the editor position when the best candidate sits right beside you. Shame on you."

"Guilty as charged, Rabbi. I humbly apologize."

"Go on, Rachel. Explain more about what you mean."

"Well, Rabbi, from talking with Pinky, it seems that the newspaper idea per se is well received. Whether it will ever happen or not is another issue. That is beyond our control, although perhaps not beyond our influence. No meeting today will lead to a definitive answer about starting the paper. Too many other folks have to be involved, as they should be.

And for the life of me, I couldn't believe that any meeting today between you and Saul was going to be to purposely dissuade us from coming to Des Moines. In my heart, I don't think you would ever do such a thing. There is nothing so horrible about Des Moines that we wouldn't have likely perceived it by now ourselves. Your job, if any, was to sell Des Moines, not discourage us. Also, I don't think anything is so terrible about us that you wouldn't want us here. You are a warm-hearted, kind man, not a mean dictator or overseer. Our family history has seen plenty of those.

So, Rabbi. If the meeting was not about our residency in Des Moines or the newspaper idea, what could it possibly be about? It can only be about Saul's capacity to create and edit the type of newspaper you'd value. That involves me. The role he would play would be very demanding. I understand our partnership and my place in it. But supporting him and his needs, setting up a home, and hopefully having children are all demanding. Saul and I have to work together in so many different ways. I must understand the time and energy demands, both physical and emotional, he will face. I must assess for myself, knowing whether he will be satisfied sufficiently to justify the effort. I also must understand what the community wants from us, not just him."

Having returned from the kitchen, wiping coffee from her blouse, Marian listened with concern and glee to what Rachel said. Then, finally, she reassured Rachel, saying,

"I applaud your insight, Rachel. Be assured that, of course, you are involved at this point. I'm afraid my husband attends too many meetings where he interacts only with men. I'm sorry to say maybe he was operating a bit on autopilot. I can assure you that the Jewish community is well united here. Women are a big part of it. They have an essential and vital role as they have created many of the institutions that function to serve and connect. Our community will understand your needs in establishing a home and family and support you joyously. "

"Thank you, Marian. That is reassuring to hear."

"Well, having been appropriately chastised," Rabbi added, "I'd like to know, Saul, what vision do you have for such a newspaper?"

Rachel jumped in, "Careful, Rabbi, you'll soon be discussing nationwide distribution, if not worldwide, if you turn my husband loose."

Saul was ready. "Rabbi, much has been done by you and others in Des Moines to provide services and opportunities to the Jewish population. My vision is to add to this by helping to create an even more cohesive community by disseminating important information from one part of the community to others. Shared data can help people feel part of a greater whole. Having a mechanism where people are informed of ideas or plans under consideration early elicits responses and feelings of inclusion. It is valuable when issues come up and decisions are to be made that people understand the impact on the entire community, not just on themselves. That supports the greater good.

Even statewide, there can be differences. One's local community might be impacted differently from those of other Jewish communities throughout the state. However, there will be a larger Iowa Jewish community. This can improve the developing local businesses and give our children chances to meet peers from other parts of the state through youth groups, travels, and conventions.

But content is going to be more than just information. There will be an editorial component devoted to advocacy. This, of course, will not interfere with the traditions of our own history. I am neither a martyr nor a proselytizer. I intend, through an editorial column, to bring ideas, thoughts, and problems to ponder relevant to the broader community. I want to awaken people, promote interest in important Jewish issues, inform people, and have the paper be part of the mortar holding a more expansive community together. I want it to be more than a neighborhood rag or organizational newsletter informing of the next potluck."

"Fair enough," The Rabbi shared, "but how are we to determine that you are the person to do this? We've not seen columns you've written or know little about your journalistic training."

"Well, no formal training. No published books under my belt. My knowledge of the mechanical know-how for publishing comes from being around it for years in the newspapers. I've always been interested in the management of papers, from journalistic to the task of publishing. I've used my time to ask many questions and learn a lot. But I know there is more to learn. I wouldn't be job hunting today by applying to take over editing or publishing the New York Times at this point in my life. But I feel comfortable handling the task we've outlined and discussed. And frankly, to deal with other small publishing jobs that will be sought out to help financially."

"David," Marian asked, "can you help me bring some more goodies and coffee from the kitchen, please?

Rachel started to offer, but Marian interjected with a shake of her head and raised a finger.

"Of course, honey. Excuse us."

Rachel and Saul sat silent.

In the kitchen, Marian gently pushed her husband. "You still seem uncomfortable with something, honey," Marian turned to David. "What is it?"

"I'm not sure… it is all so sudden. I know these two like Des Moines and would be fine staying here, but the newspaper idea is a strong inducement. I don't want to be encouraging when I'm still undecided about that issue. That just seems so unfair. The paper is a good idea, but we are not rushed to start it now. About Saul's involvement? I'm not as thoroughly convinced. Who is he, really? What does he stand for? He presents well. He is thoughtful in discussion…but…"

Marian walked over to the sink and began rinsing a dish. Both were silent, lost in their own thoughts. She admired her husband's wisdom in dealing with ideas for progress in the Jewish Community. His thoughtfulness made many comfortable having reasonable discussions and pushing forward. But sometimes, being overly cautious could risk losing an opportunity.

Finally, perhaps encouraged by Rachel's frankness, Marian said, "I can see that you are missing some key ingredients to make you more comfortable. But how many more ideas or people to implement them will you search out? No one else is coming up with a timely idea or interest. Sure, he's inexperienced, but you were when you took your first pulpit, too. Many people are around to help him with the mechanics and the economics. What you want to see are his vision, his inspiration, and his attitude or point of view. You've seen his interest. You've seen his visión for the purpose of this new community paper. I'll agree that you know little about his editorial philosophy. But, tread carefully, who else has brought this idea, this opportunity, to you? Nobody. Maybe now is the time."

"You are a bright woman. I am lucky."

"Just remember, We were inexperienced too when we got married. But we had the inspiration and opinions as to what the pulpit should stand for. Saul and Rachel could rival us there. Besides, realistically, how could Saul hurt us? A false start, perhaps? That's not a disaster. If he can't do the job, we'll find someone who can. Don't agonize. Just be happy this opportunity has landed in our laps. You know the old saying, don't look a gift horse in the mouth. A Jewish Newspaper published in English could be good for Des Moines, and an Iowa Jewish News could be even better for the state."

Rachel and Saul sat silently. Saul stared at his plate, and Rachel stared at him. Finally, she broke the silence, "I'm not sure whether I should prepare to go back to the hotel to pack our bags or just sit in agony awaiting the judge's verdict." Saul laughed.

"How can you laugh, Saul? Our futures are on the line here!"

"No honey, they really aren't. There are other roads we'll find to walk down. It's true times may be difficult. But we are young and talented and have good hearts. We'll have a family and a nice life. Our future is not in the Rabbi's hands. At most, this is one opportunity. Even if the Rabbi is not yet ready to be supportive, maybe he will be in the future. Maybe his council would think it best to wait and re-evaluate after we settle. That might be the best path. These are nice people. If we stay in Des Moines, they will be our friends. You are seeing them as judges, jury, and executioners."

Rachel sighed and shrugged her shoulders. "I wish I could be as calm as you are, Saul."

"I'm not that calm. I'm excited. Who would have imagined a month ago that we would be here, at this time even, with these notable people in a seemingly lovely city, even considering this cockamamie idea of mine? We already have friends and unearned gravitas in a town we don't live in! Just enjoy it!"

The Rabbi and Marian returned to the dining room. The Rabbi, making one last attempt to push, said, "Just one more question, Saul. As best you can, tell me who you are. Who is this Saul person you are asking us to trust? Who is the man who will decide what information is important? What issues are to be pushed? Who will know when to back off?"

"Yes, it is a big job, complex enough that Rachel has doubts. Honestly, I have some of my own. Those same questions have bombarded me repeatedly as I have walked the streets. I can offer no glowing recommendations from previous employers because I haven't been similarly employed or started anything this large from scratch. On the positive side, I know the format and the mechanics of printing. I've watched those details of publishing a newspaper for years. So, what you and I should be really concerned about is content."

"I've also seen editors struggle with content for years. They determine what is essential, accurate, fair, and problematic for any one of many reasons that must be considered. So I know the questions to ask. But I've also seen politics, biases, and money influence editors' decisions. So, the question we must ask because you and I have the same concerns is, what factors influence my decision-making regarding content? Am I purely objective? Probably not.

The next question is, how do we move forward from this point? What safety net will you have that suggests I will make the decisions in the best possible manner for the community? That safety net rests in my philosophy. A philosophy that reflects my concerns and leanings. That is best expressed in a poem I wrote in years past. It may tell you a lot. Maybe not. But at this point, it is the only thing I can offer that may reassure you. May I?"

"Of course, my boy, go ahead."

Saul unfolded a worn paper and handed the Rabbi and Marian a fresh copy. He said, "It's called 'Life: A Psychological Fantasy'. Read it if you will."

"No, read it to us aloud, Saul, if you will. We'll follow by looking at the pages." Saul read.

"Ho! My life is what I make it,"

Sang a maid of high degree.

She was proud as she was pretty,

And had glimpsed Philosophy.

All her years were spring and sunshine;

She had known no want nor woe.

In her folly she imagined

That she herself had made it so.

"Woe! My life is what i take it"

Sobbed a maid of low degree

As she sank beneath the burden

Of her life-long misery.

Hopeless child of shame and sorrow,

Doomed to perish in the mire,

Not her choice had made her shipwreck,

But Conditions dark and dire.

Hark you, Maid so vain and haughty,

Through your sister's anguished tear,

Through her wreck of soul and body.

Wisdom gives expression clear.

Life is not a plastic substance

Shaped and colored by our view,

But force both good and evil,

Damning - saving her and you.

For life is but the finding

Of conditions that are binding;

'Tis a yoke that galls and lightens,

'Tis a dream that cheers and frightens.

'Tis a struggle hard and bitter

For a tantalizing glitter,

For prize that is not real;

A conception, an ideal.

Every act, thought aspiration,

Every step that we advance

Is created, shaped, directed,

By controlling circumstance.

And no key or combination

Can the human mind invent

That will free us from the prison house

Of our environment.

As of free immortal spirit

Are you spend eternity

Were you sought in consultation

To decide your incarnation,

Or the color, creed or station

Of your brief mortality?

If the roses that are blooming

'Neath the splendor of your eyes

Had been clouded o'er with sable

By the heat of tropic skies,

Could the tears of all the ocean

Wash away the mournful stain?

Or the art of leech or fuller

Bleach the Ethiopic strain?

If your conscience and your credo

And your faith in things divine

Had been fashioned on the anvil

Of some pagan Hindu shrine

Would you then have proudly gloried

In which you now exult?

Would you then have spurned your Maker

or the Buddha and his cult?

Had the fetters of oppression

And of ignorance and want,

Chained your body, soul and spirit

From a childhood sad and gaunt

To the slums and to the sweatshop

To their stench, and toil, and strife,

Would you then have cried:" Indeed, sir!

It is I who shaped my life.

But perhaps my speculation

Does not seem to you profound,

And you ask, Is then ambition

But a hollow, empty sound?

Does not every door swing open

To intelligence and skill?

Is not talent, even genius

But a product of the will?

And I answer that ambition,

Talent, will and all the rest

By external forces only

Are implanted in the breast.

Many heart has been an altar

With prophetic rage aflame,

Burning deep its fervid message

On the monument of fame.

But for lack of molding forces,

Lack of means to fan the fire,

All unspoken is the message

All unstrung remains the lyre.

There's a pillar of cloud and a pillar of light'

To mark out your pathway by day and by night

The one called Environment pushes your feet,

The other named Destiny bars your retreat.

They guide and you follow; you may not say nay

Tho' stormy and rugged, and dark be the way;

They lead to the land yielding every desire

Or else to the Desert with serpents of fire.

So, what?"

Chapter Thirteen

Elijah continued.

Saul's voice resounded with emphasis and emotion as he read the words. Marian had a tear in her eye, and Rachel let out a sigh when he finished. Rabbi approached Saul, offering a warm hug and a simple "Welcome."

As the group settled into contemplation, Elijah prompted their reflections, acknowledging the weight of the decision before them. Discussions ensued, with individuals processing the implications of Saul and Rachel's plan to move to Des Moines and pursue the paper venture.

In the cold breeze of the balmy desert air and the glow of the campfire, the group shared personal anecdotes of starting anew, mingling laughter with moments of introspection. Nancy remarked on the importance of flexibility in Saul and Rachel's approach, while Larry highlighted the serendipity of meeting Pinky and its impact on their journey.

The conversation veered towards speculation about Saul's intentions and character, with Larry offering insights from his own experiences. The group dissected Saul's actions and demeanor, debating his sincerity and motivations.

Laura expressed a desire for a deeper understanding of Saul's poem, recognizing its empathetic tone and philosophical underpinnings. Harry offered a perspective on Saul's strategic timing in presenting the poem to the Rabbi, emphasizing its role in solidifying their relationship.

Ultimately, the group acknowledged the complexity of Saul and Rachel's decision-making process, recognizing both the risks and the potential for growth. With nods of agreement, they concluded their discussion, eager to see what the future held for the couple.

The RV campers were quiet the following evening. Some had gone for long hikes during the day. Larry had nearly fallen in an uncovered goldmine shaft. Fortunately, he tripped and fell right before he reached the unseen opening, and tragedy was everted. Sometimes, even bad luck, or in this case, Larry's clumsiness, is good luck. Such mines were a well-known hazard in the Southwest desert. Larry had wandered off to a wash, hoping to find pieces of quartz, suggesting gold might be nearby. But, he said the only exciting thing he saw was a rattler, another unexpected hazard. Larry excitedly told of his bravery in the shooting of the deadly snake. People heard the gun blast over the hills, but no one saw the snake.

Everyone knew Larry had been dying to shoot his new 45 loaded with snake shots. He'd never owned a gun before and wanted to see how the snake shot dispersed in the sand. But, instead, he found it to be very anticlimactic. So finally, after three beers over the campfire, Larry confessed that there never was a snake. But he lived with the "rattler wrangler" moniker for the rest of that winter's stay.

Elijah noticed the sense of quiet. The group was different tonight. Surprisingly, there was little conversation. He wondered, too much sun, followed by a similar amount of beer or wine? He asked, "Why so quiet tonight?"

Kathy said, "Well, we're not quite sure."

"Sure, about what?

"Well, it sounded like the end of the story. Oh, it was a good story, but is it over? Or are you going to tell us more about how this went?

"Oh, I can think of more details to give you food for thought. Yes, there is more, much more. Remember, the story so far begins with folks who lived in the 1800s in faraway lands. That's nearly a century and a half ago. As we go along, we'll learn more about our characters during all those intervening years."

However, as Rachel and Saul investigated and made their decisions, the actual world facts upon which they based their choices in the present were rapidly undergoing sea changes. The world around them was far different from the worlds of their grandparents or even their parents. But then, as of now, each generation and culture must find ways to adapt to the world they live in.

Looking backwards, an excellent example of this adaptation was demonstrated in the Broadway play Fiddler on the Roof. In it, Tevia sings of Jewish tradition and rituals adhered to through thick and thin as providing a balance between their spiritual beliefs and a chaotic, threatening, and uncertain world. He doesn't speak of the traditions as being commanded in the Torah or representative of his culture's relationship to God, but as a social salve used to keep his people afloat. At the same time, they negotiated abuse, tragedy, and the fear, helplessness, and hopelessness routinely felt. Tradition returned his people to "go" after prancing around the board game of life. Rachel and Saul's grandparents were well-steeped in those traditions.

Their parents found themselves in a different world upon arriving in America. Some traditions survived the transition, while others didn't. Rachel and Saul's world changed even more when this couple became separated from their families and settled in Des Moines. Personally, for example, they no longer lit the Sabbath candles. Nor would they fear being torn from an adolescent love by an arranged marriage, and Rachel did not go to a Mikvah before her wedding. Likewise, industrialization produced a different world with different traditions.

Significant immigration from Western Europe and Russia overlapped with rapid industrialization. After our civil war, cultures began to mix, and economic disparity occurred in America and elsewhere. This fueled a growing political upheaval worldwide. The pace of change in society was moving along with the speed of trains, which had nearly doubled over just a few decades. Saul and Rachel were born into this society, rumbling down the tracks at a breakneck speed and with unstoppable momentum.

Cultural changes between the generations were sometimes slow and other times chaotic. Sometimes, the differences offered increased gaiety and frivolity. Other times, people found more security and modern conveniences. But the new world our young couple lived in had pain and suffering of a different kind. Along with pleasantries, there were worldwide failures, uncertainty, hunger, and helplessness.

The growth and wealth led many from rural America to migrate to the cities, seeking a more prosperous life. The investors kept speculating, buying stocks on narrow margins and living high. A minor stock market crash forced stock losses in 1929. Many went from wealth or economic comfort to being impoverished, unemployed, and hungry.

Saul decided to find a new beginning elsewhere for economic and likely other personal reasons. Saul's fears were borne out nationwide in 1931. We had become a nation of debtors. We remain that way today and with similar risks. However, quantitatively, the risks were greater than they were before, and they came to the tipping point in the 1930s. Bank failures ensued, and credit was no longer available. Homes, businesses, and farms were lost. Unemployment was profound. Strikes were rampant. For the first time, we became aware of our interconnectedness in the States and the worldwide economy.

Elijah paused to let all this sink in. Then, he took the beer that Michael had handed him and enjoyed two good swallows before continuing.

It only makes Saul and Rachel's story that much more impressive. At this time, being young and inexperienced, they would try to build something out of nothing. Saul, the optimist, saw an opportunity in the country's chaos. But he was not alone. Many individuals did similarly. Some failed, and others succeeded. Saul sought relationships with like-minded men in the Jewish community in Des Moines. Finally, in the middle of a capital city, Saul found an opportunity. A history of financial acumen created a backbone in smaller Jewish enclaves going back to biblical times. This acumen became the connecting force between these men who desired to succeed and help other Jews persecuted abroad and establish a homeland in Palestine. Part of the strength of this local group lies in its size and nature. They were few in number, mutually reliant, trusting, and could make decisions reasonably quickly. Although the men's business interests differed, their support for the Jewish Community of Des Moines created unity. Saul and Rachel benefitted from this unity.

Initially, Saul needed to gain the business skills of other men. But he learned quickly and had a platform where he would make many helpful contacts. However, the reality was that deteriorating economic conditions made progress slow. Moreover, setting up a new household and starting a new publishing business during the Depression was significantly more complicated and riskier.

There was a country-wide need for government support programs for those with little or no work. However, there were only local charities under the Hoover administration and no federal government help. Moreover, Hoover made things worse by trying to isolate the United States from the rest of the world's commerce through tariffs. As a result, a crashing financial bubble spread to an entire worldwide economic depression. It was a horrible time for two newly married people to quit their jobs, leave the support of their families, and take off for parts unknown. Real risky.

"It sounds like things were horrible. Did anyone make money or do well during that time? asked Jolene."

"Well, with 80% at least somewhat employed, families grouped together, and many survived. Most helped their neighbors when they could. Some folks left one part of the country and moved to another, hoping to find jobs. Weather in the Midwest, droughts, made farming horrible. Who knows how many people were out of work? Those kinds of statistics take a lot of work to come by. But yes, to answer your question, some prospered just fine."

"Who and how?" Nick asked as he handed around an open bag of Oreos.

"Well, let's see. People still wanted and needed their entertainment. Therefore, some performers did well. The singing cowboy Gene Autry created a bundle for himself. Guys like James Cagney and Glenn Miller did just fine. Finally, Charles Darrow invented the Monopoly game, and some say he became the world's first millionaire.

"Elijah! How do you remember all these old guys?" Emma asked.

"They stand out as exceptions to how most other people lived. I've always been fascinated by wealth inequality in this country. For example, we can't forget Babe Ruth. Supposedly, he made around $80,000 in depression-era dollars. J. Paul Getty had a big inheritance. He used that cash to snatch up depressed oil stocks. He built himself a real petroleum empire. I guess those guys like Joe Kennedy, President Kennedy's old man, made his fortune in stock speculation, real estate, liquor, and movies. Then there was John Dillinger, who allegedly stole around 3 million. So, he did okay, too. Do you suppose all that money made them happier?"

Harry said, "If you want to make a fortune during a depression or recession, you should be a bottom feeder, insider trader, thief, celebrity, or inventor! Things haven't changed much! But Saul and Rachel weren't bottom feeders. So how did they make out?"

They set up in a small furnished apartment. The Jewish women assisted Rachel in the Community. They showed her around, had her over for lunch, and introduced her to new people. Everyone was welcoming and friendly. Quickly, she felt at ease in her new environment and set up a comfortable home. She especially liked cooking for Saul. She was a good cook. She was efficient at home. She faced few domestic chores in her new life that she hadn't already negotiated. Her work in the hotel gave her other experiences that would soon prove helpful to Saul.

Elijah paused to sip again from the warming beer Michael had handed him. Saul relished the support and help he got from Rachel. Yet, his work created more pressure than she could help him relieve. The newspaper supporters recognized he needed time to get equipment and set up the paper, but he would have to produce something soon. He was given a small stipend or salary to do this. He also found some small printing requests to temporarily farm out to a printer in town. Sometimes, he did some copywork for the local paper at night. These extra things helped him financially, but more importantly, they helped him make more contacts in the wider local Community, among all, not just among his Jewish investors and friends.

He also enjoyed spending time at the synagogue talking to people about what things in the paper would interest them. He intended to do this after services, but if truth be told, he found congregants frequently engaged in whispering about these things during services. In the less orthodox services of Saul's experience, religious gatherings were sometimes more about the ritual of being together than the prayer itself. Few people could translate the Hebrew language of the service.

Not really feeling connected to what the Rabbi was uttering, they quietly talked with their friends.

Whispering became part of the ritual. It firms up relationships among many in attendance. Those relationships were what offered solutions. Glares at the talkers from the Rabbi were abundant but often ignored. The Rabbi would return his attention to the Torah and drone on reading Hebrew. Saul, like some and unlike others, always felt services were more about Community than God. He didn't need buildings and Rabbis for his relationship with God. But Saul needed contact with people to learn about the Community. He was adamant about promoting that Community.

Cindy, terribly worried, wondered, "Wasn't talking so much in church, sorry synagogue, likely to piss off Rabbi Mannheimer and alienate him?"

"Good question. Saul and Rachel joined the more conservative synagogue. They had a different rabbi. The whispering didn't lead to long conversations. Instead, it was about connection, gossip, and occasional business information."

Saul was surprised at the extent of people's interest in what was happening in the other Jewish communities in different parts of the state. He needed local reporters in other cities! So, mentally, Saul expanded the geography of the relevant Jewish Community from Des Moines to the state of Iowa. As the boundaries expanded, so did Saul's job. He needed to become a traveling salesman and recruiter to create a reporter pool. His travels gave him a more comprehensive view of suffering. For example, he saw numerous eviction notices along fence lines and in specific neighborhoods.

"That's enough for tonight. Tomorrow, we can begin to get a better view of how Rachel and Saul navigated their new circumstances."

Chapter Fourteen

After lunch on one of the warmest days of the winter and a big meal, Elijah felt lethargic, as if he needed a nap. He wondered how many of the group felt the same way. Elijah planned to get the group going with the stimulation of a brief walk into the desert beyond the RVs. There, he could entertain everyone by telling them about the medicinal values of some of the cacti. He slowly descended the steps of his rig and looked over to see everyone gathered. Elijah found no one else experienced his lethargy. They were all sitting up, chattering and excited to find out whether Saul and Rachel would, tail between legs, hightail it back to Detroit, find failure in Des Moines, or, luckily, muddle through.

Excited about the state-wide possibilities, the families supporting the newspaper suggested that Rachel take a car trip around the state to get to know the communities and recruit reporters. Rachel and Saul, especially, were indebted to the loving support of Lois and Ben, who were helpful in many ways. Ben was doing just fine with his new car agency. Lois was more than pleased with mothering Rachel. Ben quickly loaned Saul a used car for his trips to explore Iowa Jewry. Lois insisted that the couple needed a car anyway and told Ben to give it to them, at cost, and be willing to finance payments. Ben agreed. Thus, a community is built as people join in the vision.

Such trips were a real luxury during a time of such hardship. Little did our couple know the profound impact their expedition would have on them. At the outset, more significant than Rachel's interest in seeing a new state was the opportunity to become part of something much broader than their own personal travel pleasures. They hoped to be welcomed into the communities, and they often were. Soon, people were anticipating their arrival. Such was the grapevine in troubled times. However, not all they met saw these 'big wigs' incursions from the East as being positive. No matter where they went, Rachel and Saul were welcomed by many who looked forward to being part of a wider community the two were attempting to create. Others viewed them with great suspicion and anger as outsiders who would threaten what was left of their financial security.

When met with such ambivalence and seeing the widespread poverty, Saul and Rachel often felt like strangers in a foreign land. Life in rural Iowa significantly differed from their "good but dangerous times" in Detroit. The rural parts of the state, even some of the larger cities, had already been impacted by economic calamity caused by the agricultural depression of the 1920s. A decade before the financial depression overwhelmed places like Detroit, financial woes were painful in Iowa and rural America. Farms were being repossessed, banks were closing, and shops on Main Street were shuttered, never reopening. Yes, Rachel and Saul were welcomed by many, but some viewed them with great suspicion and anger.

Rural and small-town Midwesterners were angry that places like Detroit and the eastern cities seemed to be doing well, but elsewhere, those less prosperous were suffering. In the East, wages were rising in 1929. In rural Iowa, most farms still had no electricity in their homes. Road repair could have been better, and schools and education needed to catch up. For many people in small-town Iowa, Saul and Rachel seemed to be outsiders, not so much a part of their community.

The couples' initial introduction to Des Moines created a deceptively optimistic view of the state. Des Moines, the State Capital, was also the nation's insurance industry capital. That business had brought prosperity and a sound financial base for the city and its citizens. The economic woes of the 1920s and even the early 1930s were less profound in Des Moines. Once Saul and Rachel moved beyond Des Moines's city limits, they were in a different social and economic climate. Saul was profoundly impacted by what he saw. Like Rachel, he had great sympathy, even empathy, for their plight. Saul also saw their anger and distrust as a barrier to his goal of more closely uniting the Iowa Jewish community. But that became a motivating factor for him. He, too, had known and felt anger at barriers holding him back, even in Detroit.

The good-time atmosphere of the roaring twenties provided the fun that Saul and Rachel enjoyed in Detroit. But many small-town Iowans viewed the swing-era dances enjoyed in Detroit as evidence of moral decay by religious crusaders. Further, the center of Detroit's prosperity, the mass production of the automobile, was in rural Iowa, seen as leading youth down the devil's road as the teens used these new devices to find secluded places to share immoral intimacies.

One day, during the trip from Cedar Rapids to Davenport, Rachel observed, "As people tell you about what is going on in the community, you seem to keep pushing them further."

"Ya, I sometimes do."

"More than sometimes! Rather than asking about current events, you're more interested in writing a history book, going back into the last century with some of your questions. Why are you so interested in all their history?"

"I'm editing and publishing a paper for the entire state, not just Des Moines. So, think about communities, not a single, united community. Hundreds of thousands of people have different backgrounds and varied moral and religious values. Learning who they are and their backstories becomes important to my effectiveness.

"Our values are often strongly influenced by our personal or family histories. The people whom I question are the audience for my columns. I need to understand their varied values as best I can. I'm interested in how these folks became who they are today."

Rachel found the research Saul implied felt overwhelming. She felt increasingly troubled by the extra burden Saul would shoulder with diving so deeply into the readers' backgrounds. She already expected that they'd be many more miles down the road at this point in their journey. Saul's discussions were neither brief nor superficial but always friendly. Even when disagreeing, most saw Saul as the warm person he was. Seeking solace, she found comfort in the organized rows of swaying cornstalks, completely contrasting to the chaos they'd witnessed in many towns.

Briefly calmed, her gaze returned to Saul. "The Jewish experience here seems well-documented since the Europeans arrived," she ventured, "wouldn't that simplify our story?"

"It would if you were correct. But your assumptions about the migration are wrong. Jewish communities are a myriad of cultures woven from persecution. Yes, many fled Europe in the 1600s – massacres in Germany, ghettos in Italy – seeking refuge like the enslaved Africans, who faced even harsher realities."

Now driving through tall cornfields on both sides of the road, Saul slowed at intersections to ensure no one else was coming across from behind the tall cornstalks. There were no stop signs at these unguarded blind intersections. Saul turned onto a bumpy road and seemed to gaze into the dust, adding, "And more importantly, who are we today? What is the underlying heartbeat? Do they feel included, excluded, welcomed, abused, involved, or alienated? Do they get along as a larger community, or is there infighting? I want to know the audience I'm serving, representing, informing, or sometimes pissing off. An entertainer would call that reading the room. I'm doing the same, reading my audience. That is as important as knowing how to lay down ink on paper or collate the pages.

Background culture and heritage are often the bedrock of peoples' attitudes and interests. The migration origin histories of the Jews of Iowa are so varied. The Spanish Jewish aristocracy might have even aided Columbus' voyage, both intellectually and financially. Columbus's first voyage might have had Jewish crewmates, including Rodrigo de

Triana, the first to spot land, and Luis de Torres. Luis anticipated that he might have a heroic role as an interpreter accompanying Columbus to communicate with the Chinese people who would welcome them when they arrived in China. The native Americans sounded nothing like what Columbus expected. Despite finding a niche by introducing tobacco (though potentially harmful), Luis de Torres' heroism was short-lived. He returned to Cuba, becoming the first European Jew in the Americas. But the Jews emigrated away from unwelcoming countries and cultures in Europe, Central and South America."

"Saul," Rachel interjected, "this is definitely more engaging than listening to the radio, but perhaps we could take a break for coffee? It would help me process all this. I understand the historical significance, but I'm having trouble relating to the enormous diversity we may find in our audience." Saul pulled into the next diner they passed.

After ordering and relaxing, sipping her coke, Rachel had a faraway look on her face. Finally, she turned to Saul, "You know honey, it's hard enough to connect with what our own parents went through, let alone ancestors from the 1600s. But all these stories we're hearing are overwhelming. What does all this mean for you and me as we drive around? Can't we just enjoy the scenery and the sunsets?"

"We can and have, but the stories are important because they are different and could influence people differently and create different attitudes. For example, Eastern European Jews may view authority figures more malignantly than some Western European immigrants. Similarly, those from Spain may carry baggage different from those from South

America. The ancestral baggage we all carry is both cultural and religious. Some Jews are strictly orthodox and rigidly interpret the Torah; others may be less rule-bound."

With a smile on her face but somewhat aggressively, Rachel, putting both arms on the table, leaned across, staring into Saul's eyes, and challenged, "But darling, as you so well put it in your poem, 'So What?' Are you just gathering more stories for a novel you'll never write?"

"Ouch, now you're picking on me."

"Novels not put to paper are just one of your foibles," Rachel jested.

"Foibles plural? You think I have more than one?"

"Hey, when you're ahead, why not keep going? But seriously, on the one hand, Saul, I understand. On another, I'm overwhelmed. Only a few weeks ago, I felt I was escaping gun fights and going on a vacation. Then, I found myself looking for a new place to live. Now, I'm accompanying you on a mission to understand world history.

Elijah added, "Saul's initial trips with Rachel began his exploration. Years later, his written history, which was about a century of Iowa Jewry, was published. True, that volume was not a novel but more a history of events and individuals. But, by learning of those events, Saul learned the struggles that produced the heart of the larger community. To know Saul, we need to know his motivation, not just his activities.

After finishing two great pieces of apple pie, Saul and Rachel left the diner and continued exploring. They would, over time, travel far and wide in the state.

Saul traveled and talked with people from the Missouri River on the West to the Mississippi on the East and many large and small towns. He heard stories of assimilation, rejection, and cooperation. But he found robust communities looking forward to what a state-wide newspaper would offer. Reporters, usually younger, quickly jumped aboard. The Des Moines community volunteers were especially helpful in sharing the names of friends living in other cities, thus developing state-wide contacts for Saul. He was very appreciative of the support. He considered his work a community project, not his own.

Feeling more overwhelmed than when they started their trip, Rachel told Saul it was time to talk the day after Rachel and Saul returned home while sitting at dinner. "We've both had significant thoughts and concerns about our future, but the time for decision-making is rapidly approaching. So, I'd like to understand your desires and intentions now. How do you see the immediate future?"

Saul sipped his coffee and stared at the not-too-distant wall as if contemplating. And he was!

"Fair questions, honey. You know, traveling the lonely, desolate back roads, considered highways here, I've thought about the newspaper project and the comfortable life Des Moines offers. But, until now, I've only invested significant time in the newspaper project. You and I have discussed at length that we want children sooner rather than later. That would be a burden on you. One that I am sure you would love. But in addition to the incredible enjoyment I would feel having children, it would and should also demand my time and attention. So that makes me wonder, should I go full bore here and now with this opportunity? An opportunity that could fulfill years of dreams and hope. Or should I back off? Should I wait a year or two to start the paper? We are still waiting for the equipment. I could slow-walk the process. The chance for success may still be there a year or two from now.

I can handle work and family if I keep up my current pace. But there will be times when I am not as present as you may like or hope for. I don't want to put you in a position where you feel that I am abandoning or neglecting you after a child is born, nor do I want to delay starting a family. On the contrary, I covet starting a family, but I am uncertain how you evaluate the situation.

Elijah felt that it was time to end the evening's story. He enjoyed leaving things dangling a bit. He stood up and said, "In those days, it was rare for a man to choose between children and work. A woman would, but rarely a man. Ultimately, Saul felt that they needed to discuss this more."

Chapter Fifteen

As the group was winding down that night, Elijah listened to a loud conversation about following one's passion, which contrasted to committing to a less exciting but secure life. At what point in life does one cash in on all the work? Is existence just a battle between pursuit and contentment? And if you are pursuing, is there a well-defined finish line that will satisfy you? Or do you keep going and going, staying on the treadmill of pursuit? Tough questions.

However, these were significant underlying conflicts in our couples' decision-making. The group members' personal stories each day were still accompanied by much laughter, but a heavy seriousness crept in. When folks become immersed in stories as if they were their own, they often become like the story's characters and introspect about their own decisions and choices. The groups' discussion began to focus on passion versus the routine or mundane, the left or right fork. Who were their own angels, the people helpfully influencing their lives?

That was the fun for Elijah. He was a storyteller for a reason. From his own years as a young child, his grandpappy would have him and his sister come to sit quietly as they had lesson times. He remembered asking, "Pappy, why do you call this 'lesson time?' It seems more like story time."

Grandpappy would explain, "Well, we can get lessons from stories, so I guess you could call it both. Many of my stories are about our family who came before us. They blazed trails for us. Or, in some cases, made things harder for us. But no matter which, there are lessons to be learned.

Some of the stories are funny, some sad, and every once in a while, messages come from ghosts that scare you. But, just maybe, someday, you'll remember some of the stories and their lessons. But in the meanwhile, we'll have a good time." Then Pappy would pass out additional marshmallows for the smores.

Elijah then mentioned that he had to be away for three or four days. His brother was having surgery in Palm Springs, and Elijah wanted to be there to support him, but he would soon be back to let them know how Rachel and Saul fared.

Some had chores to catch up with, shopping, replenishing supplies, or doing laundry. Some mentioned that they wanted to go out and enjoy the desert. Others just wanted to rest, think about the story, and reflect on their past and future choices. Finally, a few just wanted to get away from everyone else.

Some members asked Elijah if there was any place nearby where they could rent jeeps and go out into the desert. He'd heard of a place called "Safari in the Desert," where you could rent jeeps and spend a night or two with a guide. Laundry be damned, "Let's do it!" expressed a few. So, three explorers, two guys, and one woman left camp before dawn to reach "Safari in the Desert" by sunrise.

It was about a two-hour drive, mostly down dusty dirt roads without evidence of humanity or life. The roadside view provided an occasional cow skull that said, "I wandered around here once, too. See if you can fare better than I did."

Finally, they arrived at "Safari in the Desert." It was different from what the three had pictured. Having been used to cruises and guided group trips around the world with fine amenities, the desert gang of three was surprised to find an old log cabin, a corral with a few horses, and a couple of well-used, dented, and even rusty old jeeps, certainly as far from four-star amenities as you can get.

For a long time, there was no one around.

"Hail the camp," Harry shouted. He'd learned that from reading Louis L'Amour books. Only approach the door by announcing your presence and getting permission to advance.

They walked around back and saw a couple of old chairs, some saddles, and an old dog that raised his head in acknowledgment, but no one else was there to greet them. They knocked on a back door. No one answered. Finally, someone decided to try the door. It was unlocked, but no one was inside.

They walked back to the front, and a growling dog and a man with a rifle stood by their truck.

"Can I help you, folks?"

"Is this place Safari-in-the Desert?"

"Guess so."

"Are you the manager?"

"Nope."

"Well, is the person who runs the place around?"

“Guess so.”

“Can we talk to em?”

“Guess so.”

“Where would we find em?”

“Right here.”

“Would that be you?”

“Guess so.”

“I thought you said you weren't the manager.”

“Yep.”

“But you run the place?”

“Yep.”

“Why aren't you the manager then?”

“Just me, some horses, and two dogs; no one to manage. No manager.”

“Could you tell us about a Safari?”

“Yep. Jeep or horse?”

“What's the difference?”

“Excitement, noise and shake rattlin' and rollin' or solitude and a sore bum.”

“What's exciting about the Jeep trip?”

“You ever done much four-wheel driving?”

“No.”

"Ever get high-centered in a wash, maybe even with a cloudy sky?"

"No."

"Well, if you had, you'd know what excitement is."

"And the horse Safari?"

"Ever done any long horse trips?"

"No."

"Maybe best you be taken a nice walk in the desert."

"That's not really what we had in mind."

"Not sure I'm understanding what's on your mind. You plannin' on spending the night out there?"

"We thought we would."

"Ever done that before?"

"Every night. We're camped over at 'Happy Gulch.'"

"That's one of the RV parks, isn't it?"

"Ya, pretty nice, but plain. No pool or anything, just hookups."

"Got air conditioning?"

"Sure."

"Well, you could call that spending the night in the desert. I got no air conditioning on my horse or jeep."

There was a long, silent pause. Anticipation without resolution. The old man was patient. Then, just like in the movies, he spits on the ground. But that's what happens when you chew tobacco. Real life in real-time. He had no place to go and nothing to do. The threesome remained uncertain as to how to proceed.

"Well, what do you guys want to do?"

"Let us talk about it and let you know."

"I'll be inside. Just come in when you figure it out."

The three tried to decide by discussing each option's pros and cons. Finally, after a fair amount of time, they decided nothing.

Nancy piped up. "Look, guys, only three of us were excited about doing this. True, we needed to figure out what the 'this' was. We only had a name to which each of us attached our fantasies. Safari speaks to hunting or, in modern times, observing big game animals. There isn't any big game in this desert. We were lured by the name Safari. Sounds exciting, romantic, and even luxurious. We aren't hunters. We just want to go out and live not just in the desert but in ways we hadn't experienced before. Sort of explore, like on our walks, but further and different from what we share while RV camping. Isn't this where we left off with Saul and Rachel?"

Harry, confused, asked, "What do you mean?"

"Are we going to follow our passion? Are we risking doing something new and different, or will we take the safer way, go back, do some laundry, walk around, sit under the stars, and listen to the coyotes? That has been our desert experience, at least before we turn on our air conditioners."

Tim added, "We all were passionate about doing something different in the desert. Maybe not what you called an overwhelming passion. Our ideas weren't necessarily all the same, but they were still related, sort of like first cousins. So, on the one hand, we go home. Or, on the other, follow our passion and go with some old guy we don't know and who looks feeble enough to die en route and leave us stranded in the desert. Once that happens, we will wind up starving, dying of thirst or heat stroke under a blazing sun, and becoming buzzard meat. Did you guys see those animal skulls? They weren't just put there for decorations or marketing purposes."

"Well put," remarked Nancy. "Let's do it. Let's risk following our passion. Vote goes to the majority, agree?" Ultimately, they voted all in favor but with noted trepidation. But if they died, no one could take note of their worry.

"But we still don't know which approach to take, jeep or horses?" added Harry.

"Let me handle it. You men make it too complicated and bigoted."

Harry complained, "Complicated? Bigoted? What in goodness' name are you talking about?"

Nancy, trying to be patient, explained, "Well, first off, we couldn't see anyone, then when this guy appears, you ask for the manager. So why didn't you assume he was the manager?"

Harry, nearly whining, clarified, "Well, he didn't look like a manager."

The tug o'war continued between Harry and Nancy.

"And pray to tell what the run-down log cabin desert Safari business manager looks like?"

"Dunno. But not like a weary old man with skin so weathered by the sun that it looks as tough as the saddles for those horses."

"You met many Safari Desert managers, have you?" replied Nancy.

"No."

"But you assumed an image. This guy or any similar guy or heaven to Betsy female who looked like that couldn't be the manager. Bigoted!"

"But he was not in the least bit forthcoming. Answered everything with 'Guess so.'"

"That's what I mean by making it complicated. You sounded like an investigator. Is it this, is it that? What's wrong with saying, 'Howdy sir, hope we're not disturbing you. My name is Harry, and the three of us are looking for a desert experience, a trip out there into unfamiliar territory. Feel what it is like and learn more about how it operates. We heard this is a neat place to be helped. Can you help us? In other words, rather than questioning someone who probably doesn't like people being nosey about him, tell him who you are and what you'd like. Simple."

"Where did you get so wise, Ms. Nancy smarty pants?"

"I don't know about wise, but listening to Elijah's story, I remember how valuable it can be to keep learning from anyone you meet. Remember how Saul described that when he was young, he questioned everyone about what they did, what they liked, and even how much money they made? I was a little like that, and my friends would hear me and call me nosey. They were right. Indeed, I was pushy. But there is a time to be pushy and intrusive and a time not to be a pain in the ass. You kept pushing him about irrelevant things. Just be straightforward about what you want."

Nancy worked hard to help make her point. Harry seemed to listen as she continued. "I can't talk to Saul; he's just a character in the story, but I can still learn from him. Saul wanted the Rabbi and Pinky to take him on a Des Moines Safari. He enquired much about the community but not about the characters he learned from. Saul's tactic was to get what he wanted and needed without offending. He didn't let preconceived notions push him impulsively. As whirlwind as the Des Moines adventure is, he is being patient enough to take it a step at a time. He will probably do the same as he travels around the state. I'm just trying to learn from what Elijah is telling us. Now go get us a desert experience."

"OK, I'll try again. But let me go alone this time."

Harry knocked on the door.

Pete shouted, "It's open!"

Harry entered. The cabin was straightforward but neat. Bed, table, chairs, and even an old wingback chair with an ottoman. The old man was reading. Harry walked just halfway to where the man was seated.

"Hi again. Sorry if I was a little pushy out there. By the way, my name is Harry." He stuck out his hand as if to shake.

Instead, the man looked up at him, remained seated, and said nothing but stared. The silence was unsettling for Harry.

On the other hand, it was commonplace for the old man. Finally, uncomfortably, Harry spoke up. "What I should have said right off is we're part of a larger group camping a couple of hours from here. Many of us were speculating about living in the desert. Mostly what it must have been like for the characters we read about in a Louis L'Amour novel. The dangers they faced, the solutions they found, the loneliness felt, and the beauty they saw. What would it be like to have all those experiences? They would have to cope with traveling and sleeping in the desert."

But right in the middle of our speculating, Nancy, the woman with us, asserted, 'This conversation and our daydreaming about what those people experienced makes as much sense as talking about what chocolate cake tastes like. No point in describing it to someone. Just let them taste it.' So, the three of us, Tim, Nancy, and I, had a hankerin' to taste the desert. But didn't know how. Too dangerous to really spend much time out there alone. Then, one of the camp leaders mentioned we might get some help at this place. So here we are."

"Don't need to hear your life's story. What do you want?"

"That's the thing of it. We don't really know. Just an experience we couldn't get on our own, guidance, information, views. Sort of an introductory course on living in the desert. You can decide how the material should best be taught. We prepared by packing in a couple of day's worth of food, water, and bedrolls, but that was it. Horses or jeeps, whatever you'd think to be best for newbies. We have no sure way of knowing ourselves."

The old man got up, walked out the front door, spotted the other two by their truck, and walked up to Nancy. "Howdy, ma'am," taking his hat off and sticking out his hand, "I'm Pete. Hear you want to taste the cake."

Nancy grinned and stuck out her hand. "I'm Nancy, and always out to learn a new recipe. Pleased to make your acquaintance. That over there standing next to Harry, whom you've met, is Tim."

"Well, OK then, let's get you a dessert cake experience."

Tim told Harry, walking toward their truck, "What this country needs is more women negotiators. That old guy made a joke with Nancy, lame as it was."

"He was a pushover. Right off the bat, I could sense that. So, I Had him in my hip pocket."

"Yeah, right, Mr. Kissinger."

"Now, we must first decide how to do this, transportation-wise."

"Up to you, Pete. Just tell us."

"I thought you said you wanted to learn. If I just make the decision, what are you going to learn? The first thing to understand is how to go about goin out into the desert. This here truck of yours sure is pretty. Is it new?"

"Yes, pretty new."

"Dually, huh? Four-wheel drive?"

"Nope."

"Were you thinking we could go out in this?"

"OK by me, Pete. If you think this would be OK."

"OK, if you want to get marooned out there and maybe die."

"Well, by using the truck, we could go way out and see more that way in a couple of days we have."

"True, but this here place we are standing doesn't look like much, but I got shelter, food, and water. Even the luxury of an outhouse. So what would you have after two days if you got stuck 75 miles from here in the desert? If you don't mind being roasted like a pig in a hot truck, you might have shelter, but it's not very good protection. Or you could get some shade by moving from sitting on one side of the truck to the other, trying to stay away from the sun. Or you could lay under the truck. If you don't mind what's crawling around under there, there is a lot of shade. Whichever option you choose, it is like a slow cooker."

"Not sure what you mean."

"Well, you won't die right away. Instead, maybe linger longer until your food and water are gone."

Silence.

"Look, you think I'm talkin' at you like a bunch of kindergartners. Well, I am, and you are. The question is different from how we are going to get out there. Lots of ways at this point. The real question is, how are we going to get back? Now gettin' back safely might seem best if we walk. You know, plan a day out and a day back. Be OK if you don't break a leg, get a snake bit, or fall in a mine shaft. Lots of ways to become buzzard food. Later, one of them helicopters come to haul your bones off the desert.”

“You're making this sound all so appealing, Pete.”

“Yep. You ever been to New York City, Tim?”

“Sure.”

Museum?”

“Ya.”

“Which one you like the best?”

“I don't know. Museums are all so different. Metropolitan, I guess.”

“Lots of exciting stuff in there?”

“Yep, could spend days there.”

“Got people walkin' around doin' a lot lookin' in that museum, maybe even crowded?”

“Sometimes more, sometimes less.”

“So exciting museum in a fascinating city, lots of people?”

“Yep.”

“Now I'm here to tell you that there is lots of exciting stuff in the desert, too. But look far to your left and far to your right, but you see no people out there. Why not? I'll tell you why not. Because it is different from a safe, pleasant museum. It's like a fuckin' haunted house that wise people avoid because it is hard to get through alive. It's got goblins and ghosts. I'm not trying to talk down to you. That's the reality.”

Silence and sideward glances.

"But, let me ask you another question. Suppose I was planning a meal made primarily of salad and asked you to bring us the utensils. What would you get out of that kitchen drawer of yours?"

"Forks, of course."

"Sure, you wouldn't bring spoons. The right tool for the right task. But if you go out into the desert, with the agenda being sightseeing, personal growth, me time, or whatever the hell you want to call it, you just might die. The moment you get past that cabin, standing right there, the task is survival, not sightseeing. The purpose is not a new experience. It is survival. The goal is not enlightenment. It's survival. We've got to pick the right tools for the task."

Harry piped up, "Good methodology yields good results most of the time, yes, siree Bob. All for that."

Pete gave a sideward glance, recognizing wisdom but finding the sarcastic expression a pain in the ass.

"That may be how you corporate or city folk might say it. I just call it common sense. Now, here is the way I see it. I can help you taste your chocolate cake if you help with the preparation. But that involves more than just moving your gear to a jeep or horse. Do you want two days? We should be leaving at dawn. You'd be surprised how much planning that is going to take. But planning is the most crucial part of the desert experience, as you call it. Without planning, you just got hot, dry sand and danger."

Harry light-heartedly commented, "Well, Pete, you know I've been on Safaris in Africa, and it was sure nothing like this."

"Ya, a few years back, had a fellow from France come by here wanting a safari, wondering what kind of hotels we had for our overnights in the desert and whether all the vehicles were air-conditioned? After looking around, he figured we had those raised camping tents with generators set up somewhere out there. He just figured he couldn't eye them yet. I just told 'em we got no open reservation spots for two years. He couldn't wait. Left."

"Why did you name it Safari?"

"Didn't. Years back, someone called it that on one of their online blogs, so people around here just started kidding me about it. Guess the gossip spread. Besides, we don't hunt animals, but they sure as hell can hunt you out there. But we'll talk about what we do out there before you decide to venture out. It ain't no African jeep ride looking for grazing wildlife. I can tell you that."

Tell you what. Do you guys know what kind of grub you got along with you? How it's packed. How heavy it is. The same is true of water and bedroll. If you ain't sure, go take a real careful look-see at your stuff. Then we can have our planning meeting. I gotta buy some supplies at Hank's place down the road. 'Tis our saloon, hamburger place, and general store all rolled up under one roof. You get in your shiny new truck there and follow me down. Guess you'll be able to make it with all them tires on the thing. We'll have some lunch and figure what we're goin do and get anything you might need to live and talk about it."

Later, sitting around the table drinking a cold beer, Pete asked, "Why you guys wanna do this anyway?"

Nancy voiced, "They just wanted a new experience, being in and learning about the desert."

"Well, ma'am, you're already camped in the desert. So where you're staying is similar, almost exactly the same, some would say, as to where we're considering goin'."

"The idea of roughing it more. To get out of our homes on wheels, we stay here. We want to experience what it is like to survive out there without all our fancy doings. Be a different experience."

"You bring sleeping bags? Planning on being right on the ground?"

"Yes."

"You could do that outside your RV and get the entire ground experience. Be safer, too."

Tim, finally exasperated, "Pete, why are you giving us such a hard time?"

"I'm not giving you a hard time. I'm just asking simple questions you have difficulty answering because you don't know what you want. Sounds to me like you didn't ask each yourselves, and no one else bothered to ask you what we want out of this. The person who told you about the Desert Safari must have made it sound like we have an all-encompassing buffet or smorgasbord of activities to offer. So just get in line, and there will be something to eat or do."

Tim complained, "Seems we started with what kind of tour mode did we want, horse, walking, or Jeep, and now we're in some deep hole digging for clams where there is no water."

"But Tim, don't you see you're already living in the experience or tour that you're a sayin' you're wantin'. It exists right where you're camped. Just go for a nice long walk. Take along a desert guidebook and read about the plants and things. They got pretty good pictures or drawings. But be careful where you hike. Especially stay within the hills and maintain sight of your camp. Don't plan on any tall saguaro being a roadmark for your return. I guarantee you that the big, tall one with two arms looks just like all the others when you're coming back the other way. And watch the sky."

"Why the sky?"

"Any of you here last month when we had several days of monsoon-like rain?"

"No."

"You can drown out here if you're standing in the wrong place. An area that seems flat to you is a dry riverbed. Flash flood water comin' down that way can knock you down in a split second. You'd be tumbled like cement in a mixing machine. Hit your head on a rock and then drown."

"Pete, don't ever try to get a job as a travel agent."

"I'd be an honest one, for sure. Ever driven through this area on the way to someplace else during the summer?"

"Sure."

"Hot, right?"

"Hot as hell."

"There you are, driving along, maybe on a high bluff overlooking a valley, and you decide to get out of your cars and picnic along the side of the road. Even spend some time throwing the ball around with your kids. Take some of the cold cuts out of your cooler and maybe potato salad, too. Put some mustard on the bread, slap on the deli meat, and eat those prepared sandwiches. Yes, sir, just a picnic in the desert."

"True. What of it?"

"But when you opened the door, got hit by the blast furnace of hot air, not bad at first. But then the kids start complaining that it's too hot, and your wife worries the kids might get a sunburn. So you make a brief picnic of it and decide to protect the kids. You rush them back in the car and head down the road to find some roadside cafe.

OK, go back to your rigs. Mix up some flour, baking soda, baking powder, dried milk, and water with a touch of salt and, if you're really fancy, a touch of sugar. Put it in a tin and over a campfire. Pretty soon, you'll have biscuits. Get a big bag of beans and throw some in a pan over the same campfire. Eat beans, biscuits, and maybe a cup of coffee if you have enough water to make it. But take nothing else from a plastic bag or the refrigerator inside that traveling kitchen. Then, throw your sleeping bags directly on the ground and try to fall asleep as you hear the coyotes calling. Think about what is crawling around on the dirt floor under you, and then you'll have your desert overnight camping experience, complete with a meal. Sort of like a picnic."

"You guys don't need me to do that or to travel for 6 hours into the desert to have that experience. You can have it right where you're already camped. Mostly, all you'd be missing is the risk of dying."

Nancy began to see what was happening, at least within her. This talk with her friends and, most of all, listening to Pete was part of the experience. Hearing about the creepy crawlies struck home. She wasn't sure. But coming to grips with the limitations of the food and the fears she'd face was part of committing to go beyond Pete's cabin, an experiment in survival. He was right. He could offer anything else they wanted by walking with them just a short distance from his cabin. Or they could get right by their RVs. Pete gave them enough information to decide how much of a challenge they reasonably wanted to face and forced them to determine why they wanted to do it. She had taken a ropes course years before and found satisfaction in meeting the challenge, but the challenges were well-known there. Not so with the desert. There was something calling her to do this, but she didn't know why. It was something mysterious but left undone.

In the ropes course, that challenge was performing the task, not the planning. The system had already been laid out for Nancy. There was no mystery to it other than the fear of doing it. The ropes course was scary but designed to be safe. But a "desert experience," as described by Pete, was a mystery. That's what enticed Nancy. The trip depended on unknowns, weather, varmints, snakes, getting lost, or equipment failures, whether human, equine, or jeep-oriented. The group needed more experience to plan and would depend on another unknown, Pete.

This dilemma forced Nancy to look at the risk-reward aspect. She wondered, "If I'm going to take this risk, what will I possibly get out of it?" Yet, somehow, deep down, risking facing unknown challenges and attempting survival was making the "desert trip" sound like what she wanted to do. This was no longer a simple experience like going on a tour in a cave, flying over Mt. St Helens in a helicopter, or going to a museum. This was much different. She told the others. "I'm going to take a walk and stretch my legs," then got up and left.

Chapter Sixteen

Gazing at the hills in the distance, still struggling with mixed feelings, Nancy picked up a piece of dead ocotillo branch and tapped the ground as she walked. She stopped. She drew meaningless designs in the sand with a branch. Letting out a big sigh, Nancy moved on. She silently reflected on her motivation for needing silence and walking away. *I feel this strong urge to go out into the desert as if it were a quest, some meaningful passion. But I don't know what that passion or joy is. It eludes me. Here is this guy in his 80s, often coming across as brooding and wary and showing he had little trust in believing we had any idea of what we were doing. From his point of view, we're out for a sophisticated equivalent of an adolescent joyride. Maybe he is right!* She thought and thought. Questioned herself, decided, then recanted. Thought again. Finally, she was ready to go back.

Returning to the bar, Nancy approached the owner, asked for another round of beers for everyone, and then sat down. "OK, Pete. Guys, here's my take on this. I've done a lot of thinking about other trips I've been on. How I'd come back and tell a friend about a beautiful play or two we saw on Broadway, the old ruins in Italy, or the friendly people in the most colorful getups in Thailand.

But coming off an excursion into the desert for a couple of days, I'd probably have nothing to tell if it went well. When I think of the desert, I think of something that has been baked. I guess I'll see and experience that for miles and hours. Baked sand saguaro cactus, prickly pear, and organ pipe are unique, but all look the same after a while. If we get up into the mountains, there'll be a waterhole or two, maybe some animals, but nothing to rival the San Diego Zoo or Sonoran Desert Museum that I love. But it will be me surviving in nature's wilderness, wandering, crossing, and experiencing this beautiful and horribly dry place. Maybe it will be like it was for those who came before me. But, again, I don't know. If we stay overnight, we'll likely see the lovely flames of sunset come and go.

We'll probably miss seeing smaller critters crawling around under the creosote bushes. But perhaps Pete will point out the plants that, over the centuries, were earlier inhabitants' food and even medicines. But most of all, hopefully, I want, no, I demand that I experience it in utter silence and solitude just like a cowboy or Native Americans did decades and centuries ago.

Once, on a lengthy cattle drive with my dad, he told me some of the stories his father told him. His dad worked as a cowboy in this desert. He talked of the dangers and beauty of going through the canyons. But he warned that when the winds came up, the dust got so bad that you could barely see where you were going. But he talked about how much he enjoyed the desert's solitude and beauty when riding alone. So I think I want to be able, even for a few hours, to experience what my grandfather and others did, traveling alone. But you know, I can't think of one person who, if told about my experience, would be jealous and say oh, aren't you lucky? Wish I could do that.

Stop and think. How often do we marvel at or wonder about what our grandparents or great-grandparents experienced in times that seemed primitive to our existence? We think about it but can never share it. This is one time I can taste what older generations experienced. I realize it isn't even a full bite, but it will still be a taste of time travel into the past."

Everyone was silent while Nancy continued to gaze off into the distance.

"I'll surely have a guide if Pete agrees to do it and won't be alone. But at least I can taste the cake, fully aware I'm not eating the whole cake of total solitude. But even the preparation will be great. Learning to do what I need to improve my chances of survival will be part of the experience. And if I go and you accompany me, there will be no chit-chat. I want to feel as if I'm alone as much as possible. Is anybody else interested?"

Again, silence.

Pete was tired of waiting on people, obsessing as if they were deciding whether or not to ride the roller coaster at a theme park. His old bones didn't look forward to leaving his bed behind anymore. He certainly didn't want to listen to modern men whine and maybe even abuse his horses. He hoped that they would all go and leave him alone. Pete spoke up, "So what about it, guys? Do Any of you want tickets for that potentially dangerous, hot trip of boredom and misery your friend describes?"

In the end, Nancy rode out with Pete. The two of them were alone. The guys decided to return to camp, agreeing to pick Nancy up in three days. The experience was exactly what Nancy had wanted. Pete only talked when necessary, and she enjoyed the quiet. Nothing dramatic happened. Pete knew where the water holes would be found at the higher elevations. Humans and horses were adequately hydrated. One lone incident was of Pete's sorrel shying away from a rattler. Nancy and her horse were several yards behind him. But not wanting Nancy's horse to be menaced, Pete fired his 357-side arm loaded with snake shots. Ordinarily, he wouldn't have bothered the critter if it hadn't bothered him. They moved on. Not a word was spoken. Just a glance from Nancy, who mouthed the word 'thanks' and showed a small smile.

On the way back from the mountains, Nancy found herself tearful but quietly tearful. She let her mind explore. It wasn't all that complicated, yet the feelings were profound for her. What hadn't been discussed with anyone in the group was that Nancy had grown up on a large cattle ranch. She was an excellent rider and roper and familiar with the varmints and dangers of long rides. Once Nancy got into her teen years, she frequently accompanied her father and the cowboys on roundups, spending days on her horse helping to move cattle and evenings gazing at the stars before she fell asleep, alone, under the stars well away from the cowboy on his horse singing to quiet the cattle. Nancy remembered those experiences more fondly than any adolescent shenanigans she and her teenage girlfriends had gotten into.

But now, much older, Nancy hadn't ridden since graduating from college. During her first two years, she would come home for brief summer visits but mostly stayed at school, working on research that would become part of her life's work and passion and eventually earn her a Ph.D. Then, her parents were killed in a car accident in her junior year. After the funeral, she had to quickly return to school. The lawyers handled the ranch's disposition. She got a comfortable inheritance but was suddenly removed from her former life with the ranch gone. As an only child, the loss of the security and comfort of a family and home base was even more profound.

The death of her parents was a shock, of course. But what was lost was not just her parents but also the ranch and its lifestyle. That was her sense of home. She had never planned on returning to live there full-time, but it was a functioning ranch with a manager and foreman who could run it well. Upon leaving for college, she felt that if the school didn't go well and fit her, she could always return home, even for a few days or months, if needed. Once her parents fully retired or even died, she imagined "home" would continue to be there. Now, it wasn't.

Yet, there had not been the time or pressing reason to dive deeply into the loss of a home. Many changes in her life and her need to solidify the plans for her immediate future demanded her attention. All these activities enabled her avoidance, as she minimized the loss. She had painfully but briefly mourned the loss of her parents but never fully mourned the loss of her beloved lifestyle. That lifestyle had formed her self-image until the day she left for college. After the funeral and back at her school, regular classes and friends quickly took over and consumed her emotional and intellectual attention. She was busy looking forward to a whole new career. Even her closest friends in college knew little of how much the ranching lifestyle was embedded in her persona.

Today, she recognized that the passion for returning to the desert was not about a new experience, although the solitude was undoubtedly new. Moving cattle does not offer a quiet ride or much concern about survival. Accidents could happen, but there was always a chuck wagon on the cattle drives and never a worry about water. Also, she was riding among masses of noisy moving cattle and several men who would have been just as happy if she weren't there to worry about. But more than a touch of adolescent omnipotence led to her never being concerned about any danger. Even setting up camp for the night was not her concern.

Those years had been strange but wonderful times for her. She lived in two worlds: the adolescent turmoil, fantasy, and swirling culture of her wonderful friends in the city school seventeen miles away was one world. At the same time, Nancy was engulfed in a ranch life culture that she found homespun and down to earth. But riding with Pete, she reconnected with a world almost forgotten. As they rode, sometimes side by side, other times one in front of the other, things happened to Nancy. But not the kind of things you'd likely explain to your friends.

She felt the blazing sun in a comforting way. The raw, baked hills offered her certitude and power. Riding through the still-hot valley became like the comfort of a mother's warm arms. She reflected on those rides with Dad and the ranch hands, who were more like protective and adoring friends than employees. Never, during those years of rides, did she wish for a life different from what she then had. It was only when she got to college that other experiences consumed her to become the passions of her life.

The pleasure of her academic life led to an immense intellectual passion. Nevertheless, she had never fully mourned the loss of a pleasurable, social, and physically challenging life. The ranch was exciting but in a systematic daily way. Her professional explorations and research brought new issues regularly and were more varied. Yet, she was glad that just she and Pete had come together so that she could revisit the old feelings and let the tears of loss flow in an atmosphere of solitude.

One thing about your loved ones suffering an unexpected and untimely tragic death is that you never really get to say goodbye. Nancy had never lived through saying goodbye. Her tears flowed as she and Pete came off the last hill, and his cabin could be seen in the distance. Nancy slowed her horse and let Pete move ahead. Pete finally checked on her as he glanced over his shoulder. Nancy was stopped but nodded at him. Pete gave her the last few minutes of desired solitude as he knew to keep riding down the hill. Traveling the last mile alone was like letting go of her past and her parents. She also wondered if *maybe some of the fences I build between me and my friends are because I fear losing them too.* As she nudged her horse forward, Nancy thought, *I'll have to think about that.*

If the two guys had come along on the ride, they would have introduced an unwanted dimension to the experience, a foreign influence that didn't belong. Frequently, when Nancy wandered from her camp with Pete at dusk, she would become tearful. It occurred along the trail, too. But she needed one last time alone to mourn, and she did while riding that final mile. But she knew that was good. She was lucky to have had her wonderful family, the ranch, and her current adult life.

Pete was surprised that this ride seemed different from others he'd endured. Usually, he was wary of the folks he was guiding. But Nancy was a comfortable trail mate. Just being nearly alone in the desert seemed to be all she wanted. On the horse, Nancy looked like someone at home and wished to be nowhere else. As far as Pete was concerned, he was glad that just the two of them had decided to do what they did. He could not tell why the ride was so crucial for Nancy, but there was certainly something going on.

When your well-being is strongly influenced by your ability to read people, Pete's senses have become acute over the years. He could tell Nancy had her secrets. He suspected but did not know that riding horses was part of it. She never mentioned her experience, but he observed she was at one with riding within moments of mounting the horse. She rode with caution, not fear. There were little things that showed she had been in this world before. She stopped once and pushed aside some branches of a bush only to see a hoof print. Or, in the heat of the day, she turned her horse for a moment and raised her head to the sky to feel a cool breeze passing by her face. Occasionally, she would rest a hand on the saddle's cantle, not out of fear or holding on but to briefly stretch a weary shoulder. These are the kinds of things an experienced cowhand does.

Nancy felt total comfort even when she teared up.

This was no desert safari. No, this ride was the last. This was about remembering Nancy's most beautiful moments and people and saying goodbye. It was one last taste of the best cake of her life. The cake of loving parents, being entirely accepted as a competent rancher, not just by her parents, but by cowboys, the freedom, excitement, and sense of control and importance of a roundup were never to be tasted again. Her parents, the ranch, and her youth were all gone.

Her anxiety about leaving for school had been minimized because no matter how bad things got, her parents were there to have her back. Even though her demeanor and style were that of a totally independent person, she had been protected by being tethered to something greater than herself. Years ago, all that had suddenly been ripped from her. It was gone. She was now an untethered adult.

This last ride was a safari through the progressive steps of inevitable losses in life. If there ever was something called closure, this was it. That's why the tears flowed actually on and off for hours. There was no one to hear or see, just solitude, good memories, and the pain of loss.

On the third day, Harry returned as promised.

"Where's Tim," Nancy wanted to know.

"Oh, it's good he decided not to go out. He would have been miserable. He started complaining of a headache on the drive back, a slight fever and aches, all the signs of a flu bug. But he seemed a little better this morning."

"You, OK?"

"So far. So how was it? Did you pick the right fork in the road? Taste the cake? Follow your dreams and passion?"

Nancy turned away from Harry as she was answering and looked at Pete.

"Yes, it was all of those things. Perfect." As she said this, she walked over to Pete, hugged him, and whispered, "This was very important to me, and you were the perfect tour guide. I'll always be grateful. Thank you."

Pete unexpectedly hugged her back. Surprised, Nancy looked down and reached for her fanny pack to pay him. He put his hand on hers and shook his head. Then, as they backed away from each other, their eyes met, "Ma'am," he touched the rim of his hat, subtly nodded his head, whispered, "Yol Bolsun," and smiled at her. With tears forming, Nancy smiled and said, "And to you also, may that road be a good one."

This was indeed the last goodbye for her. Then, not wanting tears, she turned and left. Pete looked after them till they were out of sight. He briefly thought of his daughter, whom he hadn't seen in years, as he returned to the cabin.

Chapter Seventeen

Back at camp, the group was gathering for the evening campfire. Knowing that Harry and Nancy likely hadn't eaten, saved food was kept warm for them.

"Well, Nancy, how was your safari? Tell us all about it." Fran's eyes sparkled with anticipation as she inquired about this.

With a mouthful of food, Nancy put her hand up as if to say wait a minute and finally uttered, "Beans. Beans, dry hard bread, and robust coffee." Nancy grimaced, shaking her head at the memory.

"Beans?"

"Yep, beans and bread were the beginning and end of the menu. And I can tell you that after riding all day, they tasted damn good. But these barbecued ribs are better right now. And drinkable coffee! My stomach is still healing from the assault it got out there." She chuckled, shaking her head at the memory.

"Sounds like a wonderful time! So, you won't get a job marketing Safari in the desert?

"Probably not."

"Really, how come?"

"Too hard to explain or describe."

"Well, did you see anything interesting? Learn anything interesting out there?" Harry leaned in closer, eager for details.

"Lots to see, but you can miss it depending on how hard you look."

Fran curiously asked, "What do you mean, Nancy?"

"Well, you know how, standing on the rim of the Grand Canyon, just looking at the vastness, you could miss seeing a waterfall across from you. Gazing across, one can see a crooked white line in the rocks. But if you look through the binoculars, you can easily see that it is rushing, falling water. It all depends on your perspective. The desert is the same way. You can easily get blinded by the vastness and miss the detail."

"Was Pete a pretty good guide?" Tim asked.

"Excellent."

"So, he told you a lot?"

"No, mostly he was silent." her eyes drifted to the fire, lost in thought.

"That doesn't make sense." Tim frowned, confused by Nancy's statement.

"Well, the silence out there was golden. Lots of good thinking time. I realized that there have been experiences in life that I survived but buried. With time, my attention to those experiences waned. But there was still unresolved pain. It would have been hard to face that pain and deal with it with chit-chat going on. In this case, the silence was golden."

Sensing a therapy group was about to be formed, Elijah quieted the group by steering them in a different direction, "Are you folks ready to address Saul and Rachel's dilemma? Should they follow Saul's passion and the uncertainty it entails or, put that aside, perhaps stay in Des Moines and pursue stability and consistency?"

"I'm sure we're not going to find much agreement among us on that one," suggested Harry.

"Why not Harry?"

"Well, probably because there is no right answer. People are different. For example, I was concerned about Nancy when she got back because she looked so disheveled and tired, but when I asked her, Nancy said she was fine, adding that the experience was 'perfect.' She didn't elaborate, and I didn't ask, but those desert meals aside, to call it perfect is high praise. So, I accepted that it was perfect for her.

But for me, the whole thing sounded like it was a dusty, bumpy experience and hard work, only to climb a mountain to see what was on the other side and find that there was just another thing to climb that looked just like what you spent the last three hours climbing. I wouldn't have found that perfect. Somehow, Nancy did. What was perfect for Nancy wouldn't have been even tolerable for me. We choose what fits us. How can we tell what is ideal for Saul and Rachel? I don't think we can."

Elijah pushed further, "Yes, but now you know something about Rachel and Saul. Do you have any informed guesses about what would work for them?"

Harry, sticking to his point, "We can discuss it in the abstract, based on what little we know from what the story tells us thus far about their alternatives. But our opinions would reflect our feelings or actions in their situation. But we don't really know Saul and Rachel enough to give them advice."

Nancy replied, taking a sip of her drink, "I think that Harry is right. For example, I have a history with horses and riding. Harry is right about how he describes the physical ride, but the dusty, monotonous climbs didn't bother me. Harry felt differently. Some people like Brussels sprouts. Others hate the stuff. Experience helps you to know yourself and what you need and want. Knowing yourself well is more than helpful. It is vital. I wasn't disappointed if another hill was all I saw when I got to the top. Just enjoying the ride and satisfying my curiosity was pleasurable. For Harry, it would be boredom.

But there is more to my essential trip. That previous experience I described had left some unfinished business. So this was a way of closing the door on a chapter."

Elijah added, "So are you saying that if we try to put ourselves in Rachel and Saul's shoes and guess what they might do, that says more about us than them? Is that a projection of our own interests or biases?"

"I really think so, Elijah, but we can still have fun guessing!" offered Nancy.

Not to be sidetracked, Elijah offered, "OK, let's have some fun. We do have some objective knowledge about these two. What do you guess about why Saul is so passionate that he would risk stability for opportunity? And what, if anything, is in Rachel's background that might enable her to tolerate the risk of following Saul's passion, even though she is usually cautious and more anxious about change?"

"I guess it is sort of like trying on clothing," someone added. "You know, a sweater or dress may look great on the rack, but it doesn't fit you when you get it on. So, I guess part of life is developing an inventory of what fits you and how comfortable you are with trying new things and dealing with the fallout if it doesn't work. Saul isn't comfortably settling for just any shirt or suit. He wants to find something that fits perfectly."

Larry, the cautious investment counselor, reflected, "I help clients face the issue of risk all the time. One of the questions I always ask is, 'What kind of risk tolerance do you have?' You know, low, medium, high. Sometimes, people see themselves as having a high-risk tolerance if they have a history of doing risky things. You know, stuff like skydiving, driving too fast, skiing, gambling, or even aggressive investing. However, being a risk taker is different from having a high tolerance for risk. Tolerance involves the knowledge of experience.

So, how does one know the answer until you've experienced a loss? Therefore, I'd always ask if they ever had an investment loss and how it made them feel. How did they react if they played school football and lost the game? Or respond if their opponent unexpectedly sank a forty-foot putt on the 18th hole of a golf match to win all the money? I wanted to know if they had experienced losing much money at the poker table or on a high-flying stock. Or, how did they react if they broke a leg trying to negotiate the black run at some ski lodge? Did they go back to skiing? Questions like that. If they had no experience with losing, they couldn't possibly know their own tolerance for risk."

"How did people respond to this type of questioning, Larry?" Tim leaned forward, genuinely curious.

"It often surprised them because few investment people had been so specific or detailed with them. But it gave them a reason to pause and made it easier for most to see eye to eye with me as we began working together.

I'd reassure most that uncertainty was OK and understandable; It just meant that we needed to start cautiously rather than dive into the risky, more volatile stocks. It is much like vacationing on a lake with a lovely, inviting dock leading away from a charming cottage. If you've never been there before, you better not rush to dive off the end of that dock headfirst. Instead, just jump off that dock feet first to find the depth."

"Risk is often hard to quantify. It can be a scary force out there." Elijah commented. "But let's get back to their story. Considering the conversation between Saul and Rachel. Seemingly, they've chosen Des Moines to be their residence. What will be the choice, a state-wide Jewish newspaper or beginning a search for a different job? They had to decide. Let's find out." Elijah continued:

Sitting at the tiny kitchen table in their rented, furnished apartment, sipping her coffee, Rachel pushed Saul, knowing it was time to commit. They already had the financial backing for purchasing equipment and hiring personnel if they decided to pursue creating the newspaper. They'd had their state-wide exploration trip, made the contacts, and found the interest they sought. Their backers soon expected a report from Saul about the feasibility of the project and his intention to commit to it and proceed with it.

Rachel let out a long, weary sigh, her shoulders drooping under the weight of the whirlwind experience. First, the exodus from Detroit, then all the dinners and meetings with people in Des Moines. As gracious and warm as everyone had been, she always felt like she was on display and being judged. Of course, she'd known that feeling running a dice game in a hotel lobby, but the stakes there were getting a nice tip versus getting stiffed. The only annoying downside was parrying off overtures from drunks and high rollers who felt entitled to anything they wanted. But, even that, she had learned to handle it with grace, humor, and flattery. Usually, no matter how demanding the day at work was, she returned home to her husband or to the stability of her family.

Life had changed so much for her. Not long ago, she had an excellent job and a warm, haggling family providing meals, shelter, and a loving and supportive environment. She enjoyed her social life with Saul, their more extensive group, and her special lifelong girlfriends. There was no worry about where her next meal was coming from, fear of an uncertain future, or feeling of losing control over her destiny.

Rachel's hands trembled slightly as she cradled her coffee mug, her mind racing with the uncertainty of their future. Truth be told, she was frightened. The stakes were more significant now. She imagined the relentless ticking of the clock and the mounting pressure that would squeeze every ounce of energy out of her if the paper were to be developed. Saul could go it alone as far as the newspaper was concerned, and she could concentrate on looking for work and creating a home environment. They hadn't taken the time to thoroughly discuss their expectations about the trip west before they left. They knew what they were leaving behind but had no idea of what they would find as a replacement.

While Saul thrived in chaos, leaping into the unknown with reckless abandon, Rachel felt her chest tighten at the mere thought of unpredictability. She needed more certainty or understanding about the path forward. Instead, she was faced with the need to deal with significant uncertainties. It was likely that even more unknown issues and decisions were coming down the pike. Even anticipating having children would be a considerable change, an unimaginable joy that came with physical demands and hard work. They had talked about wanting to leave Detroit in the future. But she hadn't thought it would be this soon. Naive on my part, she thought. But they had never dreamed together about what the future away from Detroit would look like.

Just as we found out discussing Nancy, Harry, and Timothy's approach to a non-camel riding safari, knowing who and what you are is essential. Rachel believed that she knew who Saul was. He was like a captured animal led forward, tethered by a ring in his nose, tugged by his passion and things new and exciting. The highs and lows of such an existence were predictable. However, he seemed acclimated to that. Saul would carry on finding strength in camaraderie and community and believing in his own goal and passion. If Saul were not married, Rachel did not doubt that he would be in the same place today. Also, he would definitely proceed with the newspaper idea.

But he was married, and just as Rachel said when talking with the Rabbi, she needed to insist on having a position at the table. Saul was not alone. He was married, and Rachel hoped that he would consider her feelings. Rachel yearned for stability, not highs and lows. But if there were to be a hint of smooth sailing on the horizon, it had not been made visible to Rachel.

She wanted a clearer idea of what the path forward would look like. What would her role be? Was there a backup plan if the newspaper wasn't financially successful? Rachel's heart pounded in her chest, her thoughts racing with fear, while Saul's eyes gleamed with excitement as he talked about the future. But Rachel wondered why she and Saul were so different yet seemingly compatible. Her mind raced with questions, trying to untangle the mystery of how she, with her cautious nature, could be so drawn to Saul's fearless ambition. Pondering this more deeply, she thought about their backgrounds.

Yes, daily, life on the shtetl was always tenuous. It was as if there were no sunny days, only living forever under a cloud of fear. Yet, despite this similarity, there was a profound difference in the lineage Rachel and Saul each brought to the table.

This difference was emerging as the foundation of their emotional conflict. These were issues that had only occasionally breezed through Rachel's mind. But now was the time to dig more deeply.

Intellectually, Rachel knew that environment influenced much of who one becomes. Although the traumas suffered by her ancestors were various, they were probably crucial to how her parents and, subsequently, she was raised. But these were things that she, like many of us, had never even thought about. Rachel stared out the window, her gaze unfocused as her mind wandered through a maze of thoughts and uncertainties. Rachel pondered that here she was, hundreds of miles from home, alone with a guy she loved. But she didn't know him that well. She didn't know what to do. To make matters worse, Rachel didn't know herself that well. She acted as if one day she was plopped out into this world and had just been living life as it came to her.

Rachel noticed the contrast in how her parents' steady calmness clashed with Saul's parents' lively chaos. Her parents, Phillip and Celia, had immigrated many years ago as older children from Poland. They had been here twice as long as Saul's parents, who recently came here as adults. Rachel was born in America. Saul was a young child immigrant. Luckily, during Rachel's youth, her family seemed more settled and less chaotic than Saul's. She grew up with parents who already had a stable life here. This home of stability contrasted with the chaos Saul navigated as he grew up while his parents sought survival and adjusted to an uncertain life in America. But that couldn't fully explain why she was fearful and Saul excited and enthused.

Yet, Rachel's background was more complex than it might seem. Phillip and Celia's formative years in the shtetl were like many others. Daily, life on the shtetl was as if there were no sunny days, only living forever under a cloud of fear. Growing up and living in their shtetl in the old country was rugged and frightening. Travel was limited or prohibited, and owning land was illegal. The people forced to live there were poor peddlers, shopkeepers, tradesmen, and a few artisans scratching for a living.

Some fellow Jews in the shtetls acclimated by enjoying their faith's vibrant culture and mutual support. Others were buoyed with the vague hope that someday a miracle could happen, and they would migrate, perhaps to America. But all lived with the disadvantages of oppression and emotional and physical abuse. This environment was similarly shared by the ancestors of both Rachel and Saul. Yet, despite this similarity, there was a profound difference in the lineage Rachel and Saul each brought to the table. Yes, this difference profoundly influenced the foundation of their emotional conflict.

Rachel's grandparents lived in even more difficult times, knowing only a history of long-suffering and conservatism that was part of Jewish history. But importantly, living in Western Europe, conditions more easily inspired hope for a better life than for those who lived under the Tzar and Cossacks in the East. As a result, Rachel's grandparents' emigration came more easily.

Yet, upon arriving in America, Rachel's parents brought with them an all-encompassing burden, a rule they must remember at all costs. As they faced the uncertain future in the mixed cultures they found in America, the baggage her grandparents and parents carried from their orthodox shtetl to America was this ubiquitous rule of fear. It was a well-defined cultural admonition pounded into their heads by their parents. There was a right and wrong way to do everything or say anything. Or so you were warned. Rachel's parents were taught one hard and fast rule as they grew up. You should be fearful and cautious first and only act when you are confident of the outcome. As a Jewish child, everyone around you, the nobles, parents, rabbis, neighbors, and even non-Jewish children, had a right and claim to judge your behavior.

And that became the watchword for Phillip and Celia as they grew up. Gently, for sure, but this was the form of the message Rachel had heard growing up. Then, of course, the rule softened as Rachel and her siblings grew up, and Phillip and Celia created a stable life for themselves. But it was always part of the fabric that underlay Rachel's decision-making.

Saul's father, Morris, suffered even greater abuse than Rachel's parents. Yet, Sophie had instilled in him a fighting attitude. He would show the world the worth his mother saw in him. As a reaction to this, Morris was an angry optimist, full of hope. He demonstrated this by working his way up in the family business despite his brothers and sisters obstructing him. They continued to see him as the bastard who didn't belong. However, with his brother-in-law's more pragmatic approach and support, Morris knew success and a modicum of independence as he matured.

Contrasted to the fear Rachel grew up with, Saul grew up witnessing a father scraping for success. Yes, Morris was an optimist and a very wise one. He was cautious but not fearful.

Rachel thought she saw how her parents, even when raised in America, grew up feeling a self-induced fear surrounding them. Sometimes, when Rachel was more happy-go-lucky about things, it seemed as if her parents were always looking over their shoulders, waiting for the gloom and doom to descend.

Behaviorally, the adolescent Rachel rebelled against that rule of perpetual fear, but always quietly and with apprehension and self-doubt, conditions that were remnants of her earlier upbringing. Even though she might act with the bravado of the teens or young adults around her, Rachel lived in daily worry, especially about her parents finding out about her job. Rachel was torn. Her thoughts swirled in a chaotic dance, pulling her heart in two directions, leaving her feeling like she was standing on a precipice, unsure of which way to jump. She felt that she should be proud of what she did. Every day, her work demanded the skillful handling of the fragile egos of the men around her. But her parents, her Rabbi at home, and her parent's friends would all be scandalized by what she did.

Rachel always imagined that having children with Saul would bail her out. Give her a different station in life. But she carried that old baggage every day and tried to avert embarrassment or shame.

Elijah was not about to stop. "Further differences were influencing Rachel and Saul."

Each having been schooled in wariness, Celia and Phillip became acquainted as they grew as young adolescents in Detroit. Theirs was a marriage of young love, not arrangement. It was in that environment that Rachel and her siblings were born. True, Rachel had stern parents. But the family was bathed in the love created by the loving bond between husband and wife. That marital love created an atmosphere where Rachel and her brother and sister thrived. Nevertheless, Rachel grew up with parents who had lived in fear all their lives. Only after being in America for some years did they become comfortable with the gray alongside the black and white.

But the "Be fearful first and act second" rule was never forgotten. Rachel was instructed by example to worry about everything growing up. She developed a cautious, careful, analytic, and political demeanor. She was taught to learn to use "Little white lies" to get along and avoid antagonizing others. When she pressed her mother about when a lie becomes more significant than a "little white lie." The vague answer was, "You'll learn." The cloud of uncertainty hung over Rachel even as an adult. She learned to be skillful around others. But never felt completely safe. Perhaps propelled by love and foolhardy adoration, she had nearly blindingly taken the hotel job with Saul's help. But that was an exception. Rachel was usually careful to cover her bases. She meticulously double-checked every detail, her cautious nature driving her to ensure that no stone was left unturned. Other people saw Rachel as a worrier. In fact, she was. Now, she was worrying herself through this decision.

Rachel thought about her family. "We are a small group. I only have one brother-in-law, Harry. Mom and Dad say many more relatives are back in the old country. But they don't talk about them. I'm so lucky to have Roberta as an older sister. She tells me things that Mother would never mention. Thank goodness for that. I would have been out of my element in the hotel were it not for Roberta. She's kept my secret well. And Arthur! My younger brother is the apple of my eye. That kid is like my own. I love Arthur to death. He would just die if he knew about the hotel.

We are all so lucky that Dad is a generous, successful plumber and businessman. He looks so special when he gets dressed up in his three-piece suit and vest to go downtown or shul. I've been so lucky to grow up in a loving home, even with the usual bickering between us kids and my parents. Everybody has an opinion about everything. Some of my friends have parents who still need to become fluent in English. Mine are. They use Yiddish only to keep secrets from us kids. But we kids picked up enough of the language to understand what they say. They'd plotz if they found out we knew what they've talked about!"

Rachel sat and thought. "Reminiscing is pleasant. Almost a fun pastime. Then she stopped. But all that is history for my parents and me. So what? I've never thought about the future. Oh, I guess I assumed I'd get married and have kids, but married, how? To whom? To have what kind of life? I didn't imagine being rich or poor. Or imagine anything. Now, here I am, really living out Saul's life. I love him, but is this life really for me? I know one thing is true. I've learned how to worry! Oh no, another thing makes two! I know that Saul gives me a lot to worry about! But, I wonder, is the extent of my fear a product of unnecessarily needing all the pieces in place before I step forward? Or is it justified by Saul's cockamamie approach to moving forward?"

Chapter Eighteen

As Elijah sat down the next night, he noticed Al's persistent grumbling, which seemed to carry an edge of negativity about Rachel and her worrisome approach to life. Elijah had always found Al's bluntness both refreshing and troubling, but tonight, it seemed particularly pointed. He listened for a while, feeling a growing sense of unease. Was Al's criticism just an old man's gripes, or did it hint at deeper issues in Rachel and Saul's relationship? Elijah's curiosity got the better of him.

"Why does she bother you so much?" he asked, his voice trying to sound casual despite his underlying concern.

"It isn't her that bothers me. It's their marriage. I don't think it will be a good fit in the long run."

"Why not?"

"Because she is a worrier. Look, Saul seems like he's playing the long game. If you're following your passion, it will be the long road to the future, not just the here and now. That takes patience and trust on the part of your partner. Rachel is still relatively young. Before this trip, she probably hadn't thought much beyond what she would do with her friends Saturday night. Without previous experiences of trust and especially patience, this type of person or woman will be a drag on a guy like Saul. She'll obsess over problems in planning a fun evening with friends for Saturday night. How much will she distract Saul by making him justify every tactic he uses to accomplish his strategic long-range plans?

A strange silence came over the group as if the conversation was suddenly hitting too close to home.

Harry was dying to jump in but hesitated at first. Elijah could see the anxiety on Harry's face, mirroring his own feelings about the delicate nature of this conversation. The silence made him anxious too; it almost felt dangerous to appear to take sides. Elijah wondered if he should intervene, but he also feared escalating the tension.

H"Now, Fran, I don't want to be insulting with my next question, but Al, are you talking from experience?"

"Yep."

No one said a word. The pause got longer. More feet started shuffling. Even Elijah wasn't quite sure where to go with this uncomfortable confrontation. Harry had seemingly led the group right into the middle of Al and Fran's marriage.

Finally, Fran laughed, saying to her husband, "Oh, you old coot, don't leave them hanging on a cliff. Go ahead and tell them."

"Not much to tell, really. Saul and Rachel don't seem like a good working duo."

Fran sighed. "OK, I'll tell them. Al's experience is not about something that occurred between us. As some of you may know, Al worked for the Northern Pacific Railroad. He was called out many nights to do goodness knows what and saw almost everything that could go wrong. Over time, he learned to evaluate the solutions and consequences, trying to promote the good and avoid the bad. Eventually, he was promoted to Chief Engineer. By the time he was promoted, that railroad had nearly 7000 miles of track and had been an ongoing operation for years. Now, he was the supervisor of the rails and the physical cars.

Anyway, one night, the week's horrible storms hadn't ended. It had been raining for days. Flood waters rose in many rivers, flowing under dozens of trestles running over massive gorges. One of the engineers had stopped a large freight train short of a bridge, fearing it would collapse if he went over it with his heavy load. It was raining cats and dogs, and the wind was howling and strong. Al was called out in the middle of the night and was motored up to assess what to do. He knew the dangers and agreed with the engineer's decision. Al feared the bridge would collapse, even without a train, due to the pressure from the torrent of running water below. He saw the force of the water as the greatest danger. Losing the bridge was a more critical concern than getting that train across."

Harry, waiting on bated breath, "So Al, what did you do?"

Al just shrugged his shoulders. "It's her story. If she's anxious to tell it, who am I to take over."

Fran, paying no mind to Harry, went on. "A collapse of that trestle would be disastrous for the railroad. This main track carried lots of freight, which meant lots of money. Moreover, it would take a long time to rebuild that bridge. So, he came up with a plan. He had the engineer back the train up to the nearest siding and had a crane car brought up. He aimed to create a physical barrier to redirect the water flow and protect the piers. He told the men that he intended to pick up those now stranded loaded freight cars and throw them over the bridge one by one to create a wall below.

Well, all hell broke loose among the men. Arguing back and forth about this stupid idea and such. No one was willing to help him, not even to attach the freight cars to the crane. No one wanted to participate in an expensive disaster they could later be accused of helping to create. They told Al to just let nature take its course. No one wanted to be blamed for losing millions of dollars of cargo and cars. But Al was sure the bridge would collapse from the pressure of the water. He thought he could prevent it. So, he said he'd drive the engine and crane over to the middle of the bridge himself. Al wasn't going to risk anyone else's life. All he asked them was for help attaching the cars to the crane. He was taking all the physical risks and assuming full responsibility. Others were afraid of getting fired for participating in such a stupid thing.

But Al saw the bigger picture.

The men kept arguing rather than working. They were wasting precious time. Needed time. Al felt that time was of the essence, and they were delaying his plan. Rather than helping, they were worrying. Al couldn't do it alone. His voice was getting as loud as all the rest. Finally, a few pitched in to help. They dropped over a dozen cars into the river to create a barrier and divert the raging water from battering the supports. All rail cars were lost, but the bridge was saved.

When he returned home two days later, he was exhausted but managed to tell me the story. He was still pretty wrought up and so damn mad at the men. I was upset, too. I didn't know how to help him calm down. Finally, I told him they were just concerned about all that could go wrong.

He glared at me quietly but emphatically told me it was his problem to worry about. They were there to support him or not, but he didn't need them to slow him down. That bridge would have gone down if they had waited much longer. The more Al explained to me, the more intense his voice was. He was one angry guy. Finally, Al said that after a reasonable discussion, there is a time to decide when to shut up and move forward. It was as if he had laid down the rule of life, and that was that. Then he quickly went to sleep."

Elijah then stepped up, feeling a mixture of awe and discomfort. Al's story was impressive, no doubt, but it also laid bare the stark differences in how people handle crises. Elijah couldn't help but wonder how much of Al's past experiences were coloring his view of Rachel and Saul's relationship. "Wow, Al, that's a hell of a story," he said, trying to keep his tone even. "Congratulations. What did your superiors say?"

"Not much. Bosses just thanked me."

"Weren't they amazed at what you did?"

"Not really. The bosses were all seasoned railroad men. They'd seen things like this done before. So do what you have to do as safely as possible."

Then Nancy asked, "So, are you seeing Rachel and Saul's marriage as impossible? That it can't work?"

Al sighed, "I got no crystal ball. We've got no real clues about their future yet. Just their past. We'll see. But I can tell you that if I were in Saul's shoes with all he's likely going to face, I'd be a bit worried that Rachel could be a drag or, worse, a real big pain in the ass. But I'm not married to her; Saul is. And I doubt she will be a happy woman unless she always enjoys worrying. And I think that Saul just may give her plenty to worry about. Living with Saul, or maybe anyone else, I'm not sure that Rachel will ever be totally content. "

Nancy turned to Elijah and poked him, "OK, storyteller, Al wants more information, more clues. Tell us more about what Saul is made of."

Elijah: "Fair enough. I think you'll find some relevant differences in their backgrounds. Let's see what you think."

First, let's consider Saul's mother. She certainly had her early life trauma. Leah was young at the time of her mother's premature death and grew up with her father as a busy overseer on a wealthy nobleman's estate. She was casually and briefly looked after by a sister who was only slightly older. Leah and her sister raised and looked after themselves. They worked to help cook for the lumbermen in the nobleman's employment.

Although she had to work in the kitchen, Leah was industrious and curious. Fortunately, she was allowed to be extensively educated with the estate owners' children. So, when she arrived in America, Leah was fluent in four languages, including French. None of the languages were significantly helpful here, though. She, Morris, Saul, and his sister, Rebecca, communicated only in Russian. But Rebecca soon straightened them out, coming home from school and announcing, "If we want to be Americans, they say we need to learn to speak Yiddish." Yiddish was the common Germanic-based language of the Jewish community used by people from many parts of Europe.

But I digress. Yet it is essential to know that Leah was bright, observant, and clever. Growing up among the nobleman's children, Leah fell in love with one of them. The love was entirely mutual. Leah was tiny and quite pretty. The two believed the relationship to be true love. But neither her mother nor her father would have any of this.

Her father said, "Leah, you are not allowed to marry a boy who is not Jewish." The boy's father, in turn, would prohibit his son from marrying someone from such a low class, much less a Jew.

Leah's father, fit to be tied about her love affair, arranged a loveless marriage to a boy of a reasonably prominent Jewish family in the shtetl. The wealthy nobleman, Efraim, did similarly for his son Morris.

Now Morris's had his own disappointment. He, too, had been cast into a similar position. He was madly in love with a wonderful girl in town whose father would have no part of her marrying a bastard, Morris. His tainted lineage was known to most in the shtetl. Being a bastard was a major driving force in Morris's life. He grew up resented by his older brothers, sister, and father. They did not feel that he belonged in the family. The trauma to Morris was painful and significant in that he was frequently reminded he was inadequate and unworthy.

Leah and Morris's former lovers, who were of different religions and social strata, would never be in the picture again.

Elijah couldn't help but wonder, "Parents always jump in to show their children the best pathway. What kind of society could we have without the parental need to pass on such ingrained bigotry?" This thought gnawed at him, not just as an abstract concept, but because he saw echoes of this in his own life and the lives of those around him. He felt a pang of sadness, thinking about the unspoken expectations and prejudices that had shaped his own upbringing and the relationships within the group.

Morris and Leah, two young people, wound up in an arranged but loveless marriage. Capable and attractive, they were also emotionally hesitant yet needy youngsters. Unfortunately, their chaotic emotions, recent love losses, and an arranged marriage were not the best ingredients for an excellent romantic marital union.

At this point, Nancy leaned forward to get Harry's attention and called across the assembled circle, "Hey Harry, what's your prognosis for these two in marriage? Giving odds?"

Harry, in a good mood, sidestepped the issue. "Well, if Leah is as sweet as you are, Nancy, any man would be happy to have her." Some cheered, others laughed, but Charlie booed and loudly chastised Harry for failing to give odds.

Elijah continued: Unfortunately, among Eastern European cultures, such circumstances were not rare in those days. As he spoke, he thought about the parallels in his own heritage, feeling a deep empathy for Leah and Morris. Like many arranged loveless marriages, Leah and Morris became good functioning partners, often compatible, but an emotional vacuum remained. Elijah felt a pang of sadness, considering how many lives were shaped by such arrangements, and wondered how different things might have been for his own ancestors. Contrary to Rachel's positive experience, Saul grew up in a household formed around a loveless marriage.

But from Morris, Saul learned about fighting as an underdog and striving to achieve. His mother taught him the importance of language, information, and knowledge as a means of stature. Both parents were curious, a quality they needed to be to survive. They both had been taught to continually assess their situation in an unsafe environment and then decide on a path forward.

The critical difference is that Saul's parents assessed but moved forward even when the odds seemed risky, and their relationship was tenuous. Conversely, Rachel's parents found comfort and success by being overly cautious, often reacting conservatively out of fear but finding support in a strong, emotionally mutual bond.

Crucial to Rachel's current apprehension and misgivings was another barrier. The marriage between Morris and Leah was inherently shaky before Morris left for America. It became even more fragile after Morris left for America.

The newlywed couple moved into a home in the shtetl maintained by Morris's oldest half-sister, Rebecca, and her husband, Ben. They were the only ones in the family willing to accept Morris. So, all of Morris's older brothers lived there and spent their time studying the Torah, going to shul, and giving out advice. So naturally, they expressed their displeasure about welcoming Morris and Leah in their midst.

Morris and Leah's marriage was to become fractured further by Morris's older sister, Rebecca.

Rebecca's husband, Ben, was a successful craftsman with an excellent business. He had a foundry. There, they had all manner of work for designing and building wrought iron gates and closures for the large estates, palatial homes, and even the Tzar. Morris may have been careful and wary but was far from a shy young man. Being the youngest child, disrespected and unwanted, he learned to be exceptionally polite and personable, glibly trying to please those around him. He was also incredibly motivated to prove his worth. These traits also earned him an apprenticeship position at Ben's foundry.

Ben, who liked Morris and found him an admirable value in his iron works foundry, saw his other brother-in-law's attitudes of demeaning and ignoring Morris to be unnecessarily punitive. Likewise, those other brothers showed no kindness toward Leah. Nevertheless, Morris's creative design skills and craftsmanship quickly got him through the program. Soon, he was promoted to chief designer and salesman for the company. This remarkable progress led to a more opportunistic situation in Morris's life.

As the company's chief designer and salesman, Morris was away from home for many weeks supervising building projects. Leah was used to that. His absences were not problematic in their emotionally distant marriage. At best, she was barely tolerated by most of the family, but Leah had support from her one brother-in-law and, indeed, the rest of the shtetl community. In addition, she and Morris, with good financial support from work, created a living arrangement that was comfortable and congenial.

Elijah took a deep breath, noticing some people beginning to squirm. He could sense the tension rising in the room and felt a mix of relief and responsibility. Deciding this was a good time for a break, he hoped the pause would give everyone a chance to process what had been discussed and return with a clearer mind. People stood, stretched, and attended to their needs but were back sitting and ready quickly, even before Elijah!

Chapter Nineteen

As they began, Elijah continued to reveal the foundations Rachel and Saul had brought to this marriage, which some in the group seriously doubted would succeed.

Let's grasp how Saul became the man we are talking about today. Since we are unable to measure lust and chemistry, history can better help us speculate whether these two are a compatible match.

Leah and Morris's first child, Rebecca, was born in 1900. Two years later, a boy, Saul, was born. Daily, Leah took care of the children alone. Morris, in turn, was a provider for the children and his wife. Yet, despite his success, Morris wanted more. He sought freedom and respect, not more wealth. In Morris's mind, emigration to America was the one way to improve the plight of their lives and their children's futures. Intending to use his occasional absences as a cover, he developed a far-reaching plan. A plan that, if successful, could dramatically change the path of the river of their lives.

This plan was so risky and unpredictable that there was no way he could make it a subject of discussion within the family, especially with Leah. He intended to tell Leah he would go to another city to oversee a lucrative but extensive design project. However, it would require several weeks away. Such times away were unusual but not rare. Nevertheless, Morris's design and construction acumen were valued as the best among Ben's workers. Subsequently,

Morris sometimes had unique jobs for wealthy noblemen, allowing him to leave the shtetl.

Instead of working on an imaginary job, he intended to hike out of Russia and get on a boat to America, leaving Leah and two children behind and unaware of his actual whereabouts.

The family could not leave in its entirety. The shtetl was carefully guarded. Further, the specific realities of the trip were unknown to Morris. He strongly felt that his best chance for survival was to negotiate the numerous potential dangers and uncertainties alone. He had no plans as to what would happen if and when he did land on the shores of America. He intended that with his talents, he would be able to get a job as a craftsman skilled in wrought iron design and fabrication. Eventually, being more experienced, he could return and bring out his wife and children.

His brother-in-law Ben had been informed of the plan and argued against it vociferously. He didn't want to lose his best employee and friend. Nor did Ben think the plan-wise. He saw Morris's escape, once he legally left the shtetl for work, as more manageable than most but still perilous. Although Morris left Ben with enough money and jewels to finance Leah and the children joining him later, Ben was concerned he'd be left with Leah and the two children, who would grow up without a father. Ben saw nothing good coming from Morris's impulsive act.

But for Morris, it was not impulsive but a necessity. It may have been desperate, but it was planned as best he could. He was a confident optimist. Thus far, we can see Saul's father, Morris, was a risk taker in the extreme. It was as if he owed an outstanding, large debt to a bookie with whom he was now playing poker. Holding a marginal hand, Morris risks going all in on iffy cards to pay off the debt. If he lost the hand, the consequences would be severe, likely two broken legs or death. But, on the other hand, he would be free of the ever-threatening bookie if he won the hand. Similarly, death could also result if Morris was caught escaping rather than working for some wealthy landowner.

Although creative and a risk-taker, Morris was not intentionally mean or purposefully insensitive. If Leah could represent herself in this story, she'd say he was significantly cruel, self-centered, and egomaniacal. Indeed, lying to his wife moved the effrontery bar beyond being troublesome. Her opinion was not marginally disregarded but totally ignored. Morris didn't ask Leah for her opinion. He knew when told of his departure, Leah would be hurt, angry, and scared. However, Morris's yearning for acceptance and freedom was used to rationalize his decision. Even if he were killed while escaping, Leah and the children would be cared for by Ben. Everyone would eventually benefit if Morris found a successful path out of Russia. Not only Leah and the kids could join him, but the rest of his family could also. Further, his son would be saved from conscription into the Russian Army.

Mostly, Morris would prove to his birth family that he is worthy. That he is valid and belonged as much as they did.

Therefore, the winning achievement in his plan, the crowning jewel, would be when he could successfully use his skills and assets to arrange and provide for sneaking all of his family out of Russia and bringing them to the United States. He felt that he would be given stature only by providing for his entire biological family. His deeply held secret was his grandiose plan to eventually help them come to America. Best, it must remain a secret. Anyone hearing of such a bizarre intention would have only ridiculed him.

Why didn't Morris trust Leah with his plan? Shouldn't he try to make her see how important it was for him to do this? Any thought of telling Leah of his plan was readily quashed for several reasons. First, romance can distort one's thinking. We often see our partners as much better or worse than they are.

Despite their excellent working relationship, Leah and Morris lacked romance. Leah would not view Morris's plan as if he were a hero riding in on a white horse to rescue the family. She would not trust Morris's capacity but rather see it as an abandonment. Obviously, he felt that she would object. Forbid it, even pleading her case to the Rabbi who felt all Jews should stay together and eventually get to Palestine. Such a high-power objection would make it more difficult for Morris to do as he desperately wanted. Morris was sure that once a conversation about his project began, the profound, never-ending shtetl gossip would leak the phoniness of his intended work story. The guards could be alerted.

Elijah called for a brief break, quickly went to his rig, and returned with two boxes and his thermos of coffee.

Looking at Elijah's food supply, Cindy said, "Good gracious Elijah, how long do you think we will be here tonight?"

"Well, Cindy, you have much to say about what's happening in our yarn. I just wanted to be well prepared with sustenance. Don't want to die of starvation in the desert."

Charlie politely asked, "But what's in the boxes?"

"Cookies."

"Store bought, or did you make 'em?"

"Store bought."

"OK, pass them around then, must be safe and OK for human consumption."

Ruth said, "I absolutely want more than one, maybe a handful."

Elijah hospitably added, "OK, Ruth, take as many as you like, but they are big cookies. You must be famished to be so intent on gorging on cookies."

"Of course, I'm famished! Because Morris is an asshole. He pisses me off! Morris really makes me angry. He's not here to yell at. So, I'll eat. I eat when I get angry. Shouldn't, but I do."

Elijah questioned, "Did you guys take a vote on this? Is Ruth the foreman of the jury? All those sympathetic to Morris's plight, raise your hand." No one did.

Tim kidded Elijah, "You're in the deep fecal matter now, Elijah. Let's see how you rescue one of your characters, or will you drown him during the crossing of the Atlantic? You know, to satisfy the angry women here listening to you. Or you can have Morris so nauseated that he is heaving over the ship's side and falling overboard. To make it worse, no one notices him needing help or being gone once he drowns. He truly is that insignificant."

Ruth, "Attaboy Tim. Make Elijah suffer for his sins. Elijah, why would you create such a horrible man?"

Elijah, "I'm getting your message, gang. But don't kill the messenger. Remember, please, that this is how Lucas described his grandparents' plight. So, I'm not the bad guy here. And Lucas is alive and well, so Morris must have survived. But I will march on bravely, maybe stupidly, and tell you that Morris's miscalculations about people's reactions complicated everything."

Remember, Leah believed Morris to be working in a nearby town. Over time, Leah grew increasingly worried about the length of Morris's absence. What could be taking so long? He'd never been gone this long before! Also, 'Why have I yet to hear from him?' At this point, Leah knew nothing and was growing frantic. In addition, Morris's oldest half-sister, Rebecca, had become jealous of the stature Morris and Leah built in the community. Morris's ability to design and oversee projects made him almost more critical to the foundry than her own husband, Ben. As a result, she grew overwhelmingly antagonistic toward her half-brother and his wife.

Leah mentioned her worry about Morris to her sister-in-law. "My goodness, Rebecca, don't you care? He's your brother, for goodness sake! Somethings wrong. He's been gone so long. He could be hurt or get arrested. He may be suffering horribly."

Rebecca leaned in, her voice dripping with malice. "Face it, Leah, Morris never loved you. He's found someone else, gone to America, and he's never coming back."

Leah's heart pounded as Rebecca's words echoed her deepest fears. She clenched her fists, trying to steady herself. "You're lying, Rebecca. He wouldn't do that to us," Leah whispered, her voice trembling.

Rebecca smirked. "Open your eyes, Leah. He was in love with someone else before your marriage. What made you think he'd stay faithful?"

The room seemed to spin. Leah gripped the edge of the table, her knuckles white. "But he promised... he promised he'd come back," she stammered, her voice breaking.

"Promises are easily broken," Rebecca sneered. "You're just a fool, clinging to false hopes."

Leah's mind raced, recalling Morris's affectionate gestures and his earnest vows. Were they all lies? Doubt gnawed at her. She stood abruptly, nearly knocking over her chair. "I don't believe you!" she shouted, tears streaming down her face. "Morris loves me!"

Rebecca's eyes narrowed. "Believe what you want, but don't come crying to me when the truth finally hits you."

Leah shook her head, refusing to entertain Rebecca's cruel insinuations. Morris wouldn't do this to her, she thought, clinging to the image of her husband as trustworthy. However, as days turned into weeks, doubt gnawed at her resolve. Rebecca's words echoed in her mind, growing louder with each passing day until Leah found herself unable to silence them. The weight of uncertainty settled heavily on her shoulders, leaving her feeling adrift in a sea of doubt and despair. Leah was overwhelmed with the pain of loss, fear, and anger. Life's worries had climbed the highest mountain.

What would she do? Initially, she felt panicked and immobilized.

Elijah paused, his gaze scanning the faces of the group, searching for answers that seemed just out of reach. 'Could this be the turning point, the moment that shapes the destiny of generations to come?' His words hung heavy in the air, stirring unease among the listeners. Rachel shifted uncomfortably, her mind racing with troubling thoughts. What if history repeated itself? What if Saul harbored secrets like his father? The uncertainty gnawed at her, casting a shadow over her once bright hopes for the future."Whatever the impact or influence of this situation had on Saul is one thing. But even more importantly, how would the knowledge of her father-in-law Morris's behavior influence Rachel's perception of her new husband, Saul?"

Now considering himself the group prognosticator, Harry said he knew what would happen. "So, Elijah, now it is time for you to return to your rig and get, not beer, but this time vodka for all to share as we lament this screwed-up situation?"

Initially, Elijah just smiled, saying nothing. "Oh, it gets worse, Harry. But this is where we see that history can better help us speculate whether these two are a compatible match."

Elijah continued. Flash forward decades, and at this juncture in their lives, making important decisions in Des Moines, Rachel's knowledge of this background was scary. She placed herself in Leah's shoes. She wondered, "Could this happen to me? Saul was certainly a handsome man who was popular with the ladies. Was son like father? Could a good salesman, Saul, become as unpredictable as his father?"

Being scared about the worst happening, Rachel also feared creating her own firestorm. She laughed to herself, thinking about her trips through the state with Saul. The relationships he built seemed sincere. He devoured the information he gathered and liked the people he met. She had come to understand how calculating he was in whatever he was pursuing. Yet, Rachel also recognized that every new idea or plan coming from him seemed more complex and demanding.

Despite her more positive thoughts about Saul, Rachel wondered, *Can I keep up? What might he be doing behind my back?* Rachel was also aware that many people interested in becoming reporters statewide were attractive women. So, Rachel thought, *Calm down, kid. Get yourself a nice hot cup of tea, then a good night's rest. We'll figure this out in the morning.*

Elijah stared at the now cross-talking members of his group. "Well, we're unsure whether Rachel got her tea. But we find Leah immobilized," Elijah explained. "Let's call it quits for the night. You guys can figure something out for Rachel or Leah in your sleep since you haven't had any concrete solutions while awake."

Chapter Twenty

Stories can be magnetic, full of excitement, provocation, or emotion. They can draw you in. But the following evening, the entire group, including Elijah, sat silently. They were mesmerized by the serenity they felt looking toward the sky. Sitting in balmy weather, everyone focused not on Rachel, Saul, or Morris but on mile after mile of rippling tufts of brilliant orange, red, and occasionally pink-colored clouds high above the mountains. Then, finally, they surrendered to a canvas created by a sun that had sunk below their vision.

Occasionally, one member or another would turn and look toward the East, where the mountains competed in the color contest. Soft violet, nearly crimson, colors served as a welcoming sign to the campfires, which were soon to be lit.

Unlike Broadway shows, this extravaganza in the sky did not have six or seven performances a week. But for each camper in the desert, group member or not, knowing that he or she would be treated to such a performance several times a season continued to help motivate their trips to the desert.

However, the colorful sky was soon no more. And the group no longer shared the calm, enchanted attitude that the weather and Arizona sky had served up. Many of the campers were agitated and quite angry. Morris seemed to have broken the group's faith in him as he had for Leah. Everyone sympathized with Rachel's plight; some even empathized. There were more than a few divorces in the history of the group. We'll leave the "History of the Desert

Storyteller Group's Affairs" to a different storytelling session. Let's just say that by retirement age, the "golden years," more than a camper or two had some lost loves and broken hearts.

Group members, coffee mugs in hand, wandered in and out of their rigs, collecting their nighttime munchies while weighing the merits of everything to find a resolution for Morris and Leah. Shooting Morris was one frequently mentioned option. Another idea capturing several votes was for Leah to divorce Morris and change course in the story to have Leah reunite with the Russian lover of her earlier teen years.

But those options were on the group members' minds. Likely, not yet on Rachel's. Rachel would know that she must face the formidable task of confronting Saul. Group members considered many different approaches. Most included expressing the group members' anger and aggression as they identified with Leah's plight. The women in the group were both angry and more empathetic and on edge about Rachel's situation than the men. Perhaps the women more readily identified with having been left out of too many decisions themselves.

Larry put aside the small solar panel he was cleaning: "Hey, why are you guys angry at us men? We didn't do anything."

Mary Ann exclaimed, "You're all so casual!"

Larry: "It's just a story! And even so, I don't think confronting Saul is a good idea."

Mary Ann, his neighbor, said, "But a true story. And why is confronting Saul a bad idea?"

Nancy, one of the group's more introspective members, added, "Well, obviously, Rachel's fear is a reaction to the story, the history as she knows it. But her understanding might not be complete. So far, Saul hasn't done anything wrong. But his behavior suggests to her that there could be trouble brewing. It is her worry about what might happen that she needs to discuss."

Tim said, "I'd like to hear more about the story and know what happened." He paused to think, clutching his coffee mug to warm his chilled hands. "I believe Rachel should keep it simple and direct, such as, 'Saul, in resolving my mixed feelings about taking this huge project on, I've been thinking a lot about the family history. We don't know much about each other in that respect. Before my own parents arrived in America, I really knew little about their life in Europe. You told me that your father left Leah in Russia and came here alone. That feels like abandonment to me. It worries me that like father like son, and I don't want to be abandoned.'"

Elijah banged his tin cup loudly on the arm of his chair. The abrupt noise temporarily put a lid on the ideas flying back and forth. "This is why I love telling historical stories. Look at all the alternative directions I could go at this intersection. If you went on for another twenty minutes, I could have a dozen stories to tell next time, all with interesting plot lines, but let's see what factually happened."

Never to be denied, Harry chimed in, "Ya, it really happened according to the person writing the history!"

Larry joined Harry's opinion with a disclaimer, "Ya, sort of like most history we read!"

Elijah continued as all the campers laughed, nodded in agreement, and straightened their chairs.

Well, Tim gets the prize. Rachel did begin to express her concerns to Saul, as Tim had suggested. It was more of a request for information than a confrontation. But as the evening continued, Rachel asked for more details and heard more about her mother-in-law's distress. They soon ran out of time as Saul wanted to be well-rested when he met with the Rabbi the following day. But Rachel was becoming more alarmed as she began to feel that Leah had been abandoned.

Rachel awoke only somewhat calmer. She and Saul had a quiet, distant breakfast as both read their papers. Rachel politely asked Saul's feelings about his forthcoming meeting with the Rabbi but barely listened to his answer. The pot boiling her own concerns was nearly ready to blow its lid. Saul left for his appointment, and Rachel's calm lasted only briefly as she recalled how upset and inconsolable Leah must have been. But the story, the night before, left Rachel knowing only Rebecca's explanation to Leah about Morris's absence. Rachel began to fear that Rebecca's story might all be true.

Rachel's thoughts raced as she paced the living room, her fingers twisting nervously in her lap whenever she paused. Each step reminded her of the worry that gnawed at her mind. *What if Saul is like that?* The question repeated itself like a relentless drumbeat. She hesitated at the window, watching for Saul's return, her heartbeat matching the rhythm of her anxiety. She clenched her fists, trying to suppress the rising tide of panic. She was distant and cold when Saul walked in the door, far from her cheerful and welcoming self.

"OK, it doesn't take a psychic to tell you're upset. What's going on? What happened."

"Nothing."

"Nothing? You've just had this metamorphosis into a robotic zombie?" As he tried to hug her, Rachel moved backward and plopped onto a chair. Rachel, slumping like a rag doll, glared at Saul.

"Oh, Saul, I've been so worried." Rachel began, becoming an avalanche of questions. "What if you were like that? What if you became obsessed with greener pastures? You flit from one project to the next. What if the paper or Des Moines is just a passing phase? What if I am? It petrifies me to think of these things. Your being here and there and all over the place in Detroit was one thing. I had family support there, but now I'm in no man's land. In these cornfields!"

Saul took a deep breath. "I will make a cup of tea and discuss this. Can I make you one too?"

"I guess so."

Saul handed over Rachel's tea, with honey, the way she liked it, and listened to Rachel go through each phase of her thought process step by step. Point by counterpoint, Rachel described all that Morris did or might have done. Every decision or intent she ascribed to Morris was accompanied by an emotion of anger or fear that she imagined Leah experienced. Rachel successfully worked herself into a frenzy. Seemingly, she considered every possible 'What if' or

'Then you might' that she could conjure up. When she stopped and finally took a sip of the cooling tea, he asked,

"Are you done?"

"I guess. I put it all out there, my worries and fears, the long list of them."

"I can't imagine how horrible you've felt going through all that. I can see how concentrating on specific things you knew about my parents could promote questions for you. But..." then a hesitant but attention-getting pause. "Look, I know there is a lot we have to talk about, but first...." Saul began to get a smile on his face. Rachel felt herself recoil, "First, we have to look at what you did."

In a booming voice, Rachel exclaimed, "What did I? I did nothing!"

"But look, you're angry at me, and I did nothing also. I was off having a meeting with the Rabbi. So I started to smile because there is a little humor in this."

"Humor? There is nothing funny about this."

"You see, you just had a massive argument with yourself and lost. Then you were scared and pissed that you lost. So the question is, who won? I wasn't even here. But listening to you, I heard point, counterpoint, based on a combination of facts, imagined catastrophe then refuted by issues of reassurance also based on fact and then even more fear and anger, based on imagination."

"Both sides of the debate came from within your own head. You must be exhausted! As I said, you had an argument with yourself and lost."

"Yes, but no matter how you describe it, all this worries me."

"There is a good deli downstairs. After I get out of this suit, let's get a bite to eat and discuss this on a full stomach."

"I don't know. I'm pretty worked up. I'm not sure a Deli is the best place to resolve this."

"And understandably, too. And we are going to talk about it. But first, we need to get you out of the quicksand. The more you flail, the deeper you get. So, let's get safe from the pain of your imagination and deal with the realities. So, I'm going to change clothes, get out of this suit, and then we're going to get out of this apartment and go down to the deli, get a good pastrami sandwich with some Russian dressing, a giant dill pickle, a coke with crushed ice and I'll tell you about my day."

"Your day? Your day! Saul, that is one hell of a deflection. What about my day?"

"Maybe, maybe not. Why don't you wait and see."

When they returned, refreshed and calmer, the evening was still young. Once settled, Saul, seeking some diversion, tuned the radio to Amos and Andy. This was a program set in Harlem and was both funny and poignant. Of course, at that time, the "Negro" roles in broadcasting were scripted to stereotypical behavior, and the parts of blacks were played by white actors. Two white men played Amos and Andy, but many listeners didn't know the difference. Black artists weren't prominent on national networks. The program had both warmth and humor. The couple relaxed, and even Rachel laughed a time or two as they listened. But with each chuckle, she also felt a twinge of being dismissed, as if her feelings and worries were being pushed aside.

She wondered if all the deli and radio program activity was a deflection, divergence, avoidance, or maybe denial on Saul's part. Or was this another Saul tactic to create a level playing field by creating calm?

Turning off the radio at the show's end, Saul took a deep breath, his gaze lingering on the floor. "All right. Let me pick up on the history." His voice wavered slightly as he spoke. "Go back to when I was a young child and teenager. You only know about me recently as my adored girlfriend and wife." He paused, fingers tapping nervously on the armrest. "Every event you thought about and described was pretty accurate. However, my mom's impressions and conclusions, as inspired by her sister-in-law, were... not entirely accurate." He swallowed hard, the words feeling heavy on his tongue, the discomfort evident in his eyes as he met Rachel's gaze.

"Arranged marriages in that culture, in that part of the world, were common then. Yes, many of them were loveless from our standpoint today. Many parties to arranged marriages had been pulled from other relationships where they had felt the same love and lust we do today. But those arranged marriages saw many different futures. There were those ending in divorce and some ending in death, often related to childbirth. But many evolved differently over time. Let's look at what happened to my mom and dad.

Because you see the passion in me for doing something big and new like the paper, you began worrying I may be like my dad. That is a good point. His passion was, for him, a matter of fact. When Dad started working for his brother-in-law, he saw a better future for himself and his family.

But that future was different from moving to a higher rung on the financial ladder. Dad's job as a skilled laborer took long hours. He was often away from my mom and the family group they were living with. Yet, he was living the same way as his brother-in-law, Ben. People worked to survive. Comparatively, my mom and dad had a pretty good life going."

"But your dad didn't wasn't satisfied with a good-paying job. He was doing just fine but left."

"But Dad was and still is a daydreamer. Like all kids, he grew up with fairy tales with happy endings. But, when thinking about those fairy tales, he saw not myths but opportunities. For him, the end of the road was not to replace Ben in business but to get to America, the land of freedom. Even if the work or financial conditions in America were more challenging, he would be free. No more pogroms. No more rapes and children living as bastards. No more Russian conscription into the army and forced conversion to Christianity. No more watching every move and word that comes out of your mouth.

So, no. Dad didn't find satisfaction in life in a shtetl. Why should he? My dad had excellent skills as a laborer and an artisan. He was a marvelous designer. The sales expertise and management skills were things he learned along with the growth of the business. So again, Dad and Ben and their families all prospered. But there was nothing grandiose about this. Just normal progression. Their financial stability did not lessen the oppression, daily fear, and uncertainty.

And even the financial stability could instantly come to an end.

He had no untoward disregard for Mom or home. When my sister Rebecca and I were born, many people looked after us. Up to this point, Dad's passion for creating was connected to design. Much like a painter on canvas, my father was an artisan who put his love piece by piece into his ironworks projects. But, while still bound to the shtetl, the creative passion led only to a quantitative change in life and finances. It didn't bring about the qualitative change he wanted: freedom. That could only be accomplished by moving from Russia.

True. Dad envisioned something more significant for his family. He knew that someday his son, me, would be taken into the Russian army. So many never returned from that. Some people were cutting off the trigger fingers of the boys to stop them from being conscripted. As a devoted craftsman, my dad didn't want to do that. Anyway, he saw a future without pogroms, hate, and abuse. He had heard great things about America. Today, we might think that his thinking was grandiose. His passion made him imagine candy canes dancing in the skies, even though he was unrealistic. But lest not forget, millions of others wanted the same freedom, those before and after him. Maybe they pursued it differently, but the goal was the same: get to a land of liberty."

Rachel still felt she had some point to prove. "Yes, but they left as families. Men just didn't abandon their wives, their children."

"True. But in Dad's mind, he saw the trip from Eastern Europe as being risky. Frequently, discussions have arisen about other members of the shtetl leaving. Mom didn't share his passion and concluded that others were silly to take the risk of escaping. So, by the time he left, he had calculated that the chances of a large-scale escape by an entire family going unnoticed would be minimal. Although a departure in the middle of the night might catch the authorities sleeping, someone in the shtetl would have seen and reported it. He and his family would quickly be pursued.

On the other hand, Dad saw an edge in the freedom of his job. Traveling to work away from the shtetl allowed him to go beyond the walls and quickly disappear. It enabled him to get outside the walls of the shtetl and be gone a long time without raising suspicion.

Dad knew Mom's escape later would not be so closely watched. The men were most closely monitored. They were the workers and manpower sources for the armies. Even Ben agreed with that. In addition, if Dad failed alone, Mom and we kids would still be well cared for. But my mom would never have let him go alone without raising a fuss. That fuss would soon be known to everyone, including those who guarded the gates. Right or wrong, Dad had a plan. But that plan did not include an attempt to abandon his family. That was never his purpose, and in the end, Dad never did leave behind a soul. He even brought the brothers, who mistreated him growing up, to America.

Granted, he may have done it differently. But, in his mind, he was not abandoning his wife or children but risking his life to improve things. And I don't think he saw the risk as enormous, just fraught with uncertainty. But who makes a change without hope and confidence? No, the real problem was that he left Mom wondering, confused, worrying, and, I'm sure, angry. But, in his mind, he was placing her in the care of his brother-in-law, his sister Rebecca, and a more extended family. He felt they would comfort and reassure her, not provoke and scare her. He hadn't become aware of his sister's jealousy of his success and the cruel streak that would lead her to horrify his wife with the stories she made up. The extent of Rebecca's manipulation of Leah was not even known to Ben. And my father knew of none of it!

Although he didn't love Mom the way you and I love each other. He respected Mom greatly and always treated her well. He was always trying to gain favor with all his siblings. Remember, he was the uninvited child. His sister never overcame her resentment of his existence in the shtetl, living with them and being even more crucial to the company than her own husband. But there was never an indication that Ben resented Morris."

Rachel cut in, "And the other women?"

Saul replied, "There never was another woman. The existence of other women was never part of the equation, except as a figment of Rebecca's evil mind used to antagonize my mother. But, of course, my sister made all that up.

Was the situation painful, even horrible, for Mom? Absolutely, for her, but it wasn't a cakewalk for him either. But I wasn't there. I can only imagine how despicable living in a shtetl controlled by an oppressive, threatening government and marauders provoking daily fear could be. The resulting overwhelming hopelessness and helplessness are unimaginable. And many were motivated and desperate to leave this behind. Dad was further tortured by not being accepted by his own siblings.

I am forever grateful for and proud of what my parents did, each of them in their own way. Maybe Dad's approach to pursuing his dream was unique, maybe even a bit clumsy, but he was never malevolent. And perhaps he wasn't awkward but brilliantly creative. Maybe he managed to do it, which was the only way it would have successfully happened. But I know that if he didn't do it like he did, I wouldn't be here living in the United States today."

It was still early in the evening. Rachel said, "I could use some nuts and a highball." Saul jumped up, got the tin of nuts, and poured the drinks. Then, he sat back down and continued.

"Any questions so far? Disagreements?"

Rachel considered what she'd heard as she enjoyed her first sip of scotch. "No, and I am glad to get your reassurance. But I would appreciate it if you kept on your toes."

"Kept on my toes about what?"

"About behaving in a way that can easily be seen as disregarding or leaving me behind."

"Well, I can do my best to control my behavior, but that doesn't control your perception. So, the way I see it, we both have to keep on our toes about our faults."

"It's strange," Rachel continued, relaxing as her drink went down, "Sometimes one of our parents will mention that the crossing in steerage was nauseatingly cramped, crowded, dark, and damp. But they rarely complained about the difficulties they faced coming here. When I think of all those people jammed in the cargo area of those ships, it must have smelled horrible, and the sanitation even worse! Disease, rats, bugs, ugh! Yet somehow, I complain that it is awful to make a blistering car trip from Detroit to Des Moines in the summer heat and get a couple of flats along the way. Maybe I complain or worry about too many things.

Nevertheless, I need to know what really happened after your dad abandoned you, or as you put it, left your mom and you kids."

Saul's voice grew softer, almost hesitant, as he continued. "He believed Mom would be told the truth once he was safely out of the country." He paused, staring at the light hitting the cut glass tumbler they'd found at a yard sale. "But... as I continue, if you want me to, it might be better to focus on the beauty in the story, not just the pain." His eyes flickered with a mix of sorrow and determination as if trying to reconcile the past with the present. "March on?"

"Sure. With scotch in my belly, I'm ready to hear more."

Chapter Twenty-one

Without significant topsoil, the desert's hard pan became slippery and mushy in the overnight downpour. Elijah looked at puddles in the ruts in the road. "Well, we've got a blustery, rainy day in the desert. Pretty unusual for this time of the year, and most of us stayed in, but I'm glad it has cleared up, and we're left with this beautiful sky tonight. I can see most of you brought a wrap; that was a good move. But we have the fire started, and that should help some. I guess you didn't get much chance to talk among yourselves about where our characters are. What are your reactions to each of our two interrelated stories going on?"

Horace piped up, "Maybe no chance to talk among the entire group, but it got pretty hot in our rig."

"How's that?"

"Mary Ann and I had a parallel discussion. OK, maybe a conflict, well, more precisely, an argument, each identifying with the man and woman in each story. I felt that in each case, the men were doing what they needed to do for the greater good as they saw it, and Mary Ann thought that the men were insensitive and self-serving about defining the greater good. Some alternatives could have been more thoroughly discussed."

Smiling broadly, Nancy said, "Sam and I went through the same discussion, but not quite as gender specific.

Elijah queried, "Gender-specific?"

"I could see Rachel's point but not the extent of her pain. Yes, she was in the middle of making a tough decision, facing the pros and cons of how their lives would be different if Saul got involved in the paper. But what was she reacting to? It was true that she had some background information that concerned her, but the story of his parents, although dramatic, was maybe much scarier. But, once again, Rachel wound herself up before having all the facts. She had the skeleton of a story but hadn't even heard Morris's side. Rather than making it a reason for concern and discussion with Saul, Rachel made it into a federal case, full of pain for herself. In that way, she is her own worst enemy."

Sam cut in, "Saul? Saul had had an obsessively peripatetic and secretive work existence in Detroit. Probably everyone around him had suspicions about what he was or wasn't doing." He put his hand into Nancy's and continued, "His not being more open really created an environment ripe for suspicion. So, he should have been aware that any change in their lives could fuel Rachel's fire with each new change."

As she got up to throw another piece of wood on the fire, Kathy snickered, "Ya, a man thinking in that sophisticated way two steps ahead about his own behavior and impact? Right! When the sun shines at midnight."

Pulling her hand free to gesticulate and make her point, Nancy complained, "Well, Saul seemed pretty savvy in thinking ahead and anticipating what the Rabbi would feel and want to know when dealing with him. Rachel needs to grow up and learn to be a better tactician."

"Interesting and valid points, all," said Elijah, "but they all demonstrate the complexities of decision-making, dealing with the forks in our roads.

You know, most people don't talk about hope or yearning as an emotion unless maybe it gets extreme, like love. Then, we call it an emotion. But perhaps Morris's longing for a better life can be just as powerful of a driving emotion as Phillip and Celia's fear of change is a barrier to moving forward. And maybe Saul's hope of creating something new is as great as Rachel's fear of uncertainty. Is one right and the other wrong? Or are they just different and need to balance?"

"Bringing those kinds of things out into the open is often tricky. First, it demands self-awareness. Then we wonder, but if I show that side of myself to someone else, it makes me vulnerable. It might open me to criticism, rejection, and looking silly.

Since we have enough trouble knowing ourselves, let's get more information about Morris and Leah before we blow both marriages to kingdom come by projecting our feelings onto these poor people. After all, they have their own problems. They don't need our baggage too. You guys are just too creative! If I let you go on too long, you'll have Saul and Rachel in divorce court and Leah and Morris either living as bigamists or being total outcasts of their families. Great hearing your conjectures, but my story. I'm going to steer this boat down the river, not change the channel of the river!"

Saul continued to tell Rachel the story about his parents as he knew it. Leah woke before dawn each day, her hands already aching from the previous night's embroidery work.

The kitchen was her domain, yet it felt like a gilded cage. As she kneaded the dough for strudel, her thoughts wandered to Morris. Each fold and press of the dough was a silent conversation with her absent husband, questions and worries embedded in the rhythm of her work. She glanced at the empty chair by the hearth, where Morris used to sit, and a pang of loneliness tightened her chest.

Additionally, Leah crocheted and did beautiful embroidery work. But all of this was busy work. With Morris's prolonged absence, she felt rejected and abandoned.

Leah's days were filled with interactions that only deepened her sense of isolation. At breakfast, Rebecca's sharp eyes followed her every move, ready to pounce on any mistake.

"You call this strudel?" Rebecca scoffed, barely glancing at the beautifully golden pastry Leah set on the table. "Maybe you should spend less time daydreaming and more time improving your recipes."

Leah bit back a retort, swallowing her pride along with the lump in her throat. She offered a small smile and returned to her chores, the sting of Rebecca's words lingering.

She was neither a widow nor free to pursue other options as a tiny but beautiful, single young woman. As attractive as she was in later life, Saul never remembered his mother as pretentious in her manner toward others or dress. She wore baggy, plain clothes and kept her hair simple, in a bun.

Because of Rebecca's harassment, Leah believed Morris saw their marriage as loveless and cared little for her. Leah continued to suffer abuse and ridicule from Rebecca's stories about Morris's mysterious licentious absence. Ben knew nothing of what Rebecca had told Leah. Leah was ashamed and not one to complain. Therefore, Ben, unaware of his wife's lies and abuse of Leah, had done nothing to dissuade Leah from the pain of his wife's viciousness.

Eventually, the planned time came, and Ben told Leah about Morris's whereabouts. Ben informed her that Morris had spent most of the time he'd been in America living in New York. Actually, he was living with a cousin, Gayle. Morris found a much more cordial welcome from Gayle than Leah had ever seen from Rebecca. Nevertheless, Leah became distraught that Morris had not yet contacted her and arranged for her and the children to come to America. Unfortunately, this was only made worse because he sent for one of his older brothers and nephews before sending for Leah and his own children.

How could they not come first? But Morris had his reasons. Also, he couldn't help but think such a trip for Leah and two young children, one barely out of the toddler stage, to travel alone would be too difficult and perilous. For Morris, the idea of returning himself this early to accompany his wife and children risked arrest. Moreover, it could foil his plan to establish a new home base in America.

Further, it could also, out of predictable retribution, jeopardize the safety and well-being of all left behind. No, in Morris's mind, the reunion with his wife and children should wait. This was a calculation he made that was unknown to others.

Personable, talented, industrious Morris was just as successful as a skilled metal worker in New York City as he had been back home. Upon his arrival in America, Morris found it comfortable, and everyone was optimistic. Although dangerous and difficult, Morris's trip was still far more manageable than Leah's. It was faster. He had the advantages of being a man and less fearful of abuse, and he wasn't caring for a two-year-old boy and a six-year-old girl. Also, it was far more straightforward as a single man trying to navigate the confusion of Ellis Island and answer questions presented in English, a language he didn't know.

As time passed, Leah began to take on a new perspective. As a young girl, she was subservient, with little control over her future. Being a female, she was indirectly controlled by nobleman bosses, parents, elders, and rabbis who owned all decisions related to morality and one's ability to survive. The destiny of her shared love with the nobleman's son was not to be fulfilled. Yet, she saw she had some strength. She had done well in everything she pursued. She excelled in learning from the tutor to make savory brisket and mouth-watering sweets at the estate. She was only allowed to bake as a child working in the kitchen, but her specialties, including delicious challah and savory kugel, were admired and complimented by all. Once married, she was a good, attentive, loving mother.

Leah recognized that none of the older brothers held Morris in exceptionally high regard. They were all glad to see him gone. But they never said anything negative about how Morris chose to leave. Even Ben seemed to almost regard it as brave and heroic, not selfish. So, Leah decided that she and the children belonged with Morris in America. And she hoped that he felt the same way. She and Morris may not share as much love as others, but they share mutual respect and two children. Leah would go to America, and together, she and Morris would make things work. She told only Ben of her plans. He was not surprised. He felt that her decision was premature. Leah was puzzled. "Why premature?"

"Well, that was Morris's plan all along. He left money and jewels to pay for the trip for you and the children, but they are still relatively young. Are you sure they can do it? There is only enough money for steerage, and the nearest port where that is available is hundreds of miles. How would you get there alone?"

"Walk."

"Walk hundreds of miles with a 6-year-old and a 2-year-old? No way."

"We will make it work. It is time."

"No, Leah, you need one of my brothers to accompany you, but we are all busy now. You must wait. That was Morris's plan."

Leah stared at Ben, refusing to back down. She'd had enough. "That was his plan. But he never told me. You never told me. No one ever told me. I worried myself sick about what was going on. Now I must go. He implemented his plan. Now, I must implement mine."

"But what you are talking about is so risky?" As Leah continued, Ben shifted and gazed over the chickens scurrying through the yard.

"And what kinds of future life for my children and me will we have if we stay? Here, we merely exist and work but are afraid of our shadows daily. There is fear and real risk. What do my kids have to look forward to? My boy will be forced into the Army and converted to Christianity? Our daughter will be forced into an arranged marriage only to have children to continue the same cycle. My husband has forged a path. I must follow."

"He will send for you. You should be more patient."

"I have been patient. But how long should I wait? Another year? Ten? In the meanwhile, Morris and I grow apart. Staying is risky for many reasons. As is the trip. But I am leaving and will soon have a resolution. No waiting years for Morris or others to make decisions for me."

Elijah continued, "And go, she did. No one ever knew the whole story of her journey. Morris wrote about some of the things she told him. The dangerous trek was acknowledged and described, but many details were never broached. Leah had sewn the jewels in the hem of her dress. She knew where she was going, but there were no maps, escorts enabling directions or safety, or horses to provide transportation. A mother and her two young children walked hundreds of miles. Sometimes, Leah had to carry Saul. He was small. Sleep was often in fields or barns. Food was where she could find it or sometimes beg for it. People were generous.

Both for Leah and Morris, the trip was dangerous and difficult. Nevertheless, it was far easier for Morris as a single man than for Leah, a woman with children who constantly worried about noticeable diseases in others, the uncertainty of direction, feeding her children, and providing them shelter and warmth. When she finally arrived at Ellis Island, she was exhausted and overwhelmed from an arduous trek and days of dealing with her seasickness and caring for her sick children. Then, with nauseated, irritable, wandering children in tow, she had to face agony, chaos, and the language barriers of Ellis Island. Now, all but totally collapsed, Leah wasn't sure what she was in for in this strange new land."

Chapter Twenty-two

"The reception Morris experienced upon arrival was repeated many folds over for Leah and her children. Gayle's loving congeniality helped to drown out the memory of sister-in-law Rebecca's vile behavior. Gayle treated the two kids, Saul and Rebecca, and Leah and Morris's daughter, like grandchildren from when they arrived. In the home were also Morris's older brother Ira and his son Ben, for whom Morris had earlier arranged passage.

Leah found herself avoiding Ira and Ben during their first few weeks together. Every time she saw Ben helping Ira with his coat or fetching something for him, a pang of resentment tightened her chest. One evening, as she prepared dinner, she couldn't help but mutter under her breath, "Why did Morris bring them first? Why not me?" She sighed deeply, shaking her head as she chopped vegetables more forcefully than necessary.

But she soon came to view the situation differently. Once she had taken that horrible journey, she could see how difficult it could be for an aging Ira. Nephew Ben, much older than her two children, could help his much older father, Ira, on the arduous trek across Russia. Rather than having the additional responsibility of two young children as Leah had, Ira had, and would undoubtedly need, his caretaker, Ben. Leah saw Ben as a very bright and sensitive child. He welcomed young Saul and Rebecca most, cared for them, played with them, and showed them around the house and neighborhood. Leah understood why it was essential to

Morris to get his nearly teenage nephew out of Russia before the Army took him and converted him to Christianity, as was done with so many Jewish teenage boys.

At first, Leah was overwhelmed by being in America. Gone were the days of getting up without the daily stresses of a possible pogrom, fear of being kidnapped for use in sex trafficking, mass rapes, and the significant lack of personal freedom back home. Every day, cloudy or rainy in some ways, now seemed bright and sunny to Leah. Leah's shoulders sagged as she figured out the bustling streets of New York City. Each step felt heavier than the last. The faces around her blurred into a sea of strangers, moving relentlessly in every direction. She paused, leaning against a lamppost, and closed her eyes for a moment, trying to gather her strength. "I never imagined it would be like this," she thought, a wave of fatigue washing over her.

The size, the loud sounds, and the hustle and bustle in New York all seemed bizarre.

As time passed, New York and other bustling American cities were not only enormous in Leah's eyes but were enlarging rapidly. As the building continued, more tradesmen were needed. More immigrants arrived daily as people cleaning hotels and streets moved up the ladder. New York City was becoming the world's cultural capital at the time. It was significant in size and ethnic diversity, home to many immigrants, not just Jewish, but Hispanic, Italian, and Irish. People from everywhere came to the City. They contributed to the rich traditional cultures, art cultures, and image of New York, but also to the gangs and corruption as they struggled to assimilate and, at the same time, make a living.

The dynamic that Leah witnessed upon her arrival was so incomprehensible she panicked even when Ira wanted to take the children to play in the tiny outside yard. The lower East Side, where they lived, was overwhelmingly crowded with immigrants. Whereas Leah was surrounded by familiar faces in a crowded shtetl, in New York, she faced a multitude of cultures and colors.

Yet, being a survivor, Leah did recover. With time, family support, and a willingness to face the unknown, Leah became comfortable and enjoyed the sense of freedom and welcomeness of her new land. In many ways, she more than recovered. Leah prospered. She had found a sense of independence, even a bit of invincibility, out of desperate need during her fantastic trek. She became Morris's new, more independent partner and a strong yet amazingly gentle mother.

Both husband and wife worked well as a team. Casual family conversations around the dinner table or in the small parlor would initially reference things totally unfamiliar to her. Of course, she and the children were also learning the language. But the language of the time was Yiddish, not English. Immediately around her and the kids, people spoke Yiddish at home or in the neighborhood. So, she and the children quickly learned Yiddish. That was a combination of Hebrew and Eastern European languages with which they were familiar. English took longer but was still mastered as part of their commitment to a new life.

It wasn't until she and Morris eventually moved to Detroit, and she was studying for her citizenship, that she became fluent in English. But, of course, being fluent in French helped a bit. The kids? Well, they just absorbed everything and learned English early. That was the language in school. But, like so many immigrants before her, Leah sat and listened, absorbing more each day until she was fluent.

Morris did well in New York but learned he would be better paid in Detroit. So, the couple decided to move there. Morris also brought more brothers over, some staying in New York and others going to Detroit. Being so fond of Leah and the kids, Ira and Ben decided to accompany them to Detroit. Morris and Ira's families became more of a unit, tasting the fruits of a beautiful new place. The other older brothers were now freed to spend much time studying the Torah and praying without fear of retribution. Between themselves, they acknowledged Morris's gift of their new sense of safety but still showed no respect for him, even though he was the one who gave them freedom.

Talented as an ironworker, Morris became more successful in Detroit. However, he was injured when a piece of metal flew into his eye while working. Eye protection and face masks were not routinely used in those days. They had saved money. Morris, unable to do ironwork, decided to buy a horse and wagon. For a while, Morris would collect unused items from friends or neighbors and sell them elsewhere, even going into less populated areas upstate. Then Morris and Leah decided that service was more valuable than the product. They began taking the horse and cart and walking to outlying farms where they purchased milk. Trekking back to town with their weighty burden, they sold the milk in nearby neighborhoods. Carefully saving their money, they could soon buy cows and have their own dairy. Soon, they also made butter and cheese from the milk. Some say that they made cottage cheese and introduced it to Detroit. Morris and Leah were hard workers and generous in providing for the kids who wanted for little. They dressed adequately but neatly, not elegantly, and did not live as the noblemen or even as extravagantly as some wealthy relatives back home. No servants. Leah did all her own housework and cooking. Soon, Morris had an eye on buying an apartment house. He'd been raised with the idea that land ownership meant economic survival. That had certainly been true for the Russians controlling them in the shtetl.

During his property search, Morris was approached by one of their dairy customers, a lovely woman named Ford. Mrs. Ford was very polite, also friendly, and chatty. She respected that Morris had work to do but would stop and talk. She heard some of their stories and shared some of her own. Mrs. Ford was excited for Morris and Leah and hoped they would find the property they wanted. One day, she tells Morris that her husband, Henry, would like to meet him.

"I've told him all about the two of you, and he is very interested."

"In what?"

"Why your story, your ingenuity, and now your entrepreneurship."

Henry built cars. He told Morris of his plan to build a factory to produce his cars on an assembly line. This would be the first factory of its kind, and Henry was looking for investors. He offered Morris a 25% interest in the factory for the money Morris had saved for real estate.

"You are looking for partners?"

"No, not partners. Investors."

Morris demurred. Car models came and went then, which was a tricky business. The assembly line for Morris was a form of teamwork. Something he knew a little about in the ironworks company. But the opportunity just seemed too risky compared to rents from apartments. Morris also found Henry an unpleasant, pushy salesman. Refusing Henry's request. Morris told Leah, "I think an apartment building is a safer investment. It is more predictable, and besides, as much as I like Mrs. Ford, I don't trust him." Morris eventually bought his apartment building and did reasonably well. We all know the history of Ford's success in Detroit. Henry Ford was appropriately seen by many as being antisemitic. Also, some say that no Jewish investor with Henry ever saw a dime of their money again. Henry prospered well beyond Morris's expectations, but Morris never regretted buying real property.

Leah and Morris prospered. They saved and bought more real estate. Morris fixed up the buildings himself, sometimes with help from Saul. Soon, he and Leah could sell the dairy and rid themselves of the early morning, afternoon, and evening milking routines. They moved to a new, more excellent neighborhood with the birth of three more sons. Leah and Morris were very generous. Two of Saul's brothers went to college. One became a lawyer, the other a doctor. Saul and the other brother, Sidney, decided not to attend college. Morris was willing to send them all, but it was not to be. Rebecca was also exceptionally bright and took classes at the Detroit Institute of Art. She wanted to go to college, but Leah said the money needed to be saved in case the other boys changed their minds. Gender discrimination was usual in those days, even in a loving family with such a strong female leader.

But Morris and Leah brought many of their siblings over. None of the cousins went to college as Saul's brothers did. Morris was willing to help, but they weren't motivated. Yet, they very much loved their Uncle Morris and respected his wisdom. They would go to him for help dealing with life's problems and enjoyed their many discussions. All of this is important to our story about Saul and Rachel because this is the environment in which Saul grew up. Saul lived as directed by his parents' intensity, curiosity, creativity, and generosity. The genes of these two people mixed to create the forever-seeking, creative, passionate hunger Saul demonstrated as he grew up. He learned not so much from lectures or admonishment as by example. And Saul was nothing, if not observant, of what worked and didn't."

Now working on a bottle of Diet Coke, Elijah paused and took a sip before continuing.

Now, upward mobility was perhaps a more readily available path back then than today. Some of you may think that the "American Dream" seems to be getting a rougher road for many, except for techies and people with MBAs. Be that as it may, Morris and Leah's path was an exemplary map for Saul to witness. But not just a map for financial success. His parents were not only hard workers; they were fine people. They were kind and generous. Friends and family found them warm and always willing to help. Although each could be quick-tempered in certain circumstances, both calmed quickly, didn't bear grudges, and usually seemed even-tempered.

Once they were free of the day-to-day obligations of the dairy, which was sapping both their strengths, family life became more manageable. No longer burdened by the dairy, Leah could approach running her home and attending to the five active children with diverse interests. Morris, meanwhile, addressed the needed management and repairs of the apartment house. He did all this work himself. Throughout the years of owning rental property, Morris would only rent a unit that he would be willing and happy to live in. And he never did, no matter how difficult things became during the Depression.

In those days, immigrant neighborhoods changed rapidly from one group to another. Frequently, immigrants having cycled through one area would then move upwards. Some formerly immigrant communities became home to the Black Americans, Negroes then, who often found it difficult to find landlords who would accept them. Morris's property became all Negro. In no way did he ever neglect the care and well-being of those domiciles. He'd spend lots of time on sight, often accompanied by one grandchild or another. And he truly enjoyed conversing and interacting with his tenants. They found him to be a friend. Years later, when Morris died, numerous black tenants were at his funeral.

Chapter Twenty-three

"Morris, forever carrying the pain of being ostracized as a child, would never discriminate against others. Instead, his cheerful, caring approach toward others was remembered and appreciated by many.

For example, one day, years after Morris died, his daughter Rebecca returned to Detroit to care for Leah in the hospital. Staying in Leah's apartment, she had to travel a long way by streetcar to visit her mother in the hospital. One day on the streetcar, a Negro man approached her, saying, "Pardon me, aren't you Morris's daughter?"

"Yes, I am."

"I'm Al. I recognize you from when you were a child, and Morris used to visit us where we lived. But why are you on the streetcar in this dangerous neighborhood during race riots?"

"I'm going to visit my mother in the hospital."

From that day forward, Al would meet Rebecca at the streetcar stop, go aboard the car, get off, and walk her to the hospital to ensure she got there safely. She felt confident that he would have escorted her home, but an uncle came to pick her up each evening.

Morris's compassion seemed to create a legacy for his offspring. Years later, one of his grandsons would describe a similar story during the significant abuses and physical dangers arising for anyone on the streets during the turmoil in Oakland, California, in 1968. Oakland was at the center of violence in this dangerous and tumultuous time of the Black Panthers and several cultural struggles occurring in the Bay Area. The young man was beginning work as a new emergency room doctor at the largest county hospital in Oakland, California. No one felt entirely safe on the streets, and sometimes in the hospital, and for good reason. Gang gun and knife fights were ubiquitous. The difficulty in finding consistent housing, hygiene, or obtaining reasonable general medical care left the emergency room as the only option for people wounded or suffering from chronic conditions. Complicating this situation was a shift in the drug culture from the earlier hippie life to the use of harder drugs.

The nurses, clerks, aides, and doctors were immersed in twelve-hour shifts of unending shouting, screaming, anger, and cries for immediate attention, along with threats as waiting scared patients felt they were being ignored and still potential victims in danger even in the ER. Exhaustion, frayed nerves, and personal fear were felt by the staff as well as the patients.

The young intern was recently transferred from a large, well-staffed, and organized teaching hospital in the more sedate capital of New York State. To say that he faced a massive cultural change was an understatement. He was blessed that many of the nurses had served during wartime and would remind him that things could be worse. The young doctor looked at one bleeding man and said to himself, *I'm lucky that the blood on my scrubs is from someone else, not me.* He put a lid on the scramble of mismatched feelings that bombarded him when he was threatened and thought, *they need me at my best.* And that is how he performed.

Still, early as the week of his late-night shifts progressed, a black man began shadowing him when he walked home at midnight. He headed up the hill to his new apartment but was initially alarmed, seemingly being stalked. Wondering if he should be worried about the location of his new apartment, he brought it up to one of the nurses on his next shift.

She asked him if he was wearing his scrubs walking home and perhaps had a stethoscope around his neck or sticking out of his pocket. He answered "Yes" to both. The nurse said, "We're allowed to park in the front lot and are escorted to our cars each night. You are lucky. Someone must have picked up out as one of the nice guys. They've observed you for a full week in the ER, and the patients must have respected how you respected them. When they feel cared for by you, they want to care for you by protecting you. You are correct. This is not the safest neighborhood. So they have decided to make sure you get home safely. We care for the people in this jungle, and they, in turn, guard us against harm. Soon, they'll get to know you even without scrubs. That doesn't happen to just anyone."

This, of course, was many years later and unknown to Saul at the time. But it just may be part of a legacy that Saul was beginning to comprehend. Saul realized that Morris's lack of racial bigotry was part of a bigger picture. He saw that his father's inclusive nature extended beyond race. Morris had a broader understanding of what he used to call the "Gray shade of life." By that, he meant that things were not always black or white, good or bad. This philosophy influenced his approach to religion as well. Although he and Leah kept a kosher home, if they were in a non-kosher home, he would eat what was served, respect his hosts, and recognize that religious traditions do not even need to be absolute.

Years later, one of Morris's grandsons would describe a similar story during the Black Panther turmoil of the late 60s. He was beginning work as a new ER doctor at the largest county hospital in Oakland, California. Oakland was at the center of violence in this dangerous and tumultuous time of the Black Panthers and numerous conflicts in the Bay Area,

He described that as the week of late-night shifts progressed, a black man began shadowing him when he walked home at midnight. He headed up the hill to his new apartment but was initially alarmed, seemingly being stalked. Wondering if he should be worried about the location of his new apartment, he brought it up to one of the nurses on his next shift.

She asked him if he was wearing his scrubs walking home. He was. She said, "He wasn't there to harm you but to protect you. You'd been observed for a full week in the ER, and the patients must have respected how you respected them. When they feel cared for by you, they want to care for you by protecting you. You are somewhat correct. This is not the safest neighborhood. So, they do that to make sure that you get home safely. We care for the people in this jungle, and they, in turn, guard us against harm. Soon, they'll get to know you even without scrubs."

He was followed home every night he worked the ER for the year he was there.

Saul saw that Morris's lack of racial bigotry was part of a bigger picture. He soon saw that his father was inclusive in many ways. Morris had a broader understanding of what he used to call the "Gray shade of life." By that, he meant that things were not always black or white. He approached religion that way. Although he and Leah kept a kosher home, if they were in a non-kosher home, he would eat what was served, respect his hosts, and recognize that religious traditions do not even need to be absolute. Morris had strict guiding principles, but absolutes were always open for interpretation.

This ethical philosophy was consistent with Morris's upbringing. In Judaism, the Torah is considered the fundamental law, complete axioms, but often expressed in obscure terms. Early on, Jews argued about what the Torah really meant. How did it apply to their daily existence? How would they interpret it to deal with the moral situations they encountered? In Saul's mind, this was similar to the Supreme Court's haggling about our constitution. The document is supposed to explain exactly what our rules and rights are. However, just as one group of Supreme Court judges think something means "X," another may be absolutely sure that it means "Y."

When reading about Supreme Court cases in the paper, Morris used to tell Saul a story. "A rabbi and a Supreme Court justice walk into a bar. The Rabbi says, 'It is good to be here, your honor, to sit down and share schnapps with you.' The justice replies, 'But Rabbi, what is truly good?' The Rabbi replies, 'I don't know, let's taste it and find out.' "So it goes with Talmudic interpretation. For Saul, Morris was a softer, gentler, flexible interpreter of the Torah. The

Talmud? For Morris, that was something people were still debating or arguing about. He would say, "To each his own, as long as it is consistent with the Golden Rule."

Morris read widely in the field of philosophy. He found a simplified version of Spinoza consistent with his belief. Morris believed everything in nature is part of nature and follows the same laws. Since he saw men demonstrate creativity, reason, and intuition, Morris thought men would exhibit varied behaviors. He saw happiness and liberty as reasonable goals of ethical conduct. When asked how he measured this for himself, Morris would say, 'As long as I respect that guy looking back at me in the mirror each morning, I guess I'm OK.' Morris's philosophy of accepting Spinoza's belief that 'God is not the creator of the world, but that the world is part of God' would likely not get him elected president of either a Christian or Jewish congregation. But in many ways, 'Like father, like son' was an epithet that applied to Saul.

Leah and Morris, especially Morris, were also devoted to entertainment and travel. That was Morris's source of happiness. He enjoyed opera and would often attend performances and go to the Yiddish theater. Morris would play the same famous operas over and over on his beloved phonograph at home. But traveling when funds were available was the most fantastic, special treat.

They made three trips back to Russia and three times, the Torahs were smuggled out and brought back to be donated to the local synagogues of his sons. Eventually, Saul brought one to the synagogue, of which he and Rachel became members in Des Moines.

Initially, Morris was delighted about the Russian Revolution, expecting it would bring freedom to the Jews and all the people in the country. However, he later became disenchanted as his hopes never came to fruition. At that time, he bought land in Palestine so that his sister and her family could move there if she wanted to.

The trip back to Russia to visit his sister Rebecca and her husband Ben was met with some reservations by Leah. Indeed, she would be happy to see Ben, who had been so kind to her. But Rebecca, in any of the six languages Leah could speak, was a mean bitch. Before Leah left Russia, she never dwelt on how mean and vicious Rebecca's behavior toward her had been. But Leah's pain could never be forgotten. Leah, however, would not ruin the trip for Morris because of old hurt feelings. She knew she and Morris had long benefitted from their decision to leave. It led to them working incredibly well as a team and helping their children to prosper. Maybe Rebecca, by so alienating Leah, had given her the courage to come to America when she did.

When they arrived, the couple treated them warmly. There was not a mean look or sarcastic word from Rebecca. On the contrary, she was a personable and gracious host. One day, she approached Morris almost secretly and insisted that he come to the attic with her. A pair of large, ordinary candlesticks was covered with a quilt in a trunk.

"Are you allowed," she asked, "to light the candles in America?"

Morris stared at her in astonishment. "Of course." He explained how, in America, everyone was allowed to pray as they wished, even Jews!

Leah lights the candles and says the prayers every sabbath night. "So why are you hiding your candlesticks?"

Rebecca replied, "Praying is no longer allowed. If they hear or see me, even my grandchildren will report me to the authorities, and I will be put in prison or sent to Siberia as an enemy of the State. I am an old woman now, and I am afraid for my life. Even my grandchildren will renounce me." Her voice trembled, and her eyes filled with tears as she spoke, the weight of fear and betrayal etched deeply into her face.

Morris just stared in disbelief, his heart aching with a profound sorrow for his sister. He felt a surge of helplessness, his mind racing with the injustice of her plight, and he reached out, placing a comforting hand on her shoulder, wishing he could do more.

 "Please take the candlesticks with you to America and give them to your daughter to light candles on Friday nights and to remember me." Her voice broke as she pressed the candlesticks into Morris's hands.

Morris returned home with the candlesticks, the weight of Rebecca's plea heavy in his heart. Leah used them every Friday, her prayers now tinged with the bittersweet memory of Rebecca's hidden faith. When the time was appropriate, they were passed on to her daughter, who eagerly asked, "What was Aunt Rebecca like?" Leah paused, her eyes misting over. "She was a woman of great strength and sorrow, my dear. Lighting these candles connects us to her courage and her spirit. She lived in fear but never let it extinguish her faith."

"Well darling, back home, life was difficult. So let us just appreciate what we have from her."

"OK, but tell me more about her."

"Better you should not know." Keeping knowledge from kids is one thing, but Leah occasionally wondered why Morris never helped Rebecca and Ben move to America. She was not unhappy that Rebecca was in Russia and that an ocean separated them. But still, she wondered. Morris had brought the rest of the family over. Why not Rebecca and Ben? Leah had never told Morris of Rebecca's treatment of her! When asked about his failure to bring his sister and Ben to America, Morris told Leah that he'd offered, but Ben felt that he was too old to make the transition when it had become possible.

Her trips to Russia aside, Leah's favorite destination was Paris, and she especially enjoyed a resort on the sea in Dubrovnik in Croatia. Later in life, Morris and Leah wanted to enjoy spending the cold winter months in California or Florida.

On one of their trips to the Middle East, especially Palestine and Africa, they were in Ethiopia. There, Morris met and was impressed by a young Jewish man who wanted to come to America to study medicine. Morris helped the young man. After he was living in the United States, the young man would come to their home, especially for holidays. On one such visit, Morris and this medical student went to services on the Jewish high holidays. Men in the orthodox shul did not want this young man there, claiming he couldn't be a Jew because he was black. Morris's potentially hot, hasty temper rarely flared, but a giant argument ensued this time. Morris picked up the Torah he had brought back from Palestine and given it to the congregation, leaned it against his shoulder, marched out, and walked to an empty store where Morris said he was going to set up his own shul and reportedly did!

Oh my, how strongly do our genes and history repeat themselves? The same doctor grandson we talked about a few minutes ago, at the time of his Bar Mitzvah, similarly conflicted with his Rabbi. However, the details were different from what Zayde Morris encountered.

Throughout the young boy's preparations for Bar Mitzvah and confirmation, he witnessed within the congregation what he felt were significant issues of man's inhumanity to man. He thought these things should be addressed, discussed, and perhaps remedied. The Rabbi disagreed and forbade even one spoken word about this in the boy's Bar Mitzvah speech.

The yelling was likely as loud as what Zayde had experienced. However, not wanting to risk jail, stealing the Torah was not an option. Instead, the grandson said that using the Torah his grandfather had brought from Russia would insult his memory. As a result, he refused to use that Torah for his prayers. When the service was over, the boy never returned to services in that sanctuary again.

Phillip, the older brother of the bar mitzvah boy, had a similar conflict with the more senior, rigid Rabbi. The Rabbi had insisted that the two brothers pray in a specific, well-prescribed manner with the frequency, when, where, and how the Rabbi's interpretation of Jewish Law demanded. This did not sit well with the brothers. Having had his battle with the Rabbi, our bar mitzvah boy just said, "No way, no how," and ended his involvement in the conversation as Morris had. He hastily walked away.

The older brother chose to continue battling, but to no avail. He drove away, never to return to that shul again. His anger was sufficient that he would have absconded with the Torah his father had given to the shul if he could have. When asked why he didn't, he told people that the Torah was his father's gift to give and not his to take back.

But let us take a moment to examine the other gene pool from which Saul emerged, Leah's. Whereas she, too, had a temper, she also shared Morris's tolerance. Leah had many friends, Gentiles as well as Jewish. Although she kept a kosher home, did Friday night services at home, and attended school regularly, her two best friends were not Jewish. One was a Negro and a Christian; the other friend was an Armenian woman. Compared to her cousins, she was well-educated and very artistic. And whereas her husband offered the children wisdom and stability, he was sterner about discipline. Leah offered them comfort by cuddling in a down quilt when needed.

Leah was also very involved with others' welfare. She participated in many Jewish women's projects and food banks. Saul recalled that she shared Morris's broad view of everyone's worth. When Saul was a young child, he would look forward to the end of each week when his father would come home and give each child five pennies. Father and mother had a specially decorated box in the kitchen for contributions to the Jewish National Fund for Palestine. After his parents gave him the five pennies, his mother insisted that two of his pennies be put in the JNF special box.

After that, a man would come around every couple of months, enjoy tea with the family, and exchange the box for an empty one.

But in addition to the JNF box, Leah had made and decorated another box for the Armenians. She insisted that Saul and all the kids put one penny into the Armenian box. The two cents Saul had left would not buy him the coveted ice cream cone he wanted that cost three cents. Sometimes, Saul would purchase candy. Soon, he learned to save money to have cash for the ice cream cone.

Years later, when Saul was home, his mother was ill and asked Saul to do her a favor. She said the Armenian box was full and asked him to take it to the Armenian Church. When Saul arrived, he approached a priest, telling him he was there to give them the box. The priest responded, "Oh, our beloved Leah's son. Is she well?" Saul told him of her minor illness and that she would return soon. The priest then told him how, when he and a small group of poor Armenians first arrived in Detroit, Leah, a Jewish woman, was one of the first persons to come, greet them, and offer them friendship, food, and other help. Though she and her husband were relatively poor, even struggling, she regularly gave them money. "Though not of our faith and poor herself, she reached out and helped us when we were poor strangers in this new country." No neighbor or relative other than the kids and Morris knew of the Armenian box.

When Saul was beginning to approach moving to Des Moines and starting a state-wide Jewish newspaper, he understood the importance of community and a large circle of inclusiveness in that community.

"So now, my fine gathered friends," Elijah stood but continued, "I can see that everyone is very attentive, although cold, and attempting to stay near the heat of the fire while trying to move away from the smoke. I suggest that we call it a night. Before we do, please consider this a story of immigrants that still applies today. Perhaps with different variations of the struggles and resolutions, but the pains and needs don't change."

And Elijah wasn't entirely done, after all. "But out of this, what are we to learn? First, a deeper understanding of one's life partner leads to a more empathic connection. That connection is a big part of the mortar helping partnerships to survive. This is the kind of perspective that Rachel lacked, perhaps through no fault of her own."

Chairs folded and slid back under the rigs, campers quickly disappeared into the warmth of their rigs, and Elijah imagined a cup of hot tea, perhaps with some brandy.

Chapter Twenty-four

Elijah awoke at the crack of dawn, glad to see the new day. He stepped outside, stretched, and gazed around. Everything was still quiet. The sun was just short of peeking above the mountains to the East, creating dazzling, dancing colors on the substantial cumulus clouds coming in from the Northwest. Clouds that otherwise could have seemed threatening appeared alive and full of excitement. Elijah found the view inspirational. Mornings like this started the day with what he called desert charm.

Looking out the window and seeing Elijah without coffee, Mary Ann poured two cups, stepped out, and offered one to Elijah.

"Why thank you, Mary Ann. Such service!"

"Well, now Elijah, just because I haven't brought you coffee before doesn't mean you should conclude that I'm incapable of such behavior," Mary Ann said with a playful smile. "Who knows? I may be trying to entice you into revealing other secrets about our mysterious couple."

The two smiled amicably. Elijah took a sip of his coffee and chuckled. "True and well put, Mary Ann, but until I drink some of this coffee, I'm afraid I'm without witty retort."

Mary Ann glanced at the horizon, her eyes reflecting the morning's colors. "Beautiful morning, isn't it?"

Elijah nodded, taking in the view. "Yes, incredible in so many ways. So what are you and Horace going to do today?"

Mary Ann sighed, stretching her arms. "Not sure about Horace, but I'm going to nap. Didn't sleep well last night."

Elijah raised an eyebrow. "How come?"

Mary Ann looked thoughtful, her gaze distant. "Well, our discussion last night stirs something within me."

"Tell me."

Mary Ann continued, her voice thoughtful, "In some ways, you hit it on the head. There are just not enough 'tell me' requests in life." She paused, taking a deep breath. "I agree that Rachel didn't have enough information to truly understand Saul. But I started to look at my own family. I see my grandchildren suffer because they don't honestly know their parents. Or, in my mind, even their intended marriage partners. Both of my granddaughters are engaged."

She leaned back in her chair, looking up at the sky. "In some ways, the same issue is relevant for me. I try to put my best foot forward. That can be beneficial but also deceiving. It can hide a lot. And I'm not talking about putting your dirty laundry out for everyone to see. But knowing someone's history, their pains and pleasures, struggles and successes can be part of the mortar that cements a relationship."

Mary Ann glanced at Elijah, her eyes reflecting a mix of emotions. "For example, for whatever reason, I very much like to get birthday cards. No big deal, right? But to me, it's important. But I've never shared that importance with anyone. And the result is that I haven't gotten a birthday card from one of my grandkids since they were out of grade school." She sighed a touch of sadness in her voice. "That's not earth-shaking. But by withholding, I've cheated myself out of pleasure."

Elijah opened a chair and sat down. Mary Ann sat back in her chair and then continued, "It was funny. I was thinking about a move we made a few years back. There was a couple we had grown very close to in the city we moved from. We felt that we'd grown up as adults with each other. We'd met as newly married couples. We all shared some births and even deaths together. We were inseparable socially. We took vacations together and enjoyed meals together. When we moved, I missed them horribly.

But now, a few years later, I feel a more emotional loss from a couple of girlfriends I grew up with and knew through college. That seems strange to me because we've had no real connection as adults besides Christmas cards and occasional phone calls. So why do I feel more connected with my old friends than my best friends?

Because the girls I grew up with knew me better in many ways. We all knew each other's parents, what we went through with them, the good and the bad, and what we learned from them and about them. We shared the anger and love for our parents that we felt in real-time. We shared our dreams, our self-doubts, and even our silliest of secrets. Yet even though our parents would tell us old stories from when they were kids, what music they liked or classes they hated, they never would reveal their pains about losing their first girlfriend or boyfriend and not what they lied to their parents about. So, I know my school friends' fears, worries, pleasures, losses, and happiness at a different, maybe even deeper level, than I even know my parents and my best friends, and certainly my kids and grandkids.!"

Elijah saw the impact this was having on Mary Ann. "Things like that happen to us. Maybe because different times, different ages, and different relationships lead to different kinds of feelings that we share."

"I'm sure you're right. But maybe a more important reason is that we feel, 'Who cares.?' And I don't know the answer to that. But it's really bizarre."

"Bizarre how, Mary Ann?"

"Well, a couple of weeks ago, my granddaughter and her fiancé dropped by to pick something up. It was a Sunday, and I asked what they'd been doing that weekend. She told me about a movie they enjoyed. It was some exciting mystery. But they spent little time describing the mystery. Instead, they proceeded to describe the flashbacks, the back story, I guess they call it, explaining the dilemmas of the mystery. But if grandma makes comments about her backstory, they never seem to show any interest."

 Anyway, that's still what kept me up last night, wondering if I've missed so many opportunities with so many people by not even saying, 'Tell me'?"

"So, I guess you're thinking that one of the main problems between Saul and Rachel is they hadn't said, 'Tell me' before they said, 'I do.' And you may be right about that, Mary Ann. I'm sure that all of us have some lost opportunities. But that doesn't discredit the connections we do have. Use your awareness of the importance of 'tell me.' If you want to deepen those relationships, you still can. Also, you've got many years left to reveal to your kids and grandkids."

Mary Ann just looked at Elijah and smiled. "Ya, if they're the least bit interested."

"But that's my point. Your reluctance is your fear that they won't be interested or that they will think less of you in some way."

Mary Ann got up, looked down at Elijah, still sipping his coffee, and said, "Thanks for the therapy session," and left.

Elijah finished his coffee, checked the air pressure in his jeep's tires, and drove to a favorite desert spot. It is a well-used old watering hole for riders and animals alike. Elijah began to think about real people with real struggles and successes. That joy helped focus him as he contemplated the next story-telling phase. He knew what the others didn't yet. The story was about to take a sharp turn, but it was nearing 10 AM when the group would reconvene. *OK, it's time to stop daydreaming and get back to work.* Elijah thought. He finished his last piece of beef jerky, tightened the top of his thermos, and headed back down the hill.

And at 10:00, everyone met, ready as ever to continue. Mary Ann seemed rested as Elijah looked to see her smiling before he began, "OK, time to review. Are we dealing with a fairy tale or a pipe dream? After all, what do we know of Saul thus far? Growing up, he had many partial successes in a variety of settings.

Or was what looked like success really just survival? Even victory by the skin of his teeth? No one really knew. He'd shown perseverance but needed to improve in the commitment arena. He had eschewed the rigid structure and boundaries of a law school degree or a medical school education when his parents offered them. No, the routes pursued by his younger brothers were not his cup of tea.

So what was in his cards? What would be his cup of tea? Let's rejoin his story."

Hanging around the newspaper offices in Detroit, Saul would read the news feeds that chattered daily about situations in the farm belt. Some stories were horrible and shocking. So many farmers were already losing their farms, even before the Depression started. The climate was one of anger and sometimes desperation. For example, in a small Iowa town where the banks were legally repossessing many farms, a mob of angry farmers burst into a courtroom, pulled the judge from the bench, and tried to make him promise that he would not take any more cases that would cost a family its farm. When he refused, they threatened to hang him.

Saul was not an economist. But he was aware of what he saw around him. The farmers in some areas of Michigan were in trouble. From his time in Detroit, he knew people operating a loan shark business. That business was prospering. That was a tiny birdie in the coal mine for Saul. If that business is good, others must be bad. If a company is in trouble, employees wind up hungry. He had wondered if even high-flying Detroit was sputtering. He worried that the engine of growth might start to falter. But he wasn't an accurate prognosticator. He did not see that the House of Cards was about to collapse. But he did see the battles raging between the gangs, union strikes, and unavailability of credit, all occurring when an increasing immigrant population was fighting for jobs in Detroit. What did all this mean to him? That he would be better off elsewhere.

In Saul's mind, the rush to Des Moines started out only as a mission to explore new worlds and conquer them. He was also looking for an escape from Detroit. He was not just running from the law or mobs. He was also hunting for a place to 'hideout' from worsening economic conditions in Detroit. Saul hoped a State Capitol such as Des Moines would offer better opportunities. Little did he know that he was running from the ruins of the developing Depression.

If Rachel and Saul had stayed in Des Moines, it would not have been the Des Moines they had seen when they first arrived. Des Moines, too, felt the pain of the Depression. Today, we talk about the Great Depression as bad and even horrible. But the tragedy was immense. It's like one of those situations where it is easier to feel empathy for a dog whimpering by the side of the road after being hit by a car than for feeling empathy about thousands of children suffering from malaria in Africa. Similarly, it is easier to feel compassion for one starving person in the street than empathy for ten thousand starving people in your state.

Reading about the Great Depression or hearing about the Depression, one cannot truly feel what it was like.

Elijah stopped, looked around at his reading group friends, and suggested they focus. But there is a vast difference between facing forks in the road and facing the chaotic maelstrom required to negotiate a traffic circle with five or six exits and entrances. The Depression of the thirties was a three-dimensional traffic circle.

As hard as it is to feel the total weight of the worldwide Depression, let's look at the existing economic fabric, a material that Rachel and Saul would have to sew into to make a living and home for themselves. For this couple, the impact of the economic collapse wasn't something to be pitied or ignored by the side of the road. It was the road they were to travel. Let's look at what this traffic circle was like for Rachel, Saul, and many in America and the rest of the world. There were many roads leading into the traffic circle our couple was negotiating. Each lane had its own unique impact.

Before WWII, the United States economy was already badly upset due to WWI. That war had a profound impact on the underpinnings of how families or individual people lived and survived. In addition to the losses from death, many returned home from the war suffering from pain and impaired function caused by their mutilating injuries sustained during the war. For many, there were no economic or physical solutions offered by the government. One example was those soldiers with damage to their faces. Besides the pain and horrible disfigurement, these men were not seen as heroes but treated as inhuman misfits. The improved warfare technology, new explosives, gases, and machine guns far outstripped the advance of medical science to deal with such injuries. The surgeons who worked to repair war damage had no texts that outlined the medical procedures or surgeries. Instead, the doctors made it up as they went along. Warriors abandoned by their government spoke to the government's ineffectiveness in solving problems. This was a strong thread in a road full of barriers and broken promises that everyone, including our newlyweds, had to negotiate.

Likewise, the new technology highlighted the inadequacies of our own war machine should there be future wars. Our economy was pressured to develop new technologies for any future armed conflict. Yet government economic conditions limited their ability to ramp up for the next war. Inadequate funds may have limited better alternatives for defense and nondefense projects.

The end of WWI brought significant pressure to bear on the farmers who were asked to increase the production of crops and livestock to help feed the worn-torn countries of Europe. Having enjoyed good prosperity during the 1910s, the farmers were glad to buy more land, get better equipment, and respond to the challenge of feeding Europe. However, as Europe recovered, the export demand for American farmers decreased, and prices correspondingly fell. As a result, it became harder and harder for the farmers to pay the loans they had acquired to expand. As a result, farmers suffered throughout the 1920s, even before the Depression. Saul found this to be a meaningful thread as he traversed the countryside of Iowa.

The steep slope of the downhill slide quickened. Factories and stores were shutting down nationwide. At first, a thousand or two jobs were lost here or there, and soon, millions of families were destitute. There was little in the way of government support for the man or family on the street. The newspapers published the names of those who received welfare payments then, and people thought welfare was a disgrace. To this point, people who fell on hard times refused to go on government welfare only as a last resort. But, in the face of starving families at home, more signed up for welfare payments. Soup kitchens were beginning to emerge in larger cities. Unions were no longer fighting to expand and make more money but battling to save jobs.

Some people had the resources to weather the storm. Morris had been frugal and had not burdened his real estate holdings with debt. However, his position was challenging because some tenants couldn't afford to pay their rent. Yet, Morris needed to pay for utilities, taxes, and insurance. And there were maintenance costs to consider.

But whether in Detroit or Des Moines, where he and Rachel settled, the Great Depression hugely impacted the country and the promise of Saul's role as a newspaperman. The economy was far from hitting on all cylinders. The engine of growth stalled. As he prepared to develop and publish a new newspaper, Saul recognized a House of Cards in the making and anticipated the crises to come.

Saul was glad to be employed in Des Moines but wondered if the community could continue supporting his endeavor. *Would there be enough additional money floating around Des Moines to help sustain a newspaper?* Some wondered if the United States was heading for a revolution. Bread lines were forming. Soup kitchens were the last resort of many. A vast population, including Rachel and Saul, wondered what the federal government would do."

Elijah smiled at his listeners, "I guess if we were in that situation, we'd be wondering, too. But I can tell you, our story is about to enter one of those complicated traffic circles. So, to ensure you all have the strength and wherewithal to handle the stress, it might be best to get some lunch and a couple of hours of rest before we go on. Mary Ann, thanks again for the coffee." The group began to break up and head for their rigs. Many had already started to argue about the politics of the Great Depression. Elijah just looked at them, shook his head, and laughed.

Harry looked at Elijah, "What are you laughing about?"

"Just thinking about the wisdom of hindsight. It seems that we find a whole lot of wisdom in hindsight." He gave a big smile and headed for his rig.

Chapter Twenty-five

Elijah stood behind his camping chair, holding the back, not for support, but because his mood was pensive. Then, he began, "When we're thinking about complex traffic circles, it's nice to give some examples. To see how other people negotiate them. Maybe if you've been to Paris or tried to navigate an insane seven-circle circus in London, you learned the secrets from the cabbies there. But Herbert Hoover was one of the best negotiators of traffic circles, maybe not when driving, but certainly in negotiating complex decisions. But we'll see that even someone so brilliant and caring a man as Hoover will sometimes be outside his lane, unable to negotiate the complexity of a complicated circle.

Many of us living today only think of him as the person who caused the depression. But Hoover was a brilliant, caring man who was out of his element when he personally entered the political foray. For most of his glorious career, Hoover found and developed projects, both industrial and charitable, as an independent citizen. He negotiated with the governments of many nations to accomplish tasks that prevented starvation to many, feats that the governments, independently, only dream about. Yet, onto this highly successful lane in his traffic circle of life merged a lane of malignant relationships with politics. In his case, it was the Republican party of that era.

His biggest navigation mistake was a failure to not strongly oppose those in his own party, who falsely believed that limiting imports would solve the economic crises in America. And that traffic circle error precipitated a crash. His second failure, causing a multiple pileup, was not being more supportive of people badly injured in the crash. This was the opposite of his previous behaviors in life.

President Hoover was an exceptional man. He was born in Iowa but was orphaned at the young age of 9. So, as a child, he made his way to Oregon to live with a relative. That turned out poorly. Mostly, he did chores for his uncle and never went to high school. But he was self-taught in many ways and somehow managed to wangle an admission to the first class at Stanford University, from which he graduated. There, he majored in geology, where, subsequently, Hoover demonstrated his creative and critical thinking skills and applied them to a career in mining, which would eventually make him a wealthy man.

To help finance his education, he co-founded Stanford's first student housing cooperative. "Romero Hall." Although a mediocre student, he gained organizational skills by participating in student politics and was a student manager for the baseball and football teams. He helped organize the first Stanford University versus California big football game, a tradition still alive today. While at Stanford, he interned under an influential, economically successful geologist. He was encouraged to seek a career as a mining geologist.

The mining industry was chaotic. It involved working internationally from China to Australia. Others say that Hoover traveled as many as 250,000 miles in one year. He was first a consultant and eventually a partner to the most significant mining firms. He was seen as an "Engineering doctor to sick mines." At first, his only concentration was on production and product. But then he became a supporter of labor. In China, when he saw poor workers performing poorly, he instituted reforms for workers based on merit. Whether helping with laborers or creating other mining improvements, he never failed to take advantage by investing in his own successful finds and mining improvements. By 1914, he was worth over 100 million dollars in today's money.

When the U.S. entered the war in 1917, because of his organizational skills, Hoover was appointed food czar. He recruited thousands of volunteers and created policies, organizations, and rules to avoid food rationing but still feed the Allied Powers besieged by food riots and starvation in the countries at war. After the war, he was charged with providing food to Central and Eastern Europe, where 400 million faced the possibility of starvation.

He served as a close adviser to President Wilson throughout the Peace Process. He supported the League of Nations and advocated restraint from burdening the Central Powers with harsh punishments. In that strong opinion, Hoover picked the correct lane in the circus. Others, greedier and perhaps vindictive, failed to follow Hoover's lead. Many thought, and John Maynard Keynes said in a speech: "... if the totality of Hoover's realism, magnanimity, and personal disinterestedness (about the peace settlement) had been followed, the world would have had a good peace." But that was not to be.

After the war, Hoover became aware of the devastation of famine on the children of Europe. This ensured his transition from private entrepreneurial life into public life. His organizational skills were outstanding no matter where he operated. Hoover turned the government organization handling feeding Europe into a personally financed private organization specially designed to provide food for the children of Europe. Despite the opposition of Republicans, he also sent food to Germany and Russia.

As an adult, Hoover made almost every decision, and every lane he chose achieved its desired end. Maybe he was blindsided by his own success. If anything enhanced his image, it was his handling of a food shortage in Belgium. The German Army occupied Belgium but wouldn't take responsibility for feeding Belgium, which relied heavily on imported food. The British refused to lift their blockade of German-occupied Belgium unless the U.S. government would supervise the imports as a neutral party. As a private citizen and with the cooperation of the Wilson government, Hoover established the Commission for Relief of Belgium. He encouraged government and private donations, and the Commission became an independent republic of relief with its own flag, navy, factories, mills, and railroads.

Hoover used shuttle diplomacy to persuade Germany to cooperate. He crossed the North Sea forty times to arrange to set up distribution. He convinced the Chancellor of the Exchequer of Great Britain to allow citizens in England to send money to the people of Belgium. As a result, nine million war victims received over two million tons of food. An American diplomat considered Hoover the only man living, not holding public office, who had negotiated cooperation between the British, French, German, Dutch, American, and Belgian governments.

Politically, Hoover was progressive. Many felt he promoted a balance between capital and labor and included the role of government in regulation and funding. Therefore, he adhered more closely to Adam Smith's original description of a capitalistic system in his willingness to include the government in the economic equation. Nevertheless, he believed the government's role should be small, as a facilitator and regulator. He believed that business and private individuals should be financially responsible for the welfare of the people.

As Hoover was always concerned about growth, a high priority was promoting an increase in exports. As Commerce Secretary, he promoted progress, safety, and modernization. He chose to run for president as a Republican in 1928, primarily because Coolidge decided not to seek a second full term. Coolidge had served six years after President Harding died. Since Coolidge had a reputation that his greatest talent was effectively doing nothing, the Republican Party looked for a candidate who had a reputation for getting things done. Hoover was chosen and then ran against the first Catholic candidate, the Governor of New York, Al Smith, a Democrat.

If supported to do so, Hoover might have preferred running as a Democrat. Some speculated that if he had done so, the democratic party, Hoover, and, indeed, the country would have been better off. Of the two rather boring candidates, Smith stood out because he was Catholic. The 1920s were not a decade that had done much to subdue bigotry, and soon, anti-Catholic sentiment led to a widely circulated story that if Smith were elected, the Pope would rule the United States in Rome. Hoover won handily.

At the time of the crash in 1929, Hoover did not want to see people put on a permanent dole. Instead, he encouraged the private sector to maintain jobs and wages and increase investment spending to provide a fiscal stimulus. He urged state and local governments and philanthropic groups to help support people out of work. However, that philosophy could not be supported by the finances of the individual states or private philanthropic endeavors. Only the Federal government could print money and establish wider programs to support the people.

Hoover's battle to get private industry and local governments to stabilize employment was totally lost when two members of his party, Senator Smoot and Representative Hawley, passed the Tariff Act. That Act of 1930, commonly known as the Smoot–Hawley Tariff, was a law that implemented protectionist trade policies in the United States to be retaliated against other nations and resulted in a worldwide contraction of international trade. That was likely the straw that broke the camel's back. With the demise of local credit, bank shuts down, and decreased worldwide commerce, we had a worldwide depression, not just one in the United States.

Although Hoover seemed philosophically opposed to the views of the Republican congressman, when votes were taken to establish wide-reaching tariffs, many people opposed the bill, including economists. However, for whatever reason, Hoover felt that he could not break with his own party's leadership and had to sign significant legislation for his Republican Party. In doing so, he forever lost the support of that party's progressive wing. It proved to be the single worst decision of Hoover's career.

Feeling his own fatigue, Elijah called for the lunch break. Heads were swimming, imagining living during these tumultuous times.

Laura's was the loudest comment heard as the group mingled, each heading for their own rigs. It's hard to trust any politician to do the right thing. Charlie's retort was, "Maybe, but wait 'till you're on the firing line with multiple options, demands, risks, and turns in the road, and maybe you'll see it a bit differently."

During their afternoon session, many were energized by a cup of hot chocolate or coffee. Elijah assumed the additional thermos bottles near the chairs primarily represented sufficient caffeine to counteract after-lunch doldrums and keep people alert. He began:

"We left the thread with Saul and Rachel moving to Des Moines. It was a time of tragedy, poverty, hopelessness, and even starvation for man. Nevertheless, Des Moines was a city in some distress, but perhaps not as bad as many. Let's pick it up there."

Saul likes his fingers in multiple pies. He was a jack of all trades and master of none, so what did this all mean as they started in Des Moines and contemplated the start of the paper? In many ways, Saul and Rachel began life in their new location more comfortably than their immigrant parents or most folks moving to a new city. They had made friends who supported them. They were quite capable and organized and had some savings to last for a while. Saul wanted to help alleviate the suffering he foresaw starting to engulf a wider population. But he couldn't be sure how he could be of help. He had committed to creating a state-wide newspaper with editorials written by him. Would that give him a seat of influence as a community spokesperson? Could he do that?

"Now, what do folks think? Does he really have the stuff to start a successful state-wide newspaper? Or was Saul just a lightweight?

Larry, without hesitation, leaned forward in his chair and said, "Yes, a lightweight. I think he is an exciting guy, but he couldn't mine gold if he fell into a pot of it. He has no experience pulling off what he's trying to do with a state-wide Jewish Newspaper. He should get a job. Maybe even as a reporter and have a lovely family. Enjoy his life with Rachel. He's never been a leader."

Elijah, noting many murmurs and nods of agreement, suspected a nearly unanimous opinion about the dismal possibility of Saul's potential success. But, he added, raising an eyebrow, "What if I told you that in addition to the plans you've already heard, Saul was also requested to take on a job as editor of the State-wide Iowa Democrat Newspaper? What do you think now?"

Larry blurted out, "I'd think that he's in so far over his head that he'd need a lifeboat to survive." His voice carried a hint of bitterness, and his eyes darted away. "I've seen people get in over their heads before. My father tried to start his own business after the war. Thought he could handle it all, but it crushed him. I don't want to see Saul go through the same."

A few laughed, but mostly, the group sat stunned. This was new news to them. It hadn't come up in the story at all.

Charlie shook his head, a cynical smile playing on his lips. "Maybe it's a lie. You're just making up too much now, Elijah.

Next, you'll bring in little green men from outer space." He leaned back in his chair, crossing his arms. "I used to believe in big dreams too. Thought I could change things. Got chewed up and spit out by the political machine. It's a tough world out there."

Elijah smiled slightly and replied, "Nope. All true. A mystery perhaps, but all true."

Tim leaned forward, his eyes bright with curiosity. "No one else wanted to do it?" He smiled slightly. "I like to think maybe they saw something in him that others didn't. My own boss took a chance on me when no one else would, and it changed my life. Sometimes, it just takes one person believing in you."

"Could be," said Elijah, "But why give that plum to an unknown?"

Nancy said softly, "Something like that has to be because of who you know, not what you know." She glanced at Elijah, her expression wistful. "But maybe, just maybe, he's got something special. My grandmother always told me that sometimes, opportunities come to those who dare to dream big. She came to this country with nothing and built a life. Maybe Saul can do the same."

"OK, but who did this young guy from Detroit know in Des Moines? Certainly not just a rabbi and bookstore owner.?"

Mary Ann frowned, her fingers twisting the hem of her sweater. "True, this was the state's capital. That meant the center of state politics, too. Getting that type of plum job, editor! How does that happen? Was he really mafia or something and had pull or threats he could make?" She sighed deeply, a hint of envy in her voice. "I remember when my brother tried to get into politics. He was so passionate, but he didn't have the connections. It broke his spirit when he couldn't break through."

"Pretty strange, is correct. Unusual is right. Almost unheard of wouldn't be too much of a statement. But sometimes, weird things happen." Offered Elijah. "We need to take a bit of a detour and learn more about Saul and his peripatetic wanderings, maybe some things that happened even before he and Rachel got married."

Elijah quickly stood up with a tilt to his head, a smile on his lips, and a nary another word said," 'Till tomorrow." He then wandered slowly back to his rig, reinforcing the feeling that he knew something no one else knew.

Mary Ann and Nancy stayed behind to douse the fire. Then, finally, Mary Ann said, "What do you think of Saul? Could you be hitched to someone like that?"

"I don't know. Saul would keep you on your toes all right. He says all the right things when push comes to shove, but is that just part of his con, or does he mean it? There is sort of a secretive element to him."

"Just like Elijah, huh?"

Nancy stopped to think. "I've never thought about that. There is such an age difference. But they both have secrets, that's for sure." Smoke was no longer apparent, so the two hugged and headed to bed.

Chapter Twenty-six

Elijah strolled nonchalantly over to the group, the crunch of gravel under his boots punctuating the quiet evening air. "What's up, guys?" he said, his voice carrying a casual confidence.

Tim aggressively pushed. "I'll tell you what's up. We're playing poker, and you just went all in. So, I'm calling. Show me your cards."

Harry laughed, "Are you that brave, Tim, playing real poker, or is it just when you're speaking metaphorically in the desert?"

Elijah agreed. "Really pushing to see if I were yanking your chain about Saul and the new editorship, eh Tim? Ok, I'll show my cards."

"You forget Saul's background and his backstory. He was well known at the Detroit Free Press. Some considered Saul a wannabe cub reporter. That really meant little in status. But an unusual event occurred.

The country had been growing quickly. This created confusion, chaos, and power struggles in Detroit and many large cities. A tug-of-war grew between Eastern European immigrants, industrialists, and wet and dry believers regarding prohibition. Political machines were slowly being built.

With the uncertainty and turmoil occurring in the country, the editor of the Free Press back in Detroit hankered to learn more about political machines. If political machines were established in Detroit, that would change the locus of power. That could be a significant change in city governance. Such occurrences would impact reporting the news.

He decided to send a reporter out to investigate some of the ins and outs and the workings of how Tammany Hall operated in New York. This was the supreme example of a political machine. Any editor worth their weight would want to know how this organization functioned.

What was being done in New York had yet to be copied in Michigan. But as editor of the most important paper in the largest city, Saul's former quasi-boss wanted to know more. The managing editor was not looking for investigative data for a story. He wanted an education. He wanted nothing for print. His friends and contacts at the New York Herald had told him stories about Tammany Hall that had whetted his appetite for more. But listening to them over beers was like hearing rumors about a country's governance. He needed to know more about how this power base developed and operated and about its relationships with the news outlets.

The Free Press editor needed someone to educate him about the workings of Tammany Hall. Such information always gives a good editor a heads-up on newsworthy items. He wanted an outside investigator, someone not to be seen as a reporter. He needed a bright, social person who could mingle and gather information informally. He wanted this person who had no formal connection to the Free Press, "Just in case...." Therefore, he called that wannabe reporter, Saul, who always hung around and asked him to take the assignment. Saul seemed sharp and had proven himself trustworthy.

"Look around Saul, meet people, ask questions, but nothing too confrontative; you don't want to end up in the East River," the editor told him. "Use the contacts I'm giving you to make other contacts. Have a good time. Go to parties. Just learn what you can in a couple of weeks and come back. Give me calls and keep me informed. This turned out to be Saul's graduate degree in investigative reporting. Also, the contacts from that trip were to become instrumental and vital in the future.

There is much to reveal about Saul's trip that occurred before he and Rachel moved to Des Moines, but probably only a few parts are essential to our story.

First, diving into this task, Saul's interest in politics and political strategy went through the roof. He would have been happy to stay in New York for months, not a couple of weeks. Second, he spent the time of his life sightseeing and attending parties, but we'll save some of those stories for another time. This all happened before he got married. Third, he got to go to a lecture arranged by the New York Herald for reporters, given by Louis Howe, a former reporter for the Herald who had a lifelong relationship with FDR and Eleanor.

When Saul began his inquiry into Tammany Hall, he found that secrets were as scarce as untouched sand in a bustling desert. The history of the organization was known quite openly, and its rise and influence were like the sprawling roots of an ancient tree deeply embedded in the city's fabric.

So, only a little investigation was required to compile a thorough history and fulfill his mission.

Tammany was initially local, started by two brothers who'd been active in local politics for years. It began by promising support to the influx of immigrants who would gladly trade votes for jobs and other political favors, such as citizenship. But unfortunately, what was viewed as salvation by one group was seen as corruption by others.

The Tammany Society grew to have chapters all over the state. Once they gained administrative positions in city governments, they became the defacto government of not only the city but the state. They gained much power by helping the immigrants, mainly the Irish Catholics. If this were a business model, it would be: Give me your votes, and I'll reward you with the patronage of jobs and opportunities. The Tammany Society controlled the local patronage. They used that resource to build core districts with precinct leaders who served as ward bosses. The bosses marshaled the local voters and, in return, could provide more jobs, thereby satisfying the voters in turn. It was like a self-serving, self-growing glob of power or muck, depending on your point of view.

While waiting for Howe's lecture, Saul conversed with the woman beside him. It was unusual to see women at a function of reporters. Her name was Margaret. She explained that she worked for the Herald and helped make all the arrangements for the lecture. Being interested in politics and having been the main worker bee, she felt entitled to attend the speech. After a fascinating talk and Q&A with Howe, Saul, and Margaret, confined to the middle part of the row, stood and chatted, waiting for the aisle to empty. Saul had asked her many questions about working for the Herald and Louis Howe. Saul's curiosity and inquisitiveness led Margaret to say, "A few of us are meeting with him for an on-the-record interview and then just BS and drinks if you'd like to come along. It might be interesting for you.

Saul struck gold, not just in meeting a beautiful, bright woman but in being invited to sit around with a smaller group, the dim light of the chandelier casting a warm glow over the room. The scent of cigars mingled with the faint aroma of brandy, creating an ambiance of sophisticated affinity. After the interview, Howe and even a smaller group that included Saul but not Margaret went to a local speakeasy where the discussion continued until the wee hours of the morning. Howe seemed to love the attention and opportunity to pontificate about affairs near and far. Saul ate it up.

Howe became enamored with Saul's interest, attentiveness, and questions. By the end of the evening, only Saul, one other man, and Howe were left arguing. The other man thought Howe was full of shit, so Howe turned all his attention toward Saul, instructing much as a professor or father would about how the world goes around. Saul became a 'yes man' and soaked it all up.

Saul, not wanting to be easily cast aside, offered that he was a graduate student in political history. He wanted to learn more, not from books but from the people involved. "Someday, Mr. Howe, I will teach many things you discussed. So many details can be learned from what others have written. But the real history is the pain of the struggle and the strength of the tactics. That's what I learned so well from you this evening. That's the real history to be taught. I wish I could only learn more. When I think of all the people you know who've shared their life stories, I realize now how lucky you are. That's the meat that gets lost unless it is passed down." Saul knew how to prime a pump and brown nose simultaneously. He was careful to drink less than anyone else. No one noticed or cared.

Getting up and getting ready to end the evening, Howe turned laughingly toward Saul, "Well, young man, if you're so interested and want stories, gossip some would call it, why don't you join me tomorrow evening? I've been invited to Eleanor's home for a party. It's an informal affair, not a sit-down dinner. She would be delighted to meet a young man she could regale. God knows what will be on her mind tomorrow." Saul could only wonder what impact all this would have on his life.

Elijah suggested a bathroom break. Some left, others didn't, but when Elijah returned, he found the group sitting, still in disbelief, not even bothering to acknowledge Elijah joining them. They were too busy discussing the New York trip to pay him any mind. They couldn't decide if the train had gone off the tracks, the worm had turned, or any other of the adages some flabbergasted RVer opined. Frankly, none seemed particularly pertinent, and Elijah just smiled and listened. Soon, the campers were silent, and one by one, they turned to look at Elijah as if he had suddenly appeared and had more dark secrets to reveal.

I can see you all are trying to make sense of this. Let's try to understand it better. Saul described what he had learned about the internal workings of Tammany Hall to his editor in Detroit. Saul kept much to himself. Pertinent to our story, he knew that FDR would definitely run for president. Saul also learned that Roosevelt was seen as a weak, wishy-washy contender by many Democrats and didn't have overwhelming support within the party. Whatever popularity he had had been diluted by his long absence with polio and recuperation in Warm Springs, where he spent most of his time.

Both Howe and Eleanor were ever-present for the convalescence. But Eleanor had her own interests to promote on her many trips. Most of Howe's attention was focused on Franklin.

Listening to the arguing among New York City political activists, Saul heard that all the other candidates advocated top-down solutions to help people who were hungry and suffering. The mantra was that if they solved the problems of the rich, the poor would reap the benefits. Most Republican and Democratic leaders thought the same way. However, Roosevelt was different. He advocated bottom-up solutions in this crisis. Feed the poor, employ the poor, and the rich eventually will be able to use their capital to produce the products the formerly unemployed would now buy. In Saul's mind, Roosevelt seemed to be the only Democratic candidate who believed that way.

Saul felt a deep, gnawing concern for the masses who continued to suffer from the depression. Roosevelt seemed to be the man who saw it the same way. At Eleanor's gathering, Saul sat mesmerized, his heart pounding with a mix of hope and excitement as he listened to her passionate speech about the future. He saw parallels between Roosevelt's marriage and his parents.

Eleanor and Franklin's marriage was also more like a partnership than a loving relationship. This was very similar to that of his parents. After Franklin's infidelity years before, Eleanor created an independent life. Saul's mother did similarly after her husband mysteriously disappeared. Leah did share Eleanor's compassion but expressed it by ministering differently. Eleanor was independently active in politics, joining women's groups to learn more about their needs and interests and traveling to Appalachia to learn more about the poor. Eleanor operated at a higher, more majestic level. That evening she spoke earnestly, no, emphatically about these nationwide interventions. Saul's mother had her own charity boxes for other ethnicities, and Morris was especially careful and helpful in obtaining domiciles for negroes at the neighborhood level. His wife was not operating at Eleanor Roosevelt's level, but she showed no less compassion.

The similarity between the Roosevelt marriage and that of his own parents was not Saul's only new awareness that evening. Saul went over what he'd heard as he sat in his room that night, slowly undressing for bed. Initially, he concluded that the wheeling and dealing he'd experienced between the various power groups in Detroit was precisely the same as the machinations he had heard about at the national political level. There were eventual winners and losers. Politics, wherever it played out, was a power struggle. He fell asleep somewhat self-satisfied with that recognition."

Elijah stopped with this and suggested they let Saul sleep and get lunch for themselves.

Chapter Twenty-seven

As they gathered after lunch, Tim, the self-appointed group spokesperson for uncovering the great secret, attempted to stare down Elijah. "How never having a byline in his life was Saul appointed editor of the Iowa Democrat?"

Elijah smiled and said, "Tim, be patient, and it will pay off. You'll see it did for Saul." So, Elijah, keeper of the key to the secret, went on.

Tim is right. At this point, Saul's formal charge for the trip to New York had been completed. He had the information his editor would want about Tammany Hall and New York City politics. But Saul was not done with New York. He was falling in love with the 'Big Apple' as it had been called since the 1920s. The museums, the shops, and the energy of the people on the sidewalk energized Saul. He initially contemplated staying and looking around for a couple of extra days. Then, when Mr. Howe suggested they might get together for a drink the next night, Saul's decision to stay in the big city was solidified. He had quite an experience.

Drinks turned into dinner and cigars. Howe was nothing if not a man who liked to be a mentor, especially if he had an audience that rose and fell on his every word. Even an audience of one was sufficient. Saul continued to soak in the information. He learned that the Democratic convention in 1932 was likely to be brokered. That meant no one had enough votes to win on the first ballot. Subsequent ballots would be marked by much wheeling and dealing, begging for votes or bribing for votes.

"It doesn't matter," said Howe. "Just get the votes somehow." Saul learned that whoever prevailed would have to form a coalition with the power of Tammany Hall's Northeast wet votes and the Southern States' dry, racist voices. Picking up a farm state or two and an outlier state from the West would further be needed to control the convention. Saul knew that this was an extensive get. Overwhelmed, he turned his attention toward the home front.

At dinner with his new mentor that night, Saul asked, "So what does all the convention coalition stuff mean for the individual states such as Michigan?"

"Well, regarding conventions, it is essential in a state like Michigan or any state to keep the delegation together. To get them to pick one candidate and stick with that candidate through thick and thin. You need this for your own good, even if it isn't for Roosevelt."

"Why is that important?"

"Because without a block of votes to offer, your state's delegation or political party has no power at the convention. If all your voices are split between several candidates, no one will pay you much mind. Even if your party wins, you'll have little or sometimes no political patronage after the election."

"And you think that candidate should be Roosevelt?"

"Yes, son, I do. He is best for this country, and we must beat Hoover. He can do that. Do you really want to be involved?"

"Sure. But I'm not convinced Roosevelt is the best person for the job. And I'm not ready to campaign for him yet."

"Well, there are other opportunities at play. We are talking politics here. Politics is the struggle for power. Consider your home state of Michigan. As in many states, the people in Michigan are angry but feel helpless. They don't know how to remedy their situation. They don't know who or what can help them. People who are unsure of what to do often vote for their party's preference for the national presidential election.

Saul listened intently, feeling a pang of empathy for his fellow Michiganders. He knew that helplessness all too well—the frustration of seeing neighbors and friends struggle without clear solutions. As Howe spoke, Saul's mind wandered to the faces he passed daily, filled with worry and uncertainty. He felt a burning desire to make a difference, but the path ahead seemed shrouded in fog.

However, the first rung of the ladder to political power is the selection of delegates for national conventions. Here, of course, you want to decide on the best candidate. But more importantly, that selection must be unanimous. Unless you can deliver a block of votes at the convention, you will have no bargaining power, influence, and less patronage even if your candidate wins the national election. The average person doesn't recognize the political value of block voting. There are a bunch of local parties throughout the state. Someone has to pull that together."

"Sure, Mr. Howe, but what can I do about it? Community organizing is not precisely my cup of tea."

"Well, Saul, you said you wanted to touch the suffering. So, it's now your turn. But, look, nobody else is doing it either."

"Ya, but I still......"

"You have an opportunity to give the message to your editor. The Free Press is influential. Suggest he take on the job of educating his readers. This is good editorial material. And it can be used without being partisan."

It was only at the end of the very long evening that Saul had an epiphany. The more they drank, the more intense Howe became. He was adamant about beating Hoover but doubted the Democrats could turn things around without someone like Roosevelt in the White House.

Less intoxicated and desperate to learn more, Saul pushed and pushed Howe about why it had to be Roosevelt. Howe was a thin, sickly man with great enthusiasm but never demonstrated much energy. Saul was surprised to see him nearly explode. "Good god, man, this is not about a neighborhood mob brawl in Detroit. The person in the White House will be instrumental, not for the people in a four square block area off Livernois Avenue, we're talking about the lives, the welfare, in some cases the very survival of over a hundred million people."

Seeing Howe, so angry yet nearly in tears, Saul said, "Yes, I can see the national political struggle has a far wider impact than a gang war in Detroit, but why Roosevelt?"

"Because I know him. I've been with him since he was a freshman senator in the state legislature and became a leader opposing Tammany Hall control. So, I know his philosophy and his caring. Look at his plan as governor of

New York to establish a civilian conservation corps, giving young men jobs and improving public lands. He'll work from the bottom up, not just placate the wealthy. He cares about the masses. He demonstrated that better than any other candidate running. That's why it has to be Roosevelt."

The following day, Saul left New York for Detroit to report back to the editor of the Free Press. After all, they paid for this excursion. A train ride that long can be delightful or frightful. Money for a roomette almost assures a better night's sleep and more comfort. However, his New York hotel bill had been covered by the Free Press. He had to front his train ticket, hopefully, to be reimbursed by his editor. But being frugal, like Morris, Saul opted for coach fair. No sleep-inducing roomette.

Tired of holding himself upright in coach and unsuccessful in sleep, Saul decided to head back to the dining and club cars. As he walked through the cars, he couldn't help but notice the stark contrast. In the club car, people were jovial and full of laughter, seemingly untouched by the Depression. It irritated him how insulated they seemed from the reality that weighed heavily on so many others, including himself. The memory of the struggling farmers and desperate families in coach gnawed at him. How could there be such a divide, even on a train? Some talked about the depression but had not yet lost their money or fortunes. This differed from the farmers or folks who lost their homes early before the intense depression started. Coach riders were not as fancily dressed and were far from jovial; they just stared out the window. There was little conversation and no laughter.

Restless, Saul wandered aimlessly from car to car to loosen his cramped muscles and overcome boredom. Finally, late in the dark hours, he approached the end of one of the sleeping cars with nothing to see out the window. There sat the porter, waiting in case he was called by a traveler lucky enough to be able to have a roomette. The porter was as bored as Saul and had learned to sleep sitting and waiting. He was attuned to any sound or movement that might require his attention. With Saul approaching, he quickly stood up and inquired if he could help.

"No, no. I didn't mean to disturb you. I'm out for my nightly walk without my dog."

The porter chuckled, "Yes, sir, it can get rough riding at night and not sleeping. Nothing to see out the windows and a funny quiet with people trying to sleep in coach, what with the snoring, babies crying, and people coughing, but no talking. But sir, I'm sorry, but unless you have a compartment, you're not supposed to be up here."

"Ya, I guess not. But since I am here, could you answer a question or two?”

"Glad to be of help if I can, sir."

"What kind of changes have you seen on the trains, you know, the people since the stock market crash."

"Well, there aren't as many people riding. Indeed, fewer people in the sleeping cars. Getting so that they hook up with fewer of them on each trip than they used to.”

“Are any of you guys losing jobs?”

"Not at first, but fewer sleeping cars means fewer porters. So yes, I lose a trip now and then. But at least I still have a job."

"Does that make things tight at home?"

"Oh yes, sir. My wife used to work in one of the big hotels in New York. There aren't as many people traveling there, either. So some weeks, she doesn't get called in to work."

"Sorry to hear that. I know it's got to be hard, and you constantly worry about what is next."

"Yes, sir, that's true."

"Noticed any difference in the people in coach?"

"Well, I'm not allowed back there, but the conductors tell me coach ride is often down, too. Also, people seem more fidgety, on edge, and depressed. Before, they were going on vacation, at least lots of them. Now, they are traveling somewhere because they have no choice. But as I said, that's just what they tell me."

"Do you guys who work on the trains talk about all this much?"

"Well, I guess, while we're waiting in the station, sometimes hours for the next train, nothin' much to do. Lots of guys play craps, nothing big, no money. But there is always some hustler around. But guys try to keep it light, joke, and kid one another. Sort of like usual. No use beaten a dead horse."

"What do you mean by that?"

"Well, when we talk about it, the talk is when those guys in Washington are going to fix this and do something for the little guy. All those Washington people talk about is banking this, banking that."

The porter, warming to Saul, continued, "Meanwhile, we are scared to use any bank! That is if we have money to put there. That isn't happening too much these days. Sometimes, I can pick up a few bucks by hauling trash or helping people move when I'm not working the trains."

"Ya, everything is pretty crappy for a lot of people. It must be tough for you." Unknown to friends and family, there had been times in Detroit when Saul, although well-dressed and self-assured, would have gone hungry without stopping by the family home for a meal. Saul's curiosity came with an equal dose of empathy.

The two stood in the poorly lit corridor and listened to metal clanging as the giant machine catapulted forward.

"You know what the hardest thing is? My people brought me up in the South when I was younger. Then said we had to go North. They promised that everything was better up North and we'd get jobs. So, I'm used to things being challenging. But I don't like it when I see my kids hungry. They try not to complain, but I can see there are days when it's hard for those kids. But Mama is getting pretty good at stretching things out."

Saul stood, quiet and motionless, except swaying in rhythm with the train rocking. That rhythm seemed to repeatedly say, "Ho hum, ho hum, ho hum" to him as if to say, "Nothing's getting done, nothing's getting done, nothing's getting done." A sickening mantra.

Finally, Saul interrupted the silence. "Well, sir, you're a good man. I'm sure your family appreciates all you do, and it sounds like you have a wonderful family, one you can be proud of. I wish I had solutions to offer, but there is still hope. You know, there is an election coming up, maybe something better. I don't know. But I'll be good. Get back where I belong. Get out of your hair."

"Yes sir, you be no bother. Enjoy your trip now. Need any help, you just ask. We can just all hope together." What he thought but didn't say was, "Hope ain't going buy us a loaf of bread."

Saul walked back to his seat to seek some sleep.

In his kaleidoscopic mental turmoil, a moment of irony made him smile. A moment of self-awareness. It went something like this: "Well, I did it again. I inadvertently break all the rules. The first reporting rule is not identifying or becoming part of the story. I left Detroit to act as an independent investigative reporter. True, I'm returning as a political machine expert, but enmeshed in political advocacy and, even worse, leaning toward a particular candidate. I wonder what will become of all of this. I believe in what Roosevelt stands for, but what do I do about it? How do I get on his train, other than just voting?"

A lengthy ride based on coach fare gave you a spot on a stiff horsehair seat and perturbed, sometimes screaming muscles. Thinking about the pluses and minuses of his experience with Howe was exhausting. Finally, as the hours rolled by, Saul fell asleep with his head leaning against a cold window. His seat companion would have told you that in that position, Saul snored loudly. Fatigued from all his New York activities, he'd hoped to ride through the night and get some sleep. Saul felt lucky to get a window seat. This gives you the added benefit of a cold window against which to lean your head. But trains rock and roll. So do the heads placed against a cold window. As your body, including the head, seems to move a second or so behind the side-to-side movement of the train, one can suffer many minor collisions between one's head and the window while trying to rest. By the time Saul arrived in Detroit, he had a splitting headache. He vowed to get a roomette if he ever took such a ride again.

Saul returned to Detroit and gave a full report to his editor, who listened with amazement. Saul felt a mix of pride and frustration as he recounted his experiences. Yes, he had gained impressive access and uncovered valuable information about Tammany Hall, but the editor's detached fascination irked him. Didn't he see the human element, the desperation Saul had witnessed firsthand? As the editor pondered the potential for a new column, Saul's heart sank. He wanted to do more than just inform—he wanted to ignite change.

He liked Howe's idea of introducing more education about the election process. The editor thought he might have the paper run a unique weekly column discussing that. But apparently, he thought aloud, for Saul responded, "Oh, I could write that for you." The phone rang. The editor answered it, said, "Just a moment, please," covered the receiver with his hand, and said, "Thank you, Saul, good job. Just what I expected." Then he kept bobbing his head toward the door and used his other hand to shoo Saul out of the room. No column for Saul.

Nevertheless, Saul was still stoked about what he had done. He couldn't wait to tell Rachel about it. But really thought it best to only discuss his crash course in politics, leaving out all the other details, especially about the parties and the women hanging around like groupies. He had been more than chaste, likely scared by their advances. But that was not a conversation he wanted to have with Rachel. So, instead, he alluded to the political information and mostly dropped names when he told Rachel about the trip. In her mind, it was impressive, just like so much of what Saul talked about, but elusive, just like what Saul spoke about.

"Ok, guys, an excellent place to stop. Let Saul's brain rattle around, and yours as you figure out your moves if you were Saul?"

But I want to bring up another issue. We'd originally planned to move on down the road a time or two, take a break, and get different views as the story progresses. We've been here outside Parker for a while. We could move down to Brenda or Hope, but it's up to you.

"Elijah, why don't you let us talk about it tomorrow and give you some feedback."

"Seems about right to me. Happy dreams. See you tomorrow. My brandy awaits my attendance."

Chapter Twenty-eight

As the group gathered, someone questioned where Elijah was. It seemed as if no one had seen him all day.

"I saw him get in his jeep. It looked like he had lunch and one of those camera tripod things. I asked him where he was going. He just said, 'Lookin' for ghosts,' and left." Cindy said.

Horace, somewhat irritated, "What the heck did he mean looking for ghosts? Doesn't this story he's telling have enough mystery in it? So he's got to bring ghosts into the plot?"

Mary Ann laughed, "Well, you know there is that ghost town around here. Maybe some of his previous storytelling groups live out there, dead or alive."

Henry, chiding everyone, "Ya, there is that Swansea place. Mostly an old mining town with more old foundations than structures. You only get there by dirt road. It's really a lovely location that provokes memories. Maybe he went there to get away from us or from having to fess up to Tim that Saul didn't get any editorship. Think about it, guys. He prefers scary ghosts to you. How does that make you feel? Let's talk about that."

"Can it, Henry. I'm really worried. What if something happened? What if he had car trouble and couldn't fix it?" Cindy's voice trembled, her eyes wide with fear. Henry, trying to keep calm, said, "If anyone is prepared to deal with trouble in the desert, it's Elijah. He's got experience."

Nancy interjected, "True, but imagine if he's injured out there, alone. The desert isn't forgiving. Every hour counts. We can't just sit here and wait."

 The group discussed the various issues on the table without any agreement, from what to do next about moving the camp to rescue Elijah from the ghosts. No one knew anything about ghosts, but somehow, they seemed more interesting than Elijah, his potential troubles, or the issue of moving camp.

Elijah wasn't that late at all. The morning or afternoon starting times were usually suggested before breaking up. When no earlier time was decided, the group often began in the early evening or when the last person seemed to arrive after supper. Tonight, Elijah was the last to arrive. When he finally appeared, dusty and tired but safe, the group erupted in relief. Cindy rushed forward, tears streaming down her face. "Elijah! We were so worried! What happened? Are you okay?" Elijah, taken aback by the emotional welcome, nodded at everyone but remained silent. Nancy handed him a cup of hot chocolate, her hands shaking slightly. He smiled as he took it, trying to ease the tension. "OK, what's up, folks?"

Silence, Elijah frowned and thought, 'How unusual.' But said nothing as he sipped the marshmallow-laden drink. He waited. He'd spent most of the day waiting for nothing. Spending time waiting for something was easy also.

If you are a group leader, silence is almost always more anxiety-provoking for someone in the group other than you. That makes it easy and wise to wait it out. Everyone benefits more if you do it that way. Elijah waited.

"Hey Elijah, we've sort of been wondering where you've been," asked Larry hesitantly.

"Oh?" silence

Larry, more directly, "OK, where you've been?"

"Swansea." The two continued the conversation.

"How was it?"

"Quiet, beautiful."

"Just curious, any particular reason you went there?"

"Actually, yes, there was." Silence

"Mind letting us in on it?"

"No, of course not. Most stories are about people and events. Sometimes, it is easier to focus on just the events and forget about the people. That's especially true if the people are dead. Connecting with them and feeling what they felt isn't easy. So going to a place of remains to see what they saw and try to feel what they must have felt or thought helps me to connect."

Nancy, "So you're OK?"

"Sure. Why wouldn't I be?"

Tim added, "Well, we don't want this story getting you down."

"Thank you, Tim. I'm just fine. OK, fit as a fiddle and ready to move this story along. But I'm just beginning. We've got a long way to go! So, let's get started. But first, have you people decided about moving or staying put here?"

"We seem happy here, very pretty, near the river. There are things to do during the day if we don't meet. Easy restocking of provisions. Nothing to move to or for as far as we can see."

"OK then. We'll begin."

Returning to where we were with Saul before discussing his fascinating side trip to New York, we find Saul anticipated writing future editorials for the Iowa Jewish News during the upcoming elections. He continued to be interested and mine data about what was happening nationally. No one had CNN or good, comprehensive national news sources in those days. He'd frequently run over to Pinky's store and pour through papers from other cities to get information. Pinky didn't mind. He felt this was a small contribution to a larger, more significant cause. He was glad to be of help. Mostly, Pinky really enjoyed talking with Saul, especially about politics. They were fast becoming good friends.

Once back in Detroit, after his New York trip, Saul called Mr. Howe to thank him for his help. The call was warmly received and appreciated. Howe enjoyed being a mentor. The student ruse, since revealed by Saul, which had originally been used to gather information, initially irritated Howe. Nevertheless, Howe appreciated it as a reasonable step for a worthwhile journalist to use to accomplish his objective. No harm, no foul. He asked Saul to keep him informed as Saul's future unfolded, especially if he got a reporting job at the Free Press.

The subsequent move to Des Moines that Saul and Rachel made would come soon after Saul's trip to New York. That New York experience intensified Saul's concerns about the future. He more personally felt the seriousness of the current economic climate, which urged him to continue educating himself.

Once Saul was confident of his permanent situation in Des Moines, he called Howe to let him know where he had landed. Howe was fascinated to hear the story about the creation of the Jewish Newspaper and wished Saul the best of luck. He felt proud of his mentee. Saul pushed Howe for more information about Roosevelt's candidacy but got little.

These infrequent but sometimes lengthy conversations occurred between Saul and Louis Howe. Rachel couldn't shake the gnawing anxiety that had taken root ever since Saul's relationship with Howe began to deepen. Every time Saul mentioned Howe, a knot tightened in her stomach, twisting with fears she couldn't quite name."
Over lunch with Lois, her mother surrogate, Rachel finally voiced her growing unease. 'I can't stop thinking about Saul's trip to New York,' she confessed, her voice trembling. 'There's something about his connection with Howe that just feels off. I know it sounds silly, but I'm worried.'"
"Well, honey," Lois said, "Do you worry that he is doing anything illegal or unsavory with those people in New York?"

"No, not really. Saul has so little contact with the New York people that nothing could happen. There is no money being sent back and forth or something like that. At least as best as I can tell. No, just an occasional phone call."

"Well, are you worried about any of those women among the partygoers in New York? It is a pretty fast crowd, from what I hear."

"I doubt a long-distance love affair would be on Saul's plate right now! Also, I love my husband and think he's handsome and loyal. He was a snazzy dresser, dancer, and smooth talker in Detroit. But New York style? I don't think he'd be up to playing in that league."

Lois laughed, too. "What then?"

"That's the problem. I don't know. I guess the best face I can put on it is that it is another black hole, almost a secret that Saul's involved in, and I am not."

Lois, somewhat taken aback, sympathized, "Well, that could be pretty scary considering your imagination and tendency to worry!"

"Ya, I guess so. I'll just have to live with it. Sorry to bother you with it. So, what do you recommend at this restaurant?"

"They have an excellent Chef's salad. And I know you like Russian dressing. Theirs is wonderful."

"OK then, Chef's salad with Russian dressing it will be. Thanks."

Even after their conversation, Rachel's concerns about Howe gnawed at her. She lay awake at night, staring at the ceiling, her mind racing with worst-case scenarios. The distance between her and Saul seemed to grow with each passing day he spent entangled in political machinations.

Saul answered the phone a few weeks later to find Mr. Howe on the other end. Howe started and continued at length with benign chit-chat, asking questions but showing little interest in Saul's details and answers about getting the Jewish News off the deck. But, on the other hand, he asked many benign and inane questions about Des Moines.

Finally, suspicious, Saul interrupted. "Excuse me, Louis, you are not one for chit-chat. You obviously have something significant on your mind. What is it? Spill it out. Are you OK?"

"Oh yes, Saul, quite OK, thank you for asking. And you are correct. I do have something on my mind. And I won't waste more of your time beating around the bush. I have a proposition for you, but I want you to hear me out before you respond, OK?"

"Yes sir, sure. What's up?"

"Well, how would you like to help out your state."

"What do you mean, Louis?"

"Well, regarding conventions, it is important in a state like Iowa or any state to keep the delegation together. We've talked about that. You know how strongly I feel about that. I think you can help make your state important by spreading the word that whoever the candidate is, the delegation must stick together. Without a block of votes to offer, your state delegation has no political power. Picking up a few Midwestern or Western states will be important to everyone fighting for the nomination. If all your votes are split between several candidates at the convention, no one will pay you much mind. Even if your party wins, you'll have no political patronage after the election. You know we discussed that."

"Right, I remember. So what? How am I, a nobody, a citizen here but a few weeks, going to lead the lemmings up the path away from the edge of the cliff? Are you magically bestowing me that power?"

"You jest, but I'm adamant. The Democrats need to get united, pick one candidate, and stick with that candidate through thick and thin. Iowa needs this for its own good, even if it isn't for Roosevelt."

"And I suppose you think that candidate should be Roosevelt?"

"Yes, son, I do. He is best for this country, and we must beat Hoover. I think he can do that. Do you really want to be involved?"

"Yes, but you seem to suggest that I can influence that, be the savior. I'm powerless. Maybe, sure, I might be able to do something after the delegate convention within the state. But until a candidate is chosen, I must be impartial as the Iowa Jewish News editor."

"Well, there just may be an opportunity here. National political interests are fragmented and scattered around various localities in Iowa. No one recognizes the political value of block voting. There are just a bunch of local parties throughout the state. Someone must pull them together."

"Sure, Louis, but what can I do about it? Community organizing is not precisely my cup of tea."

"Well, Saul, you said you wanted to promote the interest of the suffering. So maybe it's now your turn. But look, nobody else is doing it either."

"Ya, but I still....."

"Wait up a minute. Before you keep protesting, let me tell you why I called. I have a far-fetched idea that just might work. There is a state-wide democratic newspaper in Iowa that operates out of Des Moines. That's where right where you live. Isn't it?"

"Yes, but I don't work for them."

"True, but I know that the editor is leaving to take a job with a paper in Chicago. I met this guy years ago, and he asked me to call the editor in Chicago and give him a good recommendation. He's OK, but nothing to brag about, but I did the guy a favor and indicated he'd be a solid employee. I guess that's all they were looking for. He just called to tell me that he got the job. I told him I was thrilled for him.

After I hung up, I got to thinking. This guy owes me one. What if I call him and tell him I have a recommendation for his replacement? A real go-getter who can inspire others. The party needs just that kind of person, with a national election coming up. So, I'll suggest that he recommend you as his replacement. Likely, since they have no current pathway to hiring someone else, with my friend's recommendation, you could get the job! Would you be up for that job?"

"I already have a job. Publishing and editing the Iowa Jewish News."

"Well, getting that off the ground is going to be a form of community organizing, too, isn't it?"

"Sure, a big job, in fact."

"OK, well, you could combine the two to travel the state. There is probably a lot of overlap of concern. The Jewish population in Iowa is a diverse target group searching for information about picking a leader. No actual conflict there. Right? It's not like you'd be working against competing sides. The Jews, like many groups, are impacted by the economic calamity. They'll probably be supporting the Democratic candidate. We'd like to ensure that for the general election and keep them united about someone for the primary battle."

"In theory, you are right. But doing two start-ups at a time would be overwhelming."

"Maybe not as bad as you think. There is already a publisher for the Iowa Democrat. All the production pieces are in place. So is distribution. But we are looking to control content. That is the editors' bailiwick. That's the chance you've always wanted. There are even reporters on board. So, you wouldn't have to recruit there."

"I might be able to do it, but it would also strain Rachel greatly. I'd have to discuss it with her first."

"Sure, sure. But this guy is leaving shortly and with practically no notice... He'll jump at the chance to do me a favor and maybe stay in the good graces with the publisher he's leaving behind. Take a risk, young man. Now is your moment. Grab it."

Saul softly replied, "OK, I guess, but...one question, Mr. Howe. What content are you proposing? Again, as editor, I cannot advocate for one candidate before the convention.

And when would this start anyway? What is the plan as you see it?"

"OK, the job is educational, pure, and straightforward. First, you use the power of the press to teach people the importance of having a block delegation. No splitting of votes. You let them argue, debate, yell, scream, and get it out of their system, pushing for their favorites. Encouraging them in this way will likely promote greater interest as various groups become more active competing for their favorite candidate. That will give you an opportunity to re-emphasize the importance of the issues. What candidate supports the best plans to help the people? As convention time draws near, you emphasize that not everyone can be thrilled with the choice. However, as a group, if the state has clout at the national level, you must find one candidate everyone could feel OK with, primarily through three ballots at the convention. Tell them the main overall goal is to create political power for Iowa. The importance of that power trumps anyone's personal first choice. Like it or not, that's called politics. Ride that horse. Just make it an all-Iowa horse."

"OK, how do I push for unity but support FDR simultaneously?"

"Let's begin with what you believe is a necessary governance policy for the next president. No matter what candidate the Democrats choose to push, the philosophy must be simple and straightforward and become the mantra of every article you write. Success in the primaries or even the general election does not come from debating numerous specific issues. Instead, voters ultimately rally around opposing something they are mad about or someone they trust will care about them and understand their pain.

So first, what do you believe? We've had long discussions about the Republican failure from their top-down philosophy. They think that if laws and taxes improve things for the wealthy, that success will trickle down to everyone else. It hasn't been confirmed. You can point out that the top-down policies of Hoover haven't worked nor benefited the working class. Use the power of the press to support a bottoms-up philosophy and policies to help the masses now. That is what is needed.

If you decide to support Roosevelt, you would be using the power of the press to promote his ideas and solutions, not his name. Later, mention him as someone who uses a bottoms-up approach. There are good examples from legislation that he has passed in New York. Acknowledge that there are other potentially good candidates also. But write articles about policies that benefit the people rather than candidates per se. Keep the debate alive; all balls in the air. When the time is right, you can write an editorial suggesting that Roosevelt might be a good compromise candidate, but there may be others to consider. Then, questions about Roosevelt and all the others should be raised equally.

You know my feelings about Roosevelt. But if you eventually support him, that must be based on your research, not my approval. But as the Iowa Jewish News editor, if you choose to support one candidate, notably Roosevelt or someone else, during the primaries, you'd have to resign from being editor of the Iowa Democrat. But by that time, you would have supported two fundamental ideas for the Iowa Democrats. The first is the importance of block voting to maintain convention power. Second, the importance of a bottoms-up philosophy in the candidate.

Then, you would write a final editorial saying that you can't be the editor and a partisan, but hearing everyone's arguments in good conscience, you've made up your mind blah, blah, blah...Hopefully, you'll be a leader by then, and others will follow."

"I'm just not sure I can do it or others will follow."

"Therein lies the risk and suffering you asked for, young man."

Tired from his earlier sunny day in the desert, Elijah was ready to call it an evening and started doing just that. Charlie saw him bend over to pick up his thermos. "Not so fast there, Elijah."

"Why Charlie? What's the matter?"

"Don't we have an issue to settle between Rachel and Saul? Rachel wants him to pull back from his connection to this Howe guy. Unfortunately, Saul seems to be moving full speed ahead."

Elijah stood up, stretched his back, and looked right at Charlie, but he said to the group, "I believe he's nailed it, folks. It appears that our two newlyweds are up against it again. Now that most of you've been through a few tugs of war, you could give them good advice. But when you've got significant issues to tackle? Best advice? Sleep on it. You folks should do that. I know I'm going to. I guess I'm the one who has to face the problem. But Tim should be happy knowing how Saul got the brass ring on the merry-go-round. Sleep well. I'm headin' in. Night." And he left.

Chapter Twenty-nine

The group gathered for a desert stew. Everyone brought their two cans of something, meat, veggies, soups, whatever, to put into a homemade large community pot held over a warming fire. The combined elements were blended with a long paddle until thoroughly mixed, and the stew warmed. Rolls, salads, and desserts were spread on a table potluck style. The stew was dished out. Everyone was talking about the day or the story. Several commented on how well the mysterious stew turned out. It usually did. How could it not with several cans of foodstuff all embedded in salt! Finally, as most people were munching on desserts, Elijah moved his chair into a more central position. Attention quickly turned on him.

Nancy smiled at Elijah, "OK, boss, we've slept on it, talked about it, and stewed about it. Your show now."

Elijah began, "And that stew was good. Sort of a mixture of things you'd think wouldn't all go together. So, with that in mind, let's continue in the vein of Nancy's pun."

Rachel and Saul had been apart nearly the whole day. Rachel was already home preparing dinner. She was excited to have Saul come home and try her new recipe. When Saul walked in, he walked right over and hugged her. That felt so reassuring to Rachel.

Saul wondered, "Do we have time for a drink before dinner? Maybe discuss what you did today?"

"No, not really. Everything is just about done. You've gotten home right when you said you would when you left this morning. I figured you'd be tired from being at the grind all day and want to have a good meal. I know that sometimes you don't even have time to eat. So, I'm trying something special. Hope you like it."

"OK, I'll wash up and be right in to help you."

"Just hurry because I'm ready to put things on the table."

His plate was ready for him when he sat down. Rachel had tried not one but three new recipes, and the dish was loaded. Saul looked at the mouthwatering food with anticipation, but his thought was I'm worried my plate is already too full. But nevertheless, he said, "Wow, so much looks delicious. Can't wait to see the latest in what you're dishing up."

"Well, I hope you like it. I always look forward to you getting home and sharing your stories of the day. You are doing so many amazing new things, even for you. I love to hear about the details."

"Right now, I have my mouth full on this roast. All this tastes wonderful. Give me a few minutes to enjoy your creative efforts. What else did you do today but slave away in the kitchen?"

"I'd hardly call cooking a meal slaving away, but I did go out to lunch with Lois."

"How's she doing?"

"Oh, fine."

"What did the two of you talk about?"

"Just the usual. Lois told me about Ben, his new doings at the dealership, and the issues he has with their kids. Their son, Marvin, seems to be growing up just like their father. I don't believe you've met their younger child, Gwen. From what Lois says, she's lovely and quite a bookworm. Lois just asked the usual about how we were doing and whether we needed anything. They've been so lovely and helpful to us."

"And what did you have to add to the conversation?"

"Well, they always want to know more about us. Have we talked with the folks back home? How are they reacting to our new experiences? I guess I've many stories to keep a few girl-to-girl lunches afloat. Lois wanted to know more about what it was like for you working with the Free Press. I didn't know much about it, But I told her about your special trip to New York for them and meeting all those people, especially Mr. Howe. Apparently, Louis to you now."

"Oh. What did Lois have to say about Louis?"

"Well, she was very impressed. You going to a party with Eleanor Roosevelt will probably wind up being the gossip delight of the town. Also, she was impressed that you knew Howe. She didn't know who he was but had heard his name. But I told her that you indeed were not bosom buddies with Eleanor and likely the relationship with Howe was more of a one-off thing, and I hoped it would just run down. You're busy enough without getting all involved with the New York crowd."

Saul had stalled as long as he could. "Ah, New York. You remember that story then."

"Of course. Why wouldn't I?'

"No reason. It was certainly an education for me. But since being there, the whole experience got me more concerned about political issues than I was before I went there."

"Yes, so?"

"Well, it's funny you talked with Lois about Howe today because I got a call from him."

"Oh, Saul, don't tell me you'll make another trip back to New York!"

"No, No. Nothing like that." He then told Rachel about Howe's offer of the political editorship and his significant interest in accepting the position. But, again, he braced for his wife's intense response, having such a proposition dropped on her without warning.

"You agreed to what?" Even louder. "You agreed to what?" Very loud. "Tell me this isn't true. How could you? You didn't even bring this up to me as a possibility so we could discuss the idea before you accepted. No. No. You didn't do something so dumb. What? We don't have enough uncertainty in our lives? Do you need to add this aggravation? For What?"

Rachel slumped into her chair as if worn out. "You must have lost your mind. Did rubbing shoulders with all the bigwigs make you think you could become one of them?"

As Saul started to explain to Rachel, he floundered, like a flailing fish flapping around out of water. He wondered if he should have told Pinky, even the rabbi, or helpful Ben about this rather than starting with Rachel. After all, Pinky or Ben could help Rachel understand the wisdom of what he was doing. But as Saul listened to Rachel, alternating between yelling, crying, and sitting glaring quietly, he thought, "No, bringing in the big guns and outside help wasn't going to work." Actually, it most likely was the opposite. He had hoped that Rachel would help him convince the others. "Fat chance now," he thought. "First, I must de-escalate this before convincing Rachel of anything."

He continued. "OK, OK. Honey, I get why you are not just angry but infuriated. But we will not solve this together until you're calm enough to listen. You have to be able to hear me, too. And there is so much more to tell."

"Oh great, there's more! So, what, are we leaving Des Moines and moving to DC, where you will run for office? Or no, I've got it! You've just been asked to be an advisor to the Democratic National Committee or something."

"No, nothing like that, but maybe with some time..."

"Not funny, McGee."

"You're catastrophizing. The only thing that has happened is that there was a job opening and an opportunity to do something interesting, and I expressed an interest and said yes, maybe, but that I would want to discuss it with you first."

Saul paused, feeling the weight of his words. Did I make the right decision? He thought about the excitement of the new role and the fear of disrupting their lives. This could be a chance to make a real difference, to step out of the mundane. But was it worth the potential strain on their marriage?
Saul shifted in his chair, wishing for a drink of almost anything as a divergence. "Of course, that acceptance was contingent on agreement from you."

"But you told me that you accepted the job!"

"True, but he wanted an answer right then. But there is no contract or absolute commitment. If I change my mind, so what? I change my mind. He was trying to do me a favor. Suppose we decide that it is a bad favor, no big deal. I won't do it. They'll get someone else."

"So, if I said this is not the right thing to do. It is a bad idea; even as a favor, you'd tell Howe no?"

"Well, yes and no."

"There you go with the yes and no stuff again. Is it yes, or is it no?"

"Don't fly off the handle. You gave me an ultimatum. Not vice versa. You want me to give you total control without me being involved in the discussion. I said that we would discuss it. We should both be able to see if it is a good or bad idea together."

"But what if we can't agree?"

"Well, we've been good at developing mutual solutions so far. So why not this issue?"

"But if we can't..."

"We'll face that when and if we get to that point. Why do you bring it up before you've even looked at the idea? The idea may be horrible. I don't know. I said OK impulsively, under pressure. But that served to be a pretty good holding tactic."

Rachel calmly said, "OK, I'm going to consider it. But I'm going to go out for a walk. I need to get out of the house. Please do the dishes while I'm gone."

As she left, Saul sat down heavily in his chair. The kitchen felt emptier without her presence, and the silence was oppressive. He replayed the conversation in his mind, wondering if he had been too impulsive. What if Rachel couldn't see the potential he saw? What if this decision pulled them apart instead of bringing them closer? He rubbed his temples, feeling the onset of a headache, and knew he had to find a way to make her see his vision without alienating her.

Elijah stood up, stretched, and said, "This is a good place for a bathroom break, and to call it a day. We need a night to digest that good stew. Also, with good investigative reporting, you can figure out how this couple might resolve their disagreements. That is worth a marathon session before and after dinner tomorrow. Rest up for it. It will give you a chance to ponder your own personal resolution techniques. Then, finally, we can publish a Desert Storytelling Group Guidebook on resolving couples' disputes." A couple of the men laughed. None of the women thought that was clever or funny.

Chapter Thirty

His hunger resolved by his morning breakfast and adequately caffeinated, Elijah exited his rig and opened his chair. Soon, everyone gathered.

Elijah continued. Rachel returned from her walk. Saul's editorship issue had yet to be discussed. They'd had a lovely, peaceful evening with hot chocolate and books. Rachel brought up nothing the following day, and both shared a pleasant enough breakfast. But they knew that the challenging discussion and the hard work were ahead.

After breakfast, Rachel said, "I guess we better return to the issue at hand. Where do you want to begin?"

Saul smiled and nodded, "I think you really mean; where do I want to begin explaining myself."

Rachel sighed and crossed her arms. "True, but I didn't want to start out by being so blunt."

Saul nodded, leaning back in his chair. "Thank you. But the situation as we understood it when we left Detroit has changed." Rachel uncrossed her arms, leaning forward. "Changed? How?"

"The political and economic reality risks are far more complex and scarier than just adding the work of another task, like the Iowa Democrat."

"You're losing me, Saul. I'm just concerned about adding the burden and stress of another obligation, and you're going off on a big treatise on politics. I think they jumbled your head in New York. We need to stick to the point." A long pause followed. Saul was not defensive. Likely, he felt as overwhelmed knowing what he did as Rachel felt being in the dark. Finally, Rachel broke the silence.

"I know that I'll be sorry for asking, but what could all of a sudden justify the stress of this burden? Even having to have this conversation is frankly driving me nuts!?"

Saul said nothing but slowly rose to make them both some tea. Rachel found it unusual that Saul was totally silent while heating the water. Also, unlike Saul, he was spending an unusually long time dipping the tea bags. Staring out the kitchen window at the street below, Saul's back was facing Rachel. Then, slowly, he turned, smiled, and walked to the table, where he tilted her chin up to give her another good morning kiss. Rather than "Good morning," he probably meant to say, "Sorry about all of this. Please don't feel like shooting me!"

Saul ran a hand through his hair, frustration evident in his voice. "Look honey, whether this is a new reality or one that I totally misunderstood when we started this trip, I don't know, and maybe it doesn't matter. If I missed what was right under my nose, I'm sorry. Maybe we should just pack up and go straight back home. I really don't know! But let me tell you what I know so you can tell me what you think we should do. But just be patient and hear me out. This is no cockamamie, made-up story. What I must tell you is real."

Rachel thanked Saul as he handed her the saucer with the cup of tea. She noticed that his usually stable hand was shaky.

"Let's put everything in perspective as I see it. Then you can tell me what you think and what you feel we should do. A big part of motivating me to leave Detroit was all the infighting with people competing and struggling to find work. I saw opportunities in other peoples' struggles because I helped solve their disputes and other problems. I never sought a union or manufacturing job but did small jobs for many people in all areas. Every commitment needed to be accomplished with personal attention, usually quickly, accurately, and efficiently. I was good at what I did. Then, as Detroit got busier and more chaotic, the nature of my work began to change in a way that made it harder for me to service my clients.

My work facilitated negotiating issues between disagreeing parties, often an employee to a boss, a union head with a small business manager, or an overextended family man with an understanding banker. Sometimes, individuals needed only information they found hard to access. Now, it is all large union committees fighting with boards of directors or an over-extended investor hassling with a big bank controlled by corporate directives. In past years, my personal attention to detail was instrumental in my success. For a few years, my efforts were an easy fix for many people and groups. But current needs were outstripping my capacity. I wasn't a company. I was just an individual.

There was no real future in what I had been doing. Issues of settling a gentleman's agreement by sitting down and talking were now being handled by law firms litigating the issues. Also, I lost all passion for what I was doing. Initially, I felt that I was helping people. But, as things became more litigious, winning rather than compromising seemed to be an end-all. There was no helping there, just an equal number of winners and losers."

Elijah paused and, for emphasis, walked to the side of the seated group. "Saul's explanation regarding his work is quite accurate according to what Lucas was able to find out. But we must also acknowledge that it is patently vague. There is no well-defined example of the "chores" he carried out to help others. When Lucas tried to get details from those who knew Saul when he was younger, all he heard were vague references to the law, mobs, and money lenders. No two stories agreed. So, we will live with Saul's description and accept that he felt great motivation to get out of Dodge. Let's continue. "

Saul continued to share his perspective with Rachel. "RacSo, starting in a smaller place less impacted by the growing auto industry, the unions, and the mob would be easier. Also, I wanted a well-defined job other than as a facilitator. Finally, I was looking for a city the size of Des Moines or other midwestern towns."

Rachel blurted out, "Well, all is good then. When we looked around here, Saul, we quickly felt comfortable, as if this place were better and more workable. You are a fast learner and could likely find employment in many areas."

"True. But now, with the deteriorating economy, the situation is different and worse. This goes far beyond a market crash. The problems for me of a fast-paced, chaotic growing economy in Detroit were minimal compared to those of a current depression of the economy. That is true for all people, not just me or us. Many formerly wealthy people perhaps aren't so rich anymore but can still live a very comfortable life. Others have suddenly moved from wealthy to impoverished. But millions in our middle class and lower socioeconomic groups have lost their jobs and depend on soup kitchens or relatives and friends."

"So, Saul, what does any of that have to do with the editor position for a statewide political newspaper?"

Rachel tapped her fingers on the table, her impatience growing. "So, Saul, what does any of that have to do with the editor position for a state-wide political newspaper?"

Saul rubbed his temples, a pained expression crossing his face. "That's a fair question. When I listened to all those men in New York talking about the current financial situation and their estimate of the downturn, the damage would be much worse than I thought. Unfortunately, their view has been borne out. To be honest, it scares me to death. All our current plans are now in jeopardy. How long will the community in Des Moines or even statewide be interested in a paper that frankly is rather parochial and just my passion? Under the best circumstances, we worried the Jewish paper would be a hard sell. The Iowa Jewish News readers will be more concerned about important news, not just local or State issues, but national ones. I learned in New York that the cause of what threatens everyone, including us, is much more complicated than just a stock market crash."

"Seems to me the market crash was no tiny affair."

"True, but now, hardly the biggest problem. In fact, it was as much of a symptom of the financial crises as a cause. The underlying cause was likely people, banks, and corporations having more debt than they could service. But then, attempts to fix the problems made it worse. By the time I was in New York, the guys I met could not present any convincing solutions. They had many ideas. When someone suggested a statement, the guy in the next chair would reasonably shoot it down. That was depressing. The bleak future made me appreciate the comfort of secure homes in Detroit."

"Saul, that all sounds interesting. But where's the punch line? You and I aren't having a depression summit meeting. I'd like to know whether we're discussing the editorship or a decision to move back to Detroit."

"The problem is a worldwide collapse of the economic system. That impacts Des Moines or Iowa as well as Detroit or Michigan. Depression is everywhere, not just in the United States. Do we have any more coffee?"

"Sure, but running a little low on cream. I must remember to get some."

Saul reached for his coffee and sipped it slowly, "Thanks. I'll make the editorship relevant in a few minutes. Remember? Patience. So that I don't become overwhelmed when I think about what to do, I must organize this in my head. So, I think the first problem is the one that is easy. It is a worldwide tragedy, creating destitute people because of a failing economy.

Next, I need to understand the cause. That is complicated and multifactorial. But the origins at least go back as far as WWI. Then, the US banks loaned considerable funds to other countries to rebuild. Loans that have yet to be fully repaid. That makes the banks less solvent. When a brokerage lends to a stock investor on margin, and the value of stocks falls, the loan on that margin purchase is called. The investor loses a lot and may need to withdraw banked money to pay the debt. This can further deplete banks' holdings. A bank with no money can't make loans. No money, no loaning. No loaning, farmers can't buy seed, new home buyers can't buy houses, and labor jobs vanish as industrial production halts because of lack of credit and customers have no money to purchase products. No manufacturing means no jobs. No jobs mean breadlines and suffering. That leaves excellent questions."

"Oh great. I can't wait, as if we don't have enough questions already!"

"The question is, what are we going to do about it? You can't suddenly just turn everything around; turn the clock backward."

"You know Saul, our Jewish faith doesn't emphasize prayers of supplication. No prayers where we ask God for anything for ourselves. But right now, I think I need merciful intervention, or you will go on all day! We are not here to solve all the world's problems today, but consider the wisdom of your serious, irresponsible commitment made for another editorship.".

Saul rose, seemingly because he was frustrated with Rachel's impatience in fully grasping the importance of understanding the problem before you can come up with a solution. He saw the editorship as participating in a solution. But he knew that conclusion was subtle, maybe even tenuous at best. But if Rachel didn't understand the little opportunity for an answer the editorship could provide, she'd never agree to him doing it. So, he purposefully deflected. Never underestimate Saul's tactics.

Saul placed his hand dramatically on his chest. "Oh, fair lady of my ultimate dreams, the woman of my salvation and foundation of my life, trust me. Have patience so that I can mysteriously fit all the pieces of the puzzle I am describing into a whole meaningful picture so that in the end, you will no longer wonder about the editor position but instead shout from the rooftops, 'Behold, behold! He has arrived at a genius of a solution.' So let us, as willing partners and comrades, Rachel, draw our swords and go forth together."

Rachel, taken aback by Saul's apparent silliness or temporary psychosis, quickly quashed the explosion she was about to release, a small smile tugging at the corners of her mouth.

Her growing maturity sparked a retort in kind: "Well, knight of the roundtable, pass the little cream that's left. Forgive me if I still see myself in a dingy tower high in the air. I do not see myself going forth on a rarely traveled, uneven, rocky, and dangerous path called editorship. Therein, rough with stones and crevices to trip upon, lies the cause of further pain and aggravation. But tell me, did you spend the entire car ride home practicing that monologue?"

Saul started to speak, but Rachel held up her hand for him to stop. She needed to pee, and it was time to end her agony, not getting a quick answer to what she thought was a straightforward question. She glared at him as she stirred cream into her coffee, crossed her legs, and continued, "This is not precisely Hamlet, but remember, he dies in the end with no guarantee that his sins were forgiven. Right now, you're walking close to the edge of the cliff buster. Cleverness and cuteness are not going to get you out of this. You're lucky I use the same cream as you. Remember how he died? Poison. How I see it right now, you are to be or not to be an editor on thin ice? I have yet to hear one word of justification for you, no for us taking on this extra burden."

"Please, my fair lady, faith, faith."

"Listen, dear. I already have Judaism; that's complicated enough for me. So, I don't need to join the Church of Unlimited Bullshit. But what I do have to do is pee, so please excuse me." Rachel carefully rose, held her head high with her nose in the air, and left.

Chapter Thirty-one

Group members began laughing and squirming as they thoroughly trashed Elijah's attempt at mimicking Shakespearean actors. Elijah said, "Don't laugh. I wouldn't be surprised if some of you sound this way sometimes. But while Rachel is gone, we must ask, How do these two people see the same facts so differently?"

But the painful reality was that Saul saw the situation as more widespread than his struggle with Rachel. So, it was good that he could introduce some levity. Saul felt it would be needed on the path ahead for the country, their conversation, and maybe their welfare.

At the same time Saul and Rachel were partying through the roaring 20s back in Detroit, our economy was undergoing significant change, developing like a silent malignancy. Long before leaving Detroit, Saul began to feel the pain. But he was not the only one suffering. While Rachel experienced dinner table arguing as chit-chat, Saul empathically shared the pain of those arguing, aware of their fear of the threat posed by deteriorating economic conditions. Whereas the economy seemed to be marching proudly along, especially in the eyes of the rich, there were dark clouds of warning on the horizon. The reality was that all parties were fighting for a more significant part of the economic pie long before the economy shrank by as much as a third during some years of the depression. Job security was lost long before the unemployment rate went to 25%.

In the hotel lobby, where people partied as if there were no tomorrow, Rachel was toying with men's affection and encouraging their play at the dice game. At the same time, Saul was in the streets, witnessing a house of cards with anger and battles as the socialist and communist parties sometimes pushed harder for unions for factory workers who could barely make ends meet. So maybe the gunshots Rachel experienced in the hotel manifested what Saul had witnessed, rather than some random drunks arguing over a woman.

Elijah paused, "Listen, folks, I don't want to get too personal here, but sitting on the toilet offers a moment or two for great contemplation. Rachel relieved both her physical pressure and some of her emotional pressure. She thought *I need to trust that Saul thinks that I must hear the whole story as he understands it. Otherwise, I won't understand why he wants to do this insane thing. I should let him tell it his way. Patience doesn't cost me anything. Besides, if I don't hear his full appeal, he can think my denial is uniformed!*"

Rachel returned, walking calmly in a relaxed fashion. She said nothing but went to the teapot, rewarmed the water, and prepared her cup. She shared a glancing smile at Saul, which meant, "Do you want more tea also?" Saul shook his head no. Tea prepared, Rachel sat down pleasantly, using both hands to clutch her warm cup to her bent forehead. "Saul, it's not a pretty picture you're drawing. Please continue so that I might understand what I must admit I consider an insane decision."

Saul got up to rinse his empty cup and collect his thoughts. "OK, here is my pitch regarding the importance of the political editorship."

Rachel leaned forward, curiosity evident on her face. "Alright, I'm listening. What's the big idea?"

"To solve this problem, the Republican congress, eventually supported by Hoover, decided that we should stop buying goods from Europe and the rest of the world," Saul began.

Rachel raised an eyebrow. "Stop buying goods? That sounds drastic. Why would they do that?"

"They thought it would stimulate our national economy if everything was produced here," Saul explained. "They felt isolation was the answer."

Rachel frowned. "Isolation? How did they even plan to achieve that?"

"So, the Republicans passed the Smoot-Hawley Tariff Act," Saul continued. "This act separated us from trading with other countries."

Rachel's eyes widened. "Wait, wasn't the world already interconnected through trade by then?"

"Exactly," Saul nodded. "The world was already a large trading organization. We all depended on one another."

"And what happened when world trade was halted?" Rachel asked, leaning back in her chair.

"Everything collapsed," Saul said grimly. "Just as we stopped buying from others, they stopped buying from us. Industry and farmers had less reason to produce as their worldwide customers vanished."

Rachel shook her head. "That sounds disastrous. Did it lead to the depression?"

"Yes, a worldwide depression followed," Saul confirmed. "We're not going to just waltz out of it. Things will likely worsen before they get better."

Rachel sighed. "So their great idea of self-sufficiency backfired completely."

"It sealed the fate of any chance of a quick or easy recovery," Saul concluded. "Everything has gotten worse, and that is likely to continue."

"So, Saul, what do we do? How do we fix this?"

"Short answer: I don't know. I'm curious to know if anyone else does, too. All the men I listened to agreed things would get worse before they got better."

"Saul, Is Hoover that wrong?

"I don't know. Hoover seems to have made a miscalculation in this case. I heard many poorly informed guys like me sit in speakeasies and shoot off their mouths with one opinion or another. The politicos I met sitting around the table, pontificating, sounded surer. They were well-to-do, informed, and not wet behind the ears. They were all politically active, too. They were Democrats and certainly wanted to get to the White House again. Their hunger to win may have made them overly critical. But they aren't exaggerating the problem, but maybe just crowing excessively about having better solutions."

"I'm no expert on solutions or certainly second-guessing Hoover. But an election is coming up. If things improve significantly, as an incumbent, Hoover will win hands down. But if he is wrong, and things don't get better, the Democrats have a pretty good shot at the white house."

"What does all this mean for us? Not just for the country, but for you and me?

"Well, that's where this editorship thing comes in, and I see it as a great opportunity. There will be Democrats coming out of the woodwork to run for president. Smith will likely run again. Maybe John Garner, too. Governor Roosevelt has always had an eye on the presidency, but he is seen as a lightweight and is no front-runner.

Louis Howe, of whom you are so leery, was formerly a reporter but now is a political advisor and buddy to Roosevelt. He even helped Roosevelt immensely when he was sick and did other charitable work in Warm Springs with FDR. He and Eleanor worked together to encourage Roosevelt in his recovery. Also, Howe encouraged Eleanor to return to NY and become more of an activist. She did and enjoyed it because she had some pet causes. Anyway, Howe said something that made sense to me when I asked him what was different about Roosevelt."

"What was that?"

"Roosevelt had worked his way up in the democratic party before he got sick. Remember, FDR ran as a Vice Presidential Candidate against Coolidge in 1920."

"Saul, no, I don't remember. In 1920, I was still playing with my rag doll, Loosey, not paying too much attention to presidential campaigns. Remind me."

"Loosey, really, Loosey?"

"Don't make fun. Loosey was a companion, and when I first got her, other dolls made fun of her because she was so floppy. I insisted that she was not limp but relaxed. So, I called her Loosey for Loose."

"OK, Cox got wiped in 1920, but Roosevelt had stature in the party. But then he got sick. So, for FDR to be seen as a candidate in the future, he needed to demonstrate his physical strength and capacity. This was accomplished when, in the 1928 Democratic National Convention, Roosevelt walked to the podium to nominate Smith in 1928. This was followed by his election to governor of New York.

When the market crashed, Roosevelt and Hoover waited to see what would happen. But then Roosevelt felt that he could wait no longer. He believed that he owed a better response to his constituents. Roosevelt promoted lower taxes for farmers and encouraged the state legislature to develop public power utilities. He got the legislature to pass a public works program for the unemployed to grant relief to the needy. He could be seen as a more liberal reformer willing to use the power of the government to help the people.

What was different about Roosevelt was that his proposals advocated starting at the bottom, not the top. Most other politicians offered solutions for the wealthy, assuming financial benefits would trickle down, but the trickling kept going up, not down. Roosevelt's legislative proposals directly helped the people in need at the time. Regardless of the political party, I've always considered direct help necessary. That is at the core of the editorship opportunity.

We'll start the Iowa Jewish News under worse conditions than I thought. Financially, it will be rough. Although, I'll pick up printing equipment much cheaper than I anticipated. But we'll still need good circulation, advertising, and exposure. Playing a part in the political solution will help with that exposure and have many additional benefits. Also, absent anything else, it is the right thing to do.

Starting The Iowa Jewish News, I was following my passion. I see this editorship of the Iowa Democrat as an obligation to others. It is a rare opportunity to work widely to promote the best solution I can find for helping the people who need that help the most. Such a great chance to help dramatically doesn't come along every day, Rachel."

"I'm not sure how this gets exposure and other benefits, so explain how you would do this. After all, Saul, you are just one man, and you're not wealthy and connected. So where are you going to find the time and the resources?"

"Good questions. First, remember it's an editorial position, not a publisher position like the Jewish News. Someone else cares for the mechanics, and I even get a salary. My task is to formulate an editorial format, make phone calls, write letters, and make personal contacts around the state to educate people about the issues and motivate people to prepare for the '32 election."

"But you need to find out if Roosevelt is the best candidate. So how can you honorably promote him?"

"I'm not going to. That isn't the job. The way Howe sees it is that I have two goals. First, educate people to see the problems accurately and promote interest and preference for voting democratic and getting rid of Hoover. Second. To help people understand that the state delegation must keep a united front, a voting bloc, regardless of a delegate's personal preference."

"And you accomplish this how?"

"The power of the press. I do this with columns, editorials, contacts, whatever. But at my own pace and not full-time. All my calls can have a dual purpose. The readers of both papers are interested in national and local issues. Certainly, the more state-wide contacts, the better. And the democratic party already has a call list I can start with. And there is a real role for you here also. You can help me organize all of this and even make calls. We'll need to establish a phone bank."

Rachel still felt overwhelmed. Saul was like the proverbial snowball rolling downhill. Finally, she asked, "What is the purpose of the early phone bank if you are not promoting a candidate?"

"Good question. We can write news articles all day long. Yet, who knows how much those really influence people? The best way to know what they fear, want, need, and feel is to encourage them to discuss the issues with us as they would with friends in their own living rooms. If done well, friendly phone calls can be even more helpful than news articles."

"How?"

"Because we can encourage people to tell us their opinions and concerns. It's easier to connect when you are sharing worries with people than when you are debating them about candidates. During the calls, we can educate people about the convention process and the importance of block voting. The people you talk with will likely spread the word with other friends. Knowing the inside details of the process and better understanding Hoover's failings will enable people to feel more informed and involved. The calls should be timely and not rushed. One call could educate more than one person."

"How do we get enough educated phone bank callers?'

"That's your job. We want more women involved. Tap into all the friends you're making here. Go to the women who have done a great job developing the Jewish support systems in town. Tell them that Des Moines and Iowans need them to help again. All people realize these are perilous times but don't know how to help. This allows them to be involved. Get them to invite their friends to participate. Think of who is going to be answering the phone during the day. It is women who are more likely to be home. The phone tree you can establish could be much more important than a weekly newspaper, democratic or Jewish."

"Great, but I can't educate these women. No way!"

"That's where I come in. While developing the editorial platform for the newspaper that I want the reporters to follow, I'll do a similar script for the phone bank. We'll have two or three sessions where the callers and I discuss these issues. This can also be a great help for the goal of the Iowa Jewish News."

"How is that?"

"Many of the phone bank callers will be Jewish. But as the group expands, many will not be Jewish. Sponsoring an ecumenical intermixing over a common concern creates greater visibility for the paper and acceptance and assimilation in the city."

"It sounds like you think this is a fix-all for everything."

"I'm not that naive. It may even fall flat. But it's the best we, you and I, can offer right now."

"But what about your interest in Roosevelt? You can't be partisan in this position, can you?"

"No, if I come to be convinced that Roosevelt is the best candidate, once I've got the ball rolling convincing people to see that we all need to agree on one candidate to oppose Hoover, even if that person is not our personal favorite, I'd resign the editorship and politic for Roosevelt."

"And Mr. Howe agreed to all this?" While talking, Rachel got up to fuss with dishes and pace around the kitchen. When speaking, sometimes, she would stare directly at Saul while making her point. At other times, she was more casual.

"Sure, I have something that will hold up in any court of law."

Turning to face Saul, Rachel forcefully asked, "What's that? Is there a contract or something?"

"Not exactly. We exchanged telephone numbers and addresses at the end of the last evening in New York and shook hands."

"And that's it?"

"That's it."

"And part of that handshake was that I had to agree."

Saul stammered, "Yes, I guess it was."

"You guess? You told me that was a provision."

"True, but it was my way of temporizing with Louis when he threw this at me.

"So, you really didn't mean it.?"

"I hadn't thought it through that thoroughly. The whole conversation caught me off guard. Louis said he needed an answer immediately to take advantage of the opportunity."

"So right now, Howe is convinced you will do this. He isn't waiting to hear my opinion?"

"I guess so."

Rachel returned to the table, leaned forward with her arms resting on the surface, and looked straight into Saul's eyes. "Well, you've got yourself up a creek without a paddle."

"How do you mean?"

"Louis Howe is merrily going about his business, thinking that he has solved some problems in Hicksville, Des Moines, Iowa. For him, this issue is yesterday's news, a victory in building his political superstructure for the democratic party or Roosevelt or whatever."

On the other hand, you've got me thinking that I have control over green lighting this plan. You seem to be in a bind. You can disappoint Howe, or you can disregard me to satisfy Howe, knowing I'm not in agreement. Think about that while puffing on your cigar while reading the paper tonight. Oh, yes. And consider what it will be like living with me when you neglect my concerns." Then there was a long pause. Finally, Rachel said, "You might also want to consider how that phone bank idea will go without my support." She then got up and went into the bathroom. She didn't need to go but stood before the mirror, smiling at herself, allowing Saul time to stew.

Rachel left the bathroom and went to the bedroom to change clothes and get her light jacket. Saul stood up from the table when she came out, "Where are you going? We're not done yet."

"I think I'm done. The ball's in your court." Rachel left.

Elijah figured the group had plenty to hash over and sleep on. So, he got up and announced that he would take a jeep ride the next morning. He suggested they have the day free and meet again after dinner if that was OK.

Chapter Thirty-two

After Elijah returned from a jeep ride, he settled in for a rest before making an early dinner. Looking out the window at the campfire area, he noticed people sitting around talking, listening to one another, not just the usual cross-talking chit-chat. By the time Elijah had dinner and coffee, he was ready to join the group and hear the group's reaction to how Saul's snowball was growing and whether Rachel was mowed down or had jumped aboard to go along for the ride.

"Well, folks seem active this evening. What's going on?

"Yesterday is what's going on!"

"What do you mean?

"A Trip to New York out of nowhere! Meeting an improbable group of influential people and being offered the editorship of a nationally sponsored political newspaper and, oh yes, hob-nobbing with Eleanor Roosevelt! That's a lot. This Saul character of yours seems to have gone to bed one night in Des Moines and awakened in a dream of a lifetime. Is any of this really true?

"Well, yes. You all know Hoover was president at the time of the crash."

Charlie exasperated, "You're playing with us, Elijah. You know that isn't what I meant".

Horace popped up, "Well, if all this is true, I want to know where I can reach for one of those brass rings. I've ridden many merry-go-rounds in my life but no brass rings."

"You spoiled old coot," his wife responded. So, what does that make me? Pot metal? Besides, we've gotten our share of breaks and done well. At this point, you wouldn't even know what to do with a brass ring, except bitch that you had to polish it all the time."

Laughing at Horace's expense, Mary Ann added, "Well, the events of last night's story were like bumping into all sorts of angels that Elijah believes in. You know, someone you may or may not ever see again who says or does something that significantly influences your life. The important issue is how well these two young folks recognize the opportunity and quit debating how costly or valuable that opportunity is."

Nancy asked, "But there are a lot of pluses and minuses in what they are considering. So, are you saying they should neglect those issues and forge ahead?"

"Maybe I am. But look, I understand Rachel's concern. It all seems overwhelming, and maybe the success Saul is looking for is improbable. But so what if they fall short of having a significant impact on the election? They'd likely never be able to measure that anyway. Being involved with a second paper will give Saul the experience and opportunity he wants. It's going to be a short-lived gig. They may get a little tired. So what? They're young. Rachel wants more involvement, even a job. This is her chance. Are they up for such a challenge? I think the potential negatives are being overblown. Stop bellyaching and get on with life. Dive in. The water is deep. You'll survive.

Another added, "It seems like they recognized that Rachel is somewhat of a barrier against progress. Once again, Saul and Rachel had their usual go-around because she dove into her negative, worrying imagination. Saul made that easy for her because he hadn't yet provided all the details. However, this time could be different. She is worried about the workload, and that is not crazy. It will be immense but not prolonged. But that is Saul's problem to navigate. Although I suspect Rachel will always be the worrier of the two. Pity the day she is right about something that she warned him about. When that day comes, and it will, Rachel will take no prisoners!"

Larry sat, bent over as if staring at something important on the ground. But his head was slowly but visibly shaking, perhaps in wonderment.

Elijah noticed Larry's silent communication—the tight set of his jaw and the way his eyes narrowed, staring intently at the ground. "What's up, Larry?" Larry looked up, his eyes flashing with a mix of disbelief and anxiety.

 "Well, in all my years, I've never encountered a situation like this," he began, his voice quivering slightly. "Stop and think about the stresses and risks here," he continued, his tone growing steadier but no less intense. "Let's begin with moving away from your support system to a new, unknown place. That sounds mundane and simple unless you've done it! Then, having to set up a new household without any preplanning," he said, his voice rising with each point, the strain evident in his increasingly rapid speech. "Oh, by the way, Saul also needs to find a new way of earning a living. But, hey, why not add to the fun? Take on the task of developing a whole new statewide project. Of course, don't worry about the project's chance of success or failure. Erase from your mind the consequences of failure, your long-term reputation, and your future standing in the community for years," he almost spat out the last words, his agitation now a boiling point. "A community of influential, even powerful friends and religious associates who can be supportive and cheer you on when you are successful but who can become like ghosts if you let them down."

Now, if all this bores you and you have time on your hands, why not take on the request of a nationally prominent political person to do a job that could help influence or select the next president of the United States? Insignificant right? And there is one additional chink in the armor; try to do all this without much money or experience in any of those areas. Finally, don't think about the fact that all the support around you vanishes if you fail. Suddenly, no one knows you as you go down the drain taking your new bride with you."

Larry paused for a moment or two, his hand trembling as he ran it through his thinning hair. He took a deep breath, his chest rising and falling heavily, but it did little to calm the storm brewing inside him. His agitation was palpable; his face flushed a deep red, and a vein pulsed visibly on his forehead. He seemed like a pot boiling over, on the verge of spilling its contents. When he finally spoke, his voice was loud and rapid, each word dripping with a mix of fear and frustration. The excitement in his tone was unmistakable, but it was laced with a sharp edge of anxiety, certainly not joy.

"The enormity of the perspective of stress, work, and risk is beyond my imagination. Failure in one of these fronts could sully the benefit of any success in the others. Personally, I think this young fellow is a gutsy lunatic. It is foolish to take all this on at once. If he keeps doing these things, he will fall flat on his face someday, if not this time. Talk about burning the candle at both ends; this character, Saul, is burning so many wicks that the result will look like fireworks, not a candle. For me, Rachel is the one with wisdom, but ultimately, Saul is a better debater and rationalizer."

Elijah quipped, "You've got to stop holding back your thoughts, Larry. Do I hear you saying that Mary Ann is glibly overlooking the potential realities?"

"Absolutely."

"But all kidding aside, we have Mary Ann representing Saul's position and Larry, Rachel's. Different opinions are certainly free of gender bias. So, what do the rest of you think?"

Larry's dramatic reaction made others pause and think not so much about Saul and Rachel but about themselves. Then, they shared stories of their own lucky successes and failures. It was as if there was an empathic group reaction to the situation in which Saul and Rachel found themselves. Opinions varied along the sides already drawn. However, the group found unanimity when sharing their remorse about never thanking the unique people, the angels, in their lives. To discuss that out loud was cathartic for some. The group eventually quieted, ready to hear more of the story.

Elijah moved on. "Let's look at how Saul saw things through his own eyes. Larry has brought up a comprehensive risk analysis. I suspect, Larry, that you think it would be easy to sell Saul gold mine stock from Bolivia."

"Could be a good chance," Larry laughed.

"Well, Rachel may have had some of your concerns. But as we move on with the story, Larry, we will see that Saul has a special motivation that many in this country could share, but maybe only a few in this group. Our decisions often result from what I can best call the climate of our mind."

Charlie interrupted, "What the hell is that Elijah? You're talking like a weatherman or something. Plain English, please.

"Fair enough, Charlie. I'll continue with my weatherman analysis. It's simple. What do you do in a room that feels uncomfortably cold?"

"Put on a sweater or turn up the heat."

"Exactly, you react to your environment. The environment in Saul's mind is that of an immigrant. As an adult, when someone asks him where he was born, he says Russia. After emigrating, he grew up living with the pain of his parents trying to survive and assimilate. His whole life, he has been surrounded by issues related to immigration. Remember, Saul is an immigrant. Rachel is a first-generation immigrant, and they are both Jewish and concerned about the lives of the people left in Europe. They still have relatives and friends in Eastern Europe. Saul is embedded in the Zionist movement, eventually seeing Palestine as a homeland. His father owns property there. Naturally, he has not only an interest but also emotional reactions and feelings about the immigration policies of the United States.

For Saul, the experience of the immigrants of his time was not merely a matter of bad government policy but a violation of a deeper human code, the golden rule. Do unto others as you would have others do unto you. He had already seen that the power of haves had made the climate nearly catastrophic for the have-nots. He saw that the cultures providing for labor to build America were now long neglected. He anticipated, correctly, that the pathway of oppression and disregard for suffering would continue. For Saul, this was a philosophical and moral violation. He could not stop it or stand idly by and ignore it. So, Saul would do what he could to turn the thermostat up, even if only slightly."

Elijah continued. And Saul was correct with his forecast of the storms brewing. With the depression at hand, immigrants would continue to suffer at the low end of the totem pole. Saul knows that. Current events dashed hope for slow improvement in immigrants' plight in the U.S. daily.

Remember, Europe remained unstable, and the Nazis were on the rise. Foreigners were being met with disdain. On the one hand, America is a melting pot of "huddled masses" coming to our shores. On the other hand, it has a gory history regarding its treatment of cultures different from white Anglo-Saxon protestants coming from Eastern European.

From the outset of European settlement in this land, look at how the powerful have treated those seen as less than them, especially those less powerful. First, we stole land and resources from the Native Americans, placed them on reservations, considered them heathens, and attempted to convert them to our religious beliefs. Our importation of slaves from other countries is not exactly a gold medal in our march to supremacy.

Our policies and laws have been written to find ways of using immigrant labor while simultaneously marginalizing their personhood. Subsequently, quotas were set to limit immigration from each nationality and religion from southern and eastern Europe. These quotas went into effect in the year of the crash and impacted all but Canadians and Latin Americans, who were exempt.

In the 1920s, American farmers were instrumental in helping to feed Europe. Having no cheap labor, as they previously had from the Chinese, the United States turned to Mexico for that cheap labor. Thousands of legal and undocumented workers were welcomed and supplied the work. With the high unemployment during the depression, now faced by Saul and Rachel's generation, even greater anti-Mexican sentiment grew. The United States government decided sending these Mexicans back to Mexico was cheaper than including them in any welfare program. Many of the people sent back were natural-born American citizens. Ironically, many of these United States citizens of Mexican descent were welcomed here with little consideration of legality or documentation when we needed them to harvest our crops and then again later when we needed cheap labor to mobilize for WWII.

The political guidelines for picking immigration winners and losers frequently have been one of convenience and bigotry. Morality was not an issue.

So political engagement became a passion for Saul, not because he wanted a job as an editor, but because the weather forecast for immigrants and all the have-nots needed to improve. So, in Saul's mind, his responsibility, the core of his values, and the climate of his mind demanded that he fight to help those less empowered and oppose the still significant ethnic, national, and religious bigotry he saw.

But, regarding stress and workload issues, Rachel's concerns are correct. One had to tip-toe through the tulips with one's words and deeds. Saul's philosophical beliefs and values were only universally shared by some, maybe few. Anyone writing for the Iowa Democrat or the Iowa Jewish News would be in a danger zone. The same person editorializing from both rags would forever be on thin ice.

However, Saul was more confident than Rachel. The barriers, limitations, antagonism, unfairness, workload, and bigotry that blocked Saul and Rachel's way scared Rachel but energized Saul. He grew up and developed the street smarts of negotiating his way through the neighborhoods of opposing forces within the entanglement of gangs, unions, industrial capitalists, and religious leaders of the Detroit melting pot.

Also, Saul learned lessons from his father, who had walked this path before him, first in Russia, then in New York City, and finally in Detroit. His father, with age, had grown more cautious and less willing to gamble, but he, better than anyone else in the family, knew the stuff Saul was made of.

Elijah moved his chair over a bit and sat down again. Then, considering the next chapter in Rachel and Saul's lives, he called it quits. "More coming tomorrow!"

Chapter Thirty-three

"After Rachel returned from her walk, the discussion with Saul began back up in earnest. As they sipped on their freshly brewed coffee, Rachel looked up and smiled.

"Your turn, darling. Use it well. I'm all ears."

Saul stood, knowing he'd shared the best factual and intellectual reasons for the value in him being the editor of the Iowa Democrat, pursued a more emotional appeal. Cleared his throat, looked over sitting Rachel's head, and spoke as if to an audience far and wide:

"Friends, Jewish congregants, and countrymen lend me your ears. I come to praise Saul, not to chastise him. While the good that a man can do long lives after him, the failures eventually are oft interred with his bones. So let it be……."

"Stop! Stop! Stop…boo hiss…plagiarism is not accepted. I shall ever need to sip this poison rather than eat this slop you doth provide…. Two can quote the famous words of the bard. As Hamlet said to Claudius after stabbing him, Cut the crap and get on with it. Saul! Drink the damn poison. Times a wasting."

"OK, I don't think that those were Hamlet's exact words, but I get your point. First, please consider that you might be miscalculating the burden of the workload and the stress involved in the two complementary editorships. Second, you might be underestimating the support and mission value of the help from the connections we will make.

I know my family, friends, and even you think I spent years flitting around Detroit. The reality is that I was making connections and building relationships- mutual favors, sharing information, just listening to people's problems, and offering help where I could. I became more and more accepted by many people because of one thing. They came to fully believe and understand that I could be trusted. That was my morality. But I admit, it came in handy. I was not a made man, but I encountered many unsavory characters. I never oversold anything, and I never dishonestly promised anything. Doing so satisfied my self-image as well as protected my physical well-being.

All that led to lots of part-time jobs, often just tasks. But, it was rare to find any long-term commitment, primarily because I had not found any long-term commitments that appealed to me. That's one of the many reasons for leaving. I didn't see a way to make a difference in Detroit. There, my commitment was always to someone else's project, not mine. Likely, that was not going to change. That's fine for many people. Committed workers are necessary to make projects work. There is nothing wrong with working for someone else. I just didn't want to do it. I talked with my dad about this a few times, and of course, he would once again push the 'get a profession' suggestion and lobby for university.

There were times when the path either of law or medicine seemed interesting. But the fields didn't grab me. At times, I wanted to want them to. It never happened, so instead, here we are on the brink of the Jewish News and Iowa Democrat, wondering what I will make of those. I enjoy crazy challenges and connecting people for a cause."

Rachel leaned forward, her brow furrowed in thought. 'Saul, have you considered the potential conflicts we might face? The Jewish News and the Iowa Democrat cater to distinct audiences. How do we ensure that our messaging doesn't alienate one group while appealing to the other? It's not just about content but about strategic alignment.'"

"Good points. I guess. If you build the relationships correctly, conflicts become less of a problem."

"Can you explain that, please?"

"Well, I was not much of a Democrat in Detroit. But neither am I in Des Moines. I've been a political agnostic. But I did lots of work for people of both parties. So, we respected each other's differences. I'd hope to promote any chance of a career in the news by creating relationships.

At the paper, reporters would ask me to look at a story they were composing and give my opinion or even give some editorial help. They'd ask that in preparation for showing it to their editor. Although, I knew that if I subsequently begged them to let me go out on even a little story instead of them, they'd fight me tooth and nail to prevent me from doing that. So, I didn't get much or any benefit from my connections there in that way, but my willingness to help led to them asking more. The more they asked, the more opportunity I had to learn by doing. And that was OK. I would still do them a favor. That's just how things were. Their trust in me and vice versa led to many good things and help if I was in a pinch. Success is mainly about hard work and relationships."

"OK, but how does that apply to these two tasks and the sheer volume of work they require?"

"Well, let's look at each task. And I'm entirely open to suggestions because I know this will be an evolutionary process. I can't predict every twist and turn we will face going forward. But first, the Iowa Democrat, as I've already said, 'needs no publisher support from me.' I have two jobs: increase Democratic support statewide and push for a solid block delegation."

"Ya, you told me all about that, but why is it easy and not overly time-consuming, and what about Roosevelt?"

"Well, Roosevelt is Roosevelt. I can't deal with that until after the Iowa Democrat is out of my hands. But stop and think for a moment. Most tasks for both papers right now involve making contacts to gather information. Information about what people like, dislike, want, and need. Right?

For the Iowa Democrat, I'll have to turn that information into columns stimulating interest in the democratic party. That's my strength. I can write. I can compose. And I'll have a newspaper where I can control the content.

I have a leg up on creating interest and readership in the Democratic paper. Howe has yet to learn of it, but with his help, I'll have detailed country-wide information to be sent by reporters with AP access in New York. I can get information straight from national news services. The stuff they don't even bother to send to the Des Moines Register by wire because the sources don't think we care. Some of the information will be about policy issues. Other material will be more scandalous, maybe even salacious. But don't kid yourself. The tendency toward voyeurism does not know state boundaries. Properly handled, this additional content will build readership.

Also, Iowans do care about what is happening to people elsewhere. This more widespread news coverage exposes our readers to nationwide problems and issues. They'll see the more significant needs, not just of Iowa but the entire nation. So I can introduce the idea that Iowans can be part of the solution by choosing a presidential candidate who thinks about providing help for individual citizens and their families, not just the banks and the wealthy."

"But even gathering the information is time-consuming, never mind writing and editing."

"Well, the national news is just a feed to copy. No work there. But as far as what the folks of Iowa want, worry about, or don't like, I need to enlist community reporters. Why not get some of the community reporters working for both papers? There won't be a complete overlap of interest, but I bet at least 50% will work for both. That commonality will make the relationships even easier."

Rachel looked at Saul, "OK, but much more must be done for the Jewish News. You don't even have a printing press yet!"

"True, and that's a problem, yet maybe an advantage."

"What? I'm not getting you again."

"Getting the equipment, the space, recruiting someone to sell the advertising, and all the numerous publishing aspects take time. So much of it is waiting on others to deliver or make up their minds to commit. And I can't hurry it up.

The rest is helping the reporters know what information we want from the local people. All that is included in the work we've already talked about. Having to wait on presses and other equipment to get the Jewish News up and running until I'm finished with the Iowa Democrat is a great advantage. But, gathering information will be an ongoing process. The information we collect and the news feeds I can combine as material sources of stories for both papers, just written with different slants."

Saul poured himself another coffee and asked Rachel if she wanted the same. She shook her head and said, "No, I've had enough coffee and propaganda. You've overwhelmed me with more data and argumentation than I can assimilate reasonably. Nothing I can say that will happily dissuade you from jumping off the cliff. So, I have a solution. First, I will support and help you. The amount and type of my help will be totally under my control. If I say 'no' to something you wish from me, you will no accept that 'no' without one word of discussion. Regarding the dilemma between Howe and me. I also have a solution."

"And that is?"

"Well, you might not like it, but here it is. As I said, I'll go along with you and fully support and help you however I can. But if I think it is too much and threatening you, me, or our relationship, I can immediately halt all involvement with the political paper, even if you think you are within a week of its end. I, not you, will determine if you are experiencing too much stress. Again, no debate, not even a word of discussion. If I say stop, it is as absolute as a red light. I get total and absolute veto power at all points. Further, you call Howe and tell him what the condition is. This may seem unreasonable and inappropriate to you, and it may be. However, your plan looks equally unreasonable and inappropriate to me. So, if you want to go ahead with it, those are my conditions."

Saul agreed to abide by this arrangement but probably never thought Rachel would carry through with it in any drastic way.

Elijah sighed. "Seems a bit overwhelming even as I know the ending. Maybe I'll change it. Who knows.? Anyway, they began. The dual projects were twice the amount of work Saul had anticipated and less than half the chaos and problem that Rachel expected. Yet, in a nutshell, they survived, and both enjoyed doing it."

Rachel would spend hours listening to Saul talk to sources or reporter candidates on the phone. Then, finally, she began to see how he succeeded. First, he told people who he was and what he was after. Then, if they were not interested, he readily accepted that.

He was always polite and not overly quick to get off the phone to the next call. He'd ask people why they were not interested and was appreciative of their answers, suggesting that maybe in the future, they may be able to help. He tried to learn more about their positions, concerns, interests - anything he could put on a file card and keep for future reference. Boy, did he use that material over the years? He got many good referrals from a "not interested" call.

Finally, he left all callers feeling they knew and liked him because he would kid and reveal information about himself. He got lots of personal information about them, too.

Rachel remembered that Saul told one woman, a Mrs. Jorgensen, from Council Bluffs, that if he were traveling in that area, he'd call her and see if she had baked any of that favorite apple pie she'd talked about. If so, he'd surely beg to come by and get a taste. This woman had told Saul about her work for the Christian Church and politely revealed she'd been a lifelong Republican.

Rachel doubted that Mrs. Jorgensen's positions had changed due to the call with Saul. But she wasn't surprised when, a couple of weeks later, there was a knock on the door. There stood a man from Council Bluffs who knew Mrs. Jorgensen. She had given him a pie to drop off at the office of that nice man from Des Moines, the one she had told so many people about.

Unsurprisingly, a year later, Saul was written about by a newspaper columnist in the Omaha paper as an "Up and coming, young newspaper editor in Iowa."

Rachel was impressed by how professional Saul was when he had a contact who was interested. Saul left nothing to chance. He reviewed everything that he was looking for from them. Saul often asked if there was anything they might need from him. He always made a date for a follow-up call and was good about keeping people informed of the overall progress of whatever project they were involved in.

And so the work was begun. The first glitch in Saul's plan emerged when Saul went to the offices of the Democrats and found that they had yet to publish anything. Contrary to what Howe told Saul to expect, little prepublication work has been done. No test papers had been printed. Howe failed to tell Saul the leaving editor hadn't published anything. Saul wasn't sure whether he misunderstood Howe or if he was deceived.

Saul didn't dwell on the possibilities of Howe's manipulations and instead focused on getting it running. First, he met with the staff to give them a pep talk. Saul could see no editorial content. No direction, philosophy, or discernable purpose had been defined. What he found was a shock. The staff, as they were, had in mind primarily inconsequential fluff, which Saul found shocking.

He intended a different approach and started writing to convey it. His purpose as editor was to help create statewide interest. He pushed the idea of developing more subscriptions for registered Democrats. He sent free copies to significant people in various communities who were not registered Democrats, especially newspaper editors.

Startled, one of Saul's reporters inquired. "Why are we bothering sending anything to the other papers? They have all the same news feeds we have about what is happening around the country."

"Saul picked up the phone for the most important call of his life. Probably the riskiest, too. When the person on the other end answered, Saul's staff heard, "Louis, this is Saul in Des Moines" (Elijah noted that it was no longer Mr. Howe). "You wanted better results in Iowa. You forgot to tell me you weren't getting any results here because you've got no damn paper yet. Nothing has been published. The staff is keyed up, but the material is fluff and shit. No one will care. It won't generate interest. We have an excellent team. One that I think will be top-notch. The mechanics are ready to go, but the material is fluff and shit."

Saul and Howe haggled back and forth for just a couple of minutes when, to the eavesdropping masses, Saul would at least get a chance to present his case. They heard, "OK, Louis, your project, your call. But I can't make this thing work without your help. Without help, more interesting news: all I can publish is day-to-day garbage about local meetings in Iowa. Currently, people aren't focused on meeting times and summaries. That will get old and redundant fast. But if we add more national political stuff, full of intrigue, it helps people to feel that they are really in the know about issues and are an essential part of a more significant movement. Iowans want to know what is going on elsewhere. What is their aunt in California experiencing, or are their friends in New York suffering badly, too? We can keep it fresh with each edition. Other local state papers will pick up our stories if we do that. I need insider news, not just the usual national feeds.

The Iowa Democrat can be a product where people get the information we want them to hear, and it can also be the source that other news outlets and newspapers use. Even party fights and disagreements are great material if we present them as sophisticated position discussions. But unfortunately, the national news feeds aren't going to do it that way, and they glory in making specific candidates look bad. So we won't do that. So, instead, I'll rewrite the script and follow my own format.

Do it my way, and when they pick their candidate, voters might have a more positive view of the Democrats, who they feel are more in touch with their needs and problems. But unfortunately, this paper's current path won't get you anywhere. It is a total waste of my time and energy. You said doing this would be good for my resume. I don't even have a resume, but if I did, I wouldn't want this experience to be the lead. So, I won't quit on you. So, don't quit on me as you did when you put me in this position. Don't abandon me again.

I know how to use the material to help motivate the voters, to make them mad. Hell, they're already angry. We just have to focus on who they are mad at! I only need some of the material from you, just some information about what's going on in Congress or various candidates talking to farmers in Kansas or iron workers out East. I want to show that Hoover has screwed things up, and the Republicans haven't fixed it in years. The system is rigged, and the Democrats are trying to learn what they need from the people."

Elijah continued. Saul's staff heard this as a monologue. He barely took a breath to give Louis Howe a chance to object. The barrage worked. Saul got what he wanted. Howe didn't provide much, but enough to give Saul the edge he was looking for. Saul intended to produce a Democratic party political newspaper that would remain non-partisan regarding individual Democratic candidates before the primaries. He would not print inappropriate gossip and never touch anything smelling of negative op-ed research.

The staff excitedly bought in. Reporters all started writing and readied it for print. Finally, on Saturday, January 23, 1932, Vol I of The Iowa Democrat hit the streets and the mail. Never having printed an article, much less a headline, Saul published in bold print, spread across the top of the entire page, was:

"WE WANT BREAD"

"AND WE DON'T OBJECT TO WORK."

That first headline and article were sent by wire to Reuters, AP, and newspapers across the state.

Saul had his first byline ever underneath. It was his approach that made the paper so successful. The imposing headline was followed by a single fourteen-inch column of tiny print that began, 'Acting in defiance of Hoover administration policy, the U.S. Senate manufacturers' committee Thursday voted to report favorably a bill providing $375,000,000 of federal funds for the destitute and unemployed. He then pointed out bipartisan sponsors and contrasted them to other legislators and the administration that for 2 1/2 years had left men, women, and children to go hungry and die.

The paper asked the readers to consider the question, "Why are those incumbent Republicans coming to the table now? The upcoming election? Are the Republicans no longer able to look at themselves in the mirror each morning?" The column criticized no one person by name. Instead, the Iowa Democrat attacked the administration and Congress for being absent for so long and too late to the party and did not advocate for any particular candidate. The headline, "WE WANT TO EAT," became the rallying cry.

Perhaps the future articles were not quite as dramatic, but Saul received calls from editors statewide pleased to get the additional information The Iowa Democrat provided. Staff also got more engaged because of the positive feedback. Sometimes, trying to get into the swing of things, someone would go a little overboard. Saul could be heard saying, 'Hey Jones, you're not paid to be a salesman, but a reporter. So let's tone it down a bit, OK?' But the paper staff was accomplishing much more than even Howe had hoped.

Saul wanted to make the paper more compelling. He wanted to make more sharp negative points about the Republicans. The news was current and relevant. Because of his sources, the Iowa Democrat published material different from the more influential Des Moines papers. He felt their product had done well, but he wanted to make The Iowa Democrat a home for the curious, the worried, the hungry, and the embittered. He wanted the democratic party paper kept in the hands of the reader longer. Saul felt that interest in the Democrats and circulation could be improved. He opted for political entertainment. The New York Times started publishing crossword puzzles in 1913. Saul wanted something also appealing but different.

He created a short column that was challenging but fun to read. It was a weekly letter to the editor written phonetically in the Yiddish accent by Yacob Haleetosis. Yacob was an interested reader who had much "advice for 'de Damokrats'" and wanted to convey this information. The letters were usually brief, full of honest if unsophisticated reflection, but could also be reasonably pointed.

An example would be a New Year resolution Yacob had made for 1932.

To De Iowea Damokrat,

Halo Myster Sitting Haditer:

'I gass its abott tyme I told yu abott my big taut fur 1932. Hay?'

Heers vhat Om gone do dis yier. Om gone tink abott ull tings vhat I know abott de repoblikan party. Hefter Om troo tinking abott it. Om gone rite it down on peese paiper.

Dan Om gonna tink about it some moar, and Om gone rite it down on saim pees paiper on de odderside.

Dan Om gonna tink abott ull tings dat de repoblikan party orta haff done and didn't do an Om gonna putt dam down on peese paiper too.

Hefter I gott hull bontch paipers. Om gone coppy what it say into big book, but Om rite de book in Greek, caus I wooden reed Greek and I vouldant haff to vorry about it no moar, and de hull ting vouldant be interastting to a gutt citizan anyhuh.

Dan Om gone send de book to parazij-dant Hoover so he could appreshiate vat a gutt party us Damokrats haff.

Your friend,

Yacop Haleetosis

Haspee Nu Yer: Dis is a gutt tyme to remamber not to forgat de nu slo-gun "Rite mit de Daunkee to prosparity."

Appropriately enough, the column was called Yacob Yodles, and Saul put his name on the byline. The column got more than its' share of attention; some were critical but mostly good. But for something like this, there are always detractors but seldom were the detractors sustained. It was too much work for the detractors to read the articles each week. Saul also wrote the usual erudite but down-to-earth, expected editorial for each edition. Each paper sold for 5 cents.

Saul's tenure at the Iowa Democrat was short-lived but full of accomplishments. He spent nearly as much time rewriting the format of the paper and then training the staff as he did writing columns. Meanwhile, Saul continued his work by recruiting reporters statewide for both forums.

After several weeks at the helm of publication, the Iowa Democratic Committee and Howe both appreciated the product and its impact. Finally, Saul got a call from Howe, suggesting it was time for Saul to move on. Initially feeling the bottom drop out for seemingly being fired, Saul recovered quickly. He explained, 'Mr. Roosevelt would be delighted if Saul would be Chairman of his campaign in Iowa.

After that, an article in the Des Moines Register announced Saul's resignation from the Iowa Democrat and that he accepted a statewide political position for Mr. Roosevelt. Further, the register announced that Saul was seeking a woman as co-chair. His work for Roosevelt continued throughout the campaign in 1932. Iowa did present a mostly united delegate front for Mr. Roosevelt through the third ballot at the Democratic National Convention, at which time Mr. Roosevelt was nominated.

The experience that Saul had with Howe. The Roosevelt campaign and the Iowa Democrat did not elevate Saul to national prominence. Nor did Saul seek it. But it did much for him at the local level. His work with The Iowa Democrat made him known to newspaper editors statewide. He was not a power broker but had numerous friends and connections. For Saul, that was the mortar that made his life work. Also, much of the notoriety eventually spilled over to assist the development of the Iowa Jewish News.

Chapter Thirty-four

The group members were just beginning to assemble and reminisce in wonderment about what they'd heard. Nancy mused aloud, "So much of this story reminds me of my own trip through life. When I was thirteen and proud of herding cattle, I never could have imagined that within years, I'd be doing the research I do. I wonder if that youngster Saul, as he was vomiting himself across the ocean, had any daydreams or fantasies of what life might hold for him."

Charles chuckled as he quipped, "I doubt the only thing on the mind of a vomiting two-year-old is when is mommy going to make this stop."

MaryAnn countered, "But even when he was in his mid-twenties, could he even come close to picturing what was ahead for him?"

"Probably just hoping that whoever was after him in Detroit wouldn't bother chasing him halfway across the country." Larry speculated.

Elijah smiled at the group as he sat down, just as Tim was saying, "It's sort of funny. You know how you hear of an actor or starlet getting discovered working other jobs, such as morgue beautician, firefighter, carpenter, teacher, or whatever? These people may have acted in high school, but it wasn't until someone picked them out of nowhere and gave them an audition that they struck gold."

Elijah spoke up, "Are you saying that's what happened to Saul?"

Tim replied, "Well, sort of. He was discovered in a news shop and had no more experience than someone acting in their senior play." He paused, recalling the memory. "He arrived in Des Moines with exceptional enthusiasm and the ability to deal with complex issues, but he had no experience on the big stage." Tim shook his head, a faint smile tugging at his lips. "He had no formal training or professional experience relevant to his passionate desire to be a newsman."

With a thoughtful glance at Larry, Tim continued, "With him was his pretty, petite, bright, and thoughtful wife, Rachel, who was plagued with the worry of anything new, especially her husband's tendencies to swing for the fences."

Larry nodded thoughtfully, "I guess he got an audition when he met Pinky. That in itself was incredible," he commented, leaning back in his seat. "but similarly weird was how he got a second audition sitting around a bar table in New York with a bunch of drunk politicians." Larry chuckled softly, shaking his head in disbelief. "After these guys go home, Saul is finally left alone with Howe, who loves to pontificate, and Saul is the only one left to listen. Incredibly, Saul's meeting with Howe could alter the trajectory of his life. Howe certainly is one of Saul's angels."

Elijah, who had been listening intently, acknowledged that the tale was somewhat fanciful. He glanced at the others, "Let's get back to following Rachel and Saul," he said as he directed their attention back to the matter at hand. He went on:

"OK, Saul, no longer the editor, was glad to continue to write for the Iowa Democrat as a partisan citizen. The frequency of his articles increased after Roosevelt was nominated and the election campaign was in full bloom." Elijah paused, scanning their faces to ensure he had their full attention.

"Maybe Saul's tactical idea of demanding from Howe more national news feeds better informed the Iowa readers about nationwide problems. That wider view would help Saul justify his own recommendation for a presidential nominee as he continued to write opinion pieces for The Iowa Democrat. He saw his subscribers not just as readers but as a voting group."

Elijah shifted in his seat, his eyes gleaming and his voice growing animated as he recounted. "Incredible stories have been written about the sufferings of toiling the hard-baked soil or traveling cross country in overloaded, broken-down vehicles. Some of those horseless carriages left over from the war years exist in personal collections today and are considered vintage. In 1932, they were carriages of desperation, hauling their occupants who looked for work. Those struggling to find work became the voters. However, many tones and colors, levels of interest and pain, desperation and concern formed the rainbow that would try to elect FDR."

Elijah leaned forward, "When Saul's tenure as editor ended, and before he functioned as a campaign manager, he asked Rachel to go out on a date. Most of their recent meals had been at home, brown bagged, or on the run. But Saul needed and wanted to talk.

"To what do I owe this wonderful treat, Saul?" Rachel asked, her curiosity piqued.

"I don't intend it as a treat but a necessity," Saul replied, his tone serious.

"Why is that?"

"We need to talk, I need to speak, without being interrupted by home dinner details." Saul took a deep breath, gathering his thoughts. "When I returned from New York, the train took me from the City to Detroit. The journey was not mine. Those trains were going to their destination, following the tracks no matter how I felt about or experienced it."

Rachel nodded slowly, trying to follow his train of thought. "I guess so, yes. And your point is?"

"I've been on my journey following the tracks or pathways as I see fit, which may or may not reward us with a form of golden satisfaction. The many paths I took may have curved in different directions, gone uphill or down, but they were still mine to follow. My passion was pulling and driving me, and my need to succeed fed me." Saul paused, looking directly into Rachel's eyes. "Once I started down that path, you could do little, maybe even nothing, to deter me, stop me, or even change the direction of the pathways. Before I started, you were right to worry while we discussed this. The result is that I've come out of the other end of this process, still standing and even with new opportunities."

Rachel's expression softened as Saul continued, "Thank you. I recognize how much you were a necessary help and a partner in my success. I couldn't have done it without the work you put in, the questions you demanded that I answer, and the options you suggested for me to consider. Knowing you would do that helped me to feel that someone always had my back if I was about to go too far off the rails. I know that it wasn't easy to convince me as to what too far looked like. But I trusted your creative ability to warn me if the danger was too extreme. I appreciate everything you've done, been, and who you are."

Saul reached across the table and took Rachel's hand. "Now I want to stop, take a breath, and desperately want to know how you are. How have you weathered this storm? I need you to tell me how you feel. What shape are you in? Because we are far from done. I want to measure how much energy you've got left in your wheelhouse. I want to know if you feel we are on the right track now, a doable pathway?" He paused, his gaze steady. "Or maybe you think we should slow down our efforts in planning to publish the Iowa Jewish News?"

When Saul finished, a few tears were on Rachel's cheeks. Yet, she was smiling at the same time. "First, thank you for noticing. But really, you did notice all along. There were many times you checked in with me, especially regarding the call bank. You've been a great husband as well as a boss to me and everyone who has worked with you. You never failed to express your appreciation. You never failed to answer anyone's question thoroughly, no matter how busy you were."

Rachel sighed softly. "As for a status report on my condition, in some ways, I suspect that I'm in better shape than you are, and in other ways worse, but certainly able to carry on."

"Explain more, please," Saul urged gently.

"I feel better because I don't worry about your capacity. This whole experience has been so unique and different for me. Certainly, I have never had the types of work I'm doing here. But more pointedly, I've never had the opportunity to see what you can do, too. Frankly, you amaze me. So I'm not worried about your capacity in the least! Sure, I'm tired. The exhaustion goes with the territory of engaging in such a worthwhile task. It enabled our effort. I'm young and will recover. More than ever, I feel that my efforts support your passion for journalism and, more importantly, your passion for caring about the people for whom you write. For me, that is a nice train to be on."

Saul listened intently, nodding. "And the worse off part?" he asked quietly.

"That may be a little more complicated. Your writing focus has been almost exclusively for the Iowa Democrat. I suspect you were rushing to get the Democrat off the ground. You focused there. End of story. For me, the intertwined task of getting the Iowa Jewish News off the ground and supporting the Democrat has been more of a tale of two cities or overlapping call center functions. I've been more worried about The Jewish News publication than I've been about the Iowa Democrat."

Rachel's voice wavered slightly. "A significant portion of our call bank is related to the Jewish News and the Democrat. I am more invested in the Jewish News as it is more local. The Jewish News is closer to home for me. Our friends and helpers are involved. Our reputation and acceptance in Des Moines are affected. Everything is riding on that."

She took a deep breath before continuing. "Yet, somehow, I feel that you're acting as if the preparation for the News is finished, and we are all done. Instead, I see that we are just starting. Maybe we need to get on the same page. So, tell me, honey, is the time for publication getting close? You, too, are exhausted. You've been working so hard. How close are you to being ready to print? And how worried are you about our supporters getting antsy or the community's reaction to the paper?"

Saul looked thoughtful. "I can see how you would think that my concern has mostly been for the Democrat. But that was strategic."

"How was neglecting the Iowa Jewish News strategic?" Rachel asked, her brow furrowing.

"When I accepted the editor position for the Democrat, I knew I could likely handle it because the Iowa Jewish News wouldn't yet be ready for publication. That meant I'd only have to write for one paper while I got the Democrat off the ground. There was nothing to write for the Jewish News. It wasn't circulating yet! You saw me putting all my writing efforts into the Democrat and assumed that I favored that child. No, it was just the only one born yet. The rest of my time doing outreach work benefited both projects.

So, the answer to your question is no, I'm not worried about our timeline. We are within the timeline I estimated when we got started. I'm not concerned or behind in the logistics of getting the News off the ground. I've done a lot to set up the publishing plant for the Jewish News. I've even arranged to have the benefit of using some of the machinery and reporters from the Democrat to come help with the News after the election."

Saul looked up and smiled at the waiter as he brought their soup. Beyond hungry, Rachel and Saul enjoyed their soup and looked forward to their entre. Before it arrived, Saul addressed Rachel's other concern. "You also seem worried about the community reaction. That answer involves opinions that are buried far and wide in the public's anticipation of what is to come. I won't know the community reaction until after we've gone to press."

"But what about the gossip, the talk people are hearing in the community? What are you hearing? Are people still liking the idea? Or is there resistance?" Rachel asked, her concern evident.

"Oh, there is resistance," Saul replied, setting his spoon down.

Alarmed, Rachel asked, "Why? What are you hearing? What are people saying?"

"People aren't saying anything. Nothing discouraging. Nary a bad word. I'm unaware of any negative phone calls or whispered gossip. That wouldn't likely happen this early in any case, but certainly not with such success of the Democrat."

"I'm confused, then, Saul. What do you mean there is resistance if it isn't there?" Rachel's confusion deepened.

"Oh, it's there. But people who fight this type of thing wait to attack until they see the time as right," Saul explained calmly.

"Why? Why do they wait?" Rachel pressed.

"For several reasons. First, they never want to be held responsible for shutting down the idea, killing it. Second, naysayers have many personal friends who are supporters of the paper in the community. So they don't want to come out and create a public debate, fight, or whatever. Additionally, many of their acquaintances who are supporters are also their customers and business partners. The supporters of the paper also have quiet allies. No point in ruffling too many feathers at the beginning. So, they just wait until after things are up and running. Then they will question whether this was such a good idea."

"And then, what happens?" Rachel asked, her voice barely above a whisper.

"Ah, there's the rub. When that happens, I'm on my own," Saul said, a slight smile playing on his lips.

"So, you just let it fester out there?" Rachel's concern grew.

"Oh no! No! No! No! You can't do that. You must nip it in the bud," Saul insisted, his tone firm.

"How? And when?" Rachel asked, her curiosity mixed with worry.

"Not sure. The quiet gossip, subtle innuendo, or outright criticism could dribble in. Indeed, it will if the detractors want to begin to significantly undermine support for the paper from the outset," Saul explained thoughtfully.

"Doesn't this bother you?" Rachel asked, her eyes wide.

"Sure. But it's part of the game. There will always be dissenters. Often for a good reason. My task is to prove them wrong."

"You're just seeing this as a game? A game?" Rachel repeated, her tone incredulous.

 "Easy there," Saul replied calmly. "The people who will read the paper and benefit from its advocacy and information are the ones I want to reassure and embolden. Taking the dissenters head-on is the tactic. Drawing attention to any hurt feelings I may have will benefit no one. The goal is not for me to feel good. It is to win. But there is a time and a way to best succeed in that battle."

"I understand all that, but you're putting so much time, effort, and creativity into this. Doesn't the criticism and attacks from others make it harder for you to succeed? Doesn't the idea of failure bother you?"

"Sure, to a certain extent," Saul admitted. "However, not everyone will always agree on important issues. Disagreement doesn't always lead to failure. So, we'll try many things. Some will work, and some won't. That is the risk.

Even having children is a risk and gamble. I'm not sure that even our parents feel good about us going our own way. Think of the pain my decisions have caused my parents. They struggled with existence in the old country. They went through immense pain to come to America and succeed. They offered me incredible opportunities that one could only dream about, and I said, 'No thanks.' My father must be very disappointed and pissed beyond belief.

Rachel nodded; her expression thoughtful.

"But as angry and pained as he must be," Saul continued, "my dad recognizes that he, too, went against the tide when he left. As bad as things were, people saw him as having a good job. There was financial stability. But for him, he wanted more, for himself and his wife and children. So now? He tolerates me going my own way."

"All that somehow seems different," Rachel mused.

"Different circumstances, yes, but similar issues," Saul said, his tone firm. "Community activism is not for you if you can't tolerate small battle pressures."

Rachel sighed, her eyes meeting Saul's. "I just worry, you know? About you, about us, about everything we're trying to do."

"I know," Saul said gently. "And that's why we're such a good team. You keep me grounded. You remind me of what's important. But I need you to trust that I can handle the critics and the naysayers. We've come this far together, and we'll keep pushing forward."

Rachel smiled, squeezing his hand. "I do trust you. And I'm here for the long haul."

"Good," Saul said, returning her smile. "Because we've got a lot more work ahead of us, and I wouldn't want to do it with anyone else."

Elijah paused and said to the group, "So we see Saul and Rachel not as leaders or followers, sufferers, or victims, but as facilitators. Facilitators often go unnoticed but are instrumental in allowing or even creating progress. One might wonder if Saul did a bit too much or two little facilitating in Detroit that made him so insistent to leave Detroit. But back to what we do know… "

On April 22, 1932, shortly after the first edition of the "Iowa Democrat" and Saul's mention in the Des Moines Register as Roosevelt's Iowa campaign manager, the Iowa Jewish Newspaper debuted. The introductory editorial urged support for Jewish activities and open dialogue. It encouraged readers to support Jewish activities, coordinate efforts, and share their opinions.

The paper faced immediate challenges, as Saul had anticipated. Despite the successful launch of the Iowa Democrat, doubts lingered among even his closest allies, including Pinky, the Rabbi, and perhaps Rachel, about Saul's ability to handle mounting criticism, especially given the economic climate. But Saul showed he was not merely a wannabe, a peripatetic playboy bouncing from opportunity to opportunity but fully succeeding in none.

Saul had always expected criticism and had a strategy in place. He aimed to avoid making the justification for the paper's existence an ongoing issue, steering clear of back-and-forth arguments in the editorial section. His plan was for total victory right from the start, not a prolonged battle.

His editorial response was intended to show the value of such a publication and the right of such a paper to exist. He knew how to take the high road. He was careful to write one responding editorial free from even one word of insult to or about the naysayers.

Saul headlined his second Iowa Jewish News editorial,

"CHALLENGED."

Saul began: "Several sources have challenged the publishers and team at the Iowa Jewish News as to the need for this publication. The main question seems to be: Why, after all these years without a statewide paper and especially during this economic crisis, should Des Moines and Iowa Jewry decide that they want a publication of their own?" Here, Saul was to reframe the issue.

He wrote, "Our United States of America is noted for its freedom of speech and press. Millions of Jews adopted this country as their mother country because of these liberal constitutional laws. Why should the right for this publication be challenged? Why should Iowa Jewry single-handedly be contested in exercising their rights for issuing this publication? Especially when done with fact and reason, one should be able to exercise this freedom."

Elijah noted, "Saul is raising the stakes with this tactic. The antagonists to the paper now were opposing a freely exercised constitutional freedom. This points out that the opposition was not just an affront to Saul and the publishers, but to the Constitution and all of Iowa Jewry for exercising their rights."

Saul continued to write, "But one might ask, 'What is the need or the value? First and maybe foremost, I would ask, Why is Iowa the only State in the Union with a Jewish population of over 10,000 that doesn't have one, or in some cases, multiple statewide Jewish publications?'"

Elijah continued to explain Saul's editorial approach. Saul went on to question, "Is there not value in more people knowing about public services, problems such as a robbery in one neighborhood but not another? Or is an increased awareness of others needing help of no value to the community?" The need is to create a sense of community interest and information, facts, and aspects that influence both local, statewide, and national voting decisions. Saul wrote about the importance of Jewish buying power, which should be made more evident to merchants across the state. This would help to make the Jewish community a more significant and inclusive part of the larger Iowa community. Additionally, Saul wrote that such a widespread paper would help represent Jewish voices more vocally in civic and political affairs.

Saul was motivated by history. He remembered his father, Morris, recounting how Jews became scapegoats during Russia's economic hardships, particularly by the Cossacks who blamed the Jews for every financial hardship despite the Jewish community's essential contributions to the wider community. Now, in America, Saul saw similar antisemitic sentiments, even in his favorite candidate, FDR.

Determined to protect the achievements of Iowa's Jewish community, Saul wrote that the paper would highlight Jewish charities benefiting the entire community, contributions often overlooked by the mainstream press. He envisioned the publication enhancing the coordination of educational, social, and welfare events across the state and neighboring regions. Newspapers had long fostered community cohesiveness and collective strength, and Saul believed it was time for Iowa's Jewish community to have their own voice.

Saul built a rock-solid wall for the paper in one brief editorial. He demonstrated a right to publish, a need to print, and the benefit of publishing. After that, no further challenges to the paper's existence were ever heard again.

Before retiring for the evening, Elijah commented to the group about what Saul had done. Saul employed strategic foresight and meticulous planning to fortify his nascent venture. His approach wasn't just about defending against criticism; it was about paving a path for the Iowa Jewish News to assert its significance in the economic uncertainties and communal skepticism. Nevertheless, he prepared to meet the attack. Even Rachel hadn't seen the editorial before it was published. Afterward, she asked how he came to write it.

Saul explained to her that before publication, he'd written the most intense argument he could come up with if he were personally to criticize the development of the paper. He then wrote a second argument refuting the first. Saul had learned that approach from watching the compositional process of the opinion columnists in Detroit. Then again, it had been more robust and more objectively reinforced as he watched his younger brother prepare for moot court when he was studying to become an attorney. His brother told him, 'A good trial attorney looks at both sides of the argument when preparing his closing."

Saul sighed with a mix of relief and contemplation as Rachel complimented him on his editorial. "This one was straightforward," he acknowledged, "but the challenges ahead will demand a nuanced approach. It's not just about winning arguments; it's about fostering understanding and unity within our community and reliance upon one another," he added, glancing at Rachel with a sense of understanding.

<h1 style="text-align:center">Chapter Thirty-five</h1>

After hearing about the successful launch of the Iowa Jewish News, it felt like the main issues and long-debated conflicts in Elijah's story had been resolved. It was as if, as a group, they had climbed a mountain, and after a few disagreements about which paths to follow, they safely came down the other side. Once they heard about the Iowa Jewish News successfully beginning publication, Elijah's story's main issues appeared resolved. Nothing seemed left on the table.

When they began this evening's session, the mood was relaxed, without one ounce of tension. One by one, they ticked off their summary of each issue. Rachel and Saul appeared to have a good working partnership. They recognized one another's quirks and strengths and learned to negotiate to move forward with a task. Saul was not a con but rather a diamond in the rough. He rose to heights, often unimaginable, to accomplish what others thought unlikely. Saul grew in the process. His New York trip, meeting Howe, and subsequently working with the Iowa Democrat comprised Saul's undergraduate political science education.

Many felt that the story had come to a close. The two escapees from Detroit had metaphorically negotiated the rough waters and landed safely on the other shore, just as their parents had done in reality.

Elijah smiled, listening to the light-hearted discussion. It was almost as if group members were congratulating themselves on bringing the bacon home. But Elijah's self-serving smirk reflected that he knew they were not done yet. Elijah had one more exciting episode to share.

Elijah interrupted the proceedings, "Before you begin to feel complacent about how things went for Rachel and Saul, let's hear about an exciting phone conversation shortly before the Iowa Jewish News was first published.

Saul had been at the office of the paper, scurrying from one reporter to another, everyone pushing to meet the appointed press time for their first publication. Rachel was helping out when she told Saul that Louis Howe was on the phone.

Terribly busy and annoyed at the interruption, Saul initially said, "Tell him I'm tied up and will call back later." Instead, Rachel, sitting nearby, watched him with a raised eyebrow. She then extended her arm, holding the phone further towards Saul, cocking her head and giving him a look that spoke volumes. "Really? So, you're not going to take the call from your leader?" her expression seemed to say.

Saul sighed, defeated. "Ok, ok, give it to me," he grumbled, snatching the phone. "I wonder what Louis wants now. He's probably checking up to make sure the flock is still committed," he muttered under his breath.

Bringing the phone to his ear, he forced a chipper tone. "Hi, Louis. How are you doing? You must be up to your earlobes with the convention coming up."

"Hello Saul, things are fine here. How are things coming along with your newspaper? I'm sure you're relieved to be getting the time to give it the full attention it needs. When is your press time?" Louis' voice came through the receiver.

"Probably April, real soon now," Saul answered, flipping through some papers.

"Great, is Rachel enjoying having more of your time now that the work on the campaign has slowed down?" Louis inquired.

"We do see more of each other," Saul admitted, a warmth creeping into his voice. "Rachel is as busy as ever, though. She's helping with the paper and continues making calls and chatting with people in communities away from Des Moines," he explained, glancing at Rachel across his desk. "I think she's enjoying it."

"I'm sure she's waited for this," Louis chuckled. "Your headlong dive into national politics without any initiation was stressful for you both. And I appreciate the work you did. Fine job."

"Yes, she's happy that I can now prioritize what's important to us," Saul replied as his voice softened. "However, Louis," he started, his tone now turning serious, "you are a very busy man with a convention coming up. So, as much as I am pleased to get a personal, social call from you, we both need to focus on our work. What's up?"

Louis hesitated for a moment. "You're right, of course," he conceded. "However," he continued, leaning closer to the receiver, "I wanted to ask if you felt your attendance at the convention was necessary?"

"Necessary? For what?" Saul asked, raising an eyebrow.

"To keep your group in tow," Louis said vaguely.

"As a chaperone?" Saul scoffed, a smile playing on his lips. "I doubt it. Most of them are older than I am."

"No, I mean keeping the votes tight," Louis clarified.

"Oh, ok," Saul said, understanding dawning on him. "No, not really. These people are good at their word and probably 90% committed to what Roosevelt suggested for the country. I don't need to be there to keep them committed."

"Coming from the deep well of politics, I've grown skeptical about people keeping their word," Louis admitted. "But Ok, great, I'm glad to hear that about the people in Iowa."

A wry smile spread across Saul's face. "You know, Louis," he countered dryly, "in Iowa, we too are part of the United States."

"Yes, Saul, I heard that somewhere," Louis replied with mock seriousness, "Near some pretty big rivers, so I've been told."

Saul chuckled. "But Louis, why is this so great to hear? Why so glad to be reassured? I would have called you if I were worried or had any doubts. Are you looking for an excuse to invite me to the convention? If you are, don't let me discourage you. Speak freely, my friend."

"I've always been honest and direct with you, Saul, so...," Louis began, then trailed off.

"Ya, honest and direct with some exceptions," Saul interrupted with a playful glint in his eye. "Like telling me that the Iowa Democrat was ready for publishing and only needed a new captain at the helm. All it had was a staff with no editorial direction, a few machines, and bad ideas. There was no active publisher, organization, or plan to establish one. Not much left to do there, 'ey Louis?"

Saul could practically hear Louis sigh on the other end. "Ok, I'm sorry about that," Louis finally conceded. "I was deceived, too, and it was sloppy of me. But I told you how sorry I was."

"No, you didn't," Saul countered, a hint of a smile in his voice.

"I didn't? Well, I am sorry, even if it is too late," Louis offered with a touch of resignation in his voice.

Saul grew up in wild and wooly Detroit, getting along by joking with influential people. Most seemed to enjoy the byplay. But he wasn't sure how far to push Howe. He didn't know him that well.

"Ok, Mr. Direct, apology appreciated. Still, what's this phone call about? Why are you interested in whether I think I need to be at the convention and so happy I say no? You've got me curious."

Louis took a deep breath, considering his words carefully.

"Well, before you interrupted me with grievances months old, what I was about to say was that we usually invite all state campaign managers to the convention. We pay for their room and expenses." Saul leaned back in his chair, tapping his fingers thoughtfully on the desk.

"Sounds reasonable. But I've told you the Iowa delegation shouldn't be a burden. So, are you still saying that I should go anyway?"

Louis shifted in his seat, "Honestly, Saul, I've got mixed feelings. You've earned the right. But that's not the issue. Most of our campaign managers are seasoned, not wet behind the ears. There is never a doubt about them attending. Usually, they're also delegates. But your job as manager asked a lot of you, considering everything you had on your plate. You were still writing regular columns for the Iowa Democrat and trying to give birth to the Iowa Jewish News. No energy was left to get down in the weeds by vying for a delegate role. But you were essential to our campaign." Saul nodded slowly, understanding the weight of Louis's words.

"Your value to the campaign is not the issue motivating my call. I was expecting you to attend like all the other managers. My coordinator is working on plans for all of you right now. What motivated my call was my concern about pushing you into something you didn't want to do or may not be in your best interest."

"Louis, you seem to have reservations about me going. Why?"

Louis sighed, rubbing his temple, "The other campaign managers have been in the business quite a while and have seen the seamier side of things. But unless you've operated at one of these shindigs, you have no idea how much can go wrong. A steady hand and eye on the tiller are more critical than you know."

Saul leaned forward, his gaze intense, "So? What does that have to do with me? Louis, what's the problem?"

Louis hesitated yet bluntly stated, "You're young and still untainted. These things are filthy. You wind up seeing things and even saying or doing things that you can't wash off afterward but live with."

"Louis, for goodness' sake, I'm not some innocent kid. And I do understand the national issues, not just the Iowa issues." Saul's jaw tightened, and his voice was steady but firm.

Louis raised his hands, trying to calm the rising tension through the phone, "I know Saul, I know. And I'm not trying to put you down or discredit you in any way. On the contrary, I'm trying to protect you."

Saul's eyebrows shot up mockingly as his tone shifted to sarcasm, "What, to keep me innocent, maintain my political virginity?"

Louis chuckled softly, shaking his head, "Maybe, sort of, I don't know. I don't know what you experienced in Detroit. No matter what you saw there or how seamy, corrupt, or even illegal, it doesn't hold a candle to what goes on in national politics. You may think you've seen it all, but you haven't. I'm not trying to protect you from knowing about it. But you don't need to get involved. And once you're in Chicago, you're involved if not in reality in other people's minds."

"Do you think I'll come out of it so sullied that it will ruin my reputation, my position in Des Moines, make it impossible to accomplish what I want here?" Saul rubbed his chin thoughtfully, weighing Louis's words.

"Not likely, at least I hope not. But it may change your view of the world. Sometimes, I think that you see good and bad.

And you strike me as someone who wants to take the high road, but there are a lot of grays out there. That gray road is not always a high one. Sometimes, maybe too often, we call that the compromise road. I don't know." Louis shrugged, sounding genuinely concerned. "Maybe I'm just trying to keep you the untouched optimist. Maybe I wish we could freeze things the way they are today. You know, not complicate things."

"Louis, I appreciate everything you are saying and the warning you are giving me. But, first, you can't be so naive to think I've never cut a corner or two. Some people would say maybe more." Saul's smile hinted at the determination in his eyes. "However, to participate as a journalist, especially in writing editorials, I think it is dishonest not to be aware of the whole picture. So, I guess you'll have to accept the burden of introducing me to evil. Make our reservations."

"Our reservations? Who is our?" Louis raised an eyebrow, puzzled.

"Oh Louis, after letting me wander New York alone and get mixed up with riff-raff like you, you think Rachel would let me loose in Chicago alone?" Saul chuckled, "Of course. I must discuss it with Rachel, but I suspect we'll both be there and on your dime! Isn't that a just reward for all my work?"

Louis Howe hung up without saying goodbye but likely had a smile.

Saul gave Rachel a synopsis of the call with Louis. By this time, she knew Saul well enough to know that he couldn't and shouldn't be kept from this convention. Further, working in the hotel lobby meant she was exposed to much more than Louis Howe would imagine. So, Rachel and Saul planned their trip.

Rachel was quite excited. Besides briefly visiting with Saul's sister Rebecca on their way from Detroit to Des Moines, she'd never spent time in Chicago. Rachel was elated. What she had heard about the Windy City growing up excited her. She looked forward to the unique architecture, nightlife, and beautiful walk along the Lake. Just the year before, Jane Addams had won the Nobel Peace Prize for her international efforts toward peace. She was also renowned for her work with settlement houses for immigrants and the community social services center she founded, Hull House in Chicago. Rachel was excited to visit Hull House, the new planetarium, and maybe even the new aquarium. An opportunity to stay at the Palmer House, one of Chicago's most famous hotels, was a special treat.

It was in July of '32 when Rachel's excitement grew as they rode the Rock Island Line from Des Moines to Chicago. Of course, Saul also looked forward to seeing his sister Rebecca and filling her in on all that had happened to them. But, once they got to the convention, all plans changed. They had only a short period to spend with Rebecca. In addition to Saul being busy, Rachel was put to work, and sightseeing plans were quickly relegated to nothing more than a figment of her imagination.

Saul's advanced degree came at the 1932 Democratic National Convention in Chicago. But, of course, if you like hearing about the '32 convention in Chicago sometime, check out the 1968 fiasco. Another chaotic event to behold."

Elijah stopped to measure the interest shown on the assembled faces. Everyone was very attentive. Soon, people were encouraging him to tell them what happened in Chicago.

"Ok, here we go, into the circus that makes Barnum and Bailey look calm. This can be the beginning of a long night for us," said Elijah. Let's first take a break.

Campers vanished into RVs and restrooms, craving refreshments. The fun was just starting. Storytelling group members returned, their excitement almost tangible. Were they genuinely thrilled or simply eager for the juicy convention gossip?

Elijah rose, his stance commanding attention. He wanted to set the scene for the big event, "Politics in '32 wasn't your average dogfight," he began, voice low and intense. "Sure, it's always a power struggle, but back then, the game was different. No primaries, no big announcements. It was all about lining up delegates and playing hardball before the convention even started. A few votes could be your golden ticket.

Elijah leaned forward, "The Democratic party in the 1930s was a fractured coalition - northerners who supported repealing Prohibition and immigration, with southern racists who were anti-immigrant and anti-Catholic, and western mavericks all vying for influence. It made for a chaotic and contentious convention."

Matt whistled, "Sounds like a real circus. No wonder Saul and Rachel were in for a wild ride in Chicago."

Elijah nodded, then continued, "An agreement was rare, six shooters standard, and it made for a wild ride."

He paused, letting the words sink in before he resumed. "To whatever consortium of united policy groups that existed, add into the mix the power groups interested in only gaining influence. That meant manipulating to align themselves with a winner in order to pursue their personal objectives of more local power. They were willing to compliment anyone's policy to gain favor. Whether it be the political machines like Tammany Hall in New York, the mobs or special interest forces and favorite son candidates, it was a free-for-all. With many candidates seeking support, there would likely be no clear-cut winner on the first ballot.

Elijah took a sip of water, then glanced around the group before continuing, "Roosevelt was portrayed as a weak and soft candidate by all and had an ongoing battle with Smith, whom he had nominated for president in previous conventions. In turn, Smith returned the favor to Roosevelt, supporting FDR in replacing him as governor of New York. But Smith still had great power and control over naming the New York delegate contingent. Nearly unanimously, Roosevelt's home delegation favored Smith over FDR. Even Roosevelt's national campaign manager couldn't get a position as a delegate." Elijah leaned forward, his voice growing more intense.

The result of all this was that it was going to be a brokered convention composed of threats and promises made to be kept or broken."

As Elijah sat back down, Matt rubbed his hands and said, "Ok, let's hear some good old-time politicking. You know the dirt and good stuff."

"That something you know a lot about Matt, quipped Harry?"

"Oh ya, been right in the thick of it."

"Really, what were you running for?"

"Sheriff, in this small town we lived in. Lots of corruption. The general store raised shovel prices when the old man... um, forgot his name. Anyway, this old guy who owned the hardware store got sick. They had to close it for a while 'till he recovered. The general store manager decided to open and raise shovel prices immediately. That wasn't right. So, I decided to run for Sheriff."

"Bet you made a hell of a campaign out of that issue, Matt."

"Sure did. But dirty politics was going on, probably worse than in '32. We'll see, though. Those boys were pretty rough back then."

"What kind of dirty politics in your election?"

"Well, I had posters, pictures on them, you know, a bunch of kids got paid to tear 'em down or draw an ugly mustache on them. So, I wrote a letter to the newspaper's editor saying the current Sheriff was behind it, but they didn't publish my letter."

"How'd the shovel issue play out for you?"

"Well, no one understood it as a campaign issue. I got that the voters were confused. I mean, it didn't fall under the jurisdiction of the Sheriff. But it was a point regarding personal values and moral behavior. So people agreed with me on that issue, but that didn't necessarily win any votes."

"How'd that election work out, Matt?"

"Oh, I lost, probably voter fraud," several campers smiled, unsure if Matt was serious or kidding. "But in the end, it didn't make any difference because we lived outside the city limits on our ranch, and I wasn't eligible to run anyway. But the general store owner told me I was right, that his general manager shouldn't have raised his shovel prices. He apologized and said that it wasn't a nice thing to do. Right nice fella too. But even he didn't vote for me. A year later, he bought our ranch when we moved. I gave him a good price, too."

Tim challenged, "Matt is that true, or are you bullshitting us?"

Matt laughed and shook his head, "I ain't telling. Just setting the mood for tonight. Your turn, Elijah."

"Matt, I'm not sure if I have the ammunition to match up against the corruption of your campaign, but I'll try. But to Tim's point, I'm also unsure how much of what I will say is true. So, guess it doesn't matter. As long as, in the end, FDR wins. You guys wouldn't go along with me if I changed that."

Many group members smiled, glad, freed from the burden of choosing fact from fiction. But Elijah continued, "Actually, kidding aside, we know quite a bit about what went down at that convention."

He paused, letting the tension build, "Once Saul and Rachel walked into the Palmer House as guests of the Roosevelt campaign, they were immersed in pandemonium. Orders were barked from all directions, and who should or would respond wasn't clear.

There was constant plotting for advantage between the candidates. The campaign was a high-stakes chess match, tactics shifting daily as rivals countered each other's moves. Espionage was rife, and security paramount. Though not the clear frontrunner, Roosevelt held the most initial support, making him the prime target. Howe and Farley, his seasoned campaign veterans, juggled logistics while charming delegates. Recognizing Roosevelt's powerful voice, Howe devised a personal touch: a phonograph record and signed photo for each delegate, a pre-convention blitz of intimacy.

Howe centralized the campaign at a single hotel, implementing a tightly controlled phone system monitored by his hand-picked operators. Security was paramount. The campaign's predominantly female clerical staff posed a unique challenge. Concerned about potential vulnerabilities, Howe tasked Rachel with addressing security concerns with this all-woman staff and the dangers of romantic entanglements. Identifying potential moles among the staff and opposing campaigns was a daunting task.

When Howe brought this task up to Rachel, she was flabbergasted, held both hands chest high as if trying to push away or fend off an attacker, and exclaimed, "How am I supposed to do that? Who am I to these women, most of whom are older than I am? Why would they listen to me telling them what to do? Where am I even supposed to meet with them? Where do I get a list of all the women on the staff? No, Mr. Howe, this idea just isn't possible."

Louis Howe was seasoned at dealing with someone panicking. Rachel was panicking. His go-to response was calm and reassuring, and he said it with a gentle voice and caring tone. His words were few but sufficient, most of the time to extradite himself from involvement with the panicky person who was usually standing, mumbling, and awaiting a helpful hand. That response was, "Why, I'm sure you can figure it out. It's why I picked you." Then, as he quickly turned and left, he nicely said, "Thank you so much."

And Rachel did figure it out. "Oh well, in for a penny and a pound." Rachel decided to pretend as if she belonged because now, she did. Isn't that what she did in the hotel lobby? So, without consulting with Saul or anyone else, she politely but firmly bothered hotel staff to get all the conference room reservations, hospitality service, and personnel lists she needed. Her calling card? That she was doing all this at Mr. Louis Howe's request.

She decided to use a soft approach with the women rather than a bureaucratic authoritarian one. Rachel looked too young to pull off an authority role. Rachel created a private hospitality room and sent notes inviting all-female staff to visit the space for information, relaxation, coffee, food, and plenty of time for pleasantries. There, the women had an excellent chance to get to know one another. It served as an opportunity to do informal team building because when the intense work started, they would have to back up one another when busy. It also kept them away from potential spies.

The room became a favorite for many women, as after a busy day, they could come there and eat, meet, gossip, and even find some alcoholic beverage. Rachel quickly added a light jazz quartet each night that encouraged the occasional dancing by the women.

Rachel began to feel like a den mother to older, tired women. This seemed strange, but apparently, no one resented her. Usually, she wouldn't stay late. She didn't want to seem like a monitor or chaperone. She and Saul would soon depart for dinner when the room was up and running. At Rachel's sole discretion, goodies were replenished by the hotel staff until midnight each night of the convention. The women came to view Rachel as someone there to help them, and they appreciated rather than resented her. Some even mothered her. They saw her as being a caring daughter.

At dinner, Saul asked Rachel, "How do you like your new, unpaid employment, dear?"

Rachel chuckled softly and set down her fork, "Well, it isn't the experience I feared. We laugh and make fun of all the bigwigs running around thinking they're important. The usual talk is about how women could probably do all this better. With Jane winning the Nobel Peace Prize and all these women being from Chicago, many think she'd make a better president than any of the male candidates. After all my experiences in Detroit, around the clubs and the hotel, I find it strange that so many women stay in at night, not going out with the guys."

Saul smiled knowingly, "Well, there may be a reason for that."

"What kind of reason." Rachel tilted her head, curious.

Saul leaned back in his chair, folding his arms, "Well, you know that during the first meeting Louis arranged for you with the women, you told them gently about security concerns? Then you introduced him and had him come in and say a few words and answer any of the many questions they may have about the nature and structure of a political convention."

"Of course, I remember that." Rachel nodded, recalling the event.

Saul continued, "And you mentioned that it is an exciting operation as a political convention, and you were sure that they would like hearing about it from an expert. So, you introduced him, then left."

"Sure, I remember it. You and I then went for that great walk down Michigan Avenue."

Saul chuckled, "Great walk, ya. But also, great intrigue back at the ranch."

"Straight talk Saul, not verbal hieroglyphics." Rachel frowned, puzzled.

Saul leaned forward, lowering his voice, "One piece of information Louis wanted to remind these nice ladies about is that this is a political convention. He emphasized the word political. He then reminded them of the phrase quite common for those in the know here and nationwide: Politics Chicago Style."

"And what is that supposed to mean?" Rachel's eyes widened.

Saul sighed, leaning back, "Most of these women knew. It means politics mob-style. Since the first century, politics in Chicago has been by machine. One party or another controls everything that happens: every local election, every sidewalk that is fixed or not. Until about 1920, the control in Chicago had been all Republican. Now, it is the Democrats who have total control. So, if you want anything done or to get a city job, you vote Democratic and put your request into the ward boss appointed by city hall. I learned all about that when studying Tammany Hall in New York."

Rachel nodded slowly, "Ok, I get it politics here is closely held and probably corrupt like Tammany Hall, but what does that have to do with 'Politics Chicago Style' and these nice women?"

"Well, since Prohibition, the machines have had partners from the mobs. And all the mobs, Lucky Luciano, Frank Costello, and Myer Lansky, are here or will be. All the groups are hopeful they might be able to get considerable control or influence over the White House selection. That makes the group of men dangerous combatants competing for information. You are potentially jeopardizing yourself if you spill confidential information important to the wrong person. You can never rely on anyone. Louis quickly pointed out to the women that this was not a threat but more like a public service announcement."

"And he told them, without holding back, that any forward advances from men during the coming week should be viewed as a political tactic, not a personal compliment. Anything from candy, flowers, invitations, or flattery should be seen as a technique, only to be validated after the convention, if desired."

"That is horrible to scare those women like that. And how can information and allegiance change day to day?" Rachel's face grew serious.

Saul sighed, shaking his head, "Because all the mob cares about is power, not national policy. Just what is good for the mob and the mob's buddies. The more chaos they can stir up, the more they can put people on edge, and the more control and power they can acquire. Louis didn't create or back this system. He just reminded the women it exists. In just this sort of setting, it runs amok. He warned them not to take any risks. Hence, your unexpectedly good attendance and less dating. This week is politics, Chicago style."

"Saul, this is just horrible. What can we do about this?"

Saul laughed. "Rachel, Rachel, we can't do anything. The mobs in Detroit acted similarly regarding local politics. There, it wasn't as big or organized as at a national political convention, but face it, honey, that gunshot in a hotel came from somewhere and was about something other than robbing a bank. Here, at the convention, some people do as much as possible to decrease the unjustified interference in the purely political process. Yet others are doing their best to control and distort that process."

Chapter Thirty-six

For the last day of the story, the group decided on a late afternoon potluck, complete with a Dutch oven campfire chocolate cake. Everyone looked forward to munching down on a wonderfully prepared dessert. But first, at the noon meeting, Elijah continued to set the scene.

"The 1932 Democratic National Convention was memorable for many reasons," he began, pausing to let the weight of his words settle over the group. "The event is remembered by history as the moment a world leader, FDR, was chosen to begin his ascent to power." Elijah took a deep breath, surveying the faces around him.

"The details of dates and nominating events revealed in the history books fail to express the full impact of the experience. It is best described as a litany of pieces in perpetual motion on a three-dimensional chessboard."

He leaned forward, his eyes sparkling with excitement. "Let yourselves imagine that the convention hall was like a summit meeting of the Allied powers. Chit-chat with anybody, yet nothing was disclosed to even a trusted ally. Meaningful discussions were best held only when walking or sitting somewhere no one could eavesdrop on you."

Elijah paused to let this image take root. "Each day, delegates would hear more rumors about the alignments. Often, when a delegate listened to the latest dope, it was out of date. That's how fast things changed. They moved like shadows, seeking corners to discuss alliances. It was a place where truth and lies danced closely, and you had to be sharp to tell them apart." He stood up, pacing slightly as he continued.

"Indeed, one needed to be incredibly well-informed and to be able to easily discern the difference between lies and truth. Misinformation could be made more exciting and appealing than the truth."

Elijah stopped, turning to face the group. "There were many people regaling others with descriptions of fantasy. Information was freely passed by individuals who were guessing or fabricating well-designed stories to influence others. But this melee bore more fruits than giving us the next influential world leader. As apprehensive as all parties were about security, there were few difficulties penetrating the entrances to the hall as an observer."

Walking over to the campfire, poking at the embers. Elijah looked up, his face illuminated by the flickering flames. "In walked a young man, Patrick Hamilton, an amateur lepidopterologist and expert in the life cycle of butterflies. Professionally, he had dreams of being a successful novelist and playwright.

Rather than surviving waiting for his big chance at success as a playwright by waiting on tables, he chose to find work as a journalist, a wannabe investigative reporter, as he toiled birthing his literary masterpieces."

Elijah took a step back, letting the story unfold in his mind. "Patrick was impressed by the machinations of deception marked by lies, verbal manipulations, and misdirection that flew around the room. The activity he observed was frantic and chaotic but imbued with a promise of yielding something alive and vital."

He raised his hands as if capturing the energy of the moment. "Mr. Hamilton imagined the room like the mating forest of his favorite butterfly, the Monarch."

Elijah paused, letting the image sink in. "Imbued in the Monarch is a specific type of behavioral manipulation that occurs where one horny male tries to convince another male that he is not really a male but a female. The horny attacker then attempts to mate with his coitus partner. As they drop to the ground together, the species will not be propagated. We will never know whether the victim male became convinced of any gender alteration by this attempt at deception." He chuckled softly, then continued.

"But the idea of convincing someone else of the truth, contrary to fact, struck this wannabe playwright as an exciting theme."

Elijah's voice grew softer, more reflective. "The thoughts stimulated by the chaos at the convention intertwined with his understanding of Monarch behavior emerged as the theme of a play Hamilton wrote that opened in Great Britain in 1938. The name? 'Gaslight.' This term, seemingly less significant in the FDR era but later used today as a verb, 'Gaslighting,' has widespread prevalence and impact."

He looked around at the group, his expression serious. He went to sit down, and his voice was filled with conviction. "And so, my friends, the 1932 convention produced a world leader and a descriptive theme, 'Gaslighting,' to describe much of the struggle for power, called politics."

"Whether among the monarchs or the politicians, the manipulator is trying to get someone else (or a group of people) to question their own reality, memory, or perceptions or knowledge of the fact."

Elijah stood smiling as he observed the assembled group's glances of surprise and disbelief. He enjoyed that moment and then continued.

Rachel's new role in providing hospitality for the secretarial pool was an eye-opener for her. The women she served seemed happy but unfazed by being surrounded by such powerful and influential people. Unlike many secretarial pools in large businesses, the women handling the phone messages and errands did not gossip about the people they worked for or their daily experiences. When the women were in the hospitality room, they talked about anything other than their work at the convention.

A woman named Agnes, easily old enough to be Rachel's mother, befriended her during one afternoon break. As expected, Agnes commented on Rachel's age and how unusual it was for someone like her to have been chosen to organize the hospitality room and watch over the staff. "Who do you know to get this kind of job?"

Rachel was startled by the question. Words hesitantly tumbled out of her mouth. "Well, it's not really a job. I'm not getting paid or anything like that. I was just asked to help. I guess the person they had hired couldn't do it for one reason or another."

Agnes was quite curious and pushed further about how unusual the situation seemed. After parrying off a few more pointed questions, Rachel felt that the conversation bordered on crossing the boundaries Howe had set. In turn, Rachel took the conversation in a different direction. She enquired only about how Agnes was getting along and whether she needed anything from her.

Agnes just stared at Rachel and began to laugh. Rachel, feeling totally out of her comfort zone, softly asked, "What's so funny?"

"You're not even from here, are you?" Agnes replied, a smirk still on her face.

"No, I live in Des Moines."

Agnes chuckled again. "Oh my god, you must be married to someone who knows someone."

"Agnes, I have no idea what you are talking about."

Agnes leaned in slightly, lowering her voice. "Well, I can see that you are working hard not to gossip about the convention details. I respect that. And you are right that it is an absolute no, no. But most of the girls working in our pool know each other. We work for the same organization."

Rachel's brow furrowed. "Oh, did they hire you from some secretarial agency?"

"No," Agnes shook her head, "not that kind of organization. An organization we share gossip about regularly but rarely here at the convention. But our talk is about our bosses and the women at our usual daily work, their families, not convention politics."

Rachel was still confused. "Agnes, I'm still lost."

Agnes sighed. "OK, Rachel from Des Moines, I've bet you never heard of 'Chicago Politics.'"

"It's been briefly described to me."

"I don't know what you've been told, but it refers to the all-encompassing and all-powerful organization we all work for. But it isn't your usual type of organization. It is more of a machine run by a political dynasty. The government in Chicago and much of Illinois is sometimes run by a machine. It is a powerhouse that goes back several decades. Have you heard of Marshall's Department Store or Pullman cars on a train?"

"Of course."

Chicago's power structure has deep roots. From the industrial titans like Pullman and Field to the political machines that followed, the city has been shaped by those controlling its finances. Today, that power is primarily held by the Democratic machine. Most of us here depend on it for our jobs. So, when I asked about who you work for, I meant it as a casual question about being a big convention hostess, not some deep-seated conspiracy."

"Chicago Politics seems quite interesting."

Agnes nodded. "Well, the man in the street would describe it with images of corruption, marked by shady alliances meeting in smoke-filled rooms, conniving with local bosses to steal the next election so that their mayor could maintain the power of a pharaoh. Some of that is likely true, but it works in many ways. But I guess the machine doesn't have its tentacles into Des Moines yet. So, Rachel from Des Moines just happened to get snagged up to provide coffee, baked goods, pretzels, nuts, and booze. But watch your back, kid. You can still learn a lot and have fun."

Agnes smiled at an overwhelmed Rachel, got up, and left.

Harry piped up, "Hey Elijah, before you proceed with this, I just want to ensure we aren't in jeopardy by hearing anything else you say."

Elijah paused, a faint smile playing on his lips. "No, Harry, I think you're safe. You'd definitely be considered outdated and probably too old for the modern machines."

Harry chuckled, then warned, "Be careful about how you demean your elders, Elijah. We're all members of AARP and are not to be toyed with."

Elijah raised his hands in mock surrender. "I'll behave, Harry. But you're getting the picture here. Just the kind of warnings Harry is giving me were subtly given to all the clerical help of the campaign. Now, I know that the AARP has a modicum of civility. So that makes me relatively safe. And I don't believe that Harry is a mob-made man anyway. No offense, Harry, but you don't seem like the type. So, therefore, I feel safe."

He leaned back in his seat, his gaze sweeping the group. "But many of these women could not feel safe dealing with Al Capone or any of the mob very present at the convention."

Elijah's expression grew serious. "But Howe, FDR, and his management team didn't depend on mob contacts. Remember, FDR's voice and demeanor were persuasive. Farley would get as many delegates as possible, especially those undecided or not yet committed, and bring them individually to the Roosevelt campaign room and give them a chance to talk personally with FDR by phone. They were leaving no stone unturned in urging support."

He glanced around the group, ensuring everyone was following. "Howe kept cards on each delegate, with as much personal information as possible to be used in a crunch if necessary. Preparing for the conversations with delegates and knowing the names of wives, children, and business associates could be a very personal touch."

Kathy spoke up, her brow furrowed. "Elijah, now you're telling us a story. But it's getting dicey about stuff, very creative if fiction, scary if real. Is this convention stuff for real, or are you just making it up?"

Elijah smiled, nodding slightly. "Well, I guess that is a fair question at this point. I don't want to falsely impugn anyone's character. But no, the essence of the mob stuff and FDR's campaign acumen is true. A woman named Rebecca Onion, a journalist for Slate, wrote an article about it, explaining the mob stuff. In it, she gave an example of those cards FDR had."

He reached into his bag, pulling out some papers and cards. "I don't always talk about this stuff when telling this story. But, when I have, I've been amazed at how many folks just can't believe it. No one ever questions Leah walking hundreds of miles in the winter with a two-year-old and a six-year-old while avoiding rape, mayhem, and possible starvation. But they're quickly doubtful about some strong-arming or threats in more modern times. It's as if we think everything is safer now or more civilized. That the members of our species have been tamed and won't engage in abuse.

I'm unsure about that when you look at what's happening today. But, considering they've found evidence that humans were cannibalistic, eating each other a million and a half years ago, maybe we've made some progress after all."

He handed out the cards to the one nearest to him, "As I said, this comes up every time. I have no intention of besmirching the reputation of our stalwart politicians. So, I printed out the details the Onion journalist printed on some cards for doubters like Kathy to see. I will hand these out to you to see how data is kept. The same is done by politicians today, even much more sophisticated, with giant data banks of information about you. But they didn't have computers in 1932."

Elijah picked up a card and read aloud, "So here, I'll read the first part of one of Howe's cards on a Texan named Jesse Jones: 'Money—Houston Chronicle, owner of—For himself first, last, and all the time—Ambitious—Promises everybody everything—Double-crosser.' And it goes on to deal with hobbies, like family and other valuable information. Anyway, the cards are being passed around for you to see."

He paused, letting everyone absorb the information. "Roosevelt needed the full support of Tammany Hall to secure the nomination. However, the connections between politics and organized crime were deeply intertwined. With their powerful influence, figures like Luciano and Costello weren't about to relinquish their hold on the White House. Everyone wanted a winning horse, so Costello and Tammany Hall's Hines backed Roosevelt."

Elijah leaned forward, his eyes narrowing. "Keeping track of these players is like trying to follow a dizzying football game with constant player substitutions and team switches. Luciano and Marinelli, a ward boss with control over elections, opposed Roosevelt. Their close relationship, including sharing a hotel room, solidified their alliance. Meanwhile, Costello and Hines shared accommodations, symbolizing their united front."

He gestured with his hands, emphasizing the complexity. "While all this wheeling and dealing happened, Rachel was excited and apprehensive. She was inadvertently cast into a role with women over whom she had no authority. As friendly as she tried to be, she noticed the women were extremely cordial, even warm, in the few days before the convention formally met, but no one attempted to get close after the delegates poured in. Unmitigated trust was a dangerous commodity at this political convention."

Elijah paused as his voice dropped a note, "But, like it or not, she floated around in this cloud of uncertainty of who meant what to whom. Then, she witnessed a clandestine operation in the ordinary course of moving from one place to another. Lucky Luciano and Frank Costello decided to have a personal meeting. They knew eyes were on them, each camp on the other. If anyone knew Luciano and Costello were collaborating, parties might join forces to thwart their intentions. Trust was nonexistent." Elijah leaned back in his seat, looking contemplative.

"Staying at the same hotel made it easier for their 'observers' to do their duty. It lessened the demand for excess manpower. But the colluding men didn't want to meet in the hotel. Technology then differed from today, so the meet was arranged in a place far enough out of town to quickly notice if someone was following. Also, the departure for Lucky was to be very secretive. At a designated time, his men stopped all the elevators so no one could exit on Lucky's floor. This gave him time to leave his room, get to the stairwell, and leave the hotel."

Elijah's eyes twinkled as he shared this, "As Lucky and his entourage descended the stairs, Rachel happened to be ascending the stairs. They passed with Lucky saying, 'Afternoon, ma'am.' Then, eyes averted, she muttered, 'Sir,' and they each went their own way."

He glanced around, ensuring everyone was still with him. "The rift between Luciano and Costello didn't hinge on political ideology; they were more concerned with securing a powerful position within the convention. The mob effectively hedged its bets by supporting both sides. Roosevelt, however, required the full backing of Tammany Hall. Amidst the intense investigation into organized crime, Roosevelt shrewdly distanced himself from the accusations, publicly condemning corruption while lacking concrete evidence to prosecute Tammany leaders. This calculated move earned him Tammany's crucial support."

Elijah paused, then continued, "Subsequently, FDR got the backing of their delegation, which helped gain momentum. Many factors led to a sufficient number of votes for the nomination. Roosevelt offered the VP spot to Garner, earning his delegates from the Texas and the California delegations and thereby getting the nomination by the third ballot.

At dinner, after the third ballot, Rachel asked Saul how the mob decided to join forces for Roosevelt. He explained the situation, telling her they held separate positions until late. Reading the political momentum, neither side wanted to risk being left out in the cold. So, they arranged a secret meeting somewhere."

"Oh, ya," said Rachel, "I think I saw Lucky leaving for that meeting. I met him in the stairwell as he was probably going. Luciano was very polite. Initially, I thought it was funny that he was taking the stairs. But maybe it wasn't so funny, really. Something seemed to be wrong with the elevators. I was going one floor up when my elevator got stuck, but the door would open. So, I got out, and I just walked the last flight." She buttered her bread and smiled.

But back to the convention and the election. It is worthwhile to point out an unusual circumstance. One near and dear to the main characters in our story. Near the convention's end, Roosevelt appeared on the podium before he was formally announced as the winner. This was remarkable and unprecedented. With disguised help, he walked across the stage to call attention to his strong recuperation from polio and his readiness to be president of The United States.

FDR saw this as a golden opportunity to recruit national headlines and interest, thereby gaining a wider audience for his policies. Prior to 1932, it would have been undignified to have the nominee address the national convention. No nominee had ever done that before. Usually, such an acceptance speech was given to a smaller audience, often weeks later.

However, Roosevelt wanted to show that he saw a better future. Another unprecedented move was the fact that he came by airplane to the Chicago convention. Flying was still thought to be risky by many in those years. One columnist wrote, "There was someone wanting to occupy the highest position in the land who had faith in modern new transportation.

FDR went on to boldly challenge traditional economic policies, specifically targeting the "Leak Through Theory" - a concept akin to modern trickle-down economics. While Roosevelt championed aid for the struggling, Smith, his opponent for the nomination, and Hoover, who would eventually be his Republican opponent, both vehemently opposed Roosevelt's economic plans, warning of class warfare and economic ruin. Roosevelt countered that existing laws already favored the wealthy, creating a form of class warfare. FDR argued that Smith's lack of support of even limited aid to those suffering and without jobs, along with increased tariffs, would exacerbate the plight of the lower classes.

To all of you sitting here tonight, that may seem ho-hum, but to politicians everywhere, Roosevelt's speech led to instant and oft-repeated cataplexy. The Republicans, reading his comments in the papers the following morning, nearly collapsed in glee, thinking, 'This man has just dug his own political grave.' Many democratic politicians feared the electorate would hear this as a tax increase. For some Democrats, the news in the paper shook their composure. They lamented, 'Oh my goodness, what has he done?' Saul and more than one other American, both Democratic and Republican, heard this and thought, 'Go, man, go.'

A significant postscript for the mob? After the third ballot, when Roosevelt secured the nomination for the presidency, FDR, the governor, went ahead and loosened the reins on the state prosecutor. Subsequently, many people in the mob were indicted for corruption and convicted. Even though Roosevelt had given them a reason to believe he would go soft on crime. By the time FDR took the White House in 1933, he had broken all ties with Tammany Hall and even supported LaGuardia for Mayor. This was the first break between the Democratic party and Tammany Hall in over 100 years.

Exhausted yet exhilarated, Rachel and Saul rode the train home, their minds still reeling from the day's revelations. Saul, a refugee from the oppressive grip of Russia, had played a pivotal role in a historic political event. Rachel, nestled against his shoulder, found solace in his presence. As the train clicked along the 311 miles back to Des Moines, Saul couldn't help but contrast the momentary comfort of the journey of his current life to the arduous path he traveled from his Russian birthplace to the heart of American politics. This train ride felt like a mere blink.

When they got home, Saul remarked to friends that Louis Howe had a significant role as floor manager for FDR. Saul's only contact with FDR's people after the victory in '32 was a brief telegram from Roosevelt thanking him for his work as state campaign manager. In performing that job, Saul was forever vigilant. He worked to maintain the morale of the many lieutenants he had gathered around the state, to work to register democrats and get out the vote. Saul expected FDR to win the '32 election by a landslide. He repeated that Roosevelt could lose only if they failed to get the message to the voters. He told his campaigners not to worry about the attacks, the accusations that would come Roosevelt's way. Instead, say to people, "Without name-calling or using labels, let's look at what FDR stands for. Then go back over and over and over the bread, food, jobs mantra."

And that is what Saul did every time he could put pen to paper and get it published. Final count: Roosevelt had over 22 million votes and 472 electoral college votes, while Hoover had 15 million and 59 electoral college votes. FDR carried Iowa with nearly 58% of the vote. Interestingly, he lost Polk County, where Des Moines was located. Saul was a good prognosticator because he knew the common man. At heart, he was an ordinary man. Roosevelt spent three full terms and part of a fourth working for the common man. FDR only sometimes won the legislative or legal battle, but the Second World War significantly challenged his presidency. The war's end helped to rebuild the economy, to everyone's relief.

When the election of 1932 was over, Saul and Rachel continued working on the Jewish News. Getting that off the ground proved much more complicated than the Iowa Democrat had been. Nevertheless, making it what they wanted it to be was a fulfilling challenge. The paper and Des Moines would be their home for twenty years."

Elijah took advantage of a poignant silence. The ever-present serenity of the desert was prominent. He slowly continued.

"Now, it was time for them to birth the next generation into their story. We need to get these kids growing so that they may create exciting scenarios for our next story." Elijah got up and walked toward his rig.

The group was silent. They were sure Elijah had just said, "The End," without uttering those words.

Epilogue

Many hoped maybe it wouldn't end there. Someone loudly protested, "At least tell us about the kids these two had," others applauded. As with many homespun tales, listeners had grown attached to these characters and identified with their joys, fears, and struggles. Elijah hadn't said a word! Yet the discussion among group members continued into the night. Elijah had just gone to get his nightly beer.

When he returned, Larry looked up and asked, "Elijah, why did you pick this story over others? You must know? What are the lessons of your story that encouraged you the most? What did you want to teach us?"

Elijah paused and looked like he was contemplating the question; glancing around the room, he continued, "Well, Larry, I'm a storyteller, not a teacher. My goal is to entertain you with an enjoyable and maybe provocative story. I hope that I did that. But you're right. We can learn a lot from other peoples' stories and our own if we want. Like Lucas told his wife, the purpose of stories passed on through the years is to entertain and teach lessons. Regardless of the lessons I found in this story, what is more important is what you got from it."

Nancy nodded thoughtfully, tapping her finger against her seat, "We need to take every opportunity to focus on the positive. "You know there are T-shirts and post-it notes on our walls that say, 'It's not the destination, it's the journey.' But, unfortunately, no one guarantees that all parts of the journey are easy or fun. So learning to deal with the rough spots and not bury them is a challenge."

Cindy shifted in her seat, her eyes meeting Elijah's as she added, "Rachel certainly learned to not just react to her fear but to look beyond it and live in the real world, not just her imaginary world; I could relate to that. I know that as I've worked to overcome my OCD, that is hard. But she learned something from Saul: to listen before you assume.

Harry, who had been listening intently, finally spoke up, "I really connected with Saul's ability to assess and plan."

Elijah turned to him, curiosity piqued, "What do you mean, Harry?"

"I enjoyed seeing a good strategist at work." Harry explained, leaning forward, "Morris and even Sophia had many of the same qualities as Saul.

Nancy looked over and saw Mary Ann with her head hanging down as if she were sad. "Mary Ann, you seem sad. Are you upset that this is over?"

Mary Ann was relieved by the question. It made her chuckle and momentarily moved her away from the regret that she was feeling. She chuckled. "No, nothing like that. No offense, Elijah, but I can live without a nightly bedtime story. Missing it won't drive me to tears." Others laughed, too. Elijah briefly touched his fist to his heart.

"But I was feeling gratitude but with a big dose of regret mixed with two teaspoons of loss." The group remained silent.

"What struck me so hard was Saul's relationship with Pinky. As we said, Pinky was an angel in Saul's life. This person he stumbled on accidentally changed his whole life. What if Pinky hadn't been encouraging? Saul and Rachel would probably be in Kansas City, searching for work, or back in Detroit. Instead, they are in a wonderful situation in Des Moines. I've had such events in my life. In retrospect, I'm grateful for those times and especially for those people. But I certainly wasn't aware of the value of those serendipitous events at the time. My lack of awareness meant I never took the time to thank people for their comments, advice, or help. Now, all those angels are dead. I can't thank them. For that, I feel regret. It saddens me that I lost the opportunity to make a real connection, even by briefly acknowledging their impact."

For the following hours, many logs were added to the campfire. By the time everyone was finished discussing the forks in the road and angels at intersections pointing the way, a transcript of the evening session would look like a topographical map used to plot 20 different paths.

But Fran was not about to let everything drop. "I guess one disappointment I have is not knowing what happened in the relationship between Saul and Rachel. So, what kind of emotional relationship did these two eventually have? Was the loving relationship she wanted to be consummated? That is up in the air for me. Did they even love each other, or were they more like Morris and Leah, great partners?"

Finally, Elijah spoke up. "OK, so you can all go to bed and rest easy. I'll give you a little more about our dynamic duo couple." Elijah returned to the story and pointed out that there was no time for Saul and Rachel to reflect on what they'd been through when returning from the convention. The arduous task of developing the Iowa Jewish News was yet to be faced.

"What followed for Saul and Rachel was growing success and financial stability. The progress with the paper was what they'd hoped for. The goodwill about the Iowa Jewish News spread similar positive feelings about the new young couple in the community. As a result, their personal lives also blossomed.

At the first anniversary of the Iowa Jewish News, friends held a small party to celebrate what Rachel and Saul had brought to the community. In those years, there were two types of public restaurants in Des Moines: your regular fare of chicken, spaghetti, and fine steak dining, and key clubs or country clubs where you could store and be served your own liquor, legal or illegal. Of the latter, there were two types: a club that allowed Jews and the rest.

The Standard Club of Des Moines became the private club where Jews congregated for excellent dining, drinking, and on weekends for dancing and music. This was where Saul and Rachel were to be acknowledged by their friends and colleagues. It was a wonderful evening. Unfortunately, most of the discussion and comments have been long lost to history. But I am sure that by the end of the evening, Saul and Rachel could be found dancing to the song "Let Me Call You Sweetheart," popularized by Bing Crosby, among many others.

Saul and Rachel were excellent dancers. They loved dancing with each other. Watching them, one could feel their strong emotional connection. The following years reaffirmed that a cocoon had been created. Trust, respect, and love were found in the encased package. That package housed the surviving genes of a brutalized Sophia, who was a survival victim of inhuman brutalization and mental abuse, and from a stalwart Leah, who marched bravely, alone with two young children across Russian soil, and a creative, industrious, dreamer called Morris. Together, they became the working whole called Saul. Rachel inherited the brakes that would advantage any snowball rolling downhill. Together, as Rachel and Saul were celebrated as a loving, functional whole, we can only imagine that as Saul sang the song in Rachel's ear, part of her cringed as he changed keys at least five times. But the rest of her clutched tightly into the comfort of his arms."

Elijah took a deep breath before concluding, "So that's it, folks. All you're going to get from me now about this couple. Time for bed."

There were no goodbyes among the storytelling reading group. There were still many good weeks to be enjoyed in the desert, and they remained camped close to one another. But Elijah's story was over. He, too, remained camped nearby. Soon, Nancy saw him packing up his jeep and getting ready to leave.

Elijah saw her approaching and asked, "You about ready to head home, Nancy?"

Nancy stopped in her tracks, giving him a small smile. "Possibly soon. You got another group story session beginning, Elijah?"

"Maybe, in about a week or so." Elijah stretched his arms, then let them fall to his sides. "I need time to clear my head and make some more stuff up. You know, I got to get some kids born to Rachel and Saul. I can only imagine the fun of talking about the things those kids might experience." He chuckled, shaking his head. "So, I need to get my creative juices stirred up some. I think I'm heading to Palm Springs for a few days to see the old farts follies there. It is amazing that so many damned talented people can congregate there. They inspire me. A whole group of former stage and screen performers, past their prime but still having talent coming out of their pores."

Nancy laughed softly, adjusting her bag on her shoulder. "How much of the stuff in your story is true, Elijah? And how much do you make up?"

"Does it matter?" Elijah shrugged, a playful glint in his eyes.

"No, I guess not." Nancy looked thoughtful for a moment. "But I bet if a blog were written discussing this story, there would be a bunch of discussion about truth versus fiction. I bet people would get into that discussion more than most of us did. And I wish I could stay and see what happens next. But duty calls."

"Well, Nancy, maybe you'll have to pick it up later." Elijah leaned in, his expression sincere. "Or you could decide to write the blog yourself! Oh, that reminds me. I rarely include individual issues from the group in the retelling of the story, but your experience on safari was unique. Could I use it? Do I have your permission to include it if I want?"

"Sure," Nancy agreed, tilting her head. "But I'm not sure that it has to do with how Saul or Rachel became the people they are."

"We all have things that are formative in our lives, outside influences, genetic influences." Elijah gestured broadly, emphasizing his point. "That's true even for those who consider themselves self-made. But, many times, unresolved events, experiences, or failure to address our losses or be thankful for our help can be a drag on our voyage. So maybe there was more truth to discover about your safari trip."

"Hum." Nancy furrowed her brow, considering his words. "I hadn't really thought of my parents' deaths as anything but a painful event. But it was broader than just losing them. I lost the feeling that there was always someone there to have my back. I lost the opportunity to mess up on the ranch, be laughed at by the cowboys, and then helped to succeed. No one like that is in my life now. If my parents lived, would I have been as hell-bent on pursuing my career as I have been?"

"Well, you'll have to wait and see." Elijah gave her a knowing smile. "Or figure it out in your blog. Whatever that is. But if you pull out before I'm back, Yo Bolsun, my dear."

Nancy chuckled, nodding in appreciation. "Elijah, thanks for everything, but I suspect you and I aren't done with each other yet." She smiled warmly at him.

He nodded back, a twinkle in his eye.

The End